ICE MAN COMETH

ICE MAN COMETH

C.T. WENTE

THOMAS & MERCER

Text copyright © 2015 Christopher Todd Wente

Published by Thomas & Mercer, Seattle

www.apub.com

Amazon, the Amazon logo, and Thomas & Mercer are trademarks of Amazon.com, Inc., or its affiliates.

ISBN-13: 9781477826249
ISBN-10: 1477826246

Cover design by Stewart Williams

Library of Congress Control Number: 2014941537

Printed in the United States of America

For Linda, min älskling.

Prologue

The girl looked up at the sky and smiled.

The bellies of the monsoonal clouds had darkened to steel gray as they rolled and twisted above her. She watched them with excitement, her eyes wide with anticipation as the thick autumn air began to stir. Her mother, oblivious to her state of distraction, pulled sharply on her small hand. They needed to move faster. It was nearing dusk, and the market would soon be closing. Both she and her mother were carrying newly woven saris made of *muga*, the highly prized golden silk made only here in her native Assam. They would have to hurry if they were going to sell them before darkness and the approaching rains scattered the last of the day's tourists. The girl dropped her eyes from the gathering storm and quickened her pace.

Although she was only five, the girl was expected to help sell her mother's saris in their family's tiny rented corner of the Bamunimaidan market. Not that she minded this chore. Her older sister had already taught her that a sad stare and pleading smile were powerful assets when it came to persuading the rich tourists who strolled by—and she was particularly blessed with both. Rarely did a foreigner stop to feel the lustrous silk of her mother's handmade creations without falling victim to her large, deep brown eyes. And if she worked hard and sold enough, her mother would reward her with a few *tilor laru*—the sugary sesame seed treats that were always for sale from the old vendor next to them. Just the thought of their sticky-sweet taste brought a smile to her round, mocha-colored face.

They continued down the narrow dirt path that carved a meandering line through the slums where they lived. Rubbish stirred by the wind danced at their sandaled feet. At the next turn, the girl noticed a group of young women and their children returning from the market. As usual, the burden of carrying the day's goods fell to the women and their daughters while the boys walked freely. She eyed the approaching boys warily, worried they might try to steal the heavy basket of saris slung over her back. Feeling her slow, her mother again pulled roughly. The girl stifled a protesting cry and furrowed her brow in anger as the group of women and children passed them quietly. A short distance farther, the dirt path converged with a busy road. From there they walked single file next to the road before eventually pausing at the busy intersection that bordered the market.

The girl could feel the sudden tension in her mother's grasp. Crossing here was always dangerous. An endless procession of vehicles converged without the aid of traffic signals, forcing everything into a swirling, chaotic dance. The noise of the collective confluence was deafening. Horns and engines vocalized their impatience as if competing in a mechanical shouting match. Brightly painted buses and tuk-tuks sped past in a flurry of color. A choking, blue-gray haze of exhaust hung in the air. Watching the melee, the girl edged closer to her mother, waiting anxiously for the squeeze of her hand that would signal when to go.

It was then that the clouds decided to open. Large drops of monsoonal rain fell rapid-fire with the weight of small stones, pelting them mercilessly. The girl turned her face to the sky and opened her mouth to the downpour as it cascaded down her long black hair and soaked through her brightly colored mekhela chador dress. Her mother watched the passing traffic stoically as the girl twirled and jumped in the muddy pool that quickly formed beneath their feet. She was so engrossed in the joy of the moment that she'd nearly forgotten the danger of the traffic when her mother suddenly grabbed her and pulled her roughly away from the street. Confused, the girl turned and stared out beyond her mother's protective arms. Only then did she hear the frantic screech of locking brakes coming from the intersection.

The concussion of the impact echoed like a bomb. In an instant the two vehicles were tossed spinning into the air by their own colliding inertia. The girl watched transfixed as one of the vehicles landed heavily on its side before rolling ominously toward the corner where they stood. Her mother gripped her in terror as it rolled closer. Then, just meters short of disaster, the twisted wreck abruptly slowed and came to rest on its side. Around them, an eerie silence descended as the remaining traffic shuddered to a stop.

The driver of the vehicle suddenly appeared in the upturned opening, his dark face washed in blood. Men from the gathering crowd ran over and pulled the dazed man from the wreckage as a thin wisp of smoke began rising from its engine. As they carried him off to safety, the girl looked at the ground next to the vehicle. Something strange caught her eye. A pale-colored object lay half-buried in the mud. She pointed to it and gazed curiously up at her mother. Her mother's brown eyes followed the line of her tiny outstretched arm and immediately widened in shock. Seeing this reaction, the girl realized the object must be something important. Overcome by curiosity, she pulled free of her mother's grasp and sprang forward for a better look.

The girl ignored the cries of her mother as she ran toward the smoking vehicle and knelt down next to the object. The heavy rain had exposed it further, and the girl could now finally see what it was. She reached down and gently grasped the human finger, surprised by its coldness. She tugged on the finger and watched excitedly as a hand and forearm rose stiffly from the muddy earth. The girl pulled harder, trying to free the man buried in the thick mud, but it was clear the rest of his body was trapped inside the overturned wreck. She let go of his finger and curled her nose as a foul-smelling fluid began pouring from the back of the vehicle. Something about its fluorescent-green color told her it was dangerous and she stepped back cautiously. The thin trail of smoke rising from the engine suddenly grew to a thick, acrid black column as something hissed and sparked inside.

Confused, she turned and looked for her mother. Her mother still stood at the corner but was now surrounded by a crowd of onlookers. Several men in the crowd held her arms tightly, preventing her from moving. All of them stared back at the girl with large, terrified eyes. Her mother screamed her name as others in the crowd gestured for her to come back. The girl looked at them curiously. Why were they all so afraid? Did they not wish to help the man still trapped inside?

A new sound, low and hissing like a deep breath, erupted behind her. The girl spun around to find the vehicle and the smelly green liquid that engulfed it on fire. The heat stung at her face, and she fell backward in fear. Even at her young age she could see that the fire wasn't normal. The flames twisted and rose like an angry animal, sweeping over the vehicle with an almost conscious intensity. Even the heavy rain seemed to have no effect on it. She tried crawling backward away from the inferno, but it was no use. The heavy basket of saris strapped to her back was stuck fast in the mud. Terrified, the girl cried out for her mother, but her voice was consumed by the howl of the fire. The intense heat was nearly unbearable. Steam rose from her rain-soaked dress as the flames inched closer. The hunger of the fire was simply too much. For the first time in her young life, the girl felt the soul-aching certainty that she was going to die.

And then she saw him.

He appeared like an apparition, running toward the burning vehicle with the quick, certain movements of an athlete. Afraid that he wouldn't see her, the girl flung her hands to the sky and screamed with every ounce of breath she could produce. It was only after he rolled under the flames and dropped protectively on top of her that she realized he was there to save her. He tore the thick straps of her basket away from her shoulders. In an instant she threw her muddy arms around his neck. The man then pulled her small body to his chest and sprinted from the inferno.

For the fleeting seconds she was held by him, the girl studied her rescuer's face as if she were in a dream. He was a foreign man, perhaps European or American, with brown eyes and short, curly dark hair. His white skin was tanned from the sun, and she could tell from the ease with which he carried her that he was strong. She closed her eyes and held on tightly to his neck. Despite the terror of the fire just moments before, she felt calm and safe in his arms.

When they were a safe distance from the burning vehicle, the man stopped and looked closely at the girl's arms and legs. She was lucky; the mud had protected her from any serious burns. Satisfied that she was okay, the man gently swept his hand over her cheek. The girl looked up at the man and smiled back happily as his stony expression eased into a grin. She barely noticed the rising commotion around her until a swarm of hands abruptly tore her from the man's grasp and passed her quickly through the crowd. A familiar pair of arms encircled her. The girl whimpered softly at the crushing embrace of her mother as the falling rain washed tears of relief from both of their faces. She then raised herself in her mother's arms and watched the scene before them.

The fire still burned intensely. In just minutes the twisted remains of the wrecked vehicle had been reduced to a withered shell of molten steel. The girl thought again about the man trapped inside. She glanced anxiously at the ground where his hand had rested but saw nothing more than flames churning in anger. She wondered if, like her, the mud would protect him, but deep down she knew it wasn't possible. Most likely his soul had already passed from his *jiva* and was now resting, just as the soul of her grandmother had done a few months before. The girl whispered a brief prayer of safe journey for the man's soul and glanced searchingly over the crowd.

Her rescuer wasn't difficult to find. Despite having a tan, his light-skinned face stood out noticeably from those around him. He was standing at the edge of the crowd, watching with everyone else as the unnatural fire consumed the last traces of the fatal accident in front of them. She wanted to call out to him, wanted to hug him around the neck for saving her life. But something in his expression told her not to. Something in his stare told her to remain silent. From the protection of her mother's arms, the girl looked at the man more closely. She watched the color that danced in his eyes. She watched the smile that formed on his lips.

PART I

The ecology of power will change.

By the end of the twentieth century, the balance of financial and political power within the world's developed societies will witness a rapid if not accelerating shift from their governing institutions to their largest corporate bodies. This phenomenon—fueled by corporate deregulation and governmental misguidance as well as by explosive technological innovation that will outpace lawmakers' ability to understand and control it—shall be ultimately considered by both analysts and historians as the inevitable evolution of the economic state.

By the beginning of the new millennium, the largest of these corporate bodies—particularly those directly responsible for producing or controlling the flow of energy, capital, and information—will grow into multinational and multiconglomerate entities that will individually generate revenues exceeding the gross domestic product of 90 percent of the world's countries, at the same time amassing technological and human resources more vast than any corporate complex previously conceived.

These immense corporate entities—with financial, political, technological, and above all, human resources as great if not greater than most developed countries—will define an entirely new organizational species in the evolution of modern business.

This new economic species will be defined as the *Corporate State*.

—James H. Stone, *Predictions in the New Business Ecology*

Chapter 1

A.T. Road, Guwahati
September 25, 11:35 a.m.
Planet Assam, India

Jeri—

Holy shit. I mean it. Holy shit. I have no business being here, in this gritty land of maniacally cruel humidity. There is not enough morphine in my IV drip to even begin to erase the endless torrent of loathing that pours like the monsoon rains upon this place. Everything here surely hates me. How can it not? I hate myself right now. Goddamn, what I wouldn't give for a double shot of Fortaleza and a Camel Light.

Last night I spun restlessly on the razor-thin mattress of my two-star hotel room for hours before finally kicking insomnia in the nuts. It's the goddamn heat. It burrows into your skin like a flaming hookworm and shits hot sauce into your bloodstream. I swear to god, Jeri, I'm sweating from the heat inside. Believe me, I contemplated a midnight swim in the river Brahmaputra, but this is India . . . Buddha knows what might swim up my ass and perform a hostile takeover should I doze off under the spell of my favorite nighttime muse, Lady Xanax.

But enough about my anal phobias. We have far more important matters to discuss. I imagine you're reading these words as you sit in your favorite corner behind the bar, your fingers creasing this very page as your other hand rests delicately against your cheek. Just the knowledge that this letter will soon find its way to your sublimely slender fingers makes the dull, piss-warm weight of this place momentarily bearable. Have I mentioned our kids will be gorgeous?

Enclosed is a photo of me beside a shrine to Shiva at the Umananda Temple. Please forgive my cropped head. The young miscreant I assigned the task of photo-taker displayed a level of stupidity I have not seen since the time I asked for directions in Ohio. Please also note my Joe's Last Stand T-shirt, the very one I bought at the bar so many months ago. Tell Joe I do not expect compensation for providing international advertising. As with all things, I do this out of desperate, reckless love for you.

My time here in India is drawing to a close, which is a blessing bigger than my tequila-ravaged liver. I took my last tuk-tuk ride to the market last night, which means this assignment is done. And just in time. I'm burned out, baby. Anything more than a day here and my morality and urine both become horribly clouded. I can say with an uncharacteristically high level of objectivity that this place is categorically fucked. The people worship many gods. The gods all have many limbs. When not worshipping the gods, the people eat dogs. I kid you not. Consumption gone awry, my dear.

Gods and dogs, Jeri, gods and dogs.

Right. Well, you have drinks to serve, and I'm late for another lunchtime rendezvous with Benji. You don't need to say the words, Jeri, I already know.

Ta!
Mysterious Joe's Last Stand Guy

P.S. Don't order dog.

Chapter 2

Jeri Halston laughed out loud.

The rich, warm sound of it echoed against the dark, oak-paneled walls of the old saloon. The handful of patrons sitting inside Joe's Last Stand Saloon turned and stared at the attractive twenty-six-year-old bartender sitting behind the bar, but Jeri didn't notice. She finished reading the letter and slowly stood from her barstool in the corner, a smile still lingering on her face.

"What is it, Jeri?" Chip Shepherd asked from his usual seat at the bar. Chip was a regular at Joe's, one of the sixty-something-year-old locals who considered retirement a fair excuse to drink away the afternoon hours in the ancient saloon that sat on the outskirts of Flagstaff's old downtown. He ran a hand through his scruffy salt-and-pepper hair and furrowed his brow in curiosity.

"This letter I just got in the mail. It's the funniest, strangest thing I've ever read."

"Who's it from?" the older man asked.

Jeri glanced again at the precise handwriting etched across the heavy pages of hotel stationery and shook her head in bewilderment. "I have no idea," she replied as she dropped them on the counter of the bar and picked up the envelope they'd arrived in. The familiar red and blue stripes of an airmail parcel were stenciled on its battered edges, and nearly half the front side was covered in colorful exotic stamps and postmarks. Jeri stared at them admiringly for a moment before turning the envelope on its side and shaking it gently. A small Polaroid photo fell into her hand. The photograph was just as the letter described. A large, ancient-looking temple sat off-center in the background, surrounded on both sides by a dense wall of lush, tropical trees. And in the foreground, wearing a blue Joe's Last Stand Saloon T-shirt, Jeri's mysterious admirer stood casually.

Unfortunately, as warned, the photographer had failed to include the author's head.

Jeri studied the picture closely for anything that might reveal a clue to the man's identity. His tan, muscular arms were crossed loosely, his slender frame leaning slightly back toward the right. She briefly imagined a handsome, equally tanned face with a mischievous grin staring back at her. Unfortunately, nothing in the image, real or imagined, seemed to offer any answers.

Across the counter, Chip leaned forward inquisitively. "May I read it, or is it some kind of pornographic love letter from your fan club?"

Jeri broke her stare from the Polaroid and smiled at Chip.

"Nothing pornographic, Chip. But don't blame me if that antiquated heart of yours can't handle it." She slipped the photo and letter back into the envelope and slid it across the counter.

"Wow . . . all the way from India, huh?" the older man said, admiring the envelope.

"I guess so," Jeri answered. The image in the Polaroid still hung in her mind.

"Well, let's see what was important enough to be airmailed from India," Chip replied. He unfolded the letter and slowly sipped at his beer as he read.

As she waited for Chip's inevitable opinion, Jeri gazed out the saloon's arched window at the cars that flashed by on Historic Route

66 outside. It was her favorite time of year, when the late-autumn sun bathed everything in warm, honey-golden light. She quietly admired the leaves of the maple trees planted along the sidewalk as they trembled with each passing car, their red-orange colors shimmering with an ethereal glow.

Chip dropped the letter on the bar and picked up the Polaroid with a slow, deliberate motion. He examined it carefully for a few moments before placing it and the letter back in the envelope. Jeri watched as he then drained the last of his beer, a thoughtful expression painted on his face.

"So, what do you think?" she asked, tucking an errant strand of copper-brown hair behind her ear.

Chip stared absently at his empty glass for a moment before leveling his stare on her. "I think I need another beer."

"Fine," Jeri replied as she walked over to the beer taps. This was what she loved most about the old man. Everything about him was deliberate and calculated. Even the gaze of his piercing blue eyes had a calming effect as they peered out from his handsome, weathered face. A professor of archeology in his earlier days, Chip was an amalgam of some of her favorite things—part gray-haired professor, part rugged cowboy, and part grumpy old man.

She poured him a fresh beer from the tap and handed it over with a questioning smile.

"So?"

"So I think the same thing I thought before I read the letter," Chip answered, a paternal tone creeping into his deep voice. "That I still don't understand why a beautiful, brilliant young woman like you is wasting her life pouring drinks for gruff old men like me and witless little Neanderthals like them." He pointed his thumb at a group of college-age men sitting at a table behind him. The men were too engrossed in a conversation to catch the insult, but Jeri knew Chip wouldn't have cared either way.

Jeri rolled her large, amber-colored eyes. "Do we have to have this conversation every week?" she asked, feigning annoyance. In truth, she didn't mind the older man's fatherly advice. The death of her real father just a year earlier had left Jeri devastated. Until that moment, he had been the stable center of her impetuous, wildly adventurous life. Brilliant and endlessly patient, her father had been her rational tether to reality as she bounced from one adventure, destination, and interest to the next. But all of that had changed with his death, and Jeri was still trying to accept the absence. If nothing else, Chip's occasional words of wisdom provided a comforting if only fleeting dose of the man she missed so much.

"Yes, we do have to have this conversation every week," Chip answered. "And I intend to keep having it until I'm no longer looking at the prettiest girl in Flagstaff when I order a beer."

"I'm not the prettiest girl in Flagstaff," Jeri retorted. "Not by a mile. And even if I was, I don't see how that would have anything to do with my choice of profession." She grabbed a towel and began wiping down the counter of the bar.

"I'll give you that," Chip replied, nodding. "But, then again, this particular bartender also happens to hold a handful of bachelor's degrees and a master's in economics. Isn't that right?"

Jeri ignored the question.

"Now, I may not be the sharpest tool in the proverbial shed anymore," Chip continued, "but I think I'm still smart enough to recognize talent being wasted when I see it." Finished with his sermon, he grabbed the fresh pint in front of him and took a long deliberate drink.

Jeri turned and paced quickly down the bar toward Chip. Her slender figure moved with graceful ease as her eyes burned into the older man's downturned face. Chip kept his eyes fixed on his beer as she stopped in front of him. She then slowly leaned across the counter, her fair, oval-shaped face hovering just inches from his.

"You didn't answer my question," she said, tossing the towel at his chest.

Chip looked up at her with a wry grin. "Oh, you mean the letter?" he asked.

"Yes, Chip, the letter."

"Well, I think he sounds like one helluva guy," he replied cheerfully, raising his glass. "I just hope he writes you again."

"Don't get your hopes up," Jeri replied, grabbing the letter from the counter. She turned and walked back to the far end of the bar, concealing the thin smile on her face as she stared at the envelope. She slid back onto her barstool in the corner behind the counter and looked out again at the autumn afternoon. The glow of the maple leaves was beginning to fade, their shapes tracing intricate shadows against the wooden blinds in the window. In a few more hours the sun would fall behind Mars Hill, the chill of autumn would return to the clear mountain air, and the neon sign hanging on the old brick façade outside would paint flickering crimson on the sidewalk. It was then that the magic of evening would return, bringing the nightly wave of thirty-something couples and college-age hipsters with it.

"It is rather interesting, though, isn't it?" Chip asked as he stared contemplatively at his beer glass.

"What's that?" Jeri responded.

"How well he seems to know you," the older man replied. He took a sip of his beer and looked over at her, his blue eyes still swimming with thought. "I was watching you while you read that letter. You were sitting there, in your favorite spot behind the bar, holding the letter in one hand, your other hand on your cheek—"

He paused for a moment as Jeri's eyes widened with the realization of what he was saying. "Just like he described."

Chapter 3

Tareeq 135 Madinat, Al Jubail
October 5, 8:04 a.m.
Planet Saudi Arabia

Jeri—

I'm looking nervously over my shoulder as I write you, fully expecting the twitchy coolness of morning to be chased from the room by the approaching simoon before it wrings me completely fucking lifeless. Did I complain about endless precipitation in my last letter? I'd trade a billion grains of sand for one sparkling drop of ma. Make that two billion, and throw in a double shot of Fortaleza and a Camel Light.

Camels, camels everywhere, and none of them to smoke.

The flight getting here was a disaster of colossal proportions. The mescaline and Prozac wore off somewhere high above the surreally sparkly Indian Ocean. And what I thought was a rogue band of harmless, cuddly Chia Pets turned out to be a staff of churlish Air Iran flight attendants. I swear I did nothing wrong, Jeri.

There I was, innocently floating in post-hallucinogenic meditation, when suddenly they were shouting at me from all sides. I vaguely gathered from the pointing fingers and distorted curls of their lips that it might have something to do with my shirt being inexplicably removed and my fly incomprehensibly unzipped, because the Farsi flowed from their mouths like jackals learning Hooked on Phonics. The fact that the cabin held the warm, pungent stench of a curried, oven-baked jockstrap certainly didn't help matters. I considered asking the passenger next to me how to say "What, fucknuts?" in Farsi, but EVERYONE was looking at me like I was the one who was delusional. While my memory after this is sketchy, I have compelling evidence that suggests I was bodily probed by the authorities during my layover in Dammam. Hard to say, as either the mescaline kicked back in, or they did something so terrible to my nether regions that I immediately retreated into my mental "happy place" and shut the whole thing out.

So here I am in Al Jubail, twitching and writing, waiting for a new assignment and that goddamn wind the locals call simoon to suck out what little water I have left in me faster than a parched kid can straw-suck a Cherry Coke. This has to be hell on earth, my love, just without the hookers and Justin Timberlake.

I would bitch-slap Jesus for a cigarette right now.

Let's talk about us, Jeri. There's no doubt you've chiseled your way into my enlarged, slightly atherosclerotic heart. I only hope you're as comfortable about our situation as I am. Allah knows I haven't always followed the "straight and narrow," but that's probably because I have no fucking clue what that saying really means.

Just know this, sweet pea. 1) I have solemnly relinquished my heart to the whims and circumstances of your physically oh-so-distant equivalent, and 2) I haven't felt this giddy in the groin since that time I found a stack of Playboys in my pop's closet. By this measure alone, I know I'm in deep.

The morning sirens are sounding, so I'd better sign off. Time to grab the prayer mat and square off with Mecca. We'll see who flinches first. I'm not a Muslim, Jeri. I only play one on TV.

You don't need to say it, I already know.

Ta!
Mysterious Joe's Last Stand Guy

P.S. The enclosed picture requires no caption.
P.P.S. The food here tastes like sand and shit-fed meatloaf.

Don't order dog.

Chapter 4

"Seriously, Jeri—who the hell is this guy?" Allie yelled toward the kitchen from the balcony of the third-floor apartment.

"I told you, I have no idea," Jeri yelled back, uncorking another bottle of Pinot Gris. It was Sunday afternoon, and Jeri and her best friend, Allie, were enjoying their weekend ritual of drinking, lounging, and having marathon sessions of girl talk. Jeri strolled back onto the balcony with the sweating bottle of wine in hand and dropped lazily into her chair.

"Okay, so let me get this straight," Allie said, her glass of wine perched in one hand, the two letters in the other. "Some guy is hopscotching around the world taking pictures of himself in a Joe's Last Stand T-shirt. You've never met him—or at least you don't think you have—but he writes like he knows everything about you. Oh, and he's also apparently in love with you. Does that sound about right?"

Jeri leaned over and poured more wine into her glass as Allie waited for an answer. The two of them had been best friends since the day Jeri had answered a "roommate wanted" ad in the college paper. She'd shown up at the tiny rental house on Leroux Street, exhausted and emotionally numb after a sleepless night of breaking the final cord of a pitifully frayed relationship with her live-in boyfriend. Jeri still vividly remembered the moment Allie had answered the door—her tall, thin body dressed only in a T-shirt and tiger-print panties as she stood casually drinking a beer. Allie had looked Jeri over through the screen door with a sympathetic smile. "I'm not going to ask," she'd said flatly. "Just make sure you don't give the asshole your new address." Now, years later, Jeri didn't need to look at Allie to know what she was thinking.

"Yeah," Jeri replied with a sly grin, "that sounds about right."

"I'm glad you're finding this so funny, Jer, because personally I think it's more than a little creepy." Allie kicked her feet onto the balcony's railing and sank deeper into the cushions of the chair. Her short blonde hair framed her alabaster face as she frowned. "I mean, what if he's some kind of serial stalker or molester? What if he shows up at the bar one day and says, 'Hi, Jeri, remember me? I'm that creepy stalker guy. Want to grab some dinner?' What are you going to do then?"

Jeri suppressed a laugh as she stared out at the picturesque afternoon. The distant slopes of the San Francisco Peaks shimmered like copper as the quaking aspens relinquished their summer colors to fall. A checkered sky of giant billowing cumulus clouds floated overhead, the sun casting their undulating backs in silver-gray light. And around her, shaggy army-green spears of ponderosa pines stretched upward to frame the serene valley landscape. "God, it is so gorgeous here today," she said with a sigh.

"Don't change the subject," Allie replied irritably.

Jeri reluctantly broke her stare from the view and turned to her friend. "What do you want me to do, Allie? It's not like I asked for this. It's not like I can write this guy and tell him to stop. And honestly, what's the danger in it? What has he said that would indicate harmful intentions to anything other than his own liver?" She paused as Allie rolled her eyes. "Besides," Jeri continued, "his letters make me laugh."

"I knew it!" Allie said with an accusing tone as she bolted upright in her chair. "I knew it! You actually like this guy!"

Jeri laughed reflexively. "Come on, Allie—can we be reasonable here? We're a long way past high school. I just said that his letters are funny. What the hell does that have to do with anything romantic?"

"It has *everything* to do with being romantic," Allie said as she jabbed at Jeri with her wineglass, swirling the Pinot Gris dangerously close to the rim. "Don't you see that? Every guy out there knows the best way to get a girl's attention is to make her laugh, because then we become *intrigued*." Allie drew out the last word slowly, like a teacher speaking to a first-grade class. "And god knows, once we become intrigued, we want to learn more, which means now we're *interested* in the guy, whether we want to admit it or not." She paused and leaned in closer. "And once we're interested . . . well, then we're *fucked*."

Jeri stared at her friend, trying desperately to maintain a straight face. As ridiculous as it seemed, she knew that this was Allie's best effort at heartfelt advice. "Fucked, huh? Do you mean that literally, or figuratively?"

Allie sat back and threw her hands in the air.

"Does it matter?"

Jeri shrugged and took a long sip of her wine. She was beginning to question why she'd even shown the letters to Allie in the first place.

"He's doing everything right, Jeri," Allie continued. "He's setting the intrigue trap that every woman falls into." She reached over and picked up the Polaroid from the second letter, studying it for a moment. "Even these damn photos; do you honestly think they aren't meant to make you want to know more?" She tossed it onto Jeri's lap.

Unlike the lush tropical location of the first photo, the scene in the Polaroid from the second letter was eerily empty. A midday shot of white desert sand and flawless blue sky filled the background. As in the first photo, her mysterious writer stood in the foreground, but this time his back was to the camera. In his right hand he held a small sign over his shoulder. A one-word message was written with heavy marker in the same precise handwriting as the letters—"Hell." Next to the sign, the man's dark, short-cropped hair looked disheveled and chaotic, exposing just a hint of his unshaven face. Jeri was sure she could see the edge of a wide smile in that thin, seductively hidden profile, but she was not about to mention this to Allie.

"Maybe," Jeri replied.

"Maybe what?"

She handed the picture back to Allie. "Maybe he wants me to be intrigued. Or maybe he just can't find anyone to take a good photo."

Allie shook her head and quickly shoved the letters and Polaroids back into their battered envelopes. "Fine, whatever. Just do me a favor and hold on to these. I'm sure the authorities will want to examine them when you go missing."

"Can we drop this subject?" Jeri asked as she refilled Allie's wineglass.

"Consider it dropped," Allie retorted curtly.

"Thank you. And for the record, if I ever go missing, I'll make sure you're the first to know."

"That's not funny . . . at all."

Jeri hooked her feet onto the railing and leaned back into her chair, her long legs stretched in front of her. She took a sip of wine and closed her eyes, letting the cool, sweet flavors of fruit slowly slide across her tongue. The autumn sun found a window in the clouds and drenched them both in radiant golden warmth. "Maybe so," she said as a smile stretched across her face. "But I can think of far worse things than disappearing for a while."

Chapter 5

The large black Mercedes rolled to a stop.

"So . . . what now?" he asked from the backseat.

A pair of small, petulant eyes glanced back at him through the rearview mirror. His driver was a dark, corpulent man with thinning hair and a severe expression. Despite the air-conditioning that blasted through the front console, the driver's wide head and thick, hairy neck were covered in beads of sweat that trickled down to the white cotton thobe that covered his rotund body. And he farted, a condition that he had seemed completely unashamed of since the beginning of their short drive together. "Wait," he replied tersely. "They'll signal."

"Sounds good," he replied, nodding to the driver. He gazed out through the Mercedes's heavily tinted windows at the stark landscape outside. The long two-story buildings that lined both sides of the street were nearly mirror copies of one another. Bleach white and stripped of anything ornate or memorable, they appeared intentionally designed to be forgettable. Four white doors punctured the first-floor façade in regular intervals on each side, a tiny window next to each. It was clear the windows were not designed for aesthetics but as a functional means of surveillance. The windows along the second floor were slightly larger versions of those on the first, as if teasing the idea of normalcy. He realized that, viewed under the raw, harsh light of the late-morning sun, the buildings—if not the entire area in general—gave off a serious "fuck you" vibe. It was the kind of flagrant aura of bad energy normally reserved for morgues, strip joints, and most of downtown Philadelphia.

A sudden movement caught his attention.

The second door of the building to his left slowly cracked open, forming a vertical crease of black in the stark white façade. As he watched, a hand appeared from the dark interior and quickly waved before vanishing.

"There," his driver muttered, nodding his head toward the door. The small gesture caused his body to quiver like a massive ball of gelatin. A low growl bellowed from beneath his thobe. The driver gripped the leather steering wheel and leaned forward, groaning with effort.

"Right, well, that's my cue," the passenger replied as he opened the back door and slid out of the plush interior and into the full heat of the sun. He closed the door and immediately heard a precise metallic click as the large vehicle dropped into gear and sped off. A cloud of sand and dust followed in its wake as he watched it leave. Assuming complete faith in the plan given to him, the Mercedes's flatulent, cotton-wrapped driver would be back in ten minutes to pick him up.

He walked casually across the wide, empty street and paused just outside the door, his hands shoved deep into the pockets of his khaki pants. A moment later the door cracked open again, this time wide enough for him to enter. He smiled and stepped cautiously into the black void before him.

Cool air immediately licked his skin as the door closed behind him. A heavy deadbolt clicked loudly. He took off his sunglasses and looked around. The cramped room contained only a small, flimsy black conference table and a handful of outdated chairs. Its bone-white walls were heavily scarred with smudges and dents.

Beneath it all, a hideous spread of cerulean-blue shag carpet worn by years of traffic lay sadly.

"Nice place," he remarked, smiling at the two men sitting at the conference table. The man at the door moved to the other side of the table and stood rigidly behind his two seated colleagues.

He sat down at the table and studied the faces across from him. Their dark Middle Eastern features notwithstanding, all three of the thirty-something men looked similar enough to be brothers.

"Thank you for coming," the man standing behind his two colleagues said without smiling.

"It's my pleasure," he responded, his voice warm and sincere.

"May we get you a coffee or tea?" the man seated to his left asked with a smile. He appeared to be the youngest of the three, with large, intelligent eyes and boyish, coffee-colored features. Unlike his somewhat malnourished-looking colleagues, the man's well-muscled frame was apparent under his crisp white dress shirt.

"No, thank you . . . I'm fine," he answered, returning the smile.

"Then let's begin," left-seat replied sharply. With that, his colleague seated next to him produced a large manila envelope from an unseen case beneath his chair and gently placed it on the table. His dark hand lingered on it protectively. "Four subjects in four cities," left-seat said, pointing to the envelope. "The details of each are contained here."

He glanced at the envelope and nodded. "Cause?" he asked politely.

"Our preference would be accidents for at least two," standing-man responded, his deep brown eyes studying him closely. "Of course, we leave some discretion to you. Certainly you know more about this than we do."

"Oh, I wouldn't necessarily say that."

"We were certainly impressed with your work in Assam," left-seat said with another brilliant flash of teeth.

He glanced at left-seat with surprise. "Assam?"

"We apologize for not telling you before," standing-man replied, a glint of humor in his eyes. "Assam was a test. We wanted to see exactly what we were paying for first."

The three men smiled collectively.

"I see," he replied, feigning surprise. "Well, I'm glad we've met your standards. Of course, Assam was just a typical assignment. We're capable of much more, should the need arise."

In truth, Assam had been anything but typical. It had taken more than two frustrating, rain-soaked weeks before everything had fallen into place. The fact that he'd pulled it off at all was incredible. And the last-minute use of a tuk-tuk and an untraceable fire accelerant was, in his own humble opinion, rather brilliant. If his craft was ever recognized as an art form, Assam just might go down as his *ceiling of the Sistine fucking Chapel.*

Left-seat composed his face and continued. "The subjects include three males and a female. One Middle Eastern, two Caucasian, and one Asian. Photos and your requested details are contained in the envelope."

"May I?" he asked, reaching his hand for the envelope.

"Of course," left-seat said, turning to his colleague and gesturing for him to slide the envelope across the table.

He opened the envelope and quietly studied the information. Everything appeared to be in order; the photos and personal details of the four subjects were organized just as specified. Satisfied with the material, he closed the envelope and smiled at the three men who represented his latest corporate client.

"Great, well, I think I'm all set then," he said warmly.

"Do you have any questions?" standing-man asked, a noticeable look of relief on his face that the meeting was almost over.

He nodded with a somber expression. "You've read my stipulations, correct?" he asked, pausing to look at each of them.

The three men nodded together.

"Then you understand the absolute necessity of the on-sites? The sample collections?"

"We do," left-seat answered firmly.

"Very well," he replied, standing from the table. "Gentlemen, it was a pleasure meeting you."

"I hope you've enjoyed your time in our beautiful city," left-seat said as he stood up from the table, visibly pleased to be done with the meeting.

"Very much so," he responded, smiling at the sound of his own lie. He slipped the manila envelope into his shirt pocket as standing-man walked to the door and unlatched the deadbolt before peering into the street. A white-hot shaft of sunlight fell across the carpet.

"Your car is waiting for you," left-seat said as he shook his hand, his dark eyes friendly. "Our most sincere thanks again."

He nodded and walked to the door, pausing in the narrow alcove as standing-man stepped aside to allow his exit.

"By the way," he said, turning to the three men, "I'm no expert, but it seems to me that if you really wanted to keep this meeting secret, you might have opted for a less conspicuous vehicle." He pointed through the cracked door at the large Mercedes once again parked in the middle of the vacant street.

Standing-man's puzzled face broke into a grin. "Mercedes? Ha! Everyone has a Mercedes here." He laughed as he turned to his colleagues. "It is like having, what . . . a Toyota in the US?" His two colleagues nodded affirmatively. "Bentley, Bugatti . . . maybe the latest Maybach. Those cars might get noticed. But Mercedes? No, no one here looks twice at them."

"Right . . . of course," he responded.

Standing-man opened the door and briefly patted him on the back. "Do a good job for us again, and we'll bring you back to celebrate," he said with a broad smile. "Take you out on the town . . . show you an excellent time . . . whatever you desire."

"Sounds great," he replied as he put on his sunglasses and stepped out into the intense arid heat. He looked back and grinned. "Tell your driver to have your finest Toyota ready for me."

The laughter of the three men was cut off as the door swiftly closed behind him.

He opened the back door of the Mercedes and sank heavily into the soft leather of the seat. A feeling of calm fell over him as the automatic transmission clicked into gear and the car sped down the narrow alley and back toward the hotel. He closed his eyes as the air conditioner whirred to life, ignoring the sound of the driver's bowel as it again grumbled threateningly from the front seat.

Chapter 6

Stadium Road, Rumuomasi
Port Harcourt
October 16, 1:19 p.m.
Planet Nigeria

Jeri—

This place is fabulous.

    36 hours since touchdown, and I've only been arrested by the Nigerian police once. Long story, but I was able to buy my way out of wahala (that's pidgin for "trouble"— isn't language cool?) for less than 6500 naira, which is only something like $50 bucks, though they did make me pay in US dollars. Double whammy.

    If you receive any belligerent letters from the Abuja Eko Casino demanding immediate payment on a $1,200 blackjack debt, I suggest marking the envelope "DECEASED" and sending it back. And <u>don't</u> blow up at me, sweetheart, because they were large, muscled, irate, and willing to break my hands if I didn't proffer up the faloose. I'm not exactly sure how they got the impression

I own a saloon on Route 66 in beautiful bucolic Flagstaff, but do me a favor and don't open any packages unless you are <u>sure</u> you know who the sender is.

Remember how I used to hang out with the "unofficial" supporters of the Manchester United soccer team when I lived in England? (I did tell you this, didn't I?) Remember me telling you how we'd turn the streets into a drunken mass of brutality, and how right before we tore into the supporters of the other team, all of us—hundreds of half-witted bastard men, feeding on each other's energy and bloodlust—would whisper and chant "It's going to go off . . . it's going to go off"?

Jeri, it's going to go off.

I have the sudden strange feeling that you're considering cutting your hair. If this is true, please understand that you will not only be disappointed by the outcome, you will deny the surly, wayward throngs who stumble into Joe's Last Stand Saloon the most beautiful sight to befall their eyes in recent, middle, and distant memory. That sight would be you, my love, hovering behind the bar with those long coppery locks in tow, tucking mischievous strands back into place as you fill glasses with beer and men with envy. Our children will be gorgeous, Jeri.

If the word of a wily old Texan expat can be trusted, there's a bar within spitting distance of my palatial hotel that serves Fortaleza tequila by the double shot and Dos Equis by the bottle. He asked if I'd believe that just last week two American men were kidnapped in that very bar, to which I told him I would believe no less. My odds of surviving this place are roughly one in four. For a double shot of Fortaleza, I completely accept this.

The enclosed photo captures this place at its best. This may also be considered its worst. Such is the fucking conundrum of Africa.

You don't need to say it, Jeri-girl. I already know.

Ta!
Mysterious Joe's Last Stand Guy

P.S. The food here is best described as a culinary urinal. Don't order dog.

Chapter 7

"What the heck is faloose?" Joe Brown asked as he sat at the bar and scratched his pale, mirror-bald head. The owner of Joe's Last Stand Saloon sat hunched over the counter, the latest letter clinched in his large hands.

"I think he means 'money,' Joe," Chip answered from the barstool next to him.

"Then why didn't he just say that?" the old bar owner grumbled before continuing to read. In her corner behind the counter, Jeri curled up on her barstool, slowly thumbing through a thick novel. Besides the three of them, the saloon stood nearly empty.

"Ah, shit," Joe exclaimed, slapping the letter against his hand. "Do I really need to worry about some package arriving? The last thing I need is some goddamn Nigerian casino owner mailing some kind of letter-bomb vendetta 'cause this guy didn't pay his damn debt."

Jeri and Chip exchanged grins as Joe sat with a wide-eyed look of concern stamped to his reddening face. His short, stocky frame was perched tensely on his barstool.

"I think you're safe, Joe," Jeri said with a wry grin. "I think our mystery writer is just kidding around."

"Not ours, Jeri . . . *yours*," Joe retorted gruffly. "This guy obviously isn't writing for anybody but you. But don't think for one second I won't throw out any weird shit that shows up in the mail.

I mean it. If anything bigger than a postcard arrives here smelling like Allah Ak-bar, I'm calling the authorities. Jesus Christ, I've got casino-running terrorists on my ass now."

Jeri could hear the inflection of amusement in Joe's voice. Were he really worried, she knew from experience, he wouldn't be talking about it. She went back to reading her book.

A minute later Joe dropped the letter onto the bar and slowly shook his head. "Damnedest love letter I've ever read. That's for sure."

"You should read the first two," Chip mumbled.

The saloon owner pulled the Polaroid from the envelope and squinted at the image. "Well, hell," he exclaimed, holding it close, "you can't even see him in this damn picture. Good god, why would anyone want to be in a shithole place like that?"

Jeri ignored Joe's question and pretended to read her book. In truth, she didn't even see the page in front of her; her mind was fixated on the memorized image of the photo Joe was holding. It was of a busy third-world road captured in midday, the sun hidden behind a gray-green phalanx of low clouds. The road was choked beyond capacity with a vibrant collection of cars, scooters, animals, taxis, and people, all packed tightly together in the chaos of traffic. In the background, a long row of squat one-story structures was carved into small merchant stalls, each of them filled with a myriad of colorful items that nearly spilled out onto the muddy, unpaved road. Nearly everything in the photo appeared to be in rapid, noisy, unorchestrated motion toward some unseen destination.

Everything except for him.

He stood in the middle of the road, immediately recognizable in his blue Joe's Last Stand T-shirt. As the image floated in her mind, Jeri could vividly recall every feature—his tan, muscled arms casually folded across his chest, his broad shoulders relaxed in a posture of unnatural calm, his body as still as stone in the churning melee of madness that surrounded him.

But no face.

Almost as if it had been intentionally timed, a man moving through the dense crowd stood directly between her mysterious man and the camera, effectively obscuring everything but the outline of his elusive face. Behind the blurry edges of the passing man, Jeri could almost feel his smile beaming back; could almost see his dark, intelligent eyes staring back at her smugly. The fact that his face was so tantalizingly close and yet hidden once again sent a ripple of frustration through her.

"He's either really good at hiding or really poor at being seen," Chip said in a low voice, as if reading Jeri's thoughts.

"I reckon so," Joe replied, his mouth twisted in thought. He dropped the Polaroid on the counter and looked up at Jeri, his eyes wide with excitement. "Say, Jeri, I have an idea."

"What's that, Joe?" Jeri asked as she slowly marked the unread page and laid the book on her lap.

"I don't think your mystery man is going to stop writing anytime soon, and even though he's . . . you know . . . kind of out there, he writes some pretty funny shit." Joe paused for a second, his bear paw of a hand stroking at his chin. "Plus he's wearing our world-renowned T-shirt"—his voice dropped into a low, smooth tone as he did his best TV announcer impersonation—"available for purchase exclusively at Joe's Last Stand Saloon!"

"Get to the point, Joe."

"Yeah, right," Joe stammered. He glanced around the room as his thick fingers frantically stroked his whiskered face. "So what if we posted the letters and photos somewhere in the bar where people could read them? Then everyone would get a laugh out of it. And hell, look around—it certainly couldn't hurt business." He picked up the letter and waved it in the air, his face red with excitement. "Christ, all these little college bastards raised on reality TV would eat it right up!"

Chip, sitting next to him, suddenly chimed in. "And who knows . . . maybe someone will recognize him and put an end to the mystery."

"Exactly," Joe said, nodding. He turned and smiled at Jeri. "So . . . what do you think?"

Jeri stared quietly at both men. *Why is this a tough question?* she asked herself. Did it really matter if Joe wanted to display some ridiculous letters from a man she didn't know? She probably wouldn't give a second thought to sharing love letters from others she'd received in the past—and those were from men she'd actually known. So why were these any different? And yet for some reason the idea felt distinctly wrong, as if she would be exposing something very private, something that belonged just to her.

Unfortunately, at the moment, as Joe smiled earnestly at her, she couldn't quite identify what that something was.

"Sure, Joe. Go ahead," Jeri said, unable to inject any enthusiasm in her voice. "It'll be good for the bar. And like Chip said, maybe someone will actually know who this guy is."

Joe slapped his hands loudly against the bar. "Great! Let's do it." He turned and pointed toward the wall at the front of the saloon near the arched window. "We'll hang 'em up right over there, where everyone can see 'em." He paused again as his fingers worked his chin, his eyes clouded with inspiration. "It'll be a monument to romance and love . . . a shrine to our own mysterious 'last stander'!"

Chip erupted in laughter, his broad shoulders shaking visibly. At her corner seat behind the bar, Jeri opened her book and pretended to read, ignoring the feeling of nausea beginning to grow in her stomach.

"By the way," Joe said, turning to her. "You're not really going to cut your hair, are you?"

"What?" Jeri asked, glaring at him over her book. "What are you talking about?"

"Your friend mentioned in his letter that you were planning to cut your hair. Is that true?"

"Not that it's any business of yours, but no. I have no plans to cut my hair." Jeri went back to her book for a moment before looking again at Joe. "This guy isn't a mind reader, Joe. Nor is he my friend. He doesn't know anything about me."

"Yeah, you're right . . . sorry, Jeri," Joe said apologetically, gazing at the letter on the counter. "But that's good news," he said with a thin smile. "A short-haired Jeri would definitely *not* be good for business."

Chapter 8

The red-orange light of sunset slipped through the rustic cottage windows of Augustine's restaurant and etched the wall like a shimmering fire-drawn blade. Beneath it, the old panels of mahogany glowed brightly, casting a warm radiance through the dark, densely packed dining room. From her seat in the corner, Jeri quietly admired its fading brilliance, marking its movement as dusk dragged it slowly into nothingness.

"But anyway, even if they offer, I don't know that I'd accept it," the smooth baritone voice continued.

"Right," Jeri responded as she spun a pasta noodle onto her fork.

"Right what?" the voice rebuffed with frustration. "Are you even listening to me?"

Jeri blinked quickly and looked up as she broke free of her thoughts. "What? Oh . . . I'm sorry, Rob. I faded out there for a minute." She smiled apologetically at the handsome man sitting across from her at the small table.

Rob stared back at her, narrowing his dark brown eyes.

"Is something wrong?"

Jeri looked down at her plate. The linguini she'd been molesting was now tightly wrapped around the tines of her fork, but she had no desire to eat it. She glanced back at the long smudge of sunlight on the far wall and shook her head.

"No, just tired. It's been a long day," she said quietly.

"Everything okay at the bar?" Rob said as he leaned back and returned to eating. Even in her distracted state, the derision in his voice wasn't lost on Jeri. In the few short months they'd been dating, Rob had taken every opportunity to drop not-so-subtle hints regarding his feelings about her choice of profession. As a gifted researcher and associate professor of microbiology on the fast track to full tenure at the university, Jeri knew Rob considered her job a bit pedestrian by comparison. His tone was now reminding her of it again.

"Yes. Fine," she snapped.

"Well, *as I was saying*," Rob continued, his eyes flashing her a dark look, "it looks like Biotin may actually underwrite the grant, but I'm beginning to have serious concerns about how this could affect ownership of the intellectual property."

"Really?" Jeri asked with mock curiosity. "What do you think Biotin's going to ask for?" Of course, she had no interest in the answer, but asking the question would at least buy her several blissful minutes of not needing to speak. She took a healthy sip of her red wine, some expensive new organic blend from California. It wasn't the best wine she'd tasted, but Rob insisted it was excellent.

Rob's angular, handsome face immediately turned to a brooding expression as the flickering glow of candlelight danced across his pale skin. "Well, I don't have specific details, but it looks like . . ."

Jeri watched him with an enthusiastic smile for a few moments before realizing it didn't matter. Rob's stare would remain fixed on his plate as he talked at length about the latest snag in his research-grant saga. His hands moved constantly while he spoke, meticulously cutting and organizing the items on his plate as if he were laying out samples in his laboratory.

At least she admired his passion. It was the first thing, besides his looks, that had attracted her to him when they'd met months earlier at the university's alumni summer fund-raiser she'd attended with Allie. In her black dress and styled hair, she had caught his eye within minutes of entering the ballroom. She'd even blushed when he'd walked up to her, an arresting James Bond aura surrounding him as he flashed his perfect white teeth and bowed to her in his ink-black tuxedo. Allie had quickly made herself scarce, winking like a teenager at Jeri from across the room and conspicuously mouthing the words "He's hot!" It had been an intoxicating, nearly cinematic night as they talked, laughed, and danced together for almost the entire evening.

It wasn't until a week later, on their first official date, that Rob had asked Jeri about her profession. Being in no way embarrassed of the fact she was a bartender, she had told him without hesitation. The cloud of surprise and disappointment that swept across his face had lasted only a second, but Jeri saw it as clearly as a cell under a microscope. From that moment on, she sensed that was exactly how Rob now saw her—small and minuscule, like some lesser form of life.

In the few months since, they had continued to date casually, but Jeri felt the hope of that first great night slowly drain with every subsequent dinner and conversation. As much as she wanted to believe that the handsome, brilliant young man across from her was her soul mate, she knew his heart and love were inseparably tied to a structured, predictable life of academia, and hers were somewhere else.

". . . not that we didn't consider the possibility of this happening, but the grant itself was expressly written to guarantee the university ownership of the first viable molecule . . ." Rob continued, his fork excitedly tracing circles above his plate between bites.

Jeri glanced again at the fading blade of sunlight. In just minutes it had morphed into a thin, needle-sharp shaft, its color cooling from ember-hot orange to soft, languid amber. In minutes it would be gone—a final, gentle stroke of warmth in a room of growing darkness. She took another sip of overpriced organic wine and nodded halfheartedly as Rob looked over at her, his hands and mouth in constant motion. His eyes fell back to his plate, and Jeri crossed her eyes and flicked her tongue at him like a child. She inwardly wanted him to look up at her at that moment, to stare in embarrassment or react in some unexpected way that might dislodge the dull ache of boredom that was creeping up inside her. But Rob simply droned on, oblivious of her actions.

There was nothing Jeri hated more than boredom. She would gladly take pain, fear, or exhaustion over the time-freezing, quicksand-sinking agony of being somewhere she did not want to be. Staring at Rob, she grabbed the edge of her chair and suppressed a rising urge to abruptly jump up from the table and kick her legs in the air. A vivid image of shattering plates, airborne wineglasses, and the wide-eyed gaze of horrified diners instantly filled her mind. The ridiculousness of the image and the moment suddenly overwhelmed her, and to Jeri's own surprise, a loud, high-pitched laugh erupted from her mouth.

"What the hell is so funny?" Rob exclaimed, nearly dropping his fork. His look was piercing in the dim light. Feeling like an ill-mannered adolescent, Jeri froze in place, trying to contain the laughter that continued to bubble out from behind her smiling lips as the tables around her turned quiet. She stared back at Rob with wide, watery eyes, terrified to speak for fear of another outburst.

Rob wiped his napkin across his mouth and then tossed it into his lap.

"Well, I'm glad to see that the possible failure of this research grant and the financial impact it would have on my departmental budget is so amusing to you," he said, his voice laced with ice.

Jeri squeezed the edge of the chair tightly as she sat up, suppressing the frustrated laughter that was still beating against her chest. "I'm sorry. I'm just in a weird mood tonight." She could feel his eyes burning into her as she picked up her fork and feigned interest in her food.

Rob sat back in his chair and sighed. "Is there a subject *you* would like to talk about?" he asked, his voice condescendingly sweet, as if talking to a child. "I'm sensing my stories aren't really that interesting to you right now."

Jeri shrugged dismissively. She took a long sip of wine as she considered the question. What did she want to talk about? She found herself feeling strangely vacant of curiosity, as if every interest had simply drained away. Politics? God knows where that topic would go right now. Religion? Even worse than politics. World news seemed too forced, national news too depressing, local news too trivial. And she certainly wasn't going to discuss work.

Then, unexpectedly, the image of a crowded, chaotic street in Africa came to mind. "Do you like to travel?" she asked, masking the feeling of excitement the image had produced.

Rob seemed to stare through her as he considered the question. "Depends," he said as he gently brushed away his stylish bangs of wavy brown hair. "I travel a lot for work, but I usually don't have much time to really see the places I go. I like New York City, and I think Chicago is nice, though only in the summer. Winter there is absolute hell. The last conference I was slated to attend in Chicago was in January." He chuckled as he took a quick sip of wine. "Luckily I was able to get Professor Olson to go instead."

"Well, where have you been outside of the US? Have you seen any of Europe or Asia?"

Rob nodded as he focused his attention back on his plate. "I've been to London and Paris for conferences. London was gloomy, and the food was just awful. Paris? Forget it . . . a week of pure torture. I'd been warned by colleagues about the rudeness of Parisians, but it was even worse than I expected." He paused to carefully carve a piece of gristle from his well-cooked meat and move it safely to the side of his plate. "I haven't been anywhere in Asia. There's a conference in Hong Kong in a few months that I've been asked to attend, but there's no chance of me setting foot there until that new flu has been contained."

"Of course," Jeri responded succinctly. "Where else?" she asked, prodding him. "Any exotic locations—say, Africa, for example?"

"Africa?" Rob's face twisted in disgust. "You couldn't pay me to go to Africa, or most any other third-world country, for that matter."

"And why is that?"

"C'mon, Jeri, are you kidding me? It's not safe."

Even though she could have predicted his answer, Jeri still inwardly shuddered as a heavy weight of disappointment dropped into her stomach. She nodded slowly as Rob took a sip of his wine, her face drawn taut to contain any trace of emotion. *But of course,* she thought to herself. *What were you expecting? Did you really think that James Bond lived in Flagstaff? Did you really think you'd find your soul mate here?* She looked across the table at Rob as he continued to cut, organize, and chew his food with clinical precision. He glanced up and gave her a curious smile, oblivious to the cord that had just snapped inside her. Jeri smiled back at the striking face that flickered in the candlelight—handsome, brilliant, predictable . . . utterly safe Rob.

"And you?" he asked, staring at his plate as his knife cut away neatly. "Do you like to travel?"

"I do," she said quietly.

"And how does Africa sound to *you*?" His voice was edged with indifference.

Jeri leaned forward and settled her head in her hands. Her hair glowed copper red in the candlelight. "I would say it sounds dirty, dangerous . . . real. Like anything new, I think it would be incredibly visceral. And if it's anything like what I've read, I'm sure it would be unbelievably intense."

Rob paused midcut and looked at her, trying to read Jeri's steady, intense glare. "Right. Well, I suppose I'd agree with that assessment—which is exactly why I have no interest in going."

Jeri glanced across the room. The last dying ray of sunlight clung weakly to the wall, its former fire now just a whisper of dull light. She watched as it faded into the dark mahogany, evaporating submissively into the void with a final, anticlimactic flicker from existence.

"That's okay," she said, her voice cool and crisp. "You're not invited anyway."

Chapter 9

The locals called it *harmattan*.

The dry, immense trade wind erupted from the great desert and blew downward into the moist tropical interior of Africa with the beginning of the late-autumn dry season. As it traveled south, the hot, restless wall of air sucked massive amounts of Saharan sand into its grip, turning the sky into a dull smudge of cinnamon that could veil the sun for days. It normally started blowing in late November—the desert-fired air and thick, dusty haze providing a mixed blessing of low humidity and pulmonary irritation—but this year the great wind, often called "the doctor," had come weeks ahead of schedule.

He knew this because he woke to a ruddy-orange African sky that refused to yield blue as the sunrise drew upward into morning. His throat was dry and scratched, and his mouth held the gritty, mineral taste of sand and earth that was only slightly less pleasant than the morning-after taste of Jack Daniel's. He glanced at his watch, checked his cell phone, and then slowly rose from the bed to wash in the tiny, green-tiled bathroom of the hotel room. A cockroach darted fearlessly across his path as he scratched at the short dark curls on his head, reminding him to ask the concierge for a room upgrade. If only there were a concierge. Or a room upgrade.

The torrent of Port Harcourt's morning traffic was already rolling and churning as he descended onto the street. Cars and buses jostled along the dilapidated road of potholes and pavement, a collective symphony of honking horns and screeching brakes as the smoke-farting motorcycle taxis called achabas and their daredevil pilots darted around them at fatal speeds. He fell in step with the vibrant current of locals that shuffled along the narrow line between merchant stands and vehicles, ducking his head beneath the noxious cloud of motor oil and gasohol vapor that hung suspended in the air.

Within minutes he knew he was being followed. He'd been taught how to sense it—a subconscious awareness he'd slowly learned to trust. He glanced over his shoulder and spotted them. Three small, painfully thin boys gazed back at him with large, yellow-stained eyes. He stared at them coldly before easing his face into a smile. The boys instantly smiled back at him just as they had the previous morning. The largest of the three bolted toward him, his tiny chest swelling arrogantly under a dirty, threadbare shirt.

"How now, how ya body?" The boy's thin, shrill voice asked in pidgin English as he walked beside him.

"Fine-oh," he responded with a low voice, not breaking his quick pace.

The boy's rail-thin arm lifted upward as he held out his tiny, mocha-colored palm.

"Abeg," he said confidently, his deep, ebony-black eyes liquid and intense.

He stared down at him with mock irritation as his hand worked into his pocket, slapping 300 naira into the boy's palm before gripping it in the vise of his hand. "Coke, and some hot suya," he mumbled.

The boy nodded quickly as he pulled pleadingly at his arm.

"Okay, mista, okay!"

He released his grip, and the boy shot into the dense forest of people, his two tiny colleagues trailing closely behind him. "Do quick!" he yelled after them, a sly grin creasing his lips. Within minutes his breakfast would be served.

He continued walking, weaving inconspicuously through the mob as it shuffled and flowed around him. It was market day, and the normally heavy throngs of locals clad in bright shirts and long, flowing *bubas* seemed to have multiplied twofold as they converged under the smoldering, sand-blown sky. Everything was in constant, clamoring motion. Fluttering, leg-strapped chickens dangled from tall poles. Wheelbarrows loaded with exotic fruits teetered along the pockmarked streets. Baskets brimming with plantains and yams towered over him, balanced precariously on the gele-wrapped heads of local women.

A perfect day, he knew, to go unnoticed.

A shrill young voice called out from within the crowd.

"Heavy men!"

He smiled as he considered the pidgin meaning. *Tough guy.* A moment later the boy was walking next to him, a sweating bottle of Coke in one hand and two skewers of blackened meat in the other. The boy held them up proudly, his tiny face creased with a grin.

"Thanks," he said, grabbing his meal. "Now, make you carry youself go."

The boy flashed another toothy grin. "A dey see yu lata!" he shouted as he turned to his sidekicks, and the three tiny bodies again vanished into the crowd.

He continued toward the center of town, slipping efficiently through the crowd as he chewed on the suya—steaming, pepper-hot strips of beef that were a local delicacy. He ignored the weight of the backpack that clung heavily to his shoulder. Occasionally a merchant would step out from his stall and grab onto him, urging him to see a carving or hand-sewn shirt. He dismissed them with a wave, never breaking his stride. He walked on for countless more blocks before finally, peeking through the smoky-blue haze of exhaust, his destination materialized above the market.

=====

The ten-story, immaculately finished façade of the Garden Landmark Hotel stood in stark contrast above the squat, dilapidated squalor of its surroundings. Built just a year before, the tall, graceful building was a towering sculpture of glass and steel, so anomalous to its surroundings that it appeared as if a piece of New York City or Paris had inexplicably fallen from the sky. He'd read that it was built to mark the beginning of a "new" Port Harcourt, but as he walked toward it, he thought once again that it seemed to only underscore the immense poverty of the place. To the majority of people here, the hotel was just a painful reminder of what they did not have, a mocking beacon of radiant, unattainable opulence.

He slipped easily from the stream of merchants and market-goers as he reached the entrance gate of the hotel, a large "GL" inscription elegantly emblazoned on the heavy steel gate. The massive concrete walls to both sides were intricately adorned with stylized reliefs of elephants, buffalo, and lions, artfully masking their true intent of absolute security. A short, muscular security guard with a scar across his forehead eyed him with suspicion as he stepped up and wordlessly pulled his room key and ID card into view. The guard leaned against the gate and examined the card for a long moment before fixing his dark eyes on him intensely. He nodded calmly at the guard. Satisfied, the guard nodded back and opened the gate just enough for his slender frame to pass. He smiled casually as he entered the courtyard, quickly appraising his surroundings as they transformed from the grimy, traffic-choked streets to a serene open courtyard of rose trellises and flowering acacia trees.

The nearly empty atrium lobby of the Garden Landmark stretched across a reflective sea of black polished granite. The modern, minimalist décor was an austere landscape of chrome and leather furnishings, appearing to be made more for aesthetics than comfort. Large, stunningly intricate batik textiles suspended over the check-in desk exploded with hues of ochre and phthalo blue, offering the only homage to the local Nigerian culture.

He pretended to admire them as he strolled by the desk toward the elevators, smiling casually at the beautiful, slender young Nigerian concierge as he passed. Feeling her eyes on him, he wondered briefly if she, like so many of the young women in Port Harcourt, had been "trained" in the African style of customer service. He reached the elevators and stepped into the first one that opened its golden-mirrored doors. As the floors ticked off, he mentally rechecked the contents of his backpack, absently humming to a voiceless, synthesized version of Elton John's "Your Song" that drifted from the overhead speakers.

The eighth-floor hallway curved gracefully as it followed the hotel's serpentine design. His footsteps drummed a fast rhythm that echoed out into the open atrium as he paced down the bright mahogany-walled corridor. Stopping at the door of suite 814, he glanced quickly to both sides before sliding the keycard through the electronic lock and stepping inside.

Turning to close the door, he flinched in surprise as a man's voice cried out behind him.

"Well, good morning to ya, Chilly!"

Recognizing the thick Irish accent, he rolled his eyes as he stepped through the entryway. "Christ, I should have known it would be you." He smirked, raising his eyebrows at the stout, middle-aged man sprawled across the couch. "Sleep well?"

"Fook yeah I did," the man replied. "Nicest feckin' place I've stayed at since I can remember. Never expected this in feckin' Africa."

He nodded at the man he called *Dublin*. This would be their third job together. Although he knew Dublin's real name, he would never say it. Not on a job, not ever. Nor would Dublin refer to him by any other name than *Chilly*. This wasn't just an agency rule, it was simple common sense.

"So you're my fixer on this one, huh?" Chilly muttered rhetorically as he shrugged off his backpack and looked around the swank, lavishly appointed room. "Makes perfect sense. Your mouth is the only thing filthier than this city."

Dublin's raucous laugh filled the room. "Yeah, and that's sayin' a lot," he said with the gravelly voice of a smoker. "'S'one nasty feckin' town down there. Some beautiful-lookin' girls, but I'd put on four condoms before I laid my hands on any of that strange if I were you." Dublin barely finished his sentence before convulsing once again into laughter.

Chilly wondered how someone like the loud, foul-mouthed, overweight Irishman now stretched out in front of him managed to get by in this particular profession. Then again, maybe those qualities were exactly why he got by in this profession. Whatever it was, he didn't object. As far as fixers go, Dublin was the best in the business. "Well, if anyone can get his hands on something, it's you," he replied as he walked over to the wall-sized window of glass that looked out on the decaying city. "Of course that's probably especially true for venereal diseases. Personally, I like to keep my nose and other parts clean."

"Yeah, yeah—bein' the feckin' saint that you are," Dublin retorted as he fished a pack of cigarettes from his pocket. "Prob'ly just as well. If I stay any longer, my fookin' meat and potatoes will rot off." He lit a cigarette and stared at his colleague for a long moment. "Speakin' of rot, you're really stayin' at some shite hotel in town, huh?"

"I am. It's actually much nicer than this," Chilly replied. "I doubt you even get complimentary roaches here."

Dublin's face split into an incredulous grin.

"Bugger off, mate! That's the daftest thing I've ever heard."

Chilly shrugged as he stared down at the colorful crowd swarming like ants around the market below. There was no need to defend himself on the subject of hotel accommodations. He had his own reasons for staying in the slums—none of which his colleague needed to know about. Besides, he wasn't here to live it up. In fact, blending in was a necessary part of the job. And regardless how good the money might be, this was certainly not the job of a rock star. Well, perhaps it had a *few* similarities, but not many of the good ones.

He turned from the window and dropped into an oversized leather armchair that sat across from the sofa. "All right, let's get to it."

"Right." Dublin snapped into focus as he sat upright and snuffed out his cigarette. Looks and language aside, he'd still not forgotten who was in charge.

"What's the status on the package?" Chilly asked. This was always the first question, the most important question. Without the package, nothing else mattered.

"Package acquired, of course," Dublin answered. His eyes darted instinctively to the three cell phones lying on the coffee table in front of him. "Not that it was feckin' easy. 'S'like bein' in the feckin' dark ages around here. And I'm beginnin' to think my job is almost as messy as yours, for chrissake."

"Sure," Chilly said dismissively. "And you confirmed the specs?"

"Yeah, yeah, confirmed," Dublin replied, a trace of irritation on his face. "I am a feckin' professional, ya know."

"Of course you are, Dub. Why do you think I always ask for my favorite Irishman when it comes to the tough projects?"

Dublin stared back at him with slits for eyes as he lit another cigarette. He wasn't used to being made fun of.

"And our staging area?" Chilly continued.

"Room 805. Visually checked. Everything as expected." The Irishman's mouth exhaled a long trail of smoke as he lay back on the couch. A thick roll of ghost-white skin revealed itself beneath his vintage KISS T-shirt.

"Time?"

"Package'll be delivered tonight. Nine p.m. You've got my guarantee on that as always. Room 805 will be open for business by six p.m. I managed to get it logged by maintenance as a corporate hold until showtime tomorrow, which means every employee in the building will think some executive fuckety-fuck is in there shagging his mistress. Trust me, you won't have any interruptions." He paused and took a long drag on his cigarette. "Tha rest is up to you, mate." Smoke poured from his nostrils as Dublin's mouth formed into a grin. "Got a long night ahead of you, eh? Ha! Fook yeah ya do!"

Chilly smiled and nodded. "I suppose so. And what about you? Your work's done for now. Off to some charity event this evening? Or perhaps lend a hand at the soup kitchen?"

"No rest for tha feckin' wicked, mate," Dublin said as he glanced at his watch and abruptly shot up from the couch. "I'm off to the airport. Wheels up in an hour." He shuffled into the suite's master bedroom and quickly collected his things. On the coffee table, one of his cell phones vibrated to life.

"You're being hailed."

Dublin grunted from the other room as his phone buzzed in a stop-and-go dance across the table. "Feckin' wife," the Irishman muttered as he paced out of the bedroom with two small bags of luggage. He dropped them next to the coffee table and snatched up the phone in his thick hand. "She's always harassin' me whenever I'm gone for more'n a few feckin' days."

"Aren't you almost always gone?" Chilly asked.

"Fook yeah—and thank god for that. Otherwise I woulda feckin' killed her years ago." The sarcastic smile on Dublin's face turned serious as he read the message on the screen. He looked up with surprise. "You're in luck, mate. Package'll be delivered by eight o'clock tonight. You'll be able to get an early start on making a bloody feckin' mess."

"Perfect. I guess that means you can now officially get the hell out of here."

Dublin shoved the phone into a holster on his belt and pocketed the other two. He glanced around the suite before collecting his bags. "Have fun stormin' the feckin' castle, my friend," he said from the doorway.

"Go home, Dublin," Chilly replied without turning around. "And try spending some time with your wife."

"Ha! *You* try spending time with my wife," the Irishman replied. "Then you'll know what I'm talking about!"

The door shut with a gentle click behind him. Chilly grabbed his backpack and set it on the coffee table, then emptied the contents onto the glass surface. The small steel tools reflected the light like intricate mirrors as he examined each of them. Satisfied that everything was in order, he returned the tools to the backpack and shoved it under the table, out of immediate view. He then pushed the armchair over to the window and sank into it wearily.

There was nothing left to do until the package arrived. Nothing to do but rest. He closed his eyes and inhaled the rich, earthy scent of the chair leather. The sounds of the market rose up from the street below in a cacophony of white noise, and in seconds he was asleep.

Chapter 10

It would suck to die alone.

The means wouldn't matter. Freeze to death. Burn to death. Fall from a ladder. Jump from a bridge. Whatever. This wasn't about the "how." This was about the "who cares?" This was about the simple fact that the only thing more depressing than the verb "die" was an accompanying adjective of "alone." This was about passing into the black void of eternal nothingness without a warm hand to hold or a loved face to look upon. This was about watching the nothingness creep into the corners of your vision while the pulsing rhythm of your chest stutters and fades. This was about the going, going, gone—

—and having no one there to grieve about it.

Jeri tried to push the words from her mind as she poured another beer from the tap. It was a cold October evening, and the saloon's dark, body-warm interior was busy, but not busy enough to quiet the morbid monologue playing in her head. Unfortunately she already knew the words by heart. They'd been echoing repeatedly since her disastrous dinner with Rob the night before.

She lined the drinks up along the bar and quickly glanced around the room. The usual mix of young coeds filled the bar, all giddy with the excitement of newly achieved legal-age adulthood. A twinge of jealousy coursed through her as she watched them laugh and mingle. Every face seemed to glow with the unblemished beauty of youth and optimism. The cheerful atmosphere of the room only made Jeri feel worse, her dark mood lurking like a black hole surrounded by bright, sparkling young stars.

"Are you okay, Jeri?" Chip asked from his usual spot at the bar.

Jeri glanced over at the only older person in the saloon and nodded. She realized she'd barely said three words to Chip all afternoon, and a sudden pang of guilt briefly shook her from her funk. Noticing his glass was nearly empty, she sighed and walked over to him.

"You seem a little distracted," Chip said, his blue eyes smiling at her as she approached.

"No, just busy," Jeri replied brusquely. She pointed at his glass. "Need another one?"

"Oh, yeah . . . sure."

She could feel Chip's stare burning into her as she turned and filled his pint glass. It wasn't the first time he'd sat there trying to decipher her mood and formulate the best way to shake her out of it. This was Chip the professor, Chip the problem solver, and Jeri knew he was looking at her now the same way he would have looked at an archeological site. He was reading the jagged landscape and judging where to dig.

"Here you go, old man," she said as she placed a fresh pint of beer in front him.

"Thanks, Jeri."

"Any time," she replied, a hint of warmth in her voice.

Chip latched his hand around the sweating glass and glanced around the room. "Kids," he said irritably, as if reading Jeri's earlier thoughts. "They turn twenty-one and what's the first thing they do? Come running to the bars looking for a drink."

"Don't tell me you weren't doing the same thing when you were their age," Jeri retorted sarcastically.

"No, I was," he mumbled, looking at the crowd over his shoulder. "I just don't think I looked that young. Or that stupid. Christ, just look at what they're wearing."

Jeri smiled at Chip. Even in her current mood it was hard not to give in to his cynical sense of humor. "Right. Well, obviously no one else around here is as together as you are, or I should say *were*, Chip. But most of us have to start somewhere."

Chip turned and stared thoughtfully at the amber-colored beer in his glass. "True. But you know, I never worried so much about where I started. I've always believed it's where you end up that counts." He looked up at Jeri with a shrewd smile. "Wouldn't you agree?"

Jeri felt the color flush to her face as Chip's icy-blue eyes smiled back at her. The digging had begun.

"It's probably the wrong night for this conversation, Chip."

"Why's that?"

Jeri shrugged and shook her head. What could she even say? That the night before she had blown yet another potentially good relationship? That she had once again found a single grain of fault in a handsome, intelligent man and turned that lone grain into a swirling sandstorm of doubt and disinterest? That it wasn't *him*, it was *her* who didn't quite fit right, though really in the hidden corner of her mind, an all-too-familiar voice was always blaming *him*, *him*, *HIM*? Would Chip, or any man, for that matter, really want to know that, without ever intending to, she had become a man-mashing, hope-killing, love-doubting, overanalyzing, alarmingly cynical bitch?

She tucked a loose strand of coppery hair behind her ear and looked up at Chip with wet, hazardous eyes. Chip met her stare, quietly reading the landscape of her face before shaking his head and dropping his gaze to his beer.

"Never mind. None of my business."

Jeri noticed a tall young man standing at the far end of the counter and immediately moved toward him, happy for an excuse to end the conversation. She forced her mouth into a smile as the man leaned over the bar and nodded.

"Get you a drink?"

"Sure," the man replied with a grin. "Whiskey and Coke, please."

Jeri avoided eye contact as she poured the black and caramel-colored liquids into an ice-filled glass. She could tell from her peripheral vision that the man was watching her, his eyes tracing slow lines from her hands to her face. Despite her current disposition, his stares were managing to stir a warm blush on her face. The man was extraordinarily good-looking, with a dark complexion and short, tousled curls of ebony hair. But he was young. Way, way too young.

She set his drink on the bar and looked at him, her smile coming easier this time. "There you go. That'll be five bucks, or you can start a tab."

The young man's grin stretched into a broad smile of brilliant teeth as he reached out and handed her a crisply folded bill. "Thanks, Jeri. Keep the change."

She looked at him with surprise. The warm blush on her face flared with new heat. "I'm sorry—have we met before?" she asked.

His eyes, as enticingly dark and liquid as the cocktail, widened in a mock expression of shock as he took a long sip of his drink. He studied her for a moment before waving his hand toward the wall next to him.

Jeri glanced at the wall. There, pinned to a large bulletin board made of wine corks, hung the letters and Polaroid photos from her unknown writer. Taped across the top of the board was a printed banner that read "Tales from the Last Stander," while along the bottom, another banner read "Reveal his identity and get a free T-shirt!" Wrapped limply around the board in a final tasteless gesture only Joe himself could have conceived, a single strand of silver Christmas tinsel sparkled in the dim light.

"The letters," the young man responded. "I read the letters, and, well, I just assumed you must be her." He watched with eager eyes as Jeri tucked a lock of hair behind her ear. A brief cloud of emotion seemed to cross her face as her smile twisted and faded.

"And why would you assume that?" Jeri asked.

The young man detected a new tone in her voice, as subtle and dangerous as a thin layer of ice forming on the surface of a dark road. "You just seem like the only one working here worth writing to," he replied confidently. He then grinned and narrowed his eyes, casting Jeri his most disarming expression. His fraternity friends didn't call him the *snake charmer* for nothing.

"In case you haven't noticed, I *am* the only one working here. Period."

"Right," he responded apologetically. "Well, anyway, I can see why he would write to you." He shifted his face into one his most attractive expressions, but Jeri's stare remained strangely unreadable. For the first time in recent history, the young man wondered whether his charm was working. "So, what time do you—"

Jeri quickly held up a finger. "Hold that thought."

The young man watched Jeri's slender, beautifully proportioned frame as she walked to the far end of the counter and poured a beer. His pulse quickened as she flashed him a look and handed the beer to an older, gray-haired man sitting in the corner. The two exchanged a quick word before the old man turned and smiled at him. *That's it . . . she's mine*, he thought confidently as Jeri slowly strolled back toward him. He looked away nonchalantly, feigning interest in a stack of large books tucked behind the bar next to a stool. The books all had long titles like *Global Trade in the*

Digital Communication Era, The Conundrum of China, and *Supply Chain Best Practices*—whatever the hell that meant. He was wondering who could possibly be interested in such nonsense when Jeri stepped back in front of him.

"So tell me why," she said, flashing him a brilliant smile as she rested her elbows on the counter and leaned seductively forward. He was momentarily caught off guard, awed by the silky, alabaster beauty of her face and yet confused by the cold, unblinking stare of her eyes that refused to match her otherwise inviting expression.

"Why . . . why what?" he stammered.

"You said you knew why he would write me," Jeri replied. Her amber eyes locked on his as she rested her head in her hand. "So explain it to me."

He smiled shyly and quickly ran his hand through his dark curls. *Checkmate*, he thought to himself. The boyish approach was working. It always worked. Now he just had to tell her what she wanted to hear, and this one would be in the bag.

"It's pretty obvious," he answered, staring at his drink. "I mean, you're totally gorgeous, so I'm sure he was immediately attracted to you." He looked at her with a sheepish grin.

Jeri glared at him for a moment before speaking. "And?"

"And, well, I mean . . ." He paused for a quick sip of his drink, trying to rapidly collect his thoughts. The second compliment was always harder. You had to get under the surface, take some risks. He was still searching for the right words when he once again noticed the books on the bar. *Bingo*.

"You seem really intelligent. Maybe that's not something everyone else sees right away, but I'm sure he noticed, just like I did."

"Wow. That's really . . . amazing," Jeri whispered, her lips stretching into another smile.

The young man again noticed the odd coldness of her eyes that seemed distantly focused. It was as if she were in fact looking *through* him. But he must have been imagining things. Clearly this was going well. "I guess you could say I'm perceptive," he replied.

"Oh, I agree. I would definitely call you perceptive."

He took a long sip of his drink, smiling at her with his deep brown eyes. "And I would definitely call you . . . well, actually, I would *literally* call you. That is, if I had your phone number."

"Say again?" Jeri asked.

"You know, just a little play on words," he said wryly. "But hey, since we're on the subject, I really would like to get your number."

Jeri stepped back from the bar as her smile suddenly evaporated. Her throat tightened in preparation as if her voice were now on autopilot, queuing up her words. And just as surely as she knew the words that were coming, Jeri knew she'd hate herself later for saying them.

"You know, it's interesting," she began, her voice calm and warm. "When you first walked up to me, I realized you and the man who wrote those letters have a few things in common. The most obvious is that you're both tall, dark, and—as you're clearly aware—handsome. In fact, for a minute, I thought you just might be . . . well, never mind." Jeri paused for a moment as the young man's face lit with a smile. *The poor bastard still thinks he has a chance*, she thought somberly. "The other thing you two have in common is that neither one of you knows a damn thing about me. But then, that's where the similarities seem to end."

"What about the fact that we both obviously like you?" the young man asked playfully.

"You don't *like* me," Jeri snapped. "You *want* me. Big difference. To like me would be to write me letters and tell me stories that make me curious and make me laugh. That shows creativity and interest. You, on the other hand, with your twenty-something lust, just want me, which means you'll sit here for fifteen minutes and smile your handsome smile and run your hands through your perfect, stylish hair and sneak a few peeks at my books to determine whether I'm smart or not. And if everything falls into place, you'll take me home to some filthy little apartment decorated with a beer-reeking futon and fumble me through ten minutes of mediocre sex." She paused for a moment, taking a quick breath of air as the young man slumped deeper into his barstool. "And for what? All that effort for the purpose of you going back to the frat house and telling your buddies that you . . . how would you say it? *Tapped that ass?*"

"Wait a minute, I—"

"No, don't apologize," Jeri interrupted, raising her hand. "Don't you see? I'm not asking you to like me. I'm just not interested in you wanting me. Do you understand what I mean? Of course you do. You're a smart guy. I might've just wasted the last fifteen minutes of your favorite pickup strategy, but cheer up! There's plenty of naïve young ass in this bar that hasn't learned the difference between *like* and *want* yet, so get out there and start tapping!"

The young man stared back at Jeri with wide, unblinking eyes, like an actor suddenly stricken with stage fright. His smile had fallen into his half-gaping mouth, and for the first time Jeri realized his childish shyness looked genuinely real. She picked up a towel and began hastily wiping down the counter. She was already beginning to hate herself.

"Look, I'm sorry, I—"

"You said the man that wrote those letters and I don't know anything about you," the young man interrupted. "But that's not really true, is it?"

Jeri smiled wearily as her towel made small circular patterns across the old dark oak. "No, it's not. You know something about me now that he doesn't."

"What's that?"

Jeri's smile faded as she carefully folded the towel and tossed it onto the rack beneath the counter. She glanced through the window at the blurred streaks of headlights that cut along the cold inky blackness of old Route 66.

"That I can be a real bitch."

She turned and marched toward the other end of the bar before the young man could respond. There was nothing more to add to the conversation, nothing she would want to hear. She poured a few more drinks to the waning crowd, then leaned against the back counter and waited for the night to slowly fold to a close. A young couple stood to leave, the man eagerly helping the woman with her jacket and scarf before taking her glove-sheathed hand. Jeri studied them smiling and kissing as they slid through the door, the vapor of their hot breath rising like smoke before evaporating into the frozen air. She crossed her arms and sighed quietly, the volume of a conversation beginning to rise once more in her head.

It would suck to die alone.

Chapter 11

Spotless.

Its surface radiated, glinting in the light of the room. Clean as the first time out of the box. Pure as a virgin's conscience. A tiny, glimmering sculpture of 420-grade martensitic stainless steel.

Chilly wiped down the utensil again. As always, the act rekindled a memory of his father, peering down at some tool in his workshop from behind the black lenses of his ever-present Ray-Bans, a cigarette hanging loosely from his mouth, his voice deep and confident. He would calmly repeat his favorite lesson over and over, like some goddamn religious mantra, until the words had burned into his young son's consciousness. Those same words now echoed in Chilly's head as he wiped the tiny instrument and inspected, wiped and inspected, wiped and inspected.

If you take good care of your tools,
your tools will take good care of you.

Satisfied, Chilly slipped the last instrument of machined steel into its custom-formed sleeve and rolled the kit tightly back into its original shape, slapping the thick elastic band around it before shoving it into his backpack. He stood up from the barstool and slowly stretched his arms over his head and yawned, enjoying the feeling of his tensed muscles as he wrung the exhaustion from his body. He then glanced at his watch.

2:42 a.m.

Six hours working on the package. Six hours straight. No piss breaks, no smoke breaks, no fifteen-minute porn channel jerk-off breaks. Six hours of calm-handed, clear-eyed, mind-focused, dick-flaccid attention. Some in his profession might call this heroic. Most would call it insane, but in an awed, reverential, brilliant sort of way, like Leo standing tirelessly in the dining hall of the Santa Maria delle Grazie while he toiled away at *The Last Supper* for hours at a time. Dublin would call him feckin' daft. But then, Dublin was a selfish, corpulent prick.

The package itself sat next to him in the chair at the kitchen bar, just inches away. He examined it with a critical eye and smiled. It was an inanimate mass of subtle brilliance. Then again, there was nothing subtle about the way the package itself looked. Were a stranger to mistakenly walk into suite 805 at this moment, one look at the object planted on the expensive, high-backed leather barstool would leave them suspended in the kind of paralyzing fear that usually starts with soft-spoken gibberish, ignites into involuntary shaking, and concludes with bowel-releasing spasms. It was the kind of sight that would immediately tell them that the small little corner of the world they just happened to walk into was undoubtedly the worst mistake of their lives, producing that gut feeling that this tiny circle on the map, and every unfortunate thing inside it, was about to be fully and irrevocably fucked.

Luckily, he'd never had that happen.

Chilly walked over to the window and stared down into the dark and nearly deserted streets of the city. Market day had long since ended, taking with it the usual teeming crowds. The service gate of the hotel stood directly beneath him, brightly illuminated by a high row of sodium lights that painted the seated, half-slumbering security guards in a pasty shade of jaundice yellow. Just outside of the tall, razor-wire-topped security wall stood a motley collection of roguish boys intensely preoccupied with smoking cigarettes and staring into the night. He watched for several minutes, curious why the boys fidgeted nervously, until the flickering light of a match from the darkness of the opposite street corner faintly illuminated a large gang of young men, their dark faces fixed menacingly on the boys along the fence. The scene stirred another old childhood memory in him—a warm summer day at a nameless lake, his small figure standing along the shore, watching silvery bands of panicked minnows schooling in the shallows as larger fish flashed just beyond in the murky depths.

The predators wait patiently for their prey.

He walked back to the kitchen and picked up the folder on the counter, flipping through the instructions and documents given to him by the men in Al Jubail. He paused on a page containing several images of a short, thin older man with deep-set dark eyes and a slight build, taken from various angles, revealing his facial features in a variety of expressions—laughing, serious, aggravated, and even a photo where the man appeared to be shocked—or terrified. Across the top of the page was a quickly scrawled "#1" written in heavy permanent marker and circled. He lingered on the last photo before glancing up at the package, then quietly closed the folder and tucked it into his backpack.

He was done. Installation complete.

He stumbled into the living room and fell onto the wide leather couch, rubbing his knuckles into his closed eyes for a moment before grabbing his cell phone and texting a brief message.

Batter up.

He tossed the cell phone onto the coffee table and sank into the soft cushions. The click of the entry door's electronic lock dragged him back into consciousness, momentarily disorienting him as he lifted his head wearily from the couch. A blond young man with boyish looks and broad, muscled shoulders strolled into suite 805, a large leather satchel slung over his shoulder.

"Knock knock," the young man announced, walking into the large room.

"Tall Tommy," Chilly replied as he examined the man standing in front of him. "Christ, you look like a damn college student."

Tall Tommy smiled, exposing a broad row of perfect ivory. "Aww . . . thanks, Chilly. You yourself look like that rock star from the eighties. You know, the one that tried masturbating from a hangman's noose and slipped on his own sauce?"

"To hell with you . . . I loved that band," Chilly said as he sat up slowly, his body stiff with exhaustion. "For one thing, he was from your country, so show a little respect. Second, autoerotic asphyxia is highly underrated. Maybe you should try it sometime."

"Who says I haven't?" Tall Tommy replied, his sarcasm laced with an Australian accent.

Chilly smiled and nodded. As with Dublin, this would be his third time working with Tall Tommy, but he'd liked him from the start. One look at the handsome, twenty-something Aussie told him that Tall Tommy was the kind of guy who won every athletic competition he entered, aced every class he studied, and deflowered every cheerleader he came across as a kid before heading off to college for a repeat performance. He had the naturally graced gift of chiseled looks and perfect physique that women adored and lesser men detested, but beneath his mockingly self-absorbed behavior, he seemed clean of any genuinely prickish qualities. One thing Chilly knew for certain about Tall Tommy, from their first project together in Mexico City, was that he was both razor sharp and highly skilled. Having both him and Dublin on this project was like having Michael Jordan and Scottie Pippen together on the court; he was working with a dream team of talent.

Chilly glanced again at his watch. 3:03 a.m. "Thanks for giving me a full five minutes of sleep."

Tall Tommy shrugged as his eyebrows rose in mock surprise. "Hey, mate, you called *me*."

"Yeah, but I didn't know you were practically waiting by the goddamn door when I did."

"Jesus Christ, Chilly . . . my room is two floors down," Tall Tommy snapped. "I've just spent the last two hours lying on the bed watching a fucking Barbra Streisand movie, bored out of my head. Of course, I wasn't really watching the movie as much as I was wondering why the hell Robert Redford would be interested in an emotionally unstable Jewish chick with big hair and questionable political views. Or more importantly, why the wonderful people of Nigeria would give a damn about two white Americans falling in love and having a shitty marriage."

"*The Way We Were*," Chilly replied. "Great movie. Sydney Pollack flick. I think that one won an Oscar."

Tall Tommy glowered at him for a moment before scratching his chin with his middle finger. "Yeah, that's absolutely awesome, and you know how much I appreciate your extensive knowledge of movies that suck, but that doesn't make up for the fact that I've been stuck in this fucking hotel for the last twenty-four hours."

"What do you mean, stuck?"

"C'mon, be reasonable," Tall Tommy replied, staring at his colleague as if he were mentally challenged. "Do you really think a white guy—wait, strike that—an *incredibly good-looking* white guy like me can just go strolling out on the town around here and not get noticed?"

"Good point," Chilly answered. "Especially when you're dressed like a Geoffrey Beene model."

"Fuck off."

Tall Tommy carefully rested his satchel on the coffee table and began to unpack it. He pulled out a small, brightly labeled vial and twisted the top off, catching Chilly's stare as he gulped back its contents. "Relax. . . it's just B-twelve," he said, tossing the empty vitamin container at his colleague. "Keeps me sharp. You don't honestly think I'm gonna poison this pristine temple of a body, do you?" He briefly assumed the pose of a Romanesque statue, then grabbed the air in front of him and started thrusting his pelvis slowly. "Besides, I've gotta keep it fresh for the ladies."

Chilly smiled and shook his head. "Christ, you and Dublin should hang out together."

Tall Tommy shrugged and went back to unpacking his bag. "No chance. Dublin would fuck pond scum if it had legs and a pair of breasts. He and I are not exactly playing in the same league."

"I don't think he's even playing in the same species."

The Australian laughed as he pulled a thin manila folder stamped with a six-digit number from his satchel and flipped it open. "Any surprises for me tonight?" he asked as he thumbed through the pages.

"Nada," Chilly replied, his voice low and somber. "Like clockwork so far." He watched as Tall Tommy quickly scanned the information, his brow furrowed in concentration. Even though his colleague had gotten the packet days ago, this was undoubtedly the first time he'd stopped to read it.

"When did the package show up?" Tall Tommy asked.

"About seven hours ago."

The Australian snapped the folder shut and tossed it onto the coffee table. His eyes danced around the room before settling on the object that sat at the kitchen bar. "Seven hours, huh?" he said with an edge of awe in his voice as he walked toward it. "Is that how long it usually takes to do this?"

"Depends," Chilly responded dismissively. He never liked to discuss such details. His job, like his colleagues', was a solo one for a reason. "Each one's different."

"Yeah, no shit," Tall Tommy whispered, his stare fixed solemnly on the object. "Okay, I'll take it from here, mate. Our man is doing his cameo in about six hours, so I'd better get started. Is all of your gear accounted for?" Chilly nodded as his colleague pulled two latex gloves from his pocket and looked around the room. "Anything off-list get touched?" the Australian asked as he quickly snapped the gloves over his fingers. A small cloud of talcum dust swirled in the air.

"Nope."

"Sweet," Tall Tommy said, pulling a tiny, expensive-looking pair of headphones from his pocket and placing them carefully over his ears. "Well then, Chilly, don't let the door hit your ass on the way out."

Chapter 12

"Peace Corps," the pasty-faced young man mumbled, staring at the wall of the saloon in front of him. "The guy's gotta be in the Peace Corps." He turned to his college friends and raised his arm in the air. "Ready?"

The two other young men raised their arms, and the three nodded a silent toast before slugging back the shots of vodka. A brief grimace etched their faces before turning into a conspiratorial grin.

"Whoa—shit!" His long-haired friend gasped, setting the shot glass on the bar before tightening the hair tie of his ponytail and adjusting his glasses.

"That'll fuck you up!"

"We're doing another one in five minutes," the third man replied, lightly punching both his colleagues in the chest. He was nearly a head taller than the other two, with thin, tattoo-covered arms. "And don't even try to pussy out." He looked again at the "shrine" of letters pinned to the wall inside Joe's Last Stand Saloon, his expression thoughtful as he stroked his patchy beard. "He's not in the Peace Corps, bro," he replied. "Peace Corps people don't move around that much. They stay in the same shithole place for like two years or something." He squinted at the photos. "Can't really see him, but I'd also say he looks older than most of those Peace Corps hippies. He's probably in that Doctors Without

Borders group. They're kind of like the Peace Corps . . . they go to all these fucked-up places and heal all the people that are shot and starving and shit. That's my bet."

His ponytailed friend shook his head. "A doctor? You honestly think he's a doctor?" he asked sarcastically. "No way, man . . . he's a reporter."

He stepped closer to the tinsel-wrapped display of letters and photos, then turned and looked at his two friends. "I mean, think about it. He's in places that no normal person would care about or even think to visit, but he's only there for a short time."

"True," his pasty-faced friend remarked.

"And take a look at this," ponytail continued, pointing at the Polaroids. "You can't actually see his face, which makes perfect sense if he's a reporter, because he doesn't want anyone to recognize him and find out he's sweet-talking some bartender in an old dive bar in Flagstaff."

"Right, yeah . . . that's *got* to be it," his tattooed friend muttered sarcastically before edging toward the bar. "I'm ordering another round."

"Seriously, man, it's so obvious." Ponytail's voice rose with excitement. "Look at the way he writes—he's clever and charismatic, like all reporters are. I have an uncle who was a reporter for the Associated Press—well, I mean I *had* an uncle who was a reporter."

"Like me, huh?" his pasty-faced friend asked.

"No, man," ponytail replied irritably, "he was a *real* reporter, not some wannabe college-paper reporter like you. Anyway, he's dead now, but he used to fly all over the fucking place on assignment. He was a smart motherfucker too." He leaned toward the wall and squinted, as if finding a clue everyone else had overlooked, before adjusting his eyeglasses again. "That's got to be it. Reporter."

His friends stared at him vacantly for a moment. "Damn, man, you've got me convinced," pasty-face replied. "Maybe I should write an article in the paper about this guy."

"Sure, whatever, bro," his tattooed friend declared, handing both of them an ice-cold shot glass filled to the brim. "So what happened to your uncle?"

"Bad shit, man. Drove his car into a tree," ponytail replied, a pensive frown clouding his expression.

"Fuck . . . no shit?"

"No shit. Kinda saw it coming, though. The guy was a total alcoholic. Always drunk at the holidays and making passes at my other uncle's wife. The cops that pulled his body out of the wreck said his BAC was like four percent or something."

"Is that even possible?" pasty-face asked.

"Of course it is, if you're a fucking alcoholic. Anyway . . ." He shrugged and nodded dismissively.

"Well, here's to him," his tattooed friend muttered, raising his shot glass.

"To crazy motherfucking reporters," pasty-face chimed.

"Cheers to that," ponytail added.

The three young men nodded and touched glasses. They threw back the shots and looked at each other in the weak light of the bar, shuddering and wincing with the wide-eyed grins of children.

Chapter 13

The atrium lobby of the Garden Landmark Hotel bustled with the noise and activity of midmorning check-ins and check-outs as the concierge made her rounds, gliding across the mirror-polished granite with a confident, seductive sway. Tall and dark, her body cast an exotic reflection over the black stone as she moved. She stopped briefly at one of the tables to adjust the stargazer lilies and cymbidium orchids in one of the massive flower arrangements on display, their sweet, cinnamon fragrances mixing with those of expensive European perfumes in the cool, conditioned air. A guest approached her, and she smiled instinctively, nodding at his question before tapping her phone and making a call. By eight a.m. she had already made more calls for the hotel's elite guests than she could remember. Everything from cab rides and flight confirmations for those departing to spa sessions and dinner reservations for new guests had been deftly handled. Now, seeing that the girls at the registration desk were becoming overwhelmed, she moved quickly to intercept new arrivals strolling through the massive glass entry doors.

She smiled with flawless grace, tilting her head with a welcoming expression as a group of men in tailored suits and polished Italian shoes stepped into the lobby with several bellhops in tow. "Good morning, gentlemen, and welcome to the Garden Landmark. May

I assist you in checking in?" she asked. The men nodded as they collected around her. One of the men barraged her with questions while the others stood and stared conspicuously at the curves of her body beneath her tight blue uniform. She recognized several of them. In her four years at the hotel, she'd come to know a good many of the hotel's clientele on practically a first-name basis. The majority were regular guests like these—executives from large petrochemical companies with operations in the country's oil-rich Niger delta. They were middle-aged, mostly European and American, with graying hair and soft bellies and the curt politeness of men used to getting what they asked for. But despite their egos, she admired and envied these men—or at least their wealth and power. They were refined and well mannered, a stark contrast to the hotel's other oil-feeding clientele—the large, bawdy, loud-talking roughnecks from Texas or Russia who dressed in outdated Tommy Bahama outfits and spent long hours drinking at the bar, killing time and money until their rig contracts were renewed.

She found the latter group to be both humorous and dangerous, especially at night. It was then that they would come stumbling collectively from the bar to the lobby, red-eyed and volatile, prowling for the seedier offerings of the city that sprang up like mushrooms in the night. They would collect anything in their path that they fancied, including her or any of her female coworkers, and on more than one occasion she'd had to apologetically but firmly remove the arm of a roughneck from around her waist. If personalities had a sound, she imagined that of the roughneck being the *tick*, *tick*, *tick* of a timed explosive.

Last in the social hierarchy of the hotel was the media, a disheveled, sleep-deprived fraternity of international reporters who had settled on the town like an irascible swarm of tsetse flies two years ago when the conflict between the large multinational oil companies and the local paramilitary resistance groups turned particularly bloody. Like the roughnecks, the reporters also hovered near the bar, though the two groups rarely mixed, and she'd come to recognize the mutual disdain each held toward the other. From her own tribal roots she understood this paradoxical nature of men all too well: the animosity that was born from similarity. Both were tight-knit groups of badly dressed, egotistic, womanizing alcoholics. Both hated their assignments in Port Harcourt almost as much as they hated the oil industry's executive elite. And perhaps most ironic of all, both groups ultimately earned a living from the very same source—the oil industry itself.

She escorted the group of executives to the registration desk, handing each of them her card and nodding politely before heading back toward the entry doors. Moving quickly, she glanced at her watch and noted that it was just before nine as a tall, blond man she didn't recognize brushed past her and dropped his keycard at the front desk before slipping discreetly through the hotel's glass doors. Curious, she watched as he strolled toward the street, a large satchel slung over his broad shoulders as he disappeared into the gray gasohol haze of morning traffic. It was rare for someone to be staying at the hotel she didn't know about, especially someone as good-looking as this man. He was too casual to be an executive, too well dressed to be a roughneck, and, having failed to place a hand on her backside as he passed, too well mannered to be a journalist. She was about to head back to the registration desk to inquire about him when a large black Mercedes pulled up to the entrance.

The bellhop and valet immediately converged on the vehicle as a huge, heavily muscled man stepped from the driver's seat and promptly opened the back door to release his passenger. The small, salt-and-pepper-haired head of a fifty-something gentleman popped up from behind the opened door and nodded at the driver before glancing anxiously at his surroundings.

The driver quickly assisted the bellhop with the luggage as the gentleman stood beside the vehicle, clenching the handle of a black briefcase with both hands as he shifted his small frame impatiently. Then, as if on cue, both men turned and marched toward the door. The driver walked directly behind his passenger, his square, cropped blond head fixed forward while his eyes darted left and right. His towering frame loomed in cartoonish scale above the older man as they entered the hotel.

As the concierge turned to greet them, the driver's attention immediately focused on her, his face drawn tight in a menacing stare. It was then that she realized he was also the man's bodyguard. She stepped forward and flashed both men her warmest smile. "Good morning, gentlemen, and welcome to the Garden Landmark. May I assist you in checking in?"

"Please," the gentleman said, bowing slightly. He pulled a folded reservation confirmation from his breast pocket and handed it to her. "You should have a reservation for Al Dossari." His baritone voice was measured and kind.

"Shahid Al Dossari."

She looked at the printed confirmation briefly and nodded. From the corner of her eye she could see the gentleman's massive bodyguard scanning the room. "Excellent. Thank you, Mr. Al Dossari," she said, handing the confirmation back to him. His eyes snapped from her chest to her face, a brief hint of surprise filling his expression. She smiled brightly. "As you can see, sir, we're quite busy this morning." She waved her arm toward the line of people at the check-in desk. "So please allow me to assist you directly." The gentleman nodded with gratitude as she clicked a button on her cell phone and adjusted the small headset in her ear. She smiled with a fixed stare as she waited for someone to answer.

"Good morning. This is Nnenia," a woman's voice answered brusquely.

"Nnenia, this is Abeje," the concierge responded, her voice ripe with practiced friendliness. "Could you please assist me with a special guest this morning?"

There was a pause on the line, followed by an audible grunt. "We're very busy this morning, as you can see. Why can't he wait like the other guests?"

The concierge turned and glared directly at her colleague sitting at the check-in counter a short distance away. "Our guest would certainly appreciate your assistance." Her eyes flickered briefly over at the two men. The older gentleman anxiously clenched his briefcase while his bodyguard watched her with a calm, even stare.

Her colleague glared back. "Fine. And of course that will be at the normal rate?"

"Yes, of course," the concierge responded as her smile returned. She knew Nnenia's normal rate was half of any tips. The front-desk girls weren't allowed to take tips, but the concierges certainly were— an advantage she'd quickly learned to exploit when it came to assisting the executive clientele. And an executive important enough to have a bodyguard was almost certain to be a generous tipper.

Nnenia sighed loudly into the phone. "Name?" she asked.

She recited the man's name and waited patiently for her colleague to check him in. A few moments later a bellhop walked over and handed her two keycards.

"Mr. Al Dossari, you are checked in, sir," she said, handing him the keycards. "Suite 805—one of our most beautiful executive suites—located just above us and to your right." Both men looked up silently as she pointed her thin sculpted arm toward the eighth-floor hallway that ran over their heads in the atrium. "Now, is there anything else I can assist you with, Mr. Al Dossari?"

"No, thank you," the gray-haired man responded quietly. "You are most kind." He glanced at his bodyguard, who immediately stepped forward and grabbed her forearm in his giant hand. She tensed nervously as he pressed several crisp bills into her palm. He then smiled and softened his grip, his blue eyes staring intently. She felt herself blushing at the scale of his presence. "Thank you, Abeje," he said with an American accent, his voice surprisingly soft. "And please thank your friend Nnenia too."

"Indeed I will, sir," the concierge responded, the heat in her face intensifying.

He released his grip and gave her a quick nod before falling in step behind his boss. She watched the two men stroll toward the elevators before discreetly glancing at the money concealed in her hand. As expected, her headset chirped the announcement of a call. She turned and stared wryly at the check-in counter as she clicked the answer button on her headset.

"Yes, Nnenia?"

"I was just calling to confirm the rate on room 805."

She glowered at her colleague from across the lobby. "Normal rate, as discussed."

"Of course, but what did you quote as the rate?" Nnenia pressed, her voice calm and friendly. Both women, ever suspicious that their humorless manager was monitoring their calls, always followed a strict script when discussing their side business.

The concierge pushed the four fifty-dollar bills into her pocket and began walking back toward the entrance, quietly delighting in the crisp texture of their newness. "One hundred per night," she answered. An incredulous snort crackled in her ear.

"That sounds low."

"That's the normal rate, Nnenia," she retorted. She glanced toward the desk as she passed and smiled as her friend craned her neck around a customer to frown at her.

"Fine. Well, Mr. Dossari got a very nice deal." The line immediately clicked dead.

"And so did I," she said to herself as she stood by the glass doors and watched the chaos of morning traffic slowly snake its way along the street. She rarely paid "normal rate" to Nnenia, who was undoubtedly distrustful of even her, her friend since childhood. But then again their little side business was her idea, not Nnenia's. And neither could complain about the money. The four bills curled in her pocket represented more than what most of the people on the street in front of her would make in six months. She made it in less than six minutes.

Her smile faded as she stood there, watching the women and children and men and vehicles that choked the streets of her poor, desperate city. Her childhood memories of quiet peacefulness felt painfully distant to this horrible new world: an overrun, avarice-infested version of her cherished Igwe Ocha, as her people affectionately called it. She reached into her pocket and rubbed the sharp edges of the bills, swallowing hard as she fought against the mixture of guilt and self-loathing beginning to swirl like acid in her stomach. Her eardrums suddenly popped—a side effect she might have attributed to her current feelings were it not for the glass doors in front of her immediately snapping inward as a strong blast of dry, gritty air ripped through the lobby. She instinctively closed her eyes as she turned and fell to the floor, the gasping sounds of surprised voices barely audible over the shriek of the entering wind. It was then that she felt the explosion, a concussion of energy that knocked her flat against the black granite floor with the crushing force of a mob as a flash of white light filled the atrium. She wrapped her head tightly in her arms as a pelting rain of debris fell upon her, tapping on her back and legs like the fingers of pesky children. Something large and heavy slammed hard into her back, forcing a quick scream of terror from her as she flinched in pain. Then the rain stopped.

She lay still for the long moment of silence that followed, blinking her eyes rapidly as the first wave of moans and screams echoed through the atrium. She rose slowly to her knees, catching the gaze of her own terrified reflection in the dark, polished floor as she assessed her condition. Around her, guests and hotel workers lay motionless, paralyzed with confusion and fright, vacantly watching her as she rubbed the shards of debris from her arms and legs.

"Holy Jesus! Holy Jesus! Abeje! Abeje!" Her friend screamed at her from beneath the check-in desk.

She raised her hand and nodded as she stood, wincing at the pain in her back where the heavy object had struck her. A high-pitched tone filled her ears with a deafening volume, and her head felt oddly detached from her body, as if suspended from a string.

"Get down, Abeje!" Nnenia shouted, her eyes wide with terror. "Get down!"

The concierge stumbled forward a few steps, her legs shaky. Around her, dazed guests and uniformed hotel employees began moving and cautiously sitting upright.

"I am fine. It is over," she mumbled, still reeling from the blast. She looked up at the swirling blue-gray cloud of smoke that filled the atrium and watched as a current of wind tore at its center. There, on the eighth floor directly opposite and above her, muted rays of sunlight poked limply through a jagged round hole in the marble-veneered hallway. She knew instantly which room stood in the path of that horrific hole, but counted and recounted the floors beneath to be sure.

"No," she whispered. "No, no, no . . ."

Then suddenly she froze. Something was pressed against her, something heavy on her back. She slowly stood up straight and reached behind her as the unseen object began to slide down her dust-covered uniform. Her fingers briefly touched its warm, wet surface before it detached itself and landed on the floor with a dull, syrupy thud.

"Oh, Christ! Oh, Jesus!" shrieked a man sitting next to her as he grimaced at the object on the floor.

The concierge stared at him curiously for a moment before turning to gaze at the projectile that had struck her.

"No," she whispered again, shuddering in revulsion. On the floor lay a bloody, fist-sized mound of pink, dimpled flesh, impaled with a two-inch shard of hair-covered skull. The hair, a familiar mix of neatly trimmed dark and gray, glistened under a sickening layer of wetness in the light.

———

The streets and markets of Port Harcourt were eerily still as the throngs stood captivated, gazing and pointing at the thick column of smoke that drifted lazily up from the Garden Landmark Hotel. He watched them as they stared. Mothers with children on their hips, men collected in tight circles, smoking earnestly as they noisily gestured and gawked. Heads peeked out from every bus, cab, and window in view. He pretended to share in their interest, looking back toward the hotel every few minutes as he walked, occasionally asking the obvious question, which was met with shrugs or empty expressions. As always, he found more fascination in the people watching the event than the event itself. He walked on through the city, his backpack slung over his shoulder, his pace swift but unnoticeable as he ambled through the paralyzed mob under a hazy, sand-drenched sky.

A few hours later, from the comfort of his first-class seat on a South African Airways jet, he glanced down at the tall building and briefly observed the gaping wound that still bled a thin trail of black, acrid smoke. Then, as the plane rose into the clouds, he closed the shade of his window and happily surrendered to the sleep-inducing drone of the engines.

Chapter 14

Av. Paseo Colon
Puerto La Cruz
October 25, 11:12 p.m.
The Belt of Orinoco, Venezuela

To whom it may concern,

This letter will be Xeroxed and sent to
people that I love and/or care enough about
to want to help them get their hands on big
huge wads of tax-free faloose, a.k.a. filthy
lucre beyond your wildest dreams. This is
not my usual gibbering nonsense, just a
straightforward bit of advice to lead you
down the road toward one hellacious payday.

I know of what I speak, you laconic cast
of self-absorbed cynics and skeptics, and
you know it. Who else would you ask for
tips on how to get a taxi in Cairo, or order
wine in Calcutta? Who else can safely steer
you through the running of the bulls of
Pamplona, or show you the proper way to wrap

on a mawashi before a sumo match? That's right—me.

Ever heard of the Brainybuddies? You will. Oh boy, will you ever. It's destined to become the next big toy fad in the United States and will make the Tickle My Elbow and Radish Patch Kids frenzies look like tea and Fig Newtons at Grandma's house by comparison.

According to a report I saw on the BBC just an hour ago, the Brainybuddies are poised to arrive in the United States. It's a kids' show that started in England over a year ago and in no time has knocked that weird, drug-crazed singing bitch off— completely off—the front pages of the Brit tabloids. There were near riots at Harrods and other British department stores during the last Christmas season as guards with clubs fought off gap-toothed hags screaming and kicking for Brainybuddies dolls.

There are four of these little bastards. They live in Brainyville and eat brainycustard. They have baby faces and skins of various colors and computers in their plump little bellies. Apparently two-year-olds can't get enough of them, and if the rug rats in the US are anything like their eurobrat brethren, they'll have Big Bird begging for spare change on the Sunset Strip by Jesus's birthday.

According to the BBC, the big toy launch has just started. This will give the

Brainybuddy marketing pukes just enough time for the inevitable "shortage" during the Christmas shopping season. I fully expect the eBay ads to be demanding (and getting) $500 each for these weird, mentally challenged-looking plush freaks by Thanksgiving. Anyone with a Visa card and a crisp wad of bills for bribing the inventory clerk at Toys"R"Us will be able to pay off their mortgage and send their kids to college by December 26.

Are you people getting the picture here?

If you have the luxury of choice, try to buy the pink one with the knapsack. I think his name is something like "Jo-Jo" or "Fucknuts." He will be your cash cow. Don't ask the obvious question; just know that this little pink sumbitch is drowning in charm. He prances and minces and swings his knapsack to and fro and has earned quite a following in the gay community. In other words, he has two markets, which means toddlers will be fighting drag queens in the aisles of the toy store for this little laddie, so act fast, people.

That's it. Ignore this advice and I'll be telling you "I told you so" for as long as I told you so about that other thing before. I'm not even asking for a cut, just the usual . . . a couch to sleep on, a shot of Fortaleza tequila and a Camel Light, introductions to women of easy virtue, etc. And don't think I'm not following my own advice. I've nabbed one of the little bastards, and the other three are practically in the bag.

Think Brainybuddies now, and you'll be on the long green gravy train by Christmas. Remember, you heard it here first.

Ta!

P.S. This message was typed to you ingrates on a Smith Corona Classic 10 found dusty and neglected in the lobby of my hotel. For those who haven't had the pleasure, just know that every mechanical slap of the keys chimes a whimsical "fuck you" to Microsoft, and for that I am eternally grateful.

P.P.S. The cachapas here are sublime. Pepe, a young man I befriended with a hairy forehead and a penchant for vintage belt buckles and flowery silk shirts, introduced me to these tasty little wonders. Unfortunately the capybara burgers tasted like Wayne Newton's underpants and gave me a fit of gas. Don't order dog.

Chapter 15

Jeri stared at the Polaroid picture lying on the counter with frustrated amusement as she poured a beer. She could have almost predicted the image before seeing it—a young man in a black silk shirt adorned with a grotesque pattern of white flowers sat at an outdoor table, a gap-toothed grin stretched across his light brown face. His long dark hair was pulled back tightly against his scalp and shined with the luster of heavy pomade. Despite his wardrobe and hairstyle, the broad features of his twenty-something face gazed out from the picture with a warmth and happiness that Jeri couldn't stop staring at, as if the man had just been given the greatest gift imaginable. Behind him, another man sat at the table, a beer clenched in his hand. Only his arm and a portion of his chest were visible beyond the young man in the foreground, but Jeri knew from the tanned, muscled arm and the familiar blue T-shirt exactly who he was.

Sitting across from her at the bar, Allie read the letter and sipped her wine.

"Allie, did you—"

Allie dramatically threw up her hand for silence. "Hold on, I'm trying to concentrate. And yes, I'll take another glass of wine."

Jeri poured another healthy dose of Pinot Noir for her friend and placed the glass next to its empty, lipstick-stained predecessor.

She stood quietly at the bar and watched Allie as she continued to read, a subtle grin drawn on her friend's face.

"Funny, huh?" Jeri asked.

Allie chuckled briefly before catching herself and erasing the smile from her face. "Funny? No. I wouldn't call it funny." Her green eyes flashed up at Jeri. "Unless by 'funny' you mean 'peculiar.' But that's not what you meant, is it? You meant 'funny' as in 'humorous' and 'cute.' As in 'Hey Allie, look, I'm getting chain mail from a creepy stalker who really likes me and hopes I can meet his parents one day and have his kids before he feeds me to his German shepherds or stuffs me in a wood chipper.' Am I right?"

"Yes, I meant humorous in that kind of way."

Allie glared at Jeri for a moment before snatching the Polaroid from the bar and examining it carefully. "Let's see what we have here," she said, her voice high with sarcasm. "In the foreground, a handsome young man, Venezuelan, I assume, with greasy long hair and utterly horrendous taste in clothes. He looks normal enough, though we all know that looks can be deceiving. A pleasant meal with friends at a street-side café in Puerta Whatever. Oh, and speaking of friends . . . yes . . . there behind our young, poorly dressed soon-to-be-victim is our favorite stalker—Mr. Mysterious Joe's Last Stand T-shirt Guy." She shot a snide smile at Jeri before continuing. "And how mysterious indeed. Once again our little friend has just managed to evade the camera. Another tantalizing glimpse of tanned skin and toned muscles, the oh-so-familiar faded blue Joe's T-shirt that I hope to god he washes between photos, yet nothing of that elusive face that must surely be on par with Adonis and Brad Pitt."

"Really?" Jeri replied. "I was thinking more like George Clooney."

Allie flung the Polaroid onto the bar. "Goddammit, Jeri, I can't believe you're actually walking into this. Why in the world would you even pretend to—"

"Be right back," Jeri interrupted as a young man and woman sat down at the far end of the bar. Allie bit her tongue and sighed audibly as Jeri walked away. A few stools away, a stout, thirty-something man with a military-style crew cut looked over at Allie and smiled. She could tell from his smug grin that he'd been eavesdropping on their conversation. She turned and looked at him sourly.

"Can I help you?" she asked.

"Hi. My name's Tom," the man replied. "Tom Coleman. Sounds like you and your friend are having a pretty serious conversation. Can I give you some advice?"

Allie gave him a venomous look. "Hi, Tom, my name's *not* . . . as in *not interested*. Yes, my friend and I are having a serious conversation, and as soon as she returns, we're going to continue it. Feel free to continue listening, as you've so obviously been doing so far, but do us all a favor and keep any advice to yourself."

The man started to respond, but held his tongue as Allie rolled her eyes and raised her hand for him to stop. She turned her attention back to the letter.

"Sorry, Allie," Jeri replied when she returned. "Now, what were you saying?"

"Forget it. Look," Allie said, examining the typed pages, "there's something really weird about this letter. I mean the content. Does this even make any sense to you?"

"Sure it does. There's a popular new toy coming out soon, and we should buy it before the Christmas rush. What's not to understand?"

"Go to hell, Jeri."

Jeri sighed. As much as she loved Allie, her best friend usually took the irritating position of disliking anyone who showed any interest in Jeri that didn't fit within Allie's idea of normal. She knew the attitude was simply a protective one, and the irony of Allie's own history of sordid relationships with stereotypical "bad boys" wasn't lost on Jeri, but at times these talks were simply exhausting.

"Come on, Allie . . . have any of his letters made sense?"

"No, I mean it," Allie replied, her expression stern. "Why would he be talking about these Brainybuddies? Does he really think anybody would give a shit about some weird toy for five-year-olds? And besides, he doesn't strike me as the kind of guy who has armloads of family-oriented friends with white-picket-fence houses and two kids in tow." She looked up from the letter and took a long sip of her wine. "It's just all very odd. And even stranger is the fact that he didn't write anything personal to you. I'd expect a stalker to at least take the time to write me a handwritten note."

Jeri gave her an amused look.

"What?" Allie asked.

"Turn the photo over."

Allie grabbed the Polaroid and flipped it over. A note in the same handwriting as the previous letters was quickly scribbled in blue ink on the back.

Jeri—

Sorry to make you a party to chain mail, but I never leave a friend out of "the know." Our kids will be gorgeous, Jeri, I'm sure of it.

Ta!
MJLSG

P.S. Have you made a shrine for my wellspring of romantic ravings at the bar yet? You really ought to. I'm shouting my love from the tallest aquilaria in

Bhutan, and I want everyone to hear it. Besides, people love this stuff.

Allie pushed the photo away and crossed her arms on the bar heavily. Her eyes flicked nervously around the saloon before pausing on the wall of letters. Jeri noticed that her normally beautiful face had taken on a tired, resigned expression.

"Clever, this guy," Allie whispered. "Very, very clever."

The evening crowd was beginning to trickle into Joe's Last Stand Saloon, and Jeri once again left her friend to make drink orders and fill pints of beer. She returned a few minutes later to find Allie flanked on both sides by young men. Despite the fact that this was usually her favorite position to be in, Allie sat rigidly at the bar, distracted and abnormally quiet.

"Are you okay?"

Allie looked up at Jeri with glazed eyes. She considered her friend carefully for a moment before speaking. "Don't take this the wrong way, sweetie, but I hope this is the last letter you ever get from this guy, because that's the best possible way this could end."

"I think you're overreacting."

"No, honey, I think you're underreacting." Allie leaned forward to make sure Jeri could hear her over the growing din of the bar. "You don't know the first thing about this guy, Jeri—his name, what he does, where he's from . . . Christ, you don't even know what he really looks like. But he seems to know a helluva lot about you."

Jeri shrugged dismissively.

"Lucky guesses."

"Don't bet on it. I mean, really, what good could this guy possibly be up to? He writes you from a different country every few weeks and professes his affections through these cryptic, meandering letters that somehow manage to predict exactly what you're thinking or doing. How is that possible? Now, granted, I've gotten my share of love letters, and I'll give the guy points on style, but please—if for no other reason than as a favor to your best friend—do *not* get caught up in the idea that this stranger is a harmless romantic pen pal, because I'll guarantee you . . . he isn't."

Allie punctuated her point by draining the full glass of wine and thumping it loudly onto the bar. The men on both sides of her glanced over curiously before returning to their conversations.

"Are you done?" Jeri asked flatly.

"Done? Oh, hell, sweetie. I'm just warming up."

Jeri rolled her eyes and grabbed the empty glass. "With the wine, Allie—are you done, or do you want another glass?"

Allie flashed her a radiant smile. "Like I said, I'm just warming up."

Jeri nodded. She grabbed the wine and poured slowly, filling Allie's glass only half-full before pushing it back in front of her.

"What . . . I don't get a respectable pour now?" Allie asked as she stared at the glass with dismay. "Are you punishing me?"

"No, Allie—don't you see? I'm just looking out for you," Jeri shot back. "Funny how looking out for someone can be mistaken for punishment, though, huh?"

Allie nodded reluctantly. "Touché," she replied, swirling the wine in her glass. She looked up at her friend with a soft, sad expression. "Look, Jeri, I know exactly what's happening here. And I know I'm the last person who should be giving you advice on men, but trust me. This one is different. This one is dangerous."

"He could be," Jeri retorted, stabbing the air with a shaker as she mixed a drink. "But you don't know that, Allie. You're basing that opinion on your own jaded view of men, and it's not fair. What if he's a great guy? What if he's completely normal and simply hasn't found the right person? Maybe the odds are against it, but the fact is I don't know that—and neither do you."

Allie clenched her jaw and sat straight up on her barstool. "You're right, I don't know what this guy is all about," she said defensively.

"And yes, I have a jaded view of *most* men, but I also think I've developed a pretty good ability to read people, and what I'm reading from this guy is funny, smart, and very dangerous."

She paused and leaned into the bar.

"So if you want to ignore your best friend's concerns and advice, that's fine . . . but don't say I didn't warn you when this guy shows up one day and you find yourself in serious trouble. And let's be clear about something—" Allie paused and put a hand on the shoulders of the men on each side of her. Both turned and looked at her quizzically. "I'm not talking about the normal *'I'm drunk and want to sleep with you'* kind of trouble you're used to from these harmless local pansies. I'm talking about the *'I'm chaining you to the floor of my van so we can honeymoon in my basement in Des Moines'* kind of trouble that you won't be able to talk your way out of."

Jeri smiled at the two men who had just been insulted by the attractive blonde between them. "Please excuse my friend. She has a flair for the dramatic." The two men shrugged indifferently and went back to drinking. Allie shrugged and took a sip of her wine.

"You've made your point, Allie, for probably the tenth time," Jeri replied as she angrily wiped down the bar top. "Can we drop this subject now?"

"Sure, sweetie . . . let's talk about something more fun. Oh! I have to show you something!" Allie immediately reached into her purse and found her cell phone. "A new broker was just hired at my real estate office . . . he's young, hot, and deliciously single. Here, take a look." She held her phone out to Jeri with a devious smile stretched across her face.

"Nice," Jeri replied, relieved that the topic had changed to Allie's flavor of the month. "I'm sure you'll have him under your spell by the weekend."

"I hope so. And hey, if things go as I expect them to, I might even try to keep this one around for a little while. Would you and Rob be interested in a little double date?"

Jeri winced inwardly.

"Um, probably not. I don't think Rob would be up for it."

"Why not?"

"I kind of told him it wasn't working."

"And what exactly do you mean by 'wasn't working'?" Allie asked as she tucked her phone back into her purse.

"I don't know, Allie . . . I just wasn't feeling it."

"When did this happen?"

"A few nights ago."

Allie moaned as if struck by a blow. "I'm sure you've already added these up, sweetie," she replied, holding out her hands, "but let me just remind you of a few of Rob's many attributes—young, very handsome, ridiculously intelligent, financially secure . . ."

Jeri watched sullenly as Allie ticked off the list with her fingers.

"Let's see . . . wants to have a family, free of any communicable diseases, at least as far as we know, and . . . did I already mention how drop-dead gorgeous Rob is?"

"Yeah, you did," Jeri replied. "And I know the list very well. You and everyone else, including Rob, have done a damn good job of reminding me."

Jeri glided down to the end of the counter as the heavy old entry door creaked open and a wave of cold mountain air blew a blush-faced group of young men into Joe's. Allie watched her friend as she worked. She smiled at the shy, evasive eyes of the men lined up along the bar who pretended not to watch Jeri until her back was turned, then gawked lustfully at her slim feminine figure. *It should all be so simple*, she thought sadly. *It should all be so simple, but it's always so fucking hard.*

"Don't think I haven't considered it a thousand times," Jeri said as she walked back toward her friend. She leaned against the counter and gazed at Allie, a weary, pleading light in her eyes. "Do you know how badly I want to feel it? How badly I wanted Rob to be *it*? But I can't just make it happen, Allie. I can't manufacture a feeling, and I won't stare across the table at a man who doesn't make my heart turn into lava and tell him otherwise. Rob might have had everything on my list, but the list doesn't mean love."

She glanced up at the growing crowd that had settled in the bar with the fading light of day. Her eyes flickered quickly around the room before settling on the letters pinned to the wall. "You know as well as I do that the moment either one of us falls in love, that goddamn list won't matter. We won't care whether he's a stockbroker in New York or a construction worker in Alaska. He'll just make us happy." She nodded at a man waiting to order a drink and grabbed a glass from the shelf above her. "That's the truth, Allie. The rest of this, the rest of *them*, are nothing more than a long, painful prologue."

Allie nodded as Jeri walked off to pour drinks for the new arrivals. She sat quietly for a moment, deep in thought, before glancing at the man next to her and tapping him on the shoulder. "Let's make a toast," she said as the man turned to her, her smile dazzling and eyes deceptively enthusiastic. "To finding the one," she said as they raised their glasses. "May he have all of the love, most of the list, and may he not be some crazy son-of-a-bitch serial killer."

The man laughed curiously as Allie threw back her glass and drained the blood-red wine in a single gulp.

Chapter 16

He was in paradise.

A cloudless sky stretched over him as he walked along the waterfront through the flawlessly manicured landscape. He strolled casually, following the stone-laid sidewalk that turned languidly through undulating gardens of tropical shrubs and palm trees before branching into the numbered pathways of the Bahia Redonda Marina's endless rows of docks. A pungent smell of stagnant salt-water hung heavily in the humid air, tempered by the sweet, musky aroma of flowering gardenias. Before him, a forest of sterile white masts, yards, and rigging stood sharply in the bright morning sun. As he neared the dock gates, a waiter in a pressed white uniform promptly approached him, a silver tray of tall champagne flutes perched on one hand.

"*Buenos días, señor,*" the short, dark-skinned waiter said with a bow. "Would you care for a mimosa?"

"*Si,*" he replied, shifting his backpack as the waiter handed him a crystal flute filled with champagne and fresh orange juice.

"May I assist you with anything else, *señor?*" the waiter asked, standing rigidly at attention.

"*Gracias*, no," he replied.

"Very well. *Buenos días,*" the waiter replied, bowing again politely.

He watched the waiter disappear down the path before continuing toward the massive marina, ignoring a flock of seagulls swooping and screaming overhead, until he came to dock gate 32. There, he produced a small key from the pocket of his white cotton pants and unlocked the gate. Once inside, he moved slowly down the dock, enjoying the sound of his flip-flops on the sun-bleached teakwood as he scanned the names of the luxurious super-yachts that flanked him on both sides.

Halfway down the long dock, a familiar yacht floated peacefully in its slip.

He stopped and gazed up at the polished, cobalt-colored hull with an air of envy that was bordering on the genuine. Mentally noting its slip number, he continued on, nonchalantly examining the other multimillion-dollar ships that fidgeted in their slips like sleeping giants as he sipped his morning cocktail. A few minutes later, the teak-and-chrome-finished stern of another familiar ship came into view. He drained the last of the champagne from the delicate crystal flute and placed it on a nearby bench before stepping on board.

The deck of the fifty-six-foot sailing yacht *Lorelei* stood pristine and empty. After a quick check of his surroundings, he silently unlatched the door at the front of the cockpit and made his way below. The yacht's interior was no less impressive. Polished maple walls and white oak floors glimmered in the well-lit and surprisingly large salon, with matching leather-trimmed furniture neatly fitted around a large table and desk. It was apparent that every inch of material that completed the cabin was both practical and perfectly finished, designed to meet the demanding expectations of both the sea and the ship's owner.

He stood quietly for a moment, taking stock in his surroundings, before moving to the desk across from him and opening an overhead cabinet. A row of worn, well-used travel books filled the small compartment, their titles advertising exotic worldly destinations. He grabbed a thick volume on Russia and had begun thumbing through it when a dull knock echoed from the stateroom behind him. He returned the book to the cabinet and moved cautiously toward the closed door, listening intently. A low grumbling noise came next, followed by another all-too-human sound that forced a smile onto his face.

He turned the latch and walked in.

The dim light of the master stateroom revealed another lavishly functional arrangement of cabinets and fixtures, all following the gentle sweeping lines of the ship's hull. Centered in the room, a king-sized bed that appeared sculpted from a single piece of wood was covered in a mess of sheets and pillows. Sticking out from beneath the sheets were a pair of pale, stout legs that appeared lifeless.

He walked over to the bed and cleared his throat loudly. The legs didn't move.

"Dublin! Wake up!"

Dublin's portly torso immediately snapped upright as his arms frantically pulled at the sheets that covered him. He blinked wildly as his unshaven face popped out from under the bedding, his thick, hair-blotted chest heaving rapidly.

"Fookin' hell, Chilly!" Dublin snapped as he scratched at his disheveled head of hair. "What the feck are you tryin' to pull?"

Chilly stepped back from the Irishman and waved at the air.

"Christ, Dublin, do you always fart in your sleep?"

Dublin sat silently, his hands fumbling around for several seconds before pulling a wrinkled T-shirt from beneath the sheets. He put it on slowly, eyeing his colleague grumpily from behind half-closed eyelids. "How the hell should I know what I do in my feckin' sleep?" he replied. "Of course, I wasn't asleep for that long," he continued, his lips peeling back to reveal a waxy grin of yellow, smoke-stained teeth. "Thirty minutes earlier and you'da walked into a veritable Brazilian orgy."

"Right, of course."

Dublin reached for a pack of cigarettes on the nightstand. Next to them, his ever-present cell phones were neatly lined in a row. "I'm not shitting you, Chilly," he said, shaking his head wearily. "I've never had a better time. The girls here are fookin' amazing." He stabbed a cigarette into his mouth.

"I believe you, I really do," Chilly replied. He reached out and grabbed the cigarette from Dublin's mouth and flung it onto the bed. "Now put your cigarettes away and stop farting. It's time to go to work."

Dublin stared down at the bed, weighing the request, before irritably collecting the cigarette and stuffing it back in the pack. "Right, fine," he said as he stood up from the bed. "But first I need some coffee."

The two men walked into the galley. Chilly sat down at the table while the Irishman made coffee. A few minutes later Dublin placed two steaming mugs on the table and dropped his pale, heavy frame into the chair across from his colleague.

"Jesus, 'tis a nice feckin' boat," Dublin whispered, looking around with envy. "I could def'nitely get used to staying here for a while." He looked over and prodded Chilly with his mug as his thin, whiskered lips stretched into a broad grin. "I can only imagine what kind of rat-infested turd-hut you're staying in."

Chilly stared at him for a moment, feeling uneasy. Beyond the fact that his colleague was a hungover mess, something about Dublin didn't seem right. "Actually, I'll be staying on the boat for this one," he replied, sipping his coffee.

"The fuck you say," Dublin replied, looking back at him with wide, bloodshot eyes.

Chilly took his colleague's surprise as genuine, if for no other reason than it was the first time he'd heard Dublin say "fuck" without an Irish accent. "You don't mind, do you?"

The Irishman considered him for a moment, his temple twitching under his shaggy mess of dark hair. He abruptly drained half his mug of black Colombian and shrugged. "Fine by me, but why the sudden change of heart? Finally gettin' a taste for da finer thangs in life, eh?"

Chilly leaned in and looked at Dublin closely. "What did you take last night?"

"What?" Dublin said as he tensed in his seat. He set his coffee mug on the table and crossed his arms defensively. "What are you talking about?"

"You heard me," Chilly replied. "What was it?"

"Nothin'," his colleague snapped. "Besides, that ain't your business."

"No, it absolutely is my business." He watched as Dublin tried his best to conceal the twitches and shudders that were now noticeably plaguing his body. "Now what did you take?"

Both men sat quietly for a moment, listening to the muted sounds of the *Lorelei* creaking in protest to her mooring lines. Dublin's expression was now a dangerous mixture of fear and rage.

"It isn't easy, ya know . . . this feckin' job," he said as his eyes flickered wildly around the galley. "No nine-ta-five gig like the rest of tha normal feckin' world."

"You were never told it would be," Chilly replied, watching his colleague with calm interest.

Dublin fixed his stare on him, the tremors in his body momentarily subsiding. "Yeah, well, hearing it and living it are two completely diff'rent things, ain't they?" he retorted, holding Chilly's gaze for a quick, frightened moment before fumbling at his pocket and fishing out a pack of cigarettes. In an instant he had a cigarette in his mouth and was frantically groping at his pockets for a lighter, mumbling obscenities in an accent too thick to comprehend.

"Don't," Chilly commanded.

Dublin pretended not to hear him. A relieved sigh escaped his pursed lips as he finally pulled a single match from his pocket.

Chilly reached over and snatched the match from his hand. "You're compromised, Dublin," he said, snapping the match in two before dropping it in what was left of his coffee. "Given the fact that you can't sit still, I'll assume you took a psychostimulant. Probably meth. Which means right now your head is suffering from a very pleasurable torrent of dopamine and serotonin. Unfortunately, that amount of euphoria-inducing chemicals is highly unnatural, and coming down can be a bit nasty. But you already knew that, didn't you?"

Dublin sat glumly, his fleshy shoulders slumped forward like those of an overgrown child being reprimanded. He stared at his hands as they repeatedly balled themselves into fists, seemingly indifferent to the fact that his head was twitching every few seconds. "You don't . . . you just don't understand," he muttered. "It keeps me sharp."

"I'm sure you think it does," Chilly replied. "And just how sharp do you feel right now?"

"Hey, fuck you!" Dublin screamed as he smashed his fists on the table before pressing his hands into his temples until the knuckles of his fingers turned white. He rocked his fleshy frame back and forth in the chair until the swollen lids of his eyes crept open and his brown eyes peered out menacingly. "You don't know anythin' about me," he said in a tired, hollow voice. "You don't understand what this job demands." He stood and walked over to the coffee-maker. "Sure," he continued, watching the steaming black liquid fill his mug, "you know what I can do for you, what I can *get* for you. But you've got no feckin' idea what it takes for that to happen. If you did, you'd understand why I need a little boost sometimes."

Chilly watched as the Irishman threw back a long slug of coffee before tossing his mug angrily into the sink. The sound of the ceramic mug crashing into the stainless steel basin echoed through the boat. "You're right, Dublin," he replied, "I don't know *how* you do what you do. Nor do I have any idea what it takes to pull it off." He paused and drained the last of his coffee. "I'd say that's partly because I'm rather busy doing my own job. As you may have noticed, my job can also be somewhat demanding at times. Mostly because of the type of people I deal with from day to day. You know the sort—those cold, slimy types who can stare right through you without blinking."

Dublin twitched nervously as Chilly looked up at him, his dark eyes hard and frigid.

"But mostly it's because I don't give two shits what it takes to do your fucking job, as long as I know you can do it."

Chilly calmly examined his empty coffee mug for a moment before hurling it toward the sink. His colleague barely lunged out of the way before it exploded against the granite backsplash, showering him with sharp fragments of ceramic.

"Are you feckin' daft, mate?" Dublin shrieked, brushing himself off.

"Well, at least you're still quick," Chilly replied. A slight grin curled his lips.

"You're goddamn right I'm still quick. And you're goddamn wrong if you think I can't still do the job."

"That's not for you to decide. Unfortunately we don't have time for other options."

Chilly stood and walked over to the Irishman, pausing just a few inches from his face. "You know the protocol in this kind of situation as well as I do," he said as he rested his hands on Dublin's shoulders. "And you know what I have the authority to do if you royally fuck this up."

Dublin nodded solemnly.

"But let's not worry about that just yet. Right now, I just want to know one thing." He pressed his hands deeply into Dublin's shoulders. "Is my package going to be delivered on time tomorrow night or not?"

Dublin raised his head and met his stare directly. "Fookin' hell. Have I ever let you down before?"

"Is that a 'yes'?"

"Yes, for fuck's sake. That's a 'yes.'"

Chilly stared at his fixer for a moment before abruptly releasing his grip. "Great. Then there's nothing else to worry about." He patted the Irishman affectionately on the shoulder and walked into the salon. Dublin watched curiously as he opened a cabinet door and removed two large blankets to reveal a safe. Chilly quickly spun through the correct combination on the dial and opened the heavy door.

"How in feckin' hell did you know there was a safe in there?" Dublin asked, dumbfounded.

"I'm going out for a while," Chilly replied, grabbing something and shoving it into his pocket before closing the safe and returning the contents of the cabinet. He then threw his backpack over his shoulder and started up the stairs to the main deck. Halfway up, he turned and glanced at Dublin.

"Clean up that mess in the galley, will you? And while you're at it, put some new sheets on my bed. I didn't travel halfway around the world to clean up whatever your drugged-up ass farted into my Egyptian cotton."

"What do you mean, *your* bed?" Dublin muttered. He looked at Chilly with a puzzled stare, then his bloodshot eyes abruptly widened in surprise.

"Are you fookin' telling me that this boat is—"

"There's more than fifty pounds of plastic explosives expertly fitted into the corners and crevices of the *Lorelei*," Chilly interrupted.

"More than enough to ruin your day ten times over. How the hell you managed to get on board and deflower Puerto La Cruz's ugliest prostitutes without blowing half of this harbor into next week is beyond me. I guess you're one helluva fixer after all—meth or not."

Dublin grinned sheepishly.

"Of course," Chilly continued, gingerly patting the pocket with the object he'd taken from the safe. "That's not to say I can't still ruin your day. You have until two p.m. tomorrow to get me the package. In the meantime, I want you to shower, sober up, and move your shit out of my room. You and Tall Tommy can fight over the guest cabins."

Dublin nodded as his colleague disappeared up the stairs and quietly slipped off the boat. The sharp tendrils of a soon-to-be-massive headache were beginning to work their way deeply into his head, and his stomach suddenly felt as if the boat were pitching in high seas. He looked over at the shattered remains of the mugs strewn across the galley and shrugged. "Feck it," he muttered to himself as he stumbled into the salon and fell heavily onto the couch. His eyes were barely closed before the rhythmic tapping of footsteps across the *Lorelei*'s top deck echoed painfully in his skull. He looked up to see a perfectly built young man in white slacks and a polo shirt gliding down the teak stairs, a leather satchel hanging casually over his shoulder.

"What's up, Dub?" Tall Tommy asked as he tossed his satchel on a chair and removed his headphones. His muscled arms and chest stretched the fabric of his shirt as he pulled off his baseball cap and ran a quick hand through his thick blond hair. "You look like shit, dude."

Dublin eyed him sourly for a moment before responding.

"Yeah, well, you shoulda seen the feckin' girls that—"

"Man, is this a nice boat or what?" Tall Tommy interrupted, running his fingers along the handmade cabinets next to him. He whistled in awe as he disappeared into the galley and aft stateroom.

"Yeah, nice feckin' boat," Dublin muttered under his breath before closing his eyes and folding his arms over his head. His aching skull felt like it was in serious danger of cracking like glass under the pressure and shattering into a thousand pieces. Part of him was hoping that it would.

"Oyster . . . fifty-six-footer," Tall Tommy mused as he walked back into the salon and stood over Dublin. He kicked the Irishman in the leg to get a response but roused only a feeble moan. "Somebody must have gotten a nice bonus to afford this sweet little bitch," he continued. He sniffed at the air and looked around, a confused expression clouding his handsome face.

"We've gotta do something about the smell, though. It smells like whores and stale nachos in here."

Chapter 17

CONFIDENTIAL

Memorandum #RO-1423.09

Date: October 27

To: Thomas R. Coleman

Re: Candidate Entrance Evaluation/Case File:
#6253-76

Subject: Evaluation Summary

Candidate #6253-76 Coleman, Thomas R. has
completed the requisite entrance examinations
and evaluations as defined.

Candidate completed the Psychological
Evaluation portion of the examination with a
score of: NON-PROFILE/ATYPICAL.

Evaluator's notes:

Candidate's written test scores display a
high potential for Impulse Control Disorders
(ICD) that may significantly compromise

judgment while active in the line of duty.
Candidate's psychological assessment
interview was completed on the same day of
the written evaluation as required by the
Agency's Psychological Evaluation Standards
(PES). Candidate's PE interview also
indicated a high potential for ICDs.

Failure to meet the mandated psychological
profile as defined by section 45.32 of the
Mental Profile Guidelines disqualifies the
candidate from acceptance into the Central
Intelligence Agency at this time. As defined
by section 4.12 of the MPG, candidate's
failure to meet the mandated psychological
profile at the time of evaluation disallows
any subsequent attempts for entry into the
program.

——

Agent Tom Coleman read the one-page memo he'd received in the mail for a fifth time before neatly folding it twice and tossing it into the wastebasket. He then organized the items on the desk of his cramped, windowless office and stared vacantly at the Landscapes of Sedona calendar pinned on the wall next to him. His mind was still processing the news when someone knocked on the door.

"Yeah, come in."

A male colleague, dressed in the customary button-up blue shirt and black slacks of the Department of Homeland Security's Immigration and Customs Enforcement, the ICE office, walked in and smiled. Like most of the people that worked in the Flagstaff Field Office, the man was several years younger than Tom.

"Hey, Tommy boy," his coworker said, flashing a broad smile, "workin' hard or hardly workin'?"

"What's up?" Tom replied curtly.

His colleague sensed Tom's mood and immediately eased his smile into an awkward smirk. "A few of us are heading out to lunch. It's Rick's birthday, so we're going big. Wanna come along?"

"So it's Agent Martin's birthday, huh?" Tom shook his head as he once again organized the folders on his desk. Like him, Rick Martin had started his career with ICE as an investigation agent about eighteen months earlier. In that time, Tom had worked with him on enough cases to know that the young man had all the requisite qualifications for a successful career in any governmental agency—he was endlessly cocky, flawlessly unimaginative, and brilliantly adept at turning investigative mistakes into departmental triumphs in the final draft of every report that he filed. Even so, it was still a surprise to Tom when Agent Martin was promoted to a coveted position in Undercover Operations six months ago, with the speed and attention normally reserved for the offspring of nepotistic senior officials. The two had been cautiously cordial since, but Tom knew from that moment on that Rick could never be counted as a friend.

"Where are you guys going?" he asked.

"Burger King."

Tom's dark brown eyes flashed up at his colleague. "Burger King? Are you serious? Christ, you guys eat there every other day of the week."

"I know, but it's Rick's birthday and that's where he wants to go." Tom's colleague shrugged and looked at his watch. "So, are you in?"

"Sorry, can't do it," Tom said, gesturing at the neatly stacked case files on his desk. "Too much work piling up."

"Suit yourself," his coworker replied, backing out the door. "Should I tell everyone you're working a serious case? Maybe closing in on an illegal taco stand, or hot on the trail of a pack of rogue landscapers trying to sneak black-market piñatas through Nogales?" He gave Tom a sardonic wink. "Keep it up and you might just get a promotion like Rick did while you're still young. After all, you're only what . . . forty?"

"Thirty-four."

"Oh shit, sorry Tom," his colleague replied, barely containing a grin. "I think it's the crew cut. It makes you look, you know . . . older."

Tom opened a case folder on his desk and waved his hand dismissively.

"Go eat your fucking Burger King."

"Right. Later." His colleague spun and disappeared down the hallway as the steel door to Tom's office closed loudly behind him.

Tom stared blankly at the case documents in front of him for a few moments before closing the folder and carefully returning it to the stack on his desk. He then glanced at the wastebasket. The discarded memo was sitting upright on its edges on top of the other trash in a way that annoyed him. He reached over and quickly poked it onto its side.

"Fuck you," he muttered.

He poked it several more times before punching it deep into the wastebasket with his fist.

"Fuck you!"

Tom sat up and took a deep breath. He shrugged embarrassedly at himself as he opened the top drawer of his desk and grabbed a small bottle of antibacterial lotion. After methodically wiping his thick hands with the lotion, he turned to his computer and pecked "impulse control disorder" into an online search engine. A second later, the first ten of 340,000 results appeared on his screen. Tom scanned the first page of results and clicked on the first one that had any resemblance to English. The link flashed to a medical website with the image of a doctor smiling compassionately. Tom winced at the bold "Understanding Psychological Disorders" headline on the page and scrolled down to read the relevant text.

Impulse control disorder (ICD) is a set of psychiatric disorders including intermittent explosive disorder, kleptomania, pathological gambling, pyromania, trichotillomania, and dermatillomania.

Impulsivity, the key feature of these disorders, can be thought of as seeking a small, short-term gain at the expense of a large, long-term loss. Those affected with impulse control disorder repeatedly demonstrate failure to resist their behavioral impetuosity.

Impulse control disorders are considered to be part of the obsessive-compulsive disorder spectrum.

The page included several links to related disorders, treatment options, and mental facilities with calm-inducing names like Pleasant Acres and Heritage Ridge, but Tom ignored them and quickly closed the web page with an irritable click of his mouse.

There was no point in investigating the matter further, he concluded, because the whole idea was completely and utterly ridiculous. Kleptomania? Not possible. The only thing Tom had ever stolen in his life was a toy from a department store when he was a kid, and that was only because it was Superman, his favorite superhero. He'd been six years old, for chrissake. Pathological gambling? A few weekends in Vegas years ago with his ex-wife and the occasional lottery ticket were the extent of his gambling history—certainly nothing in the pathological category. Pyromania? *Give me a fucking break*, he thought. He couldn't remember the other disorders that had been listed, but it didn't matter. He didn't have any form of this "ICD" bullshit. Period.

The more he thought about it, the more obvious the answer became—the examiner who interviewed him must have grossly misread his psychological condition.

Tom thought back to the day of the evaluation. He remembered the examiner—a short, fair-skinned, midfortyish woman with a beaked nose, heavy makeup, and a demeanor that had been friendly to the point of flirtatious. *Was that it?* he wondered. Did he not give her enough attention and she had decided to retaliate by pinning a disqualifying "disease" on him? The questions during the evaluation had been easy enough; he'd been concise and polite in his responses, and he even recalled her smiling warmly as she noted his responses. God knows how, but he must have pissed her off in some way. But how could he explain the written test results that apparently pointed to the same conclusion? Were they trying to weed him out for other reasons? *Am I too old?* Tom thought. *Am I too aggressive? Is this memo itself a test?*

Tom froze with fear as another possibility suddenly came to mind.

Did they know what really happened in Afghanistan?

No matter how slim the possibility of someone knowing—and worse, revealing—what the truth might be, Tom had always known it existed. But why now? And who could have possibly known? He had to figure this out. He needed an answer. A real answer. He had not just spent the last thirteen years of his career in service to his country to now be disregarded and diagnosed with a fucking disorder.

He clicked on his e-mail and reread the message that his brother-in-law, CIA Agent Alex Murstead, had sent him that morning.

Tom,

I assume by now you've gotten an official notice from the agency about your candidacy. Sorry for the bad news, but don't get too down over it. The CIA isn't for everyone, and you should be proud to already be serving your country in the Department of Homeland Security.

—Alex

Tom spent the next fifteen minutes drafting a response to Alex, several times erasing and starting over, before finally concluding that he sounded like a jabbering idiot and clicking the Delete button. Despite the fact that Alex was part of the CIA's highly secretive Special Operations Group—or SOG, as it was usually called—out of Langley, Tom knew there was probably little more he could do to help. Even if he could, his brother-in-law was not willing to risk breaking the rules. At least not for him. Maybe if Tom and his sister, Jane, were on speaking terms it would be a different story, but that was a moot point. The two of them hadn't spoken in years, no doubt for something Tom had done, if he were to ask his sister. Now the only communication he had with her came in the form of a photocopied letter Jane sent every Christmas, informing the family in nauseating detail how she, Alex, and Tom's two perfect nieces were doing. Most years the self-absorbed bitch didn't even bother to sign it.

Tom smacked his hands against the keyboard in resignation and sat back heavily in his flimsy, torn-upholstery chair. "C'mon, think," he muttered to himself, locking his thick fingers together and resting his hands against his brown crew-cut hair. He sat quietly for several minutes considering the situation.

The idea that the CIA had an ulterior motive for barring him seemed unrealistic. Ever since his first day of Marine Corps boot camp in San Diego more than a decade ago, everything Tom had done was in service to his country. He'd graduated from his platoon and proudly served with the 1st Battalion, 5th Marines, completing a tour in Iraq and two in Afghanistan before being discharged with honors. From there, he'd spent six years battling gang violence with the Phoenix Police Department's Gang Enforcement Unit while he earned a bachelor's degree in criminal justice. Despite the stress, he'd actually considered making the PPD a permanent career choice, until an argument between Tom and two young Latino men at a downtown bar where he and his now ex-wife were celebrating one night escalated into an altercation that left both of the young men in the hospital. The incident led to a three-week paid suspension while the matter was investigated. The conclusions of the investigation led to little more than a slap on the hand, but it didn't matter; the damage to his career and his already unstable marriage was already done. When his sergeant met with him on the morning of his reinstatement, Tom handed him his badge and told him he was resigning from the force. The next day Tom's wife told him she was resigning from their marriage.

Two months later he took a job with the Department of Homeland Security's ICE agency, and he'd been quietly pushing paper for the government ever since. A multiple-homicide case he'd been investigating in the border town of Douglas gave Tom his first opportunity to work with the CIA, and he was immediately enamored. He still vividly remembered the first morning of the investigation, when two gray-suited men walked in and flashed their agency credentials before moving through the crime scene with an aura of unchallenged superiority. The rest of the team, including the local PD and Border Patrol investigators, whispered expletives about them behind their backs, but not Tom. To him, they represented the best of the best—highly trained, experienced men who had the brains, the balls, and the federal brawn to get the job done.

It was at that moment that Tom decided he wanted the gray suit and badge of the CIA for himself.

Certain that his official record was clear, Tom again considered the possibility that the CIA recruiters had stumbled upon the facts of what happened during his second tour in Afghanistan. After all, they were the CIA. As his brother-in-law, Alex, had once mentioned during a rare family get-together, *they just have ways of knowing.* But how could they know anything more than the details he'd officially reported?

Despite years of suppressing the memory, a storm of images began streaming through Tom's mind. His heart rate immediately began to race as a horrifying montage of scenes—pitch-black night, shouts of surprise and anger, blinding muzzle flashes, and deafening gunfire, running, falling, stumbling—collided and twisted together. He quickly pushed the images from his mind and concentrated on the hard facts. Eight Marines had set out for a routine patrol in the southern district of Arghandab on that clear night of May 23. Approximately three hours into their patrol, Tom and his men had come under heavy fire from a large group of insurgents. Less than an hour later it was over. Of the eight men who had set out on that patrol, seven didn't come back.

And that was all that anyone could possibly know.

Tom rapped the knuckles of his hand against the corner of his desk as he considered his next move. He knew it would be pointless to speak with the psych examiner who'd diagnosed him and try to persuade her to reconsider, assuming he could even find her. Besides, pressing the issue would only weaken his case—or worse, help justify the agency's ridiculous conclusion about his condition. As remote as his chances might be, Tom wasn't giving up. He was used to tough challenges, and the Marine Corps, the Phoenix PD, and certainly his current job with the Department of Homeland Security had taught him that patience was the key to overcoming almost every steep pile of shit heaped in front of him.

One way or the other, he was going to be a CIA agent.

He just needed to find another way in.

Tom spent a few unfocused hours reviewing case files and scratching notes before conceding to his distracted state of mind. He needed more time to sit and think. He needed a quiet place to clarify his thoughts and start developing a strategy. More than anything, he needed a drink.

After quickly filing cases and meticulously cleaning his desk, Tom grabbed his leather jacket and gloves and switched off the yellow overhead fluorescent lights. He strolled past the large Homeland Security crest mounted in the hallway as the concussion of his office door slamming to a close signaled his departure.

Chapter 18

"What the hell's going on around here, Jeri?"

From across the counter of the crowded saloon, Chip stared wide-eyed at Jeri with a genuine look of surprise. He gazed again toward his usual barstool, which was now hidden within a large group of flannel-clad coeds, and shook his head irritably. "That's my spot," he muttered as he sat down at the opposite end of the bar and brooded.

Standing at the beer taps busily pouring drinks, Jeri glanced over at him and smiled. "You know the rule, Chip. First come, first served."

The older man nodded. "But it's Monday afternoon, for chrissake. What are all these people doing in here on a Monday?"

"Drinking, just like you," Jeri replied as she loaded the drinks onto a tray and ducked under the bar. She collected the tray and headed off to the tables before the old man could respond.

Rust-orange rays of late-afternoon sunlight drifted into Joe's Last Stand Saloon as Jeri slowly wove her way through the crowd. Looking around her, Jeri could understand Chip's surprise. On what should have been a quiet October afternoon, heavy with the scent of burning leaves and approaching snow, Joe's Last Stand was packed. Groups of hip, twenty-something students along with their middle-aged professors were crowding into the saloon, filling the warm, dark interior with the incongruous aromas of perfume, patchouli, and beer. Jeri maneuvered her way into the densest part of the crowd—the corner where the shrine of letters and pictures from her Mysterious Joe's Last Stand Guy were hung. The men around her turned and stared intently as she passed. "Four Guinness and a Smithwick's," Jeri called out loudly, trying to recall a previous time when the noise of the saloon required her to yell.

A short man in faded corduroys and an oversized wool sweater turned and waved her toward his group of friends. "Yo—right here," he replied. He passed the drinks to his friends, who nodded and smiled at Jeri in thanks. The man then looked at Jeri as he sipped at the frothy head of his beer.

"So, are you her?" he asked.

"Her who?" Jeri responded, assuming an air of obliviousness.

"Jeri. You're Jeri in the letters, right?" His eyes flickered over her figure before returning back to her impassive stare. "You've got to be her."

"I am indeed." Jeri nodded. "That'll be twenty-four dollars, please."

"Right." He quickly pulled out a wad of crumpled bills and handed them to Jeri, smiling up at her with an earnest smile. "I can see why he writes to you. You're a very beautiful woman."

Jeri stopped counting the money and glanced at the man as he raised his glass to her and took a drink. She studied his face for a trace of sarcasm or humor before realizing he was offering an honest compliment. "Oh, well, thanks," she replied, surprised by the remark. "Do you need change?"

"No, we're good. Thanks, Jeri." The man gave her a lingering stare before joining his friends as Jeri turned and headed back toward the bar. A dull, unsettling feeling began to take weight in her stomach as she slipped through the dense crowd. Along the way, Jeri noticed with growing alarm that the conversations around her would suddenly pause as she passed, and she could feel the eyes she'd spent years getting used to now staring at her with renewed interest. As much as she wanted to pretend otherwise, the vibe in the saloon was very different, and it had something to do with her. For some reason beyond her understanding, Jeri was now the center of interest, and the idea was making her sick.

Jeri was just beginning to imagine the reason for this sudden interest when a thin, pasty-faced man who looked closer to puberty than drinking age abruptly stepped in front of her.

"Hi, Jeri, I'm Josh!" the man exclaimed excitedly as he held out a gaunt hand. "It's great to finally meet you!"

Jeri instinctively stepped away from the young man, unsure whether his enthusiasm was drunkenness or a slight social handicap. "Hi, Josh," she replied warily, clenching the tray with both hands to avoid shaking his hand. "How can I help you?"

"I just wanted to introduce myself," the young man said, smiling back at her with large, dark brown eyes that darted nervously under a flat crop of shapeless black hair. His pale, waxy skin seemed to glow in the dull light of the bar. To Jeri, he looked exactly like the type of smart, nerdy kid who provided comic relief on a TV sitcom.

"Okay . . . well, nice to meet you, Josh," Jeri replied, pointing at the bar behind him. "Now, if you don't mind, I really need to get back to work."

"Oh . . . yeah, sure," Josh replied, still standing in her way. Jeri was about to push past him when he raised his hand and smiled. "Hey, I just wanted to ask . . . did you like my story?"

"What story?"

The young man gave her a dumbfounded smile before laughing awkwardly.

"Oh, c'mon, you . . . you know," he stammered. "The story I wrote in the *Jack* about you and your, uh . . . pen pal. It came out this morning."

Jeri shook her head in confusion. It was odd enough that the nerdy kid standing in front of her was old enough to be in college, let alone allowed in a bar. He was also apparently writing stories about her in the university paper. She dimly noticed that the noise of the crowd seemed to be rising with her impatience.

"Do you know me, Josh?" she asked bluntly.

"Know you? Well, um, no . . . not really. That's why I—"

"Then how did you manage to write a story about me if we haven't even met?"

"Oh, that," Josh replied, swallowing. "Yeah, well . . . you see, I was in here drinking with some buddies one night and we were reading the letters and staring at the photos and I . . . you know, I thought, 'Man, I should totally write a story about these,' and yeah . . . so, I did."

"Of course you did," Jeri muttered, shaking her head.

"I was, like, really hoping we'd get a chance to talk before I submitted it," he continued, his dark eyes watching her nervously. "But you know how it goes with deadlines and stuff. Luckily, Joe the bar owner was nice enough to give me a quote when I called him."

"Do you have a copy of the story on you?" Jeri asked.

"Oh . . . yeah, sure!" Josh replied as he reached into his laptop satchel and pulled out a copy of the paper. "Here you go. You can have that one!"

Jeri glanced at the paper before grabbing it and leveling an angry stare at the young man. "Are you even old enough to be in here, Josh?"

Josh smiled and bobbed his pale head. "Oh, yeah . . . totally! I know I look young, but I'm actually twenty-two."

"Good." Jeri nodded. "Then you're old enough for me to sue you if I find anything libelous in your story. Now step aside."

A frightened stare was plastered on the young man's face as Jeri brushed past him and headed toward the bar. Through the crowd she could see her male coworker—a tall, heavyset college senior named Owen—frantically trying to keep up with the drink orders. Owen normally only worked weekends, but Jeri had called him in to help with the unexpected mob. He gave her an obvious look of relief as she slipped back behind the counter.

"Just in time," he muttered, nodding toward the door. "More coming in."

Jeri looked up to see the heavy oak entry door groaning on its hinges as more bodies pushed their way into the saloon. "Oh god," she said as the new wave of patrons headed toward the bar. "Please tell me this isn't all because of me."

"What—you didn't know?" Owen replied, flipping the handles of the beer taps as he filled another order. "Of course this is all because of you. You and those strange fucking letters." Before Jeri could respond, her coworker produced another copy of *The Lumberjack* from beneath the bar and slapped it down on the counter in front of her. "There you go," he muttered, smiling at her sarcastically. "Enjoy your fifteen minutes of fame."

Jeri scanned the front page. On the lower left-hand corner was an article under the Local Beat section written by a Josh Wilhelm. The pale face and dark eyes of the young man she'd just met peered back at her from the small photo beneath the author's name. Jeri moaned as she read the title: "Local Bartender Romanced by International Mystery Man."

"You've got to be kidding me."

"I need three Long Islands, Jeri," her colleague shouted over the din of the bar. "Can you help a brother out?"

Jeri nodded dully as her eyes stayed fixed on the paper. Her hands seemed to work automatically at mixing the drinks as she read the article.

In a manner more befitting of a Hollywood screenplay than a late-night bar romance, a local woman has become unexpectedly intertwined in an old-school courtship by an international man of mystery.

And she doesn't even know his name.

Jeri Halston, an alumnus of NAU who bartends at the Joe's Last Stand Saloon in old downtown, has been receiving cryptic love letters since September from an unnamed gentleman who only refers to himself as the "Mysterious Joe's Last Stand Guy." In the letters, which have been enshrined on a wall in the old saloon for the enjoyment of its patrons by owner Joe Brown, the mystery author provides a comically convoluted and very unconventional perspective on his travels and daily affairs. But the one message he states clearly is his love for Halston.

"Three Long Islands," Jeri yelled as she pushed the finished drinks to her colleague. A man standing at the counter in front of her yelled and waved to get her attention, but Jeri ignored him as she continued reading.

It is also clear that the mysterious author likes to stay on the move. In just over a month, Ms. Halston has received letters from India, Saudi Arabia, Nigeria, and most recently, Venezuela.

Adding to the mystery is the inclusion of a Polaroid photo in each of the four letters Halston has received, the subject of which always seems to be a dark-haired man, presumably the letters' author, in the location of the letter's origin and always wearing a blue Joe's Last Stand Saloon T-shirt. In each of the photos, the man's face is tantalizingly obscured by something that hides his identity.

Halston, who was not available for an interview, is apparently neither excited nor concerned by the sudden romantic attention. Bar owner Brown, Halston's close friend and employer, says Halston is handling it like any other unexpected advance, finding it "entertaining like the rest of us, but nothing to be taken seriously." According to Brown, "Jeri's way too smart to let this be anything more than a flattering joke. It was even her idea to put the letters up for our patrons to read and enjoy."

I'm going to kill Joe for this, Jeri thought with conviction.

While nothing in the letters indicates that Halston's mysterious admirer plans to be in Flagstaff any time soon, Joe Brown hopes to meet him one day.

"I'm not sure about Jeri, but I'd love to have a drink with him," the saloon owner said, adding, "as long as he isn't some complete wacko."

"Hey, Jeri!" Owen called out over his shoulder. "Can I get two rum and Cokes and a shot of Jägermeister, please?"

Jeri looked up from the paper and stared out at the loud, packed room. Around her, the crowd inside the saloon was acting as it always did—laughing, arguing, boasting, flirting—as tensions and sobriety drained with the afternoon light. As usual, her eyes met the fleeting stares and furtive glances of men and women who smiled and lingered before moving on. But something in their stares was different.

And now she knew why.

In all her life, Jeri had never sought out attention. The closest she'd come to anything resembling fame was when she'd somehow been nominated for homecoming queen, and even that little taste, the nods and stares in the hallways of high school, had left her literally nauseated with anxiety. In her time as a bartender, Jeri had come to accept the attention that came with the job, rationalizing it as simply part of the occupation. But she'd certainly never been comfortable with it. To her, there was no worse feeling than the raw, penetrating sense of exposure that came from the knowledge that someone knew more about her than she knew of them. And now, thanks to Joe and a nerdy little college reporter, she once again felt the gut-wrenching sensation of being looked at, talked about, and—worst of all—analyzed by everyone in the bar.

"Jeri! Yo . . . Jeri!"

Jeri realized Owen was standing next to her.

"Hey," he said quietly, placing a worried hand on her shoulder. "Are you okay?"

"Yeah, fine," Jeri replied, forcing her gaze away from the crowd. "Sorry, I'll get those drinks for you. Rum and Cokes and a Jäger, right?"

"Already taken care of," Owen replied, watching her closely. "Look, I'm sorry. I thought you knew today's little boom in business was because of that lame article." He glanced up at the crowd. "By the way, the little fucker who wrote the article is here . . . do you want me to throw him out for you?"

"No, it's fine," Jeri said, waving her hand dismissively. "I've already been introduced. Besides, I can only imagine what his next story would be if I had you give him the rough treatment."

"Okay. Well, hey, look, do you want to get out of here?" he asked, patting her back. "Seriously, I've got this covered. You should just go home."

Jeri looked at her colleague. While she was not one for finding excuses to avoid working, at the moment every bone in her body was aching to slip away from the stares in the bar and crawl into the warm privacy of her apartment. Besides, the more she considered the substantial profits Joe was making on the attention surrounding her letters—which really meant the substantial profit he was making on *her*—the more her guilt of walking out on the busiest afternoon in recent history began to fade.

"Are you sure?" she asked, a genuine smile of appreciation lighting her face.

"Go."

Jeri quickly grabbed her bag and jacket before noticing Chip sitting in the corner, his blue eyes watching her gloomily. She sighed and walked over to him.

"I'm out, Chip," Jeri said, tossing the copy of *The Lumberjack* in front of him before ducking under the counter and popping up next to him on the other side. "I can't seem to get any privacy around here tonight." She watched the older man's eyes widen in surprise as he read the headline.

"My, my," Chip said under his breath. He scanned the article for a moment before glancing at the crowd over his shoulder, his eyes deep in thought. "So that explains it, huh?" he asked quietly. He muttered something else to himself before taking a sip of his beer, but the words were lost to the noise of the room. Jeri leaned in close to him.

"Do me a favor," she said, putting her arm around his broad shoulders. "If you see Joe, my close friend and self-appointed press agent, before I do, please inform him that I would like his resignation immediately. In the meantime, I'm going home to my paparazzi-free apartment."

"This is why you need a *real* job, Jeri," Chip replied, looking at her with a solemn expression. He tapped the paper slowly with his finger and leaned toward her. Jeri felt the soft scratch of his gray stubble against her cheek as he whispered in her ear. "This is the only thing this place will ever give you—grief and disappointment."

Jeri nodded as she pulled on her jacket and threw her bag over her shoulder. She looked somberly into Chip's blue eyes for a moment before tousling his salt-and-pepper hair. "Don't worry about me, old man. We both know this is just a stepping stone until that gig at the strip club opens up in Vegas, right?"

Chip smiled back at Jeri, seeing once again the dark ember that smoldered and gave light to her beautiful eyes. He knew the source of that fire all too well, and like any fire, he knew to regard it with caution. "You're right," he replied, giving her a thin smile as he went along with the joke. "But only if it's a day job. You'll want to keep your nights free for prostituting. That's where the real money is."

Jeri's eyes softened as her smile stretched wide. She hugged Chip tightly and kissed him on the cheek. "Thank you for understanding me."

Chip shrugged. "Oh, I don't ever pretend to understand you, but that doesn't mean I won't keep trying to persuade you otherwise. Now go home." He smiled as Jeri gave him a final squeeze, then turned and watched as she slipped quietly through the crowd, a wake of curious stares following behind her. His eyes lingered briefly on the throng before he turned back and took a long sip of his beer. He then grabbed the newspaper lying on the counter in front of him and began slowly reading the article.

===

Tom Coleman looked up at his surroundings in surprise.

Nearly an hour after leaving the Homeland Security offices to clear his mind, he found himself walking along Historic Route 66 at the edge of the old downtown. He glanced up at the sky. The fading rays of late-afternoon light were smothered behind a low, dirty-gray blanket of clouds as small, cotton-white flakes of snow fell in a meandering dance before dissolving on the brick-lined sidewalk. Noticing the chill in the air, Tom raised his collar and considered what to do next. He didn't want to go home. It was too quiet at home. Too alone. A fleeting image of his ex-wife abruptly came to mind, forcing him to shrug. No, he wasn't ready to go home. And besides, he still had more thinking to do.

A flash of light caught Tom's attention. He looked up to find the neon sign of Joe's Last Stand Saloon flickering to life above him, its red-orange colors warm against the cold sky. Remembering the promise of a drink he'd made to himself a few hours earlier, he turned and headed for the entrance.

Tom opened the door and immediately recoiled with shock. The old saloon was packed. He'd been in Joe's a few times before, but the crowd had never been anything like this. His first instinct was to pull an about-face and find a quieter bar, but as the patrons closest to the door turned and stared at him, the idea of leaving suddenly seemed childish and rather cowardly. Deciding that his need for a drink was stronger than his aversion to the crowd and the germs that came with it, Tom cautiously worked his way inside.

He headed toward the bar and noticed that luckily a single bar-stool in the corner was still open. He pushed his way through the mob and sat down wearily between a young couple busily groping each other and an older man quietly reading a newspaper. "I'll take a Bud Light when you get a chance," he shouted as the heavyset bartender passed by. The man didn't acknowledge him. "Bud Light, please!" he repeated.

"Heard you the first time," the bartender replied, giving him a petulant sidelong glance as he poured a fresh beer from the tap. "Be with you in a minute."

Tom glanced around the old saloon. He wasn't familiar enough with the place to know if this type of crowd was common, but his instincts told him it was extreme even for a busy night. As he always did in public areas, Tom pulled a sanitary wipe from the inside pocket of his jacket and quickly wiped down the bar top in front of him before tossing the cloth discreetly under the bar. He then glanced at the young couple beside him as they continued to kiss, their hands in constant motion to find exposed and loosely concealed skin. Seeing no chance of a conversation there, he turned to the older man sitting next to him.

"Hell of a night here, huh?"

The older man looked up from his newspaper and leveled his piercing blue eyes on Tom. "Indeed it is," he replied.

The bartender hastily placed a beer on the counter in front of Tom and yelled out the price as he moved down the bar, his hands stretched full with drink orders. Tom considered wiping the glass with a sanitary wipe before irritably pushing the thought from his mind. "I don't think he likes me," he muttered as he pulled out his wallet and dropped the money for his drink on the bar.

The older man seemed to weigh the thought for a moment before shaking his head. "I say he's too busy to have an opinion of you just yet."

"You're probably right," Tom replied as he studied the man next to him. He looked to be in his late fifties, with wavy, gray-streaked hair and a rugged-looking face that gave him the incongruous look of both outdoor adventurer and philosophy professor. Despite his age, he appeared to be remarkably fit, and something about his demeanor told Tom that the man was still quite capable of handling himself. Given his relaxed manner, Tom also sensed the man was a regular at Joe's.

"So, is it usually like this around here?" Tom asked, slightly out of curiosity and mostly just to kill time.

"No," the older man replied, his eyes still scanning the paper. "Today is a uniquely busy day."

"Any particular reason why?" Tom pressed.

The older man looked up from the paper and drained the final drops of his beer. With a quick gesture of his hand he caught the attention of the bartender, who wordlessly nodded and smiled before immediately bringing a fresh replacement. Tom knew without trying that he could not replicate that response.

"There's always a reason, my friend." The old man turned and stared at Tom with a stern, empty expression. "Whether you can know it or not, whether you can see it or not, whether you can understand it or not, the reason is always right there in front of you."

Tom stared back at the old man, trying to decide if they were still talking about the same thing, when the older man smiled. "By the way, my name's Chip," he said, extending his large hand.

Tom nodded and shook the older man's hand, surprised by his strength. "I'm Tom. Nice to meet you, Chip."

"Nice to meet you, Tom," Chip replied, extending his arm and sweeping it theatrically around the room. "And welcome to gay and lesbian night at Joe's Last Stand Saloon."

Tom froze for a moment as the words sunk in, then nodded as he reached for his beer. He glanced quickly at the couple kissing next to him as he took a drink, trying to catch a glimpse of their sex. The one farthest from him was definitely a woman, and a good-looking one at that. Although he couldn't see her partner's face, by all accounts it appeared to be a man with short-cropped hair in an oversized flannel shirt. Unfortunately, Tom knew that description also matched the look of every bull dyke in northern Arizona. He sat his drink back onto the bar and sighed heavily.

This was turning into a total fucking disaster of a day.

"You okay there, Tom?" Chip asked next to him.

"Yeah, I'm fine," Tom muttered, stealing a few more quick glances at the crowd before smiling at the older man. "I just didn't know it was a homo—I mean, I didn't know Joe's was a—"

"I'm just kidding you, Tom," Chip said as he slapped him on the shoulder. "You just looked like a homophobe, and I couldn't resist."

"Right, got it," Tom said, forcing a weak laugh at the joke. He wasn't a homophobe, he thought defensively. He just didn't go out of his way to hang out with queers.

Chip pushed the newspaper toward him and tapped on the story at the bottom. "Here's the real reason for tonight's little party," he said, staring at Tom with a wry smile. "In case you didn't already know."

Tom leaned forward and read the headline: "Local Bartender Romanced by International Mystery Man."

He pointed his finger at the heavyset bartender behind the counter and glanced at Chip. "Him?" he asked with a disbelieving look.

Chip considered the question for a moment, watching Tom's expression for any hint of humor before realizing he was serious. "No, Tom, not him. As I said, this isn't a gay bar."

"At least not yet," Tom muttered cynically, shaking his head. "The way these young people are nowadays, you just never know." He scanned the first few sentences of the article. Before now, Tom had never bothered to read the local college paper. He'd always assumed that if it was anything like the people he saw walking around campus, it was a useless expression of naïve liberal viewpoints written by people who'd never stuck their heads out of the ass of academia long enough to see how the real world works. Based on the subject matter in front of him, his opinion wasn't changed. He took another drink of his beer.

Reading further, Tom realized the bartender mentioned in the story had to be the good-looking woman who'd served him the last time he was here. He vaguely remembered the heated discussion she was having with her friend. A hot flash of anger passed through him as he recalled the way her bitchy blonde friend had dismissed him when he'd tried to speak to her. *I should have shown that bitch who's boss*, he thought with a shrug. He finished the article and ordered another beer.

"So let me get this straight," he said, turning to Chip. "Some kind of James Bond wannabe is sending letters to a female bartender with a nice ass, and the story makes the college paper?"

"Apparently it does," Chip replied, focusing his blue eyes on Tom. "By the way, the bartender with a nice ass is a friend of mine, so please mind what you say about her."

"Oh . . . my apologies," Tom replied. "I didn't mean to offend . . . just making conversation." He silently scolded himself for his lack of judgment. *The old man is a regular. Of course he'd be friends with her.*

Chip's expression softened into a wide smile, but his stare remained ice cold. "I'm sure you didn't."

The bartender returned and dropped a fresh pint in front of Tom. Both men drank in silence for a few minutes as Tom studied the interior of Joe's. Despite the untold number of dive bars he'd frequented in his younger years, Tom still marveled at the predictability of their features. The morose collections of decaying pictures and cobwebbed debris that cluttered the walls under the dull incandescent light. The sturdy, ass-worn barstools and stained, gummed, knife-carved tables. The amalgamated scents of tobacco, mildew, perfume, and breath. And most important, the bar counter itself—ancient and coffee-black, shellacked and relentlessly wiped like a revered altar until it gleamed with a waxy pallor that was both dull and brilliant at the same time. All were the requisite features of Joe's Last Stand Saloon and its dive-bar kin, this ubiquitous archetype that, as its name implied, sat lowest on the social scale. As Tom glanced around the room, he surmised that whatever glory had ever dwelled in this ancient saloon sitting alongside old Route 66 had long since vanished, its remnants entombed beneath the thick layers of varnish on the counter where his beer now rested.

"They're over there," Chip said, his finger pointing toward the far wall of the bar, "in case you're interested."

"What's that?" Tom asked, glancing over his shoulder.

"The letters that he wrote her—they're posted on that wall," Chip replied as he stared into the dark amber of his beer. "The photos are there too."

Tom looked toward the far wall but could see nothing beyond the huddle of people that stood in the muted light. He considered getting up to have a closer look, then decided against it. It would be better to wait until he was buzzed enough to manage the germ-filled congestion of humanity he would have to deal with. He turned to Chip instead. "So all this started a few months ago, huh?" he asked. To his own surprise, Tom realized that he was beginning to relax. The beer was soaking in, the din of the crowd was beginning to fade into the background, and the conversation with the friendly older man sitting next to him was beginning to get interesting.

"The first letter arrived a little over a month ago," Chip replied matter-of-factly. "I was actually sitting here when Jeri opened it."

"And what was your take?" Tom asked.

Chip rubbed his stubbly beard for a moment while his eyes darted quickly around the bar, as if his mind was assembling the answer to a long, complicated mathematical equation.

"Well, I thought it was all very interesting," he said thoughtfully, his pale eyes flashing at Tom before settling back on his beer. "But then, everything is interesting to me. I mean, come on . . . why else would I sit here for hours on end if I wasn't fascinated by the mundane and trivial?" The hint of a smile curled the edges of Chip's mouth. "Christ, I could sit here all day watching someone eat corn nuts without getting bored."

Tom smiled at the older man. While he'd never admit it, he could empathize with Chip's condition. That simple ability to find interest in the smallest of details sat right at the core of his own personality. He took another swallow of beer, enjoying its cold, bitter taste. "And you're telling me nobody knows anything about this guy? Who he is, what he does, or . . ." Tom paused as the image of Jeri's face, almond-shaped and beautiful in the soft light of the bar, flashed through his mind. "Or what his intentions are?"

Chip shook his head. "No. And if anyone does, they're not talking," he replied laconically. "Of course, every idiot who walks in here and reads the letters seems to have a theory or a hunch. And I've heard just about all of them."

"Care to repeat a few?"

"Oh god, you name it," Chip muttered, his hands drawing wide arcs in the air. "There's the obvious ones—he's a hippie in the Peace Corps; he's a hungry young reporter on some shitty-gritty assignment; he's a good-doing doctor selflessly fighting disease in the worst places on earth. Then there's the creative ones—he's a location scout for a reality TV show; he's a recruiter for an offshore development firm; he's a buyer of rare antiquities and artifacts." He paused to take a drink before continuing. "And then there's the cryptic ones, like the guy tonight who swore if you traced the locations of the letter's origins in chronological order on a world map, you'd see that it forms the shape of a pentagram. There was even a cute little redhead sitting on that barstool earlier who was convinced the names of the letters' origins were some form of anagram. She must've sat there for two hours trying to patch the letters together . . ." Chip's baritone voice trailed off, leaving a flagrant question lingering in the musty, warm air of the saloon.

"So . . . did she come up with something?" Tom asked.

"Only if your definition of 'something' includes total gibberish," Chip replied, shaking his head. "I tell you, if the kids I listened to tonight are any indication of the level of intellect we're producing these days, this country is in serious trouble." He smiled a quick thanks to the bartender as the man dropped off another pint. "So anyway, that's the story," he said quietly, taking a long drink as if to punctuate his sentence.

Tom nodded. He could tell that the older man was done with the topic, but his interest was too aroused to let it drop just yet. He figured he had an even chance at asking one more question before Chip gave him a dismissive wave of the hand.

"You seem to be pretty good at reading people, Chip . . . so what do *you* think this guy's up to?"

Chip's expression softened for a moment as he glanced around the saloon, his gaze scanning the faces of the patrons and briefly the wall of letters before settling on Tom. His blue eyes seemed to hold a turbulent wash of ideas, swirling and colliding as they were drawn inward, like leaves drawn into a deep whirlpool. "What I think this guy is up to is a game that could be very innocent or very serious, and we won't know which until he chooses to show us. Either way, he's got the advantage. We know nothing about him, and yet he knows something, perhaps a great deal, about Jeri and this place. He could be sitting next to you right now, or sitting on the other side of the world. None of us have a clue."

He paused for a moment, examining the pint of beer in front of him as if seeing it for the first time. A smile dimpled the edges of his handsome face. "As to what he *is*, well . . . all I can say is that I've lived long enough to know that sometimes a person who's after something never really reveals what or who they are until they have it. And as much as I hate to say it, I've learned from long personal experience that the best endings come from planning for the worst possibilities."

Tom nodded. "So if I'm hearing you right, and applying your reverse logic, we should assume that the funny, romantic, and seemingly harmless guy who's writing these letters is—"

"Anything but harmless," Chip replied, finishing Tom's sentence as he held him with his stare. "Until I know otherwise, I think it's safe to assume this guy could be capable of anything." His mouth curled into a wry grin. "Hell, for all we know, he could be an international terrorist."

Tom considered the older man's statement before smiling back at him.

"I suppose he could."

An hour later, sufficiently drunk enough to wade through the crowd, Tom shuffled his way to the corner of the room where the shrine of letters and pictures was hung. He stared with fascination at the various sheets of exotic hotel stationery and read every one of the odd, neatly scripted letters, all of them signed by the Mysterious Joe's Last Stand Guy. He examined the Polaroid photos and smiled at the clever obscuration of the writer's face in each one.

Then, for reasons even he wasn't quite sure of, Tom pulled a pen and sheet of notepad paper from his pocket and began slowly writing down the dates and origins of each letter.

Chapter 19

Jeri sat under the heavy flannel-covered comforter of her bed and stared at the open book on her lap. The bottle of red wine she'd opened moments after getting home now sat half-empty on the nightstand, perched precariously on a stack of books along with an empty wineglass. Outside her bedroom window, light wisps of snow drifted past the frost-covered panes of glass.

Her mind was now reasonably calm, the wine having successfully dulled the edge of anger she'd felt since leaving the saloon an hour before. She once again picked up the romance novel Allie had given her and started to read. Two pages into it, she reminded herself how much she hated fiction—romance novels even more so—and resignedly tossed the book onto the already overburdened nightstand next to her. With nothing left to distract her, Jeri sank deeply into the thick pillows of the bed and sulked. Her thoughts drifted randomly for several minutes before inevitably settling on the events from earlier that evening. The image of a packed room of people watching her move through the bar filled her mind, causing a tinge of nausea in her stomach. She shook her head to dislodge the thought, desperately searching her mind for something else to concentrate on. As she closed her eyes and breathed deeply, a favorite memory slowly drifted into her thoughts. Jeri focused her mind on the memory, and within seconds she was asleep.

They were hiking.

The morning sun filtered through the emerald-green leaves of the aspen trees and fell in beautiful, shadow-wrapped patterns around her as she walked. The midsummer air was already warm, filled with the orchestra of countless buzzing insects as they whirled and zagged around her. She brushed a nagging fly away from her face and looked up. Ahead of her, the thin trail along the Coconino National Forest's Inner Basin turned and disappeared within the green underbrush of the forest. Jeri sighed loudly. She knew from the map she'd studied during their predawn drive into the park that the trail continued upward into the San Francisco Peaks in the distance, a long and grueling hike that her dad was convinced would be a piece of cake. She looked back at him and frowned.

"What's up, buttercup?" her father asked. His large brown eyes peered down at her from his tall, thin frame with an ever-present glint of curiosity and humor.

"I don't feel like dying in the mountains today," she replied grumpily. "And please stop calling me buttercup."

Her father replied with a deep rolling laugh that echoed through the forest, forcing Jeri's frown upward into a smile. She loved her father's laugh, loved the way its low, resounding rhythm surrounded and embraced her like a comforting hug. Even her nascent sense of teenage independence was no match for its disarming warmth. She swatted at the tall blooming stalks of yellow columbine in front of her and continued walking.

"Anything you want to talk about, honey bunny?"

"Dad!" her fourteen-year-old voice screamed as she turned and shot him a venomous look.

"What? I didn't call you buttercup, did I?" He smiled at her with his handsome face, his dark brown hair held back from his forehead by a tightly wrapped bandana. "Besides, we're ten miles from everything . . . you don't have to worry about me embarrassing you in front of anyone out here, Jer-bear."

Jeri shook her head and stomped up the trail as her father's deep laughter embraced her again. She brushed a lock of hair from her already sweaty face and listened to the chorus of birds and insects around her. She didn't feel much like talking. In a few days her father would again be leaving on a long trip, and Jeri knew no amount of questions—or his infuriatingly vague answers—could take away the impending sense of loneliness she would feel when he was gone. All she wanted now was as much time with him as she could get before he left—and to make him feel endlessly guilty for dumping her once again on Aunt Patricia and her mothball-smelling house.

"How long will you be gone this time?" she asked grimly as she plodded ahead of her father along the overgrown trail.

"Two weeks, give or take a few days," he replied, a hint of regret in his voice. "Not too long."

Jeri grunted. "And where will you be?"

"New York City . . . conferences and meetings . . . boring stuff."

Jeri nodded her head. Her father always had a knack for making his business trips sound like nothing short of pure torture, but she knew for a fact he loved his work. An economist and business analyst, her father was a ridiculously intelligent man who in the last few years had become highly sought as a business consultant to large corporations. After years of barely scraping by, the results of his newfound fame had been mixed: more money for their little two-person family, but less time together to enjoy it. For the first time ever, Jeri had all of the material things her school peers had—fashionable new clothes, a brand-new bicycle, and best of all, all the books and music she could get her hands on. But what she wanted more than anything was the same commodity that was in great and growing demand—her father's warm, brilliant, and always-laughing presence.

They followed the trail upward past the groves of quaking aspens and towering Engelmann spruce into a long, open meadow of wildflowers and waving golden grasses. Jeri heard her father whistle and looked back to see him standing on a rock with a hand cupped over his eyes, staring admiringly out at the view.

"You see that?" he said loudly, pointing at a mountain on the opposite end of the valley. It looked to Jeri like its top had been carved out with a giant ice cream scoop. "That's Sunset Crater."

"Yeah, Dad, I know," Jeri answered, staring at her hiking boots. "You've pointed it out before."

"Sure I have. But . . . well, look how beautiful it is in the morning light."

"It's great. Can we eat now?"

Her father stared at the distant peak for another moment before looking over at her with a dazed grin that Jeri knew all too well.

"I know you didn't hear what I said, Dad," she said, exasperated. "Can we please eat now?"

"Oh, course we can, buttercup."

"Daaad!"

They laid a blanket across a large flat rock and sat down next to each other. Jeri pulled two canteens of water from her backpack as her father unwrapped a large sandwich and laid it out on a bright red bandana in front of them. They sat in silence for several minutes, eating hungrily and watching the colors of the panoramic landscape change under the rising sun. Both of them burped in fullness and laughed out loud at each other. Jeri's father pointed out a few more things of interest in the distance, then moaned in mock exhaustion and sprawled his long frame against the sun-drenched rock. Jeri studied the view for a few minutes longer, quietly remembering everything her father had pointed out before lying down next to him and resting her head on his chest. She stared up at his tanned, youthful face, relaxed and friendly with its ever-present grin. Even now as he pretended to sleep she felt the nagging ping of dread in her stomach as she remembered he'd soon be gone again. His strong heartbeat thumped loudly in her ear.

"Dad?" she said softly.

"Yes, sweetheart," her father replied with closed eyes, his tone eager as if he'd been waiting for her question.

"Why did things have to change? I mean, why do you always have to leave now? I know you're making more money and stuff, but . . . but don't you miss the way things were before?"

His chest rose and fell slowly as he lay quietly against the rock. Jeri knew this meant her father was thinking very seriously about the question. After a few seconds, his low voice spoke softly back to her.

"I do miss it, sweetheart, much more than you can tell. I know these past few years have brought more than their fair share of changes. Change can be such a difficult thing sometimes . . . even for me. You're too young to remember, but when your mother died, I was convinced that nothing ahead of us could ever be as good as what was already gone. But I still had you, my little drooling, diaper-wearing bundle of joy and terror. And as time passed, I came to realize something."

"What's that?"

"That all things have no choice but to continually change. And that nothing can escape this fact. Just look at how much you've changed in just the past few months—you're turning into a young woman faster than I can believe! Even this rock we're lying on is changing . . . fracturing, eroding, sinking back into the soil." His hand found her forehead and slowly stroked her hair. "The key to accepting change is realizing the great things you have now, at this very moment in time, because one day I guarantee you'll look back on today and wish things were just as they are right now."

"I doubt that," Jeri replied dejectedly.

Her father lifted his head and gave her a look of feigned surprise. "What? You're not having fun out here with me?" he asked sarcastically, tousling her hair.

"Well, yeah, I'm having fun, I guess. But I keep thinking about the fact that you'll be leaving soon, and when I think about it I get sad all over again."

Her father laid his head back and said nothing for a few minutes. Jeri was beginning to think he'd fallen asleep when his head nodded slowly and his lips pursed like they always did when he was about to say something important. "It's okay to be sad sometimes, sweetheart. It helps us appreciate the good times even more. Just try your best not to let it get in the way of making new good times, okay?"

"Okay."

"Promise?" her father pressed, tickling her neck.

"I promise!" Jeri replied, shrieking with laughter as she swatted his hand away.

"Good. And I'll make a promise to you too. I promise to be home soon, and when I am, I promise to give you as much of my attention as you could possibly want . . . which I'm guessing will be less and less as the next few years go by."

"Why do you say that?"

"Just a hunch, Jer-bear . . . just a hunch."

Jeri pressed against her father, feeling a warmth inside her that was even better than the sun against her back. She closed her eyes and listened to the steady beating of her father's heart, her thoughts drifting and fading toward a deep, effortless sleep.

The dream began to change.

Jeri dimly noticed the sound that followed her father's heartbeat, a sharp, high-pitched chirp that seemed to chase every faint beat. The warmth of the morning sun faded from her back, replaced by the chill of artificially conditioned air. As she stirred, she noticed the light that filtered through her closed eyelids had mutated to a cold, dull white. A familiar voice whispered her name as a warm hand lightly stroked her arm.

She opened her eyes and looked up at her father.

The hospital room was small and cramped. The air held the lingering smell of strong antiseptic. An army of stark metal machines crowded around her father's bed, beeping and humming as they monitored his vital signs through a swarm of thin plastic lines that ran to his chest and head. Lying in the center of the chaos, wearing a green gown and covered with a thin blanket, her father looked up at her and smiled.

"Hey, kiddo," he said weakly. "Did you get some rest?"

Jeri nodded in a state of shock, blinking back tears as the full weight of reality came rushing back to her. In an instant she remembered everything.

Her father's illness had come on without warning. He had called her late one night while she was writing her thesis for her master's in economics in her apartment, her head buried deep in notes and thick volumes on global economics when the phone rang. He'd tried to make small talk with her at first, but Jeri knew her father too well to know he wouldn't have called without a reason, and quickly asked him what was wrong. His voice trembled with emotion as he reluctantly told her about the strange headaches and dizziness he had been having for the last few weeks, and how he'd finally relented and gone to the doctor that morning. After a few tests and an MRI, the horrible truth was pointed out to him on a computer screen—her father had a massive brain tumor. Ten minutes after hearing the news, Jeri had packed a bag and was already breaking the speed limit in her old Toyota Corolla as she wiped away a torrent of warm tears and drove to the hospital.

Now, two sleepless days later, she was sitting beside her father's hospital bed in the middle of the night and staring into his exhausted, deep brown eyes.

"How are you feeling, Dad?" she asked as she grabbed his hand and squeezed it reassuringly. Her father shrugged with an indignant look.

"Physically, I feel fine . . . no pain at all," he said slowly, his eyes wet with frustration. "It's the symptoms that are killing me."

Jeri nodded and looked away for a moment to fight back the tears in her own eyes. Less than a day after the diagnosis, the effects of her father's tumor had begun to manifest themselves in terrifying new ways. Growing deep in the center of his brain at the critical juncture of tissues that control cognition, the tumor had created a condition her father's neurosurgeon called transcortical sensory aphasia, a condition that, to her father's horror, had left him completely unable to comprehend written language. The irony that a man who'd spent his life as an economist and analyst was now incapable of understanding a single line of text was nearly beyond bearable. Realizing that her time with this brilliant, humorous, and loving man was short, Jeri had stayed glued by his bed, vowing, much to the irritation of the nurses, to stay by him until the end.

She blinked away the last of her tears and turned back to her father with a smile. "Would you like me to read to you?" she asked.

Her father closed his eyes and shook his head. "No, just talk to me, buttercup."

"Oh god, Dad, you haven't called me buttercup in ten years."

He opened his eyes and smiled mischievously at her. "Has it been ten years? Wow . . . time flies, huh? Of course, from what little of my mind I have left, I seem to remember you weren't a big fan of that name. What do you say we just blame that little slipup on the tumor?"

"Deal," Jeri replied, laughing with her father at his morbid joke. She stared down at his still-handsome unshaven face and forced herself to remember every last detail of the moment, struck once again with the heavy weight of knowing these could be her last memories of their time together. As if reading her thoughts, her father's warm laughter eased into a long, punctuating sigh. He squeezed her hand gently.

"It's okay, sweetheart, I'm not ready for this either. God knows I wasn't expecting something like this . . . but I certainly don't have any regrets about my life and how I've lived it. It's been a wonderful ride. And how could I be any more proud of you?" He paused and wiped a tear away from her cheek. "My beautiful, brilliant daughter. Graduating summa cum laude with a master's in economics practically under your belt . . . just like your old man. You'll be kicking some serious ass in this world before you know it."

Jeri smiled and shrugged dismissively. Her father gave her a solemn stare.

"Just promise me something, Jeri. Promise me that you'll always trust your own instincts and pursue everything you do with passion. No matter what you choose to do, just remember that if you follow your heart, it will always lead you to happiness. Okay?"

Jeri nodded in response to her father's request, ignoring the fresh flow of tears on her face.

"Promise?" he asked, his voice deep and uncharacteristically serious.

"I promise," she replied.

"Good."

Her father smiled peacefully as he glanced over at the machines beside the bed. The bright green line of his heartbeat monitor raced frantically across the small screen next to him, rising and dipping in a life-affirming rhythm. He watched it keenly for a few moments before looking over at Jeri with a worried expression.

"Sweetheart, there's something else I need to tell you . . . something about my work. It's probably nothing, but . . . I'm . . . I'm being cautious."

Jeri leaned in closer toward her father as he fidgeted uncomfortably under the thin blanket. "What is it, Dad?"

"Like I said, it's probably nothing. I . . . I've made a lot of friends in my career, but, well . . . unfortunately a fair number of enemies too. Not that this should be surprising. I suppose you can't analyze matters involving the world's largest economies and corporations without occasionally gaining the attention of the men who run them, huh?" He looked up at Jeri and gave her a tired smile.

"The truth is, sweetheart, I've collected a fair amount of information over the years from my work. Information that some would consider sensitive at the very least."

"Like what?" Jeri asked.

Her father looked toward the door nervously. A moment later he looked up at her and began speaking in a low whisper. "All sorts of things.

Top-level operational memos . . . unrecorded executive orders . . . buried procedural doctrines . . . even personnel files. You have to understand, after people began to know who I was, they started coming to me. Disgruntled employees with information, rich executives who suddenly grew a conscience, even corporate spies who wanted to seed negative information about their competitors. I became something of a priest of the corporate confessional. Of course, most of it is relatively benign if not completely outdated at this point." He paused and gazed at her with a grave expression. *"But some of it . . . well, some of it is simply too dangerous to expose."*

Jeri looked at her father, hoping for a punch line that his expression told her was not going to come. *"Dad, why are you telling me this?"*

Her father squeezed her hand gently. *"Because when I die, you'll be the only person who knows that this information exists. More importantly, you'll be the only person who knows where to find it."*

"But I don't . . . I have no idea where to find it."

Her father's mouth turned into a shrewd grin. *"Do you remember the last time I called you buttercup?"*

"You mean other than two minutes ago?"

"Yes."

Jeri thought for a moment and then nodded. *"You mean the time we—"*

Her father quickly placed his index finger over his mouth and smiled conspiratorially. *"If you remember the time, sweetheart, then you know the place. But be careful."* He reached up and gently stroked her hair. *"I've learned from all my years chasing stories that there are some stones you simply shouldn't look under."*

Jeri stared at her father suspiciously. *"Dad, are you okay? I mean, are you sure this isn't a . . . a hallucination? You haven't had any sleep since early this morning. You've got to be exhausted."*

"I am," her father said as he nodded wearily. *"And while we're on the subject, you haven't slept much yourself lately. I want you to go home and get some sleep."*

"I'm not leaving."

"Go home, sweetheart."

"No chance."

Her father grunted his annoyance. *"God, you're as stubborn as I am."*

"Even more so," Jeri replied as she smiled back at him.

"Well, I expected as much," her father said. *"That's why I asked the nurse with the pretty green eyes if you could stay in the nearest available room. She said you could. By the way, I think she likes me."* He laughed and waved his hand toward the door. *"Go ask her to set you up."*

Jeri hesitated for a moment, terrified to leave his side, before finally relenting to his logic. *"Okay, fine,"* she replied as she leaned forward and kissed her father on the forehead before standing. *"But I'll be back to say good night."*

"That sounds good," he replied, staring up at her with warm, affectionate eyes. *"I love you, Jeri . . . more than anything in this world."*

Jeri grabbed his hand and squeezed it tightly. *"I love you too, Dad."* She walked to the door, then turned back to him and smiled. *"How about we take that hike again when you're feeling better. Is that a deal?"*

Her father flashed her a broad smile. *"That's a deal."*

The nurses' station for the third-floor patient ward was a short walk down the hallway. As she approached the large elliptical desk, Jeri could see one of the nurses on the night shift eyeing her suspiciously.

"I'm sorry, miss, but visiting hours are over," the small, gray-haired nurse said with practiced briskness as Jeri stopped at the counter.

"I know . . . I'm here with my father, James Halston. His nurse said I could stay in an open room for the night if one is still available."

The nurse glared up at Jeri over her bifocals and frowned, deepening the framework of wrinkles around her small features. *"Oh, she did, did she?"*

"Yes, she did," Jeri replied, glaring back.

The older woman huffed and dropped her eyes to the computer screen in front of her. *"Room 307 is empty—for now,"* she said tersely, *pointing in the opposite direction from her father's room. "Down the hall and to the right."*

"There's nothing closer to room 324?" Jeri asked.

The nurse gave her an exasperated glare. "No, there isn't."

Jeri nodded and thanked the crusty nurse as she turned and headed down the hallway. She walked slowly, feeling the full weight of exhaustion sinking deep into her body. A few moments later she was standing outside of room 307. She was just beginning to open the door when the loud buzzing of an alarm echoed from the nurses' station. Jeri turned and stared in confusion. Almost immediately, two of the nurses stood up and began running down the hallway. A third nurse appeared from a patient's room and fell in behind them. As she watched, a sudden jolt of alarm shot through her as she realized where they were heading. Her exhaustion instantly vaporized as she ran after them in terror, crying out a single word.

"Dad!"

She flew into her father's room, nearly crashing into the nurses as they hovered over his body. Between their bent figures and quickly working arms, Jeri caught a glimpse of her father's writhing body and cried out in horror. Caught in a massive seizure, her father's limbs were flailing wildly against the restraining hands of the three women. The nurse closest to Jeri turned and shouted at her to leave, but she could only stand and stare in frozen fear. The woman grabbed her, pulling her toward the bed, shouting for her to help. Jeri grabbed her father's hand and held it tightly to her chest. As she did, she looked down at his tortured face. Her father's head was thrown rigidly back, his jaw clenched tightly, his face crimson red as he fought desperately against his own body.

"Help him!" Jeri heard herself scream as the nurse next to her steadied a large syringe over his body. The nurse was about to plunge the needle into her father's leg when suddenly his convulsions stopped. The room grew eerily quiet as her father's body relaxed and his eyes rolled

slowly back until they settled on Jeri's face, their deep brown intelligence replaced with a cold and vacant stare.

Jeri woke to the sound of her own scream as she opened her eyes and shot up from the bed. She glanced anxiously around the dark bedroom, struggling to catch her breath as reality now rushed back to her. Outside, a deeper veil of snow rested against the corner of her window as the wind whispered lightly. She sighed and fell wearily back against her pillow, closing her eyes tightly before the forming waves of sobs could overtake her.

Chapter 20

The wake of the *Achilles II* stretched like a long white scar as its deep, cobalt-colored hull cut swiftly through the warm tropical water. Cruising at a steady fifteen knots off the Venezuelan coast, the ship's massive twin diesels hummed quietly as they powered the 130-foot yacht through the calm Caribbean Sea, their sound unnoticed by the partygoers above.

On the main deck, Christina Lynch stared out at the distant lights of Puerto La Cruz as they flickered in the fading light of dusk. Warm tropical air stirred across the deck, rippling the handmade linens on the tables around her and teasing the chartreuse silk of her Valentino evening gown. Christina leaned lightly into the rail as her manicured nails tapped the empty crystal flute in her hand impatiently. Behind her, another two dozen guests lounged around tables adorned with extravagant hors d'oeuvres, picking lightly at plates of caviar, lobster, and foie gras that were delicately arranged between intricate ice sculptures of dolphins and whales.

A middle-aged man wearing a white jacket trimmed in gold suddenly materialized next her. "Miss?" he inquired as he held up the dark green bottle of Krug Clos d'Ambonnay she'd been waiting for, a polite smile trained on his placid face. Christina shifted her long legs and gave the server an irritable stare before holding out her hand. A torrent of shimmering gold filled the crystal flute as the priceless champagne flowed from the bottle, and she watched the ensuing eruption of impossibly small bubbles with mild admiration as they shimmered and sparkled with perfection. Her glass filled, the servant smiled again before curtly bowing and heading toward the next guest. Christina arrogantly waved the air with her fingers, as if brushing the aura of the servant away. She knew that the modest pour of champagne swirling in her glass was worth more than the servant who poured it would make all month. But of course Christina felt no remorse for this fact. In her mind, this simple fact merely reinforced the significance of everything that now surrounded her—the importance of the evening, the power of the people standing around her, and, thanks to her relationship with the man she arrived with, the importance of Christina herself.

She took a sip of champagne and quietly watched the other guests. Most of the men around her appeared to be in their late sixties or seventies, all of them wearing tailored tuxedos and trailing forty-something trophy wives on their arms. Although by far the youngest and undoubtedly the best-looking guest on the ship, Christina distanced herself from everyone else. She had no intention of socializing alone, especially when her boyfriend had abruptly left her to "wrap up some business" with his team of lawyers belowdecks. Irritated by this fact, she took another sip of champagne and decided a more powerful form of relaxation was in order. Discreetly reaching into her Lana Marks clutch, Christina found the small vial she relied on for just such an occasion. She deftly extracted two pills from the container and popped them into her mouth, swallowing them *sans aqua* as she'd learned from her years as a model. A few minutes later, just as their effect was beginning to take hold, a hand touched her shoulder.

"Excuse me, miss," a deep, confident voice said from behind her. Christina turned to find a tall, exceptionally good-looking man in his midtwenties standing a few steps away. His tanned, chiseled face was fixed with a practiced smile as he waited for her to meet his eyes, which Christina eventually did after slowly admiring the way his trim, athletic figure filled his Brioni tuxedo and the stylish cut of his blond hair. Finally succumbing to the pull of his hazel-colored eyes, she smiled and slipped a lock of her long, wind-blown brunette hair behind her ear.

"Yes?" she replied with a falsely irritable tone. Despite his looks, the man was apparently part of the ship owner's staff, and Christina couldn't resist the urge to treat him as such.

"Mr. Birch has asked for you downstairs," he said warmly, his smiling eyes reflecting the last dying rays of sunlight as he held up his arm. "May I escort you there?"

"I suppose," Christina said with a sigh. "But first—" She pointed her little finger to the sky and drained the last of her champagne before dropping the crystal flute on the tray of a passing waiter. "Okay, let's go," she commanded, her green eyes tracing over him. She took his arm and squeezed it casually, feeling the toned muscles beneath his jacket. They walked past the evening's entertainment—a four-piece band playing '80s tunes. Christina recognized the song that was playing and began swaying her hips seductively. Had the circumstances of the evening been different, she was sure the man now leading her would have made a deliciously nimble partner for both dancing and more private activities belowdecks. As if reading her mind, the man tensed his arm as they descended the grand stairway of inlaid marble toward the staterooms below.

"Beautiful night, wouldn't you agree, Miss Lynch?" he asked as they entered a long corridor that ran through the center of the ship.

"Yeah, sure," she mumbled, silently wishing a waiter with a fresh tray of champagne was within sight. Her little pharmaceutical friends had taken their full euphoric effect, and she was craving more of the swirling bubbles of carbonation that tickled her throat with every sweet sip. Unfortunately they were alone in this area of the ship. She glanced at her escort with a cynical smile. "Just like every other night I've seen since I arrived here."

"Of course, Miss Lynch."

"Oh, Christ, don't call me *Miss Lynch*," she replied flirtatiously, squeezing his arm roughly. "My name is Christina."

"Okay. So I take it you're not a fan of Puerto La Cruz, *Christina?*"

Christina winced at the sound of her own name and gave her escort a surprised, questioning look. Even in her chemically altered state, she couldn't miss the venomous tone he had managed to inject into the pronunciation, as if her name were a choice curse word. "Haven't seen enough of it to say, really," she replied flatly. "Other than the resort and this ship, I wouldn't know what this godforsaken place even looks like."

"Well, if you get a chance, I would highly recommend a day trip to the small town of Santa Fe. It's a beautiful little town, nestled in the foothills of the Turimiquire Mountains. And the view," he exclaimed, raising his arm in front of him, "is truly breathtaking."

Christina's arm, wrapped around his, was swept up in the motion, which ripped her purse from her hand and sent it sliding across the floor.

"Fucking hell," she muttered as she bent down to pick it up.

"Please . . . allow me." Without breaking stride, her escort deftly reached down and grabbed the small clutch, holding it for her as they walked the last few steps.

Arriving at the last stateroom in the corridor, the man unwrapped his arm from her grip and tapped lightly on the door. Inside, Christina could hear the muted shuffling of someone moving clumsily toward the door. Her escort then gave her a heart-stopping smile as he gently opened her hand and placed the small purse in her palm.

"Thank you," she said, leaning seductively toward him. "What was your name again?"

"Call me Thomas."

"Thank you, Thomas. And thanks for the advice. I'll do my best to visit Santa Fe if I ever get off this damn boat."

"I hope you do. Good night, Christina," he said as he bowed, holding her with his stare. He turned and disappeared into the narrow servants' corridor next to her as the click of the stateroom door lock sounded.

"Good night, Thomas . . . you tall, handsome bastard," Christina whispered, staring longingly into the dark corridor as the door to the stateroom flew open. A half-dressed man with brown, thinning hair and a round cleft chin stood in the doorway.

"Oh, well . . . *there* you fucking are," her boyfriend, Derrick, said, glancing down the corridor before grabbing her arm and pulling her into the room. He slammed the door and spun around to face her. "What the fuck took you so long?" he asked, pushing her aside as he made his way to the wet bar behind her.

Christina glared back at him, her large, oval-shaped eyes cold and hard.

At thirty-six years old, Derrick Birch was already a well-known and highly respected entrepreneur in the world of alternative energy development. After getting his degree in chemical engineering at MIT, Birch immediately landed a coveted researcher position with Reich-Walston Laboratories, a key research firm for the world's largest energy companies, where he quickly proved his genius by developing a hydrogen fuel cell design that was three times more efficient than anything before it. Armed with the rare gift of having people skills that matched his engineering genius, Birch skillfully ascended the politically fortified ranks at Reich-Walston until, at age thirty, he decided he could start his own energy research firm and avoid the bureaucratic bullshit altogether. Eighteen months and thirty million in angel investment dollars later, Birch and a handpicked team of researchers and lawyers were a tour de force firm specializing in energy-innovation research, development, and patenting. With each major innovation, almost always the result of Birch's own inspiration, the company spun off a new corporation. Covering a wide spectrum of technologies that ranged from cutting-edge fuel-cell development to fossil-fuel refinement, the nascent companies were almost always caught in a bidding war between the world's largest energy companies and conglomerates, all of them salivating for technologies that promised new market opportunities and competitive advantage. Along the way, Birch had found himself a very rich man.

And as Christina had learned early on in their short, turbulent relationship, Derrick Birch had an ego and a temper to match.

"What are you talking about?" she snapped. "Up until five minutes ago I was upstairs trying not to stick out like a pathetic, lonely loser when your manservant found me and dragged me down here." She walked to the bar and roughly opened the wine chiller, grabbing the first bottle of Dom Pérignon she could find. "Where the fuck have *you* been?"

"You know exactly where I've been, *Chrissy*," Derrick replied, using the nickname he knew she hated. "Stuck on this fucking boat for ten hours, trying to hack out an agreement that won't completely fuck me." He poured a tall glass of straight vodka over ice and took a long sip before staring at her solemnly. "Christ almighty, even after all these years it's still David versus fucking Goliath in these things." He paused for a moment, as if expecting her to speak, but she returned his stare with a vacant expression. "The deal's almost done, and suddenly they're trying to break my fucking balls over some tax records from four years back. I'm sitting there with three high-priced lawyers on my side of the table, and I still had to call

Roger in fucking Houston and get him to explain every tax shelter we've used since god knows when. It's fucking unbelievable."

He walked over to the bed and sat down heavily on the corner.

"And of course, the whole time you sit in these meetings with these guys and their lawyers, they try to make you feel like they're doing *you* some kind of fucking favor. As if what I do could've just come from *anyone*." Derrick drained the rest of the strong drink in a single gulp and walked back to the bar. "Assholes. I should tell them to fuck off and reopen negotiations with Exxon. At least they aren't a complete bunch of pricks."

"Sure, do it," Christina remarked distractedly, admiring her shoes as she leaned against the bar next to him. Derrick grumbled as he poured another vodka and settled his pudgy frame onto the chaise lounge in the corner of the room. He sat quietly for a few minutes, staring into his glass as his thoughts drifted around him.

"You know," he said finally, gazing at her with glassy, bloodshot eyes that seemed to be staring through her, focused on the memory he was seeing, "when I was a kid, I used to have the best fucking dreams. Better than anything fucking Hollywood could've made. And I'm not talking about that silly flying shit either. No, I had the best dreams imaginable. I could just see things the way they were supposed to be . . . the way they *should* be."

His eyes focused back onto hers. "Do you even know what that feels like?"

Christina stared at him without answering. She'd seen Derrick drunk enough times to know that his questions were simply rhetorical statements, like lines in a one-man play.

"That's what I always wanted to be, you know . . . a director. A fucking Hollywood director. Christ, I even became a fucking thespian in high school out of sheer eagerness to make it happen. Of course, I spent more time designing sets and tinkering with the shitty video equipment than hanging out with all the damn wannabe drama queens, but I was convinced it was my destiny." He threw back another slug of his vodka and laughed. "Fuck, I was a naïve kid back then."

Christina raised her eyebrows in surprise as Derrick swirled his drink and smiled dejectedly. She'd never heard him talk about his childhood before, and she wasn't sure how to take it. Could it be that there was actually an emotional, god forbid *vulnerable*, man behind the abrasive, egotistical genius? The idea made her shudder.

"Then again," he said, looking at her with sharp, lucid intensity, "I suppose I am a director in a way. Not on film, of course, but in a much bigger way. Anybody can make shit up and put it on film, but how many can say they have the power to truly make their dreams a reality?"

"Not many, D," Christina replied in a tone that bordered on the patronizing. "You're definitely one in a million." She quietly commended herself for being supportive of Derrick, even under these circumstances. Her mind drifted for a moment as she contemplated the shopping trip it was going to take to get him out of the doghouse when he sobered up.

Derrick gave her a thin smile and nodded. He drained his second vodka and placed the empty glass on the floor as he stood up unsteadily from the chaise longue. "Fuck it. It's all nothing more than smoke and mirrors in the end."

Christina rolled her eyes. "God, you are such a buzzkill. Was there a reason you asked me down here?"

"Actually there was," Derrick replied, clumsily tucking in his white tuxedo shirt as he walked toward her. He stopped just inches from her slender figure, his stare moving mischievously up her long tanned legs and past her modest cleavage before slowly focusing on her face. Christina gave him an irritated frown. A twinge of nausea struck her as he leaned in close and his warm, alcohol-laced breath washed over her. He swayed slightly and pointed at her purse.

"I need some of your little friends."

Christina instinctively clutched her purse tighter as his hand moved toward it. "What the fuck are you talking about?"

"You know exactly what the fuck I'm talking about," Derrick replied, his eyes fixed intently on her. "Did you honestly think I didn't know?"

"Know *what*, Derrick?"

"Jesus Christ, Chrissy—will you stop fucking around? You've got a small pharmacy in that tiny fucking purse and we both know it. Now listen . . . I don't need coke or E or any fancy bullshit, I just want something to help me fucking relax." He took a step back and smiled. "So are you going to stand there and play fucking stupid, or are you going to pull out one of those little vials from the Lynch treasure chest like a good little girlfriend?"

Christina stared at her boyfriend in shock. This was not normal Derrick. Even in her clouded state, she knew something was seriously off with him. It was strange enough that he was reminiscing about his childhood—a subject that, for as long as she'd known him, had been walled off from her like the safe in the bedroom of his Malibu estate. But the fact that he was now asking for drugs—and drugs from *her*—was beyond comprehension.

"I can't believe you're asking me this," she finally said, glaring at him.

"Come on, stop being so fucking dramatic. I've just spent a whole goddamn day down here dealing with a school of sharks in suits, and now I have to go upstairs and act like I actually like these motherfuckers. Alcohol by itself isn't gonna cut it tonight, so I'm asking you for a little extra help. So please, drop the fucking Mother Teresa act and show me what you got."

"Fine," she said, handing him the clutch. "Knock yourself out. And I mean that literally."

Derrick walked over to the bed and dumped the contents of the purse onto the mattress. "Holy shit," he exclaimed, staring at the bed. "I was just kidding when I said you had a small pharmacy. I didn't realize you really did."

"Fuck you, D. Do you have any idea how much I dislike you right now?"

"I'll make it up to you," he replied as he leaned down and began rummaging through the collection of small vials and bags that contained an assortment of brightly colored pills and white, sugar-like powder. "So, what should I go with?"

"Why don't you try them all," Christina answered dryly, pouring more champagne for herself.

"C'mon, be serious. You're the expert with this shit."

She walked over to the bed and brushed his hands away before quickly sorting through the paraphernalia. "No . . . no . . . no . . ." she remarked as she tossed the items one by one back into her bag. "Definitely not . . . no . . . no—"

"How about these?" Derrick asked, picking up a vial containing two pink, oval pills.

Christina stared at the container in his hand, perplexed. Though the pills were inside one of the handmade, silver-capped glass vials she'd found in Venice a few years ago, she had no idea what they were.

"Let me see those," she said, reaching out her hand.

Derrick closed his fist around the vial and stepped back. "Oh, so these must be the good ones."

"Give me the fucking pills, Derrick."

He flashed her a boyish smile and walked over to the bar. Christina looked on as he poured another tall vodka and then popped the pills into his mouth. "Bottoms up, baby," he said as he swallowed half of the glass. She shook her head disbelievingly.

"Oh, for fuck's sake, Chrissy, what's the problem?" he asked as he finished getting dressed. "Did I just rob you of dessert?"

"I have no idea what you just took, you idiot." She tossed the last of the vials back into the small bag. "So when you're experiencing projectile vomiting in five minutes, or having a full-on epileptic seizure in the middle of this trivial little social event, don't look at me."

Derrick put on his jacket and quickly studied himself in the mirror. Despite his thinning hair and soft, fleshy build, he held the posture of a man who commanded respect and attention. Watching as he adjusted his tie, Christina realized he was once again transforming back into the rigid, razor-sharp businessman and genius that everyone upstairs was expecting.

Satisfied with his appearance, he turned and gave her a pensive stare.

"If you can handle those little pills, I have no doubt I can too. But don't worry—if I manage to get myself into some form of socially compromised position, you'll be the last person I look to for sympathy and comfort. Now let's go."

=====

The top deck of the *Achilles II* was washed in the vibrant colors of dance lights and disco balls as Derrick and Christina made their entrance. The same crowd that Christina had earlier avoided now smiled and greeted her excitedly, and she surmised from the relaxed stares and the jovial sounds around her that a considerable amount of alcohol had been flowing in the short time she'd been belowdecks. A waiter immediately approached them with a fresh tray of champagne. Christina grabbed two while Derrick abruptly excused himself and started walking toward a tall, muscular gentleman wearing a perfectly fitted gray suit standing nearby. She shot Derrick a fatal look as he glanced back at her, but he simply shrugged before turning and greeting the man warmly.

Once more abandoned by Derrick and surrounded by strangers, Christina wandered toward a quiet corner of the railing to drink and sulk in peace. Dusk had deepened into a clear, moonless night, and the ship hummed peacefully as it moved across the calm, ink-black waters of the Caribbean. Christina stared out at the horizon, trying to determine exactly where the tapestry of diamond-baguette stars ended and the lights of the town along the shore began. The warm wind that had teased her dress earlier now rushed around her in short, angry gusts. She drank her champagne and breathed deeply, trying to forget the drama with Derrick downstairs. As much as she tried to focus on the enjoyment of her buzz, a heavy knot of frustration and anger twisted dully in her stomach.

She stared out over the water, thinking about their relationship, and realized Derrick had grown more and more detached from her in the last several months. Not that it surprised her. Derrick had made it entirely clear from their first casual drink together that his business and his "ideas" came first. But what did surprise Christina, as she looked into the dark emptiness in front of her, was that she cared.

Until now, she'd been content to enjoy Derrick's company when he was in a good mood, and even more content to enjoy the benefits of epic, worldwide shopping sprees as atonement for when he wasn't. Not that the relationship was one-sided. She wouldn't have even looked at Derrick a few years earlier when she was an up-and-coming model for the Brooks & Hanna agency in Los Angeles. Back then, she was up to her twenty-two-inch waist in coveted advertising deals, flying from LA to New York or London almost weekly to fling attitude at the camera or the catwalk.

But the on-camera stress had begun to fuel an off-camera drug addiction, and the only person who'd failed to see the destructive effects was Christina herself. Rumors of her being an "impossible, drugged-up bitch" were just reaching full circulation around the modeling agencies when a leaked security cam video of Christina having sex with a respected agency executive went viral on the web and turned her ridiculously lucrative modeling career into vapor practically overnight. A year later, unemployed and semisober, Christina had found herself with limited options and an empty bank account. By the time she'd met Derrick, the playing ground was level. He saw the opportunity to date the hottest girl he could ever imagine, and she saw the opportunity to keep paying her mortgage.

And now here she was, she thought contemptuously, half-drunk and half-high and staring into a dark night on a beautiful boat full of rich strangers and a boyfriend who didn't give a shit about her. *If only things had gone differently*, she thought to herself. If only she were still a model. If only the drugs didn't feel so goddamn good.

If only everything she touched didn't end up so fucking *ruined*.

Christina was so deep in thought that she barely noticed the needle-thin trail of white that was moving across the water where she was staring. Even with a full sky of stars shining brilliantly overhead, without the moon it was too dark to see what it was, and she quickly dismissed it as the wake of a small fishing boat heading out to sea.

Feeling slightly dizzy, she drained the flute of champagne in her hand before impulsively tossing it overboard, leaning her head over the stainless steel rail to watch it plummet three stories into the dark water below. "Oops," she whispered shamelessly, giggling to herself. Still armed with a glass of champagne in her other hand, Christina turned and scanned the lively crowd. The band was playing a familiar Rolling Stones cover, and she watched with mild amusement as a group of senior-aged men lurched and strutted around the dance floor as their younger, doll-like wives laughed and clapped with encouragement. Just beyond the dance floor she noticed Derrick talking with his large friend, his head nodding slowly as the other man spoke intently.

"Fuck this," Christina mumbled to herself with sudden conviction. She drained the second flute of champagne and tossed it into the water below before straightening her dress and striding purposefully toward Derrick. She was halfway to him when a thin, forty-something blonde woman dressed in a floral-patterned shibori ruffle, most likely Oscar de la Renta, stepped in front of her.

"Oh my *god*," the woman said, drawing out the words with a reverential Southern accent. "That green looks absolutely *amazing* on you." She dramatically held out her arms and arched her back to reveal a recent breast augmentation. "You simply *must* tell me where you got it."

Christina blinked at the woman quizzically, wondering where this cosmetically altered cliché for annoying trophy wives had come from. "Excuse me?" she said.

"Where did you get that sublime dress, darling?"

"I don't remember," she replied impatiently. Christina knew in fact that she'd bought the dress at a boutique in Monaco two months ago, but at the moment she had no desire to discuss such details.

"Well, it is almost as gorgeous as you are," the woman replied, flashing a perfect smile as her significant cleavage cantilevered unnaturally over her slim frame.

"Thanks. And where did you get those?" Christina asked, pointing at the woman's chest as her eyes darted to find Derrick.

"Get what, dear?"

Christina gave her a sardonic smile.

"Oh, these?" the woman gasped with mock surprise, sweeping a hand gently across her bosom. "Well, let's just say my third husband—god rest his soul—was good for something." She laughed at her own joke before looking at Christina earnestly. "Though I must say, Dr. Drennon did a remarkable job. Are you in the market, dear?"

"No," Christina replied, "I just wanted to confirm they're as fake as the rest of you. But thank you," she said, grasping the hand of the woman affectionately. "At least now I know who to swim to if this fucking boat happens to sink tonight. Would you excuse me for a moment?"

The stunned woman stared aghast at Christina's lithe figure as she walked away. Christina grabbed another full flute of champagne from the tray of a passing waiter, sipping it with a menacing smirk as she walked toward her unsuspecting boyfriend. As she approached, the large gentleman Derrick was talking with locked his eyes on her and noticeably stiffened.

"Hi there, fellas," she said, resting her hand on Derrick's shoulder and giving him an affectionate squeeze. She could feel him recoil in surprise under his Armani tuxedo. "Am I interrupting anything important?"

Derrick looked at her with wild, dilated eyes for a brief moment, his expression a mixture of surprise and annoyance, before composing his face into a smile. "Hi, babe. No, you're not . . . not interrupting anything at all." He wrapped his arm limply around her waist. "This is . . . uh, this is—"

"Max Delaney," the man said as he offered Christina his massive hand. "You must be Christina. Pleasure to meet you."

"Likewise, Max," she replied, shaking his hand. Standing next to him, she realized that Max was even larger than he had looked from across the deck of the boat. As he released her hand, Christina couldn't help but feel like a miniature person next to his sheer physical presence. "And thank you for not crushing my hand."

"Of course," he replied, smiling warmly.

"Max and I got caught up talking and . . . sorry, didn't mean to ignore you. Yeah, so anyway, I was . . . what was I talking about?"

"Derrick and I were just talking business nonsense," Max said, folding his large arms across his massive chest as he rocked slowly on his feet. Christina noticed that, unlike every other guest on the boat, Max wasn't drinking. "Nothing that interesting, really . . . wouldn't you agree, Derrick?"

"Yeah, right, right," Derrick replied quickly.

"Well then, I'm glad I wasn't invited to the conversation," Christina said sarcastically, giving Derrick a harder squeeze as she smiled at him. He forced a strained smile before shooting a quick glance at his large companion.

Max smiled back at both of them.

Christina was just about to speak when the band abruptly ended its set and the singer handed his microphone to a short, stocky bald man with a large nose and small, hawkish eyes.

"Ladies and gentlemen, could I have your attention please?"

Christina stood listlessly next to Derrick as the speaker wasted a few minutes thanking the band and cracking several outdated jokes that were marginally funny the first time around. She noticed that nearly everyone in the audience, including Derrick, laughed on cue at the short man as he paused after every punch line, and decided he must be someone of importance to command such a communal ass-kissing. Only Christina and the towering pillar of muscle named Max standing next to her watched straight-faced as the man finally got to the point.

"But anyway, we're not here tonight to listen to my bad jokes," he continued, his face turning serious as his dark, narrow eyes searched through the crowd. "We're here to celebrate a momentous milestone for our company, and to honor and celebrate the man whose vision will help lead us into the future."

Christina jumped in surprise as the people around her erupted in applause. Several faces turned expectantly to Derrick as he glanced around with a smug grin on his face. He took a sip of what appeared to Christina to be another large vodka on the rocks as his eyes flickered over to Max. She looked over at Max, who met her gaze with a wide, cautious grin as his large hands slowly clapped with a distinctly audible concussion.

"Ladies and gentlemen, all of you know Derrick Birch, a man whose genius in alternative energy development is perhaps only matched—as I've certainly learned today—by his skills of negotiation."

The crowd again erupted in laughter.

"Derrick represents the kind of rogue visionary who can radically change the course of even large multiconglomerate companies like our own," the little bald man continued, his baritone voice measured and authoritative. "And as CEO, I've learned all too well what can happen when companies fail to recognize the need for change, or fail to cultivate the people who provide the ideas and innovations upon which we all come to depend."

Christina listened as loud murmurs of agreement were echoed around the crowd. The importance of the evening once again struck her, as the CEO of one of the world's largest companies looked over at Derrick with a practiced smile and continued his speech.

"And so tonight, in recognition of this endless pursuit to find the idea makers and innovators who hold our future, I am honored to announce one very large victory."

He paused and dramatically raised his glass in the air.

"Ladies and gentlemen, shareholders and executive colleagues . . . it gives me great pleasure to announce that Derrick Birch has officially agreed to head our alternative energy division for the next five years!"

Christina flinched again as the crowd erupted with shouts and applause. Hands quickly brushed past her to pat Derrick on the back, and she resignedly assumed the role of a loving and loyal girlfriend, smiling and nodding to the men and women around her. Derrick tightened his grip around her waist, and she turned to find him staring at her intensely.

"Are you okay, D?" she whispered, her mouth brushing against his ear.

"Not in the least," he replied, smiling back at her with unfocused eyes. A pang of fear flashed through Christina as she held Derrick's unnerving stare, and she wondered again just what the hell those pills were that he'd taken from her purse earlier.

"Do you want to go downstairs?"

"Are you kidding me?" he exclaimed, slurring his words slightly. "I'm a fucking rock star right now. I can't leave in the middle of the moment these magnanimous-sounding pricks are pretending to like me."

"Jesus Christ, you are the most stubborn goddamn asshole on the planet," Christina hissed under her breath. "Do you know that?"

"Yes I do."

"Now, we've spent a long, grueling day ironing out the details of this little agreement," the CEO continued, rolling his eyes sarcastically. "And, yes, we still have some more documents to sign in the morning, but I wanted each and every one of you to be present tonight to share in the celebration of finally acquiring Petronus Energy's newest secret weapon"—he paused for effect, then swept his arm toward Derrick—"Mr. Derrick Birch!"

Derrick released his hold on Christina and took an unsteady step forward. "Thank you! Thanks, everyone," he shouted, raising his glass to the CEO before draining it. Applause once again swept through the crowd as the band erupted into the opening chords of "Start Me Up" by the Rolling Stones. The crowd toasted and cheered, then refocused their attention on the music and the dance floor. Christina crossed her arms and glowered at her boyfriend as he stumbled back to her.

"Need another drink?" he asked as he stood swaying in front of her, his hands fumbling as he tried to tear the bow tie from his neck.

"Derrick, what the fuck are you doing?"

"I'm securing my future," he replied, grinning at her with the hint of a sneer. "What the fuck are you doing?"

"I'm wondering if the man I'm here with is going to make a complete ass of himself in front of his new boss this evening." She grabbed the empty glass from his hand. "Is stumbling around drunk and high on god-knows-what your idea of securing your future?"

Derrick threw back his head in laughter, stumbling back and nearly falling in the process.

"Jesus Christ," Christina hissed, keeping her expression neutral as she grabbed his arm. "Is this honestly funny to you, D?"

Derrick took a moment to compose himself before smiling at Christina with large, drug-glazed eyes. "It's hard to say, really. Yes . . . and, um, no." He wrapped his arm around her and pulled her roughly into his chest. "But I know you'd be acting the same way as I am if you knew even half of what's happening right now. So do me a favor and wipe that judgmental fucking expression off your face."

Christina stared at her boyfriend. Even now, while she was pressed against him, he seemed miles away, and growing more distant with each second.

"I have no idea what you're talking about, D."

"I know," he said quietly, releasing her from his grip. "And you never will."

Christina sensed the presence of Max's huge figure looming next to her even before she looked over to see him. He nodded at her politely before fixing his eyes on Derrick.

"Sorry to interrupt. Derrick, can I speak to you for a second?"

Christina saw a flicker of something in Derrick's face as he looked up at his colleague and nodded. Something that looked eerily close to terror. But as quickly as it appeared, it was gone. He turned and met her stare.

"I'll be right back," he said, flashing her a brief smile. "And I'll bring some more champagne with me."

"Great. Have fun," she said, giving him a dismissive wave as she turned to watch the band. She felt Derrick linger for a moment before walking off with Max. A few minutes later, Christina glanced over her shoulder to see the two men talking at the front of the ship. She noticed with alarm that Derrick was sitting on the bow rail, perched precariously over the water as he laughed at something his colleague was saying. She started walking toward them, but then stopped herself. If Derrick had made anything clear in his actions and words tonight, it was that she was becoming an intrusion in his life. The last thing he'd want would be his annoying girlfriend looking out for his safety. "Whatever," she mumbled, as she turned around and glowered at the dancing crowd.

And then the sky above her exploded.

Christina kneeled down and shrieked in terror as an intense flash of light erased the darkness of the Caribbean night and its shock-wave washed over her. She looked up to see fiery embers streaking overhead, trailing long fingers of ruby-red sparks that burned into nothingness as they fell toward the ship's deck. A moment later, as the outer embers of red began to fade, a second explosion followed, filling the sky with a brilliant display of arching blue showers.

She quickly stood and straightened her dress, glancing around with an embarrassed smile as the rest of the partygoers stared transfixed at the unexpected fireworks show. She looked behind her to see Derrick still slumped awkwardly on the bow rail, gazing upward with a silly, childlike grin on his face. Next to him, Max caught her gaze and waved back politely.

A quickening tempo of explosions signaled the coming crescendo, and Christina hastily grabbed another flute of champagne from a passing server as the volume of the band rose with anticipation. She emptied the glass in a single swallow, feeling the effervescent cascade of bubbles tease her throat as they flowed over her tongue. Then, with a climactic display of exploding color and perfectly timed music, the show ended, and the lights of the ship went dark. Christina and everyone around her immediately raised their glasses and roared with excitement under the beautiful starry night, clapping and cheering as the lights were slowly brought back to life. She turned to see Max standing at the bow, staring up at the smoke-filled sky as his massive hands clapped with the crowd.

Next to him, the rail was empty.

Christina's mind seemed to process the moment in slow motion as the color drained from her face. She took a half step toward the bow of the ship as her eyes darted quickly across the faces around her. *Derrick could have gone to get another drink*, she thought to herself, but instinctively knew this wasn't the truth. From halfway across the ship, Max's eyes dropped from the sky and locked onto hers. His smile faded as he read the terror in Christina's expression. In an instant he turned his huge frame and seized the railing where Derrick had been sitting a moment before. At that same moment, beneath the vacuous silence that had settled over the crowd in the wake of the fireworks, the sound of the *Achilles II*'s engines rose in protest as their props tore through an object beneath the boat.

Christina turned and walked calmly to the stern, slipping past the rest of the partygoers as they glanced around in confusion. She dimly registered the trembling of the ship as the engines were stopped and the anxious shouting of the crew as they frantically pulled ropes and rescue equipment from marked stations and ran past her. She seemed to float above her Ferragamo stilettos on legs that weren't her own until her hands reached out and wrapped tightly around the railing at the back of the ship. There, Christina felt her body lean dangerously over the rail, and the scream that was lodged in the pit of her stomach erupted in a spray of champagne-colored vomit just as the ship's spotlights illuminated the water below.

Thirty feet beneath her, the mangled torso of a man bobbed lifelessly in the wake of the ship, centered in a wide slick of black-red blood. Christina stared at the torn fabric that covered the floating remains and absently noted that it was Armani before strong hands grabbed her from behind and pulled her from the railing. The screams of the passengers around her faded as she surrendered to the bliss of unconsciousness.

PART II

Like an apex predator introduced to a new, prey-rich environment, the Corporate State will rapidly expand its presence across the global economic landscape, commanding a dominant share of its core markets while at the same time cultivating a new generation of corollary submarkets. Ironically, it will be at this advanced stage of development that normal regulatory barriers such as domestic and international antitrust laws will have little real effect or meaning. The inherent legal and organizational complexities of the Corporate State, combined with its nearly limitless financial resources, shall thwart any normal means of governmental intervention.

This is the Corporate State in its mature form of existence—a massive and massively complex global business organism that possesses the financial, political, and human resources necessary to control and consume at will.

—James H. Stone, *Predictions in the New Business Ecology*

Chapter 21

Jeri-girl—

I left the bar last night in that most seductive of moments when lust and ambition wash over the rocks of fear and inhibition on the currents of nicotine and cheap vodka. I fell straight into bed and found myself trapped in a deep orifice of musty, flesh-colored dreams where the women hovered elusive and kind and the men sat drunken and heated. Dark eyes were drinking me, Jeri, and I wanted to drink them back. This was a place of restless hands and hot breath; sticky-stained tabletops and raw, twitching skin sweaty from the friction of impatient urges. Voices of strange tongues curled around the white cloud of my cigarette, as ethereal and haunting as the gummy, glistening sclera that flickered behind the veil of mascara-stained lids.

It's the goddamn vodka, Jeri, I swear it.

I know you keep asking yourself who this crazy

handsome bastard of loose literary chops and oodles of air miles on Air Iraq must be, but this isn't important. As for the "what" I am, well, Jeri-girl, we're cut from the same fleeting fabric. Like you, I'm just a voyeur of the human condition, a lowly vending machine in the loathsome global cafeteria. Our professions may be different, but the endgame is still the same. We cater to the need, baby, and the need is all we need to know. If corporations were cigarettes, my love, I'd be the secondhand smoke.

It's cold here, Jeri, but nothing like the cold I knew before you.

Our kids will be gorgeous.

Ta!
Mysterious Joe's Last Stand Guy

P.S. You'll be pleased to see that I finally got my full mug in the Polaroid.

P.P.S. The lamb shashlik at Podvorie's was better than losing my virginity to Cindy Arlington in the fourth grade. Don't order dog.

P.P.P.S. What are people saying about me there? I hope you placed my letters in the southeast corner of the bar. It really is the optimal viewing place.

———

Jeri read the letter twice before pulling out the Polaroid and laughing out loud. In the background, a large, redbrick gothic cathedral sat at the end of a long courtyard flanked by rows of dark, leafless trees. In the middle of the courtyard, a lone man stood with his hands on his hips, his heavy winter jacket unzipped to reveal the Joe's Last Stand Saloon T-shirt he wore underneath. A black wool scarf was tightly wrapped around his neck and lower face, and a massive fur hat covered the top of his face to his dark eyebrows, its ear flaps hanging comically down to his collar. Peering out from between the oversized hat and scarf, a pair of silver aviator sunglasses reflected the gray wintery sky, and Jeri could see the distorted image of a small, childlike figure holding the camera. Only the man's nose, tanned and perfectly ordinary, was exposed to the camera.

Jeri stared at the photo as a long, heavy sigh parted her lips. She stood from her barstool behind the counter and strolled slowly over to the southeast corner of the bar where the rest of the letters and photos were hung. As she pinned the photo to the wall, her eyes met those of the sunglassed man in the photo, and a quiver of excitement slid like the soft touch of a finger down the back of her spine.

Chapter 22

Tom Coleman looked up from the open folder in his hand and glanced at his watch. It was 3:32 p.m. He sat back in his chair and listened. The silence that filled the corridor outside his tiny office told him that the Immigration and Customs Enforcement offices were nearly deserted. Unlike Tom, his colleagues were already practicing their early escapes from the office in preparation for the upcoming holidays. No doubt most of them were busy planning parties, buying gifts, and making the endless arrangements that came with this most wonderful time of the year.

In other words, their lives were now something of a living hell.

Tom shook his head at the thought as he closed the case file and placed the thick manila folder carefully on the "pending" pile on his desk. He opened the top drawer of his desk and found one of the small bottles of antibacterial lotion he kept in his office. A subconscious grin appeared on his face as he squeezed a large portion of the wonderfully sterile-smelling liquid onto his hands and began slowly rubbing them together. For reasons he couldn't explain, Tom found the act calming. He methodically rubbed the strong disinfectant into his skin, happily imagining a billion little germs being purged from his body. With his hands clean, he grabbed another file from the tall stack of new cases and began thumbing through the dull, photocopied pages. A few pages later, his concentration abruptly faded.

Something else was weighing on his mind.

He closed the file, stacked it neatly on top of the "new" pile on his desk, and once again wiped his hands with lotion. He then turned his attention to his laptop. The latest reply in a string of e-mails between Tom and his brother-in-law, CIA Agent Alex Murstead, was still on the screen, and Tom found himself once again reading the tersely worded response.

Tom—

I'm not having this conversation with you any longer. The rules are the rules, and you need to stop entertaining any more ridiculous ideas for getting around them. It's time to accept the fact you're simply not cut out to work for the CIA.

There's nothing wrong with working for the Department of Homeland Security. It's a good job. It suits your skills. Hell, in this day and age you should consider yourself lucky just to have a job.

I'm serious, Tom—stop pushing this. I've got far more important things to be doing right now.

—Alex

Tom closed the message with an agitated press of his finger. Nearly two weeks had passed since being told he'd failed the psych portion of the CIA entrance exams. While the initial shock of the news had subsided, a lingering feeling of anger still burned like a hot coal in his stomach.

And now he was on his own.

Of course, the realization that he was on his own wasn't surprising or even intimidating to Tom. Quite the contrary, in fact. He'd been trained from his first day in the Marines to overcome difficult, if not impossible, hurdles. Hell, his entire career up to this point was defined by obstacles he'd taken on and conquered. Sure, not every obstacle had been conquered without sacrifice—he quickly shook the images of Afghanistan from his mind—but he'd always managed to find his way out of odds-against-him shitstorms alive and kicking. And that was the point. That was how he'd find a way to become an agent in the CIA. He'd tackled bigger challenges than this and survived, because that's what he was—a survivor.

Hoo-rah, motherfuckers.

Tom leaned back in his chair and stared stoically at the ceiling, trying to piece together another solution in his head. Unfortunately, nothing was materializing. He sat deep in thought for several more minutes before finally curling his fists in frustration. If there was anything Tom begrudgingly admitted to himself, it was the fact that he was much better at investigation than strategy. As much as he hoped otherwise, a plan to get him back in front of the CIA was not going to come easily.

Conceding this reality, Tom reluctantly decided to call it a day. He stood and carried out his usual routine, straightening the stacks of files on his desk and lining up their corners neatly before wiping down his laptop. When he was finished, he cleaned his hands once more and grabbed his coat to leave. He was halfway out of the door to his office when he reached into his coat pocket for his keys and felt the sharp edge of a folded piece of paper. Puzzled, he pulled it out and unfolded it. Scrawled across the page was his own barely legible handwriting.

Guwahati, Assam, India 9/25
Al Jubail, Saudi Arabia 10/5
Port Harcourt, Nigeria 10/16
Puerto La Cruz, Venezuela 10/25

As Tom stared at the list of cities and dates, the memory of the night at the bar a few weeks earlier came slowly back to him. Against his better judgment, he'd ended up having more than a few drinks that night, and the details were now embarrassingly hazy. He remembered sitting next to an older man at the bar—*what was his name? Skip?*—and talking about some letters one of the bartenders had received. He also recalled reading the story in the college paper—how the letters had unexpectedly started arriving a little more than a month earlier; their cryptic, ranting tone; the mocking anonymity of their author; and perhaps strangest of all, the obscure photos of the writer himself. Tom and the old man next to him had discussed it for some time, and he now vaguely remembered staggering over to where the letters were hung and jotting down the places and dates they'd come from on the notepaper in his hand.

Unfortunately, he couldn't remember why he'd done this.

Tom wadded up the piece of paper and started to toss it into the trash when a nagging thought stopped him. Was there something more to this than he remembered? Hadn't the old man said something else? Something about *terrorism*? He hovered in the doorway trying to recall before finally relenting to his curiosity. Cursing at himself under his breath, he turned and paced back into his office.

Dropping the note on his desk, Tom sank back into his chair and pulled up an online search engine on his laptop. He glanced at the first city and date on the list before typing "Guwahati terrorist attack September" into the search engine. The screen instantly flickered with the first of more than 164,000 results. Scrolling through the first few pages, Tom found a few general articles on cases of terrorism in the city in the northeastern state of India, but nothing on any recent incidents. He typed in "Guwahati homicide September" and a fresh list of more than 200,000 results popped onto the screen.

"Jesus," he muttered to himself as he scrolled through the first few pages of results. He skimmed through several articles, many of which were written by human rights organizations. One article accused the local police of outright murder and cited a recent incident where a driver was pulled from his vehicle for speeding and mercilessly beaten by several officers before being tossed into a lake to drown. Another article described a freak accident involving two vehicles that collided and caught fire near a local market, killing a young Italian scientist. Tom shrugged dismissively and moved on. While the stories were tragic, he knew firsthand from his tours in the Marine Corps that police corruption and freak accidents were an everyday reality in third-world countries like India.

Deciding Guwahati was a dead end, Tom glanced at the next location and date on the notepaper and typed "Al Jubail terrorist attack October." To his surprise, the search engine came up with a fraction of the previous results. Apart from a few cases of murder, including two men who were gunned down in public for displaying homosexual behavior, Tom found nothing of particular interest.

After a few more minutes of searching, he concluded Al Jubail must be one of the safest cities in the Middle East, at least for heterosexuals, and went to the next city on his list.

The search results for "Port Harcourt terrorist attack October" exceeded 1,200,000. Tom shook his head as he started scanning through the first few pages of results. He was beginning to think the entire effort was a waste of time when, at the bottom of the second page, a headline caught his attention.

"Terrorist Explosion Kills Petronus Energy Executive"

Tom clicked on the link, and the browser immediately jumped to the bright colors and flashy graphics of an international news agency's website. A large image of a luxury hotel atrium littered with dust and debris appeared beneath the headline. Inset in the corner was a photo of an older, distinguished-looking man in a suit and tie smiling at the camera. Tom read the caption beneath the image:

"The scene from inside the Garden Landmark Hotel in the city of Port Harcourt this morning, where an explosive device planted inside a guest room killed Shahid Al Dossari, a director of research for Petronus Energy."

Intrigued, Tom grabbed a notepad as he quickly scanned the article. The first thing he noted was the date. The attack on the hotel had occurred on the nineteenth of October—just three days after the letter at the saloon had been dated from the same city. The second thing Tom found odd was the anonymity of the terrorists themselves. Contrary to most such attacks, no one had claimed responsibility for this particular bombing. He scratched down the name of the victim and the name Petronus before searching under the fourth city on the list.

The search results for Puerto La Cruz numbered more than 400,000 results. After ten minutes of scrolling through a seemingly endless list of incidents in the coastal Venezuelan city, Tom paused and leaned back in his chair.

What the hell am I doing? he asked himself. He was poking blindly for a connection to a man he knew nothing about, and for whom he obviously had no evidence of being a criminal—let alone a *terrorist*. Why was he even suspicious? Because of what some drunken old man had told him at the bar? Admittedly, there was something about the older man that Tom had found persuasive, and yet the absurdity of it was obvious. A *terrorist*? Terrorists were maniacal, remorseless extremists who killed innocent people and disappeared into the shadows. Terrorists sent bombs in the mail, not letters. Terrorists didn't write love letters. And even if they did, certainly no terrorist would write love letters to a bartender in fucking Flagstaff, Arizona.

The more Tom considered it, the more ridiculous the idea sounded. He leaned forward to close the search engine on his laptop, but paused as he glanced at the name written on his notepad.

Petronus

He stared at the name for a moment. *What did he know about Petronus Energy?* On a whim, Tom typed the name into the search engine and clicked on the first link in the results. Almost immediately a friendly looking corporate website appeared. Filling the screen was an image of a handsome young couple with two kids standing in a large grassy field. Across the bottom of the image, the words "Tomorrow's energy today" were written in large type next to the company's logo. Tom scrolled past the image and stopped at the mission statement.

> Clean energy. It's the dream of every environmentally conscious energy company, and the driving force behind everything we do at Petronus Energy. From responsibly using fossil fuels to tirelessly searching for new sources of clean, viable energy, Petronus is dedicated to the passionate pursuit of delivering tomorrow's energy today.
>
> Learn more about our mission, our environmental policies, and our global operations.

Tom clicked on the "global operations" link. A new page immediately opened displaying a large world map. He looked at it with surprise. Each continent with the exception of Antarctica was covered in a myriad of pulsing red dots. As his cursor moved over one of the dots, a small window appeared with the name and image of a company facility along with a brief summary of the operational details.

After scrolling over a few locations, it was clear to Tom that Petronus Energy was a major multinational corporation, operating everything from oil rigs and refineries to research laboratories and corporate campuses.

Looking closer at the Middle Eastern area of the map, Tom noticed that Saudi Arabia was saturated with red dots. He moved his cursor over several and quickly found Al Jubail. Again a small window popped up next to the location. Tom scanned the summary and immediately realized the city was a major operational hub for Petronus Energy, containing the company's largest petrochemical processing facility and the primary Middle Eastern office.

Going back to the top of his list, Tom next turned his attention to India. A brief search of the northeastern corner of the country revealed another major Petronus Energy operation in Guwahati. "Isn't that interesting," Tom muttered to himself as he scrolled over the African country of Nigeria. To his surprise, Port Harcourt also turned out to be home to several of the company's drilling operations. Excited by this emerging pattern, he checked the last city on the list. A moment later, Tom leaned back in his chair and smiled.

Petronus Energy had operations in every city on his list.

Whatever this mysterious letter writer was doing, it seemed to be linked to the large petroleum company. *So what are you up to?* Tom wondered as he picked up his pen and slowly circled the name "Petronus" written on his notepad.

Simplifying his earlier approach, Tom typed "Guwahati September" into the search engine, this time adding the word "Petronus." The first page of results flashed in front of him. As he read the second headline on the list, Tom's pulse quickened.

"Petronus researcher killed in accident"

Tom clicked on the link, and a British news site filled the screen. A large image of a busy city street corner appeared above the brief article.

September 28
Guwahati, India—The collision of two vehicles at a
busy intersection resulted in the death of a 31-year-old
Italian man this evening after unidentified materials in

one of the vehicles caught fire and quickly consumed both vehicles. Marcello Avogadro, a chemical engineer employed by Petronus Energy, was traveling in one of the vehicles, a motorized rickshaw called a tuk-tuk, near the Bamunimaidan market when the accident occurred.

The drivers of both vehicles managed to escape prior to the intense fire observed by witnesses, but neither has been found since for questioning. No other injuries were reported. Authorities are now investigating the source of the materials that caused the fatal accident.

Tom glanced at the date of the Guwahati letter and shook his head ominously. Like the bombing in Port Harcourt, the letter was written and sent just three days before the accident. He quickly copied the text from the online article and pasted it into a document on his computer, then created a folder titled "Research" inside his personal folder and saved the document under the name "Petronus incident report."

Going back to the search engine, Tom then typed the phrase "Al Jubail Petronus October." The laptop screen flickered with results. After scrolling through the first eight pages of results, he again decided Al Jubail was a dead end and moved on to Puerto La Cruz.

More than 4,500 results were returned for Puerto La Cruz. Scrolling through them, Tom's hand froze when he came to the fourth link on the second page.

"Renowned energy scientist fatally wounded after falling overboard"

The article linked to the headline was predictably brief, but Tom's pulse again quickened as he read the summary of details.

October 30
Puerto La Cruz, Venezuela—Renowned American energy scientist and entrepreneur Derrick Birch was killed late

yesterday evening after falling overboard from a private yacht and sustaining fatal injuries. Birch, who was reportedly in negotiations with Petronus Energy for an undisclosed position within the company's alternative energy division, was attending a private corporate function at the time of the tragedy, which occurred in calm waters approximately six miles offshore.

The 36-year-old Birch was considered a leading scientist in the areas of oil refinement and fuel-cell development, and owned controlling shares in more than four separate energy-development companies. According to witnesses on board at the time of the incident, Birch appeared heavily intoxicated prior to the accident. At this time authorities have no reason to suspect foul play.

Tom read the article twice before saving a copy to his Petronus incident report. He then wrote a quick summary of the facts.

Guwahati, India:

Letter written—9/25
Marcello Avogadro—Petronus Chemical Engineer
Killed—fatal accident—9/28
Location of Petronus research lab

Al Jubail, Saudi Arabia:

Letter written—10/5
No known incident
Location of Petronus refinery

Port Harcourt, Nigeria:

Letter written—10/16
Shahid Al Dossari—Petronus Director of Research

Killed—homicide/bomb—10/19
Location of Petronus drilling operations

Puerto La Cruz:

Letter written—10/25
Derrick Birch—Scientist in negotiations with Petronus
Killed—fatal accident—10/29
Location of Petronus drilling and refinery operations

Tom sat back and contemplated the summary on his laptop screen. The facts were eerily similar. Three men, all of them researchers or scientists for Petronus Energy, were now dead. All three had died under extraordinary circumstances, and all three had died exactly three days after an unknown author had sent a letter from the very same location. Even the location that wasn't tied to a death, Al Jubail, was linked to Petronus. And certainly none of the locations were common travel destinations.

Another thought occurred to Tom as he studied the dates on the screen. He sat up and quickly punched "Joe's Last Stand Saloon Flagstaff" into the search engine. Almost immediately the address and phone number appeared on the screen. He grabbed his desk phone and dialed the number.

"Joe's," a low, gruff voice answered.

Tom hesitated, not sure what to say.

"Hi, yeah . . . I uh, I had a few drinks at your bar a few weeks back and I happened to notice those letters the bartender had gotten."

"Okay," the man said impatiently. "So?"

"Oh, well, I was just curious, has anyone figured out who that guy is yet?"

"Nope, not to my knowledge, and I own the place. There's a free T-shirt for anyone who knows who he is, though."

"That's what I heard," Tom replied with mock enthusiasm. "By the way, have any more letters arrived lately?"

"Yep, Jeri just got another one today. Same deal as before, a letter and a photo."

Tom froze in his chair. "Oh, really? Would you mind telling me where it came from?"

"Russia this time," the bar owner answered.

"From where in Russia?"

"Oh, hell, I don't know," Joe replied irritably. "Why are you asking?"

"Well, I think I might actually know who this guy is," Tom responded, lying to the bar owner. "But I'd need to know what city he sent that last letter from to be sure."

There was a brief pause on the line before Joe acquiesced with a loud sigh. "Hold on, I've got to walk over there and look. It's not like I take the time to remember some Russia goddamn city."

"Thanks," Tom replied.

"Yeah, yeah," Joe replied sourly. "Let's see here, it says Ka . . . Kaliningrad."

"You mind spelling that for me?" Tom asked as he picked up his pen.

"K-a-l-i-n-i-n-g-r-a-d. Now is there anything *else* I can do for you?" Joe said sarcastically.

"Do you mind telling me the date written on the letter?"

"November twelve," Joe replied tersely, "and if you want to know anything else, you can come down here and look for yourself. We've got three-dollar beers on tap tonight."

The line went dead before Tom could respond. He set the phone down and immediately reopened the global map on the Petronus Energy website. As expected, a red dot was located over the city of Kaliningrad. Without looking at the details, he opened his summary and typed in the newest location.

Kaliningrad, Russia:
Letter written—11/12
Incident—?

Tom leaned back in his chair and stared again at the short summary with a growing feeling of excitement. Just what the hell had he stumbled onto? He glanced again at his watch. Today was the fourteenth—just two days after the letter had been sent. This obviously meant the author of the letters was sending them express mail.

It also meant something else. If the pattern of deaths was real, and this mysterious letter writer was in fact involved, there was still time to act before another incident occurred in Kaliningrad.

The question that plagued Tom now was the "if" itself. Did any of this actually mean something, or did it mean absolutely nothing at all? During his days in the Phoenix PD, Tom had quickly learned that the biggest errors in any investigation were often caused by the bias and prejudices of the investigator himself. Given enough time and resources, any investigator can find circumstantial evidence against a suspect, but it's their motivations for doing so that determine the methods and value of what they find. Tom knew that even "good" investigators could be driven by prejudices, even ones they weren't aware of, while in the pursuit of justice. It was a key reason why investigators almost always worked in teams.

Despite the information that was now staring at him, Tom had to consider whether his own motivations had brought him to this conclusion. After all, he had been looking for a homicidal connection to the mysterious letter writer when he found it. This fact by itself represented a significant bias. He also had to consider the potential consequences for himself. Pursuing an unsanctioned investigation sparked by the drunken rant of an old man and driven merely on a hunch could land him in one serious shitpile of trouble.

But his days on the force also taught him to trust his gut, and Tom's gut told him this situation was different. This wasn't a coincidence. The circumstances were too well aligned, the odds too far against it. Biased or not, Tom was convinced he knew what he was looking at, and what he saw was the trail of an international killer. He nodded as the certainty washed over him.

The only question was what to do about it.

Tom knew that if he had any desire to climb the ranks within the Department of Homeland Security, this could easily be his ticket. Of course, he had no such desire—and no intention—of giving up the most important information he had ever stumbled upon to an organization that would most likely give him a promotion and a pat on the back before kicking him into another life-sucking desk job. On the other hand, not communicating to his superiors knowledge or information pertaining to criminal—let alone *terrorist*—activity was in itself a criminal offense.

Tom stood up from his desk and began pacing. His office felt even smaller under the droning hum of the fluorescent lights as he moved back and forth, considering his next move. He needed to deliver the information to the appropriate authorities before another homicide or "accident" occurred, but he had to find a way to do so in his favor. He continued moving, deep in thought, when an idea struck him and stopped him in his tracks. He stood motionless for several minutes, his mind turning over the idea, until his mouth slowly curled into a broad grin.

He bolted back to his laptop and opened his e-mail.

Tom's fingers punched rapid-fire across the keyboard as he glanced at his notes and typed the message he'd quickly composed in his head. Five minutes later, he read the finished draft, fixed a few typos, and hit the "Send" button. He then sat back in his chair and smiled at his incredible good fortune.

It was brilliant. Tom didn't need to solve the case, or even lead the investigation. He simply needed to spoon-feed the right dose of information to the agency that should be investigating the matter in the first place—the CIA. Of course, if he happened to get noticed for his incredible investigative skills along the way, it certainly wouldn't hurt his chances of getting back into the agency's good graces.

Either way, he had nothing to lose.

Tom was still smiling to himself as he shut down his laptop and carefully wiped down his desk with disinfectant. *I'm not such a bad strategist after all*, he thought as he flicked off the lights and shut the heavy metal door behind him. He decided a few drinks were in order, and whistled happily as he strolled out of the empty Homeland Security offices and into the cold Flagstaff evening.

Chapter 23

"I thought Venezuela was crazy, but this one takes the cake."

Tall Tommy sat in the sparse cabin of the parked delivery truck and blew quietly on his mug of coffee. Sitting next to him in the driver's seat and wearing the same crimson-red uniform as his colleague, Dublin shook his head incredulously.

"Yer feckin' eh right it takes the cake," he responded with a dour expression. "This is a goddamn suicide mission."

Both men stared solemnly out the windshield of the Red Apple Vending truck, its sides painted in blocky, bright red Russian, as the pewter-gray morning sky slowly brightened. Across the alley from where they were parked stood a long, windowless, two-story brick building flanked by a high steel fence. Like most of the buildings in the old Pregolsky industrial park, the drab building sat unmarked and inconspicuous. The two men poured more coffee from a large thermos and waited patiently.

"There," Tall Tommy said a few minutes later, pointing with his coffee cup at an approaching van. "That one's going in."

They watched closely as the van turned into the building's service entryway and braked roughly before the gate. The driver rolled down his window and yelled into the small metal intercom beside him, slapping his hand impatiently until the gate opened with a loud metallic groan. The van then sped quickly past the entryway, turning and racing along the long front façade before stopping abruptly at a large gray service door scarred with rust.

"Why is everyone in Russia always in such a damn hurry?" Tall Tommy asked nonchalantly as he watched the driver of the van jump from the cab and quickly walk to the door. Just as he reached it, a short, stocky man with a thick mustache peered out from behind the door and nodded.

"Russians are not unlike us Irish," Dublin replied with a sympathetic grin. "We find work to be an unwanted distraction from our true passion, which of course is drinkin' ourselves into oblivion."

"Yeah, I've noticed that."

The two men watched as the driver unloaded several boxes onto a handcart before disappearing into the building. "Okay, I think we have our entry point," Tall Tommy remarked flatly.

"Dah," Dublin replied.

Tall Tommy glanced over at his colleague. "I hope to god you know more Russian than that, Dub. Otherwise we're fucked."

Dublin grunted humorlessly as he drank his coffee.

A few minutes later, the driver reappeared at the service door with the mustached man and exchanged a few quick words before climbing back into the van and driving off. The mustached man glanced around quickly before slipping back into the dark interior and shutting the large steel door. Tall Tommy nodded at Dublin.

"Okay, that's our cue. Are you ready to impersonate an angry, half-drunk Russian? It shouldn't be too hard considering you're already an angry, half-drunk Irishman."

Dublin smiled back at him. *"Spasiba, dolboeb."*

"What the hell did that mean?"

"Thanks, fuckhead."

"Now see, that's more like it!" Tall Tommy said with a wide grin as he punched his colleague in the shoulder. "I feel better already. Now let's go make some magic!"

Dublin steered the delivery truck onto the street and accelerated toward the entry gate a few hundred meters ahead. "Just remember," he said, his normal Irish accent now replaced with heavy Russian. "You're my Swedish-born coworker. You don't have to say anything. Just sit there and look like the fucking Aryan poster child that you are."

"A mute Swede. Got it," Tall Tommy replied as he adjusted the Red Apple Vending cap on his head.

Dublin turned the truck into the service entry and stopped next to the gate. A cold blast of Baltic Sea air blew into the cab as he rolled down the window. He lit a cigarette and took a deep drag before slowly leaning his head out.

"Dobraye utro," he grumbled at the intercom as smoke poured from his mouth.

"Yes, good morning," the gruff, tinny male voice from the intercom responded in Russian. "Pickup or delivery?"

"Delivery," Dublin replied, matching the petulant tone of the Russian voice. "Vending machine." He calmly smoked his cigarette as a long moment of silence passed. Finally the heavy entry gate began to open as the intercom crackled to life.

"Main service door," the voice replied tersely.

"Spasiba," Dublin responded, flicking his cigarette out the window before rolling it up. He cast a quick look at Tall Tommy as the truck rolled past the gate.

The same mustached man they'd witnessed earlier appeared again as the truck groaned to a halt next to the service door. Tall Tommy stepped down from the cab and smiled stupidly as the man barked out a question in Russian.

"He can't understand you," Dublin responded sourly in perfect Russian as he rounded the back of the truck. "My comrade is Swedish."

"What the fuck is a Swedish brat doing here in Kaliningrad?"

the man asked, his small eyes fixed suspiciously on Dublin as Tall Tommy unlocked the back gate of the truck.

"Delivering your fucking vending machine," Dublin shot back with a sneer.

The stout Russian glared at Dublin, then shrugged and nodded. "Yes, of course," he muttered. He watched impatiently as the two men quickly unloaded their cargo before gesturing with a peevish wave of his hand for them to follow him into the service room.

Dublin and Tall Tommy followed as instructed.

The massive interior of the service room was cold and poorly lit. Around them, large square frames of rusting steel were haphazardly stacked, and Dublin grimaced at the heavy garlic-like smell of welding-torch acetylene that filled the room. The mustached Russian led the two men toward a gray, desk-sized device in the corner of the room and then stepped aside and pointed.

"Take it over there," he ordered.

Dublin and Tall Tommy exchanged a brief look. "What is that?" Dublin asked the Russian as he lit a cigarette and nodded at the machine.

"Scanner," the Russian replied as he watched them. "Everything that comes in gets scanned for security."

Tall Tommy rolled the large vending machine up to the scanning device and lowered it gently onto the floor before stepping out of the way. Dublin gave him a quick hand signal as the Russian walked over to the scanner and immediately began typing onto a small keyboard. Tall Tommy nodded and moved quietly toward the Russian.

"So how the hell do you scan something this big?" Dublin asked indifferently as he took a drag of his cigarette. The Russian said nothing as he picked up a small device attached by a cord to the large machine and glanced at a small monitor mounted on top.

He then stepped over to the vending machine and began slowly running the handheld scanner across the front.

Tall Tommy took another step toward the Russian.

"Chto za huy," the Russian grumbled as the image on the small monitor flickered and went dead. He angrily slapped the handheld device with his palm a few times, then cursed and walked back to the machine. Tall Tommy glanced at Dublin with a questioning look as the Russian punched at the keyboard. Dublin gave him a hint of a smile.

"Is there a problem?" he asked the Russian.

"Fucking thing just died," the Russian replied gruffly as he continued punching keys.

"Does this happen often?"

The Russian paused and looked up. "No," he said as he glared at Dublin. "Not often."

Dublin nodded, taking a long final drag of his cigarette. "Are you thirsty?" he asked as he dropped his cigarette butt onto the concrete floor and crushed it under his boot.

"What?" the Russian man replied.

Dublin walked around to the back of the vending machine, unraveled the power cord, and handed it to Tall Tommy to plug into the wall.

"What would you like, comrade?" Dublin asked as the lights on the vending machine flickered to life. The Russian man's mustache twitched with confusion for a moment before his mouth slowly drew into a smile.

"Kvass," he said eagerly as he walked over to Dublin.

"A kvass it is," Dublin replied as he fed coins into the machine and punched one of the large buttons. Almost immediately, a can of the fermented, mildly alcoholic drink dropped into the dispensing tray.

"*Spasiba,*" the Russian said as Dublin handed him the drink.

"*Pazhalusta,*" Dublin replied as he lit another cigarette. "So comrade, since nothing gets in without being scanned, should we sit here and wait for the scanner to fix itself, or should we load the vending machine back into the truck and come back next week?"

The Russian man looked at Dublin and the smiling face of Tall Tommy for a moment before drinking the can of kvass in a single gulp. He crushed the empty can and tossed it at the scanning machine. "Follow me," he muttered gloomily, oblivious to the foamy traces of kvass still clinging to his mustache. "I will show you where it needs to go."

Chapter 24

Dr. Tatyana Aleksandrov looked up from her computer and noticed with surprise that it was already 8:23 p.m. She turned and glanced at the window. The view from her second-floor laboratory offered little more than the concrete and corrugated steel that composed the buildings within the large industrial complex, now muted under the ink-black lid of night. The cold Baltic wind whispered incessantly against the thick glass.

Tatyana leaned back in her chair and slowly stretched her small, five-foot-four-inch frame before taking off her wire-frame glasses and methodically rubbing her tired, deep green eyes. Her stomach grumbled in hunger, and she remembered that the silver-rimmed teacup sitting on her desk was empty. She looked at her computer screen, noted the speed of the data compiling in her latest thermal simulation, and decided she had at least another hour before she could call it a night. If Tatyana had a husband or significant other, her work schedule might have created an issue. But she did not have a husband or significant other. In fact, despite being only thirty-four and reasonably attractive, she didn't really have any close male friends. Tatyana considered this as she grabbed her teacup and started walking toward the cafeteria.

The second floor of the Baltisky Research Center was silent as Tatyana paced quickly down the long corridor of empty laboratories and offices. The emptiness didn't bother her. She'd spent enough late nights in the building to be comfortable with this, and she knew Pavel the night guard was sitting in the security room downstairs. Of course, she also knew that Pavel very much liked his vodka, perhaps almost as much as he liked his naps. But still she didn't worry. Regular exercise had kept the muscles on her lean frame toned and strong, and nearly a year of boxing lessons had given Tatyana the confidence to rarely worry about her own personal safety.

She slowed slightly to peer into the dark office of Dr. Volkov as she passed. He had probably left hours ago, but for the last several months Tatyana often found excuses to walk past his office to steal a glance. Even at this late hour she couldn't resist the urge to look. It had been this way since April, when she had noticed him watching her intensely during a staff meeting. He had approached her afterward with an unexpected proposition, and that same evening they had quietly locked themselves in Volkov's office after the rest of the staff had left. Tatyana still vividly remembered the feeling of her colleague's warm breath against her neck and his muscular chest pressing down on her as she'd lain across his desk.

She still didn't know why he'd acted so coldly afterward, barely saying good night to her as he left, but Tatyana assumed it had something to do with a wife and a family that had never been mentioned. Apart from a few quickly averted glances, he had avoided any contact with her since, and she now passed by his office with a lingering tinge of frustrated excitement.

As usual, the lights in the second-floor cafeteria were turned off. Tatyana stepped into the darkness and swept her hand along the wall until she found the switch. The long rows of overhead fluorescents stirred to life, filling the large room with flickering yellow-white light. She winced at the sudden brightness before turning toward the corner of the room where the vending machines were located.

"Dobroi nochi."

Tatyana jumped in shock, nearly dropping her teacup as the low male voice pierced the silence. She looked up to see a lone man sitting in the corner of the room, smiling at her from the table where she normally sat and ate her dinner.

"Good evening," Tatyana replied breathlessly in Russian.

"Please," the man said, gesturing for her to come and sit at the table.

Tatyana stood motionless, examining the man. He was young and didn't look Russian, with noticeably tan skin and short, curly hair that was dark like his eyes. His outfit, comprised of a sweater, jacket, and pants, was a matching shade of black that gave the man the sophisticated look of an artist, or perhaps a cat burglar. But his handsome face, stretched with a welcoming smile, appeared warm and genuinely friendly. Sensing no threat, Tatyana stepped toward the table and slowly sat down across from him.

"Vy govorite po-angliyski?" the man asked her.

"Yes, I speak English," Tatyana replied in crisp English, nodding.

"Oh, good," the man replied with a relieved sigh. "Because I've just recited everything I know in Russian, and if you didn't, this conversation would be very awkward."

Tatyana smiled. "Are you American?"

"Yes. Well, sort of," the man replied. "I mean, I'm probably more American than anything else. But I really hate to be defined so categorically."

Tatyana stared at him, confused.

"Look, I'm sorry. I know my presence here must be very odd to you." The man reached into the breast pocket of his jacket as he spoke and felt around for something. "I doubt you often get unexpected visitors showing up in the cafeteria at this hour of the evening. But if you had any idea what I've gone through to be here, I think you would start to appreciate the seriousness of the situation, and the importance of this meeting."

Tatyana's eyes widened in surprise. "So you are here because of me?"

"Indeed I am," the man said with a smile. His eyes flashed with excitement as his hand found the item he was looking for and pulled it from his jacket. "In fact, Dr. Tatyana Aleksandrov, I'm here to end your life as you know it." He extended his hand toward her, a small object wrapped in foil pressed between his fingers. "Would you like a piece of gum?"

Tatyana blinked vacantly at the man, wondering if she'd heard him correctly. "What did you just say?"

"Would you like a piece of gum? It's spearmint."

Tatyana pushed her chair back from the table. "What did you say before offering me a piece of gum?"

The man looked at her with a blank stare. "I said I'm here to end your life as you know it. But please, don't get up."

A thin glaze of cold sweat coated her skin as Tatyana slowly stood up. She could feel her heart pounding beneath her blouse as she stepped behind her chair and glanced around the room. "Is this a joke?" she asked. "Are you completely a lunatic?"

"Not that you're in the mood for an English lesson, Tatyana," the American replied, holding her stare, "but the correct way to say that would be *'Are you a complete lunatic?'* I know it seems like a subtle difference, but that's the right way to say it. Now please, sit back down and try to relax."

"Who the hell are you?" Tatyana demanded. The sound of her own voice, shaky and frightened, was even more unnerving than the man sitting in front of her.

"Me? Oh, I'm afraid we just don't have enough time to get into that right now. Honestly, Dr. Aleksandrov, I don't think you'd find me all that interesting even if we did."

Tatyana continued looking around the room. *What the hell is happening?* she thought as the dark-haired American calmly sat and watched her. She considered throwing herself onto the man and using everything she'd been trained in her boxing classes to physically subdue him, but another, more rational voice in her head told her this was a very bad idea. She glanced at the nearby wall and noticed the old intercom box, just a few steps away. There was a chance that the intercom was connected to the security office downstairs. Tatyana decided even if it wasn't a good chance, it was probably her only chance. She swallowed back the fear in her throat and met the American's eyes.

"Why you would want to kill me?" she asked matter-of-factly. "I'm hardly worth the trouble."

The man grinned as he slowly unwrapped the piece of gum in his hand. "You're a very modest woman, Dr. Aleksandrov, but please. That's like Yuri Gagarin landing after the first manned voyage into space and saying, 'It was just a little spin around the planet.' As for killing you, I—"

Tatyana bolted toward the wall and smashed her fist against the speaker button. "Pavel! Pavel! *Te nuzgna mne v kofetirie sechas!* Pavel! I need you *now!*" She released the button and stared desperately at the speaker, waiting for a response from the security guard. A numbing silence filled the room.

"I'm afraid Pavel is in no condition to join us right now," the man replied. He crossed his legs and glanced nonchalantly at his watch. "Last time I checked, his blood-alcohol level was about three times the local definition of intoxication, and he was pretty comfortably stretched out on the floor of the security office."

Tatyana stepped away from the intercom and turned to face the American. A sudden awareness of her own breathing came over her as the air in the room seemed to take on a dense, oppressive weight. The man met her stare with a knowing, almost sympathetic softness.

"You didn't let me finish. You asked me why I would want to kill you."

Tatyana gave him a slight nod. The American examined the unwrapped piece of gum in his hand for a moment before popping it into his mouth. He stared absently at her as he chewed, appearing to Tatyana to be deep in thought. She found the man's state of calm to be nearly unbearable.

"The truth is that I do *not* know why anyone would want to kill you, Dr. Aleksandrov. I only know what I've been asked to come here and do."

He paused and looked down at something next to his chair. Tatyana noticed his backpack for the first time as he reached down and quickly pulled out a small, cloth-wrapped object and placed it on the table. She glanced at the object and noticed a long cylinder of matte-black steel protruding from the end. A paralyzing wave of fear struck her as she realized she was looking at the barrel of a handgun.

"Now," the man continued, "there are some things I need to explain to you, but I know this information isn't going to be easy to process. Dr. Aleksandrov, are you listening to me?"

Tatyana pulled her eyes from the gun and looked at the American.

"Physiologically speaking, Dr. Aleksandrov, you're starting to go into a state of stress-induced shock. Your pulse is becoming more rapid, but ironically also more weak, and as a result your body is not getting the oxygen it needs to function properly." He rested his hand on top of the weapon and gave Tatyana another sympathetic smile. "It's really a study in contradictions when you stop to consider it," he continued. "Your skin is becoming wet from the fear-induced production of sweat, but a lack of blood flow is causing your skin to become cold. Your mind is racing to find a solution to this dilemma, but the reduced blood flow is impairing your ability to complete even basic cognitive tasks. Put simply, your body is literally fighting *itself* right now—and I can tell from experience that the outcome is going to go one of two ways."

He paused and carefully unwrapped the handgun.

"Either your adrenal glands are going to start pumping a truckload of epinephrine into your system and turn you into superwoman for about forty-five seconds. Or your oxygen deprivation is going to lead to syncope, which is just a fancy term for fainting, and you're going to end up sprawled across the floor."

Tatyana stood motionless as the American quickly inspected the weapon, then laid it gently back on the table with the barrel aimed at her chest. Her legs felt like lead weights attached to her waist.

"Either way, I don't have much time to tell you a few things."

"What does it matter if you're going to kill me?" Tatyana asked.

"I know it seems strange, but I'm required to do this before we continue."

"You Americans are all completely fucking insane!" Tatyana yelled at the man with a sudden rage. The sound of her own heartbeat seemed to grow to a deafening level. The American studied her intently, recognizing the change. He began speaking in an even, practiced tone.

"Dr. Aleksandrov, there are times when we are asked to make sacrifices for the greater good. This necessity doesn't make the sacrifice less painful, nor can we allow the pain of what's to come to make the sacrifice seem less than necessary."

Tatyana only half listened as the crazy American calmly recited his speech. She was convinced the man was going to shoot her the instant he finished his rehearsed monologue, and the certainty of this knowledge sent another wave of terror through her body. Her hands began to shake beyond her ability to control them.

"The circumstances in which you now find yourself are not directly the result of your actions, but whether you recognize it or not, you are a key part of something much bigger than anything you can now imagine."

Tatyana ignored the pounding in her head and kept her eyes fixed on the man. She sensed that she had only a few moments left, but she forced her body to remain still. She knew if she simply ran, she had almost no chance of making it out of the building alive. The research facility's security system was old, but it still took several seconds to disarm the night alarm that unlocked the main personnel doors.

She needed another option.

"Last year, during your research into a phenomenon known as thermal resonance, you uncovered something highly unexpected. Something that surprised your scientific colleagues, not to mention yourself. What you didn't—and apparently still don't—fully comprehend is the magnitude of the potential impact those findings could have on . . . well, on everything."

Tatyana shook her head. She had no idea what the American was talking about, but apparently he knew something about her research. She had indeed published most of the findings of her twelve-month study on thermal resonance in the *European Energy Review*, but hardly a word had been spoken in response by the scientific community. Certainly nothing shocking, and certainly nothing to be killed for. Or was there? Tatyana vaguely recalled the highly irregular outcome of the final two experiments she had conducted using depleted uranium, but she had disregarded them as anomalies stemming from a faulty thermographic imager. Her scientific comrades had generally agreed. The outcomes could be found in exacting detail in her notebooks in the archive room next to her laboratory. She could even show him . . . Tatyana's mind suddenly seized on an idea.

The archive room.

Built of thick, lead-lined walls, the archive room was essentially a large, fireproof safe designed to protect the lab's paper-based research. A relic of the past, the room's once massive library of information had long ago been digitalized, leaving it to now serve as little more than a glorified storage closet for outdated or broken lab equipment. Nevertheless, the room was still accessible only through a single, vault-like door armed with a sophisticated electronic keypad. *And I know the code,* Tatyana thought excitedly as she stood there staring at the American. Of course, the hardest part of the plan would be finding a way to get a head start on her assailant. But if she could somehow get to the room and lock herself inside, Tatyana calculated she would have enough oxygen to survive until her colleagues arrived the next morning. Her legs quivered with anxiety as she considered her next move.

"Dr. Aleksandrov, on the day your research was published, a chain of events was set in motion that you couldn't begin to imagine, nor would you want to." The American's voice trailed off as his fingers stroked the dark steel barrel of the gun. "As I'm sure you've learned in your professional career, business and science make for strange bedfellows. They both see the world very differently. As in any doomed relationship, the only thing they seem to agree on is that they can't live without each other."

Tatyana tensed as the American casually cupped the pistol in his hand as he continued talking. She had to make her move soon.

"Whereas the mind of science is focused purely on the joy of discovery, the mind of business is focused purely on the exploitation of that discovery." The man paused and looked her in the eyes. "Tonight, Tatyana, you're unfortunately experiencing the business side of your discovery."

Tatyana sprang forward and grabbed the edge of the table just as the American raised the gun. She screamed in terror, feeling a torrent of strength-giving adrenaline course through her arms as she pulled the heavy table into the air and tossed it forward on top of the man. She turned and sprinted from the cafeteria as the muffled sound of surprised laughter echoed behind her. As she bolted through the door and began running down the long corridor, her heart felt as if it was going to explode from her chest.

Faster . . . faster! she told herself.

A hundred meters ahead, the door to the archive room stood quietly next to her research laboratory. The distance appeared maddeningly far, and Tatyana felt like she was in the middle of a slow-moving nightmare as she rushed toward it.

"Dr. Aleksandrov!" the American's voice cried out behind her.

Tatyana ran even faster. She knew stopping or even looking back would only make her an easier target.

"Tatyana!"

The door to the archive room was tantalizingly close when something sharp stabbed forcefully into the right side of Tatyana's back. She cried out in alarm when a second, more intense sting pierced the back of her neck. To her horror, her limbs immediately began to feel sluggish, forcing her to slow to a stumbling walk. Tatyana reached back frantically to find the source of the pain. Her fingers touched something hard protruding from the base of her neck. She pulled it free and glanced, terrified, at the object in her hand. It looked like a child's toy, a tiny rocket comprised of a long metallic tube and four miniature, winglike fins at its base. Only the short needle at its tip revealed the object's true purpose.

"Move!" Tatyana screamed, pleading with her body as she angrily tossed the tranquilizer dart to the ground. But it was no use. Just a few short steps from the door to the archive room, her legs went numb, and she collapsed heavily to the floor.

Within seconds, Tatyana's paralysis was complete.

She lay motionless, sprawled on the cold linoleum floor, gazing helplessly at the door to the archive room. The sound of the American's footsteps echoed closer. Finally, after an agony of terror-filled waiting, a pair of black leather shoes stepped into view just inches from her face.

"Amazing, isn't it?" the man asked as he dropped his backpack on the floor next to her. He kneeled down and took her pulse. "It's a paralyzing agent that targets a receptor in the skeletal muscles. Turns any human being into a drooling pile of inanimate flesh in seconds." He removed the other tranquilizer dart before turning Tatyana onto her back and carefully straightening her limbs. She stared blankly as he examined her, his hands pressing and feeling with the practiced touch of a physician. Satisfied, he then reached into his backpack for something. Tatyana felt her pulse rise as a large needle and syringe came into view.

"It's okay," he said, giving her a reassuring smile. "I just need some blood samples."

Tatyana distantly felt the needle as it penetrated deep into her vein, as if her body had become a strange inanimate object uselessly attached at the neck. A moment later she watched as the American quickly shoved three large vials of blood into the backpack next to him.

"All done."

She stared unblinking back at him, consumed by a mixture of terror and rage. She tried to command her hands to reach out and grab the man by the throat and kill him, but she couldn't summon so much as a twitch. Even her eyelids, succumbing to the effects of the paralyzing drug, were unable to close, and a steady stream of tears began rolling down her temples into her dark brown hair.

His smiling face hovered over her. "Okay, Dr. Aleksandrov, it's about that time. I want you to know that, having now personally suffered through a few weeks in Kaliningrad, I can say with absolute certainty that you are, as they say, going to a better place."

Tatyana steeled herself as the American lightly touched her shoulder. *I'm going to die now*, she thought as she watched him reach into his backpack. He pulled out a small phone and punched a single button. "Be ready in five," he said curtly before tossing the phone back into the bag. He then pulled out a long coil of nylon rope and began tying some form of knot, pausing when he caught Tatyana staring at him.

"I'm sorry, Tatyana, just one more little prick," he said, pulling a small syringe from his pocket. Tatyana didn't feel the needle this time as she watched his finger push the contents of the syringe into her neck. A soothing warmth began to cascade through her body, replacing the fear and rage in her chest with a calming sense of peace. She watched as he went back to forming a knot with the cord, his fingers deftly moving at what seemed an impossible speed. He then stopped and looked at her again.

"By the way, your plan to escape to the archive room was a very good one. Unfortunately, I know the combination as well." The American then reached out and gently closed Tatyana's eyelids. She distantly felt the tightening of a rope around her ankles and exhaled with a long, submissive sigh.

The sound of her heartbeat faded as the warmth overtook her.

She was ready for the darkness.

Chapter 25

"Christ, you're starting to become a regular around here."

Tom Coleman smiled at Chip as he sat down next to the older man at his usual spot at the bar. "Funny, I was beginning to think the same thing," he replied as they exchanged a quick handshake. "How's it going, Chip?" Tom asked as he glanced around for the bartender.

"Can't say it's going too badly," Chip replied cheerfully. "At least it's getting quiet around here again."

Tom nodded and glanced around the room. The attention generated by the article in the college paper seemed to have receded in the last few days, leaving the usual mix of dejected students and alcoholic professors scattered around the room.

"This must be the third time I've seen you in here this week," Chip said, giving Tom a quizzical look. "Any particular reason why?"

"Well, it is the holiday season," Tom replied cynically. "As far as I see it, drinking's as much a part of the holidays as turkey and dressing."

"Well said." Chip raised his glass of beer and toasted the room.

"Jeri working tonight?" Tom asked nonchalantly.

"Yeah, she's around here somewhere."

Tom pulled out a sanitary wipe and quickly wiped down the counter before taking off his gloves and carefully placing them in front of him. As with past nights, he used them as armrests to avoid direct contact with the bar top. He then reached into his jacket pocket and quickly checked that his notepad and pen were in their usual spot. Satisfied that everything was in order, he removed his coat and laid it across his lap.

"If you're planning on being a regular, you need to start acting like one," Chip muttered as he pointed with his thumb. "There's a hook under the bar for your coat."

"It's fine on my lap," Tom replied.

Chip stared at Tom for a moment, then grunted loudly. "Suit yourself."

Tom gave him a friendly nudge with his elbow. "So what's new, old man?" he asked.

"Nothing worth telling." Chip shrugged. "The world and the beer are still ice cold."

"Gotcha. And is that a good thing?"

Chip gave Tom a sidelong glance. "Depends on how you like your beer."

"Well, I suppose that's my cue," a female voice replied. Both men looked up to find Jeri leaning against the opposite side of the counter, staring at them with her arms folded. Tom immediately sat up straight.

"Jesus, Jeri, you've got to stop sneaking up on people like that," Chip chided mockingly.

"It's an old, loud bar, Chip," Jeri fired back. "Almost as old and loud as something else in this room. An epileptic elephant could sneak up on you."

Tom watched Jeri as she spoke to the older man, her face soft with affection. Her jaw tightened when she caught him staring, the softness vaporizing as she turned to speak.

"Something to drink?" she asked.

Tom ordered a beer and then watched in admiration as Jeri turned and walked away. His eyes followed her body as it moved beneath her worn jeans and faded blue Joe's Last Stand T-shirt. He watched as she reached up to grab a glass, exposing a thin strip of pale unblemished skin along her lower back that led him to imagine the smooth, warm texture he would undoubtedly feel if his hands were pressed against her. After a moment of enjoying the fantasy, Tom realized he was staring. He turned and looked at Chip.

"Anything new from her mysterious admirer?"

Chip shook his head as he drained his beer and rested the empty glass on the bar. "Nope . . . not that I've seen. But then, he's not a once-a-week kind of writer." He glanced at Jeri pouring beer on the other side of the bar. His expression softened with affection as he watched her, like a proud father finding perfection in the simple act of a daughter. "If the past is any indication, she'll be getting another letter from him in the next few days or so."

"From another new town, I'd guess," Tom muttered.

"I'd say that's a safe bet."

Both men fell silent as Jeri returned with their drinks. She smiled at Chip as she handed him his beer, then glanced suspiciously at Tom. "Everything okay over here?" she asked, placing his glass on the counter. Tom nodded, unable to remove his eyes from her.

"Everything's great," Chip replied. "Just discussing the consistency of my bowel movements with my friend Tom. Tom here thinks my once-a-week schedule is grossly inadequate. Fortunately, my enlarged liver is keeping all other bodily functions flowing like a fresh beer tap." He gave Jeri a wide grin. "Speaking of my liver, I think I'll excuse myself for a moment." The older man slid from his stool and headed off toward the restroom.

Tom glanced over at Jeri and smiled awkwardly. "I owe you for my beer," he said, reaching into his pocket.

"Don't worry about it," Jeri replied. "Anyone who keeps Chip entertained is entitled to one on the house." She picked up a thick hardback book lying on the counter and slipped back onto her barstool in the corner.

"Thanks," he replied, giving her a thin smile. "But Chip probably considers me to be more annoying than entertaining."

"If he lets you sit by him for more than five minutes, he must find something useful about you."

"Then I suppose I'll consider myself lucky."

Tom sipped his beer and watched Jeri as she quietly read her book. He was feeling lucky. For the last week he'd spent half of his evenings occupying the corner stool of Joe's in the hopes of getting to know Jeri and the people at the saloon she associated with, only to come up with almost nothing of substance. Most of that time had been utterly unrevealing, and Tom had finally given up on the idea that Jeri was anything other than a reclusive, reticent young woman who preferred books to men and had the rare quality of being as beautiful as she was aloof. In fact, the only men she'd had more than a passing word with were Joe the owner and Chip the old regular. The few sentences Tom had just exchanged with her were the closest he'd come to a conversation, and he now felt oddly privileged.

He decided it was time to press his luck.

"Mind if I ask you a question?" he said, glancing at her with a keen expression.

"Shoot," she replied, her eyes still fixed on the page in front of her.

"What's Chip's story?"

Jeri appeared to ignore the question and continue reading. Tom was about to ask again when she abruptly shut the book and turned to face him. "What makes you think I know anything more about

Chip than you do?" she asked defensively. "You're the one who's been sitting next to him for the better part of a week."

"True," Tom replied, "but he seems more interested in talking about you than himself." He noticed Jeri's eyes narrow slightly at his remark. "Anyway, he just seems like a nice guy, and I was curious to know what brings a man like Chip to the saloon every night. Given the way you two talk to each other, I figured you knew him well enough to know the answer. But hey, it's no big deal," he said, shrugging. "Forget I even asked."

"He was a professor at the university," Jeri said quietly. "Archeology."

Tom looked over at her slowly, masking his surprise at the fact that she was finally speaking candidly.

"He walked in one summer afternoon not long after I started working here," she continued. "Strolled up to the bar wearing some ridiculous cowboy hat and those intense blue eyes and sat down on that same barstool he sits on now. Before long he was a few beers down and explaining how he'd just wrapped up his last archeological dig with a group of grad students. Apparently the university had forced early retirement on several of the tenured professors in the department to make room for 'fresh blood,' as he put it. Chip was one of the professors forced out. Not that he seemed that upset about it. A few hours after walking into the saloon he was toasting his freedom and talking to me like I was his long-lost daughter."

Jeri paused and glanced around the room. "God, that was more than a year ago. I can't believe it's been that long."

"And he's been coming in ever since, huh?" Tom asked.

"More or less. He's been around more than usual lately . . . ever since the letters started arriving. But that's probably because he's convinced himself this mystery writer is out to kill me." Jeri rolled her eyes and gave Tom the slightest hint of a smile.

Tom nodded. *If only you knew the half of it*, he thought as he smiled back.

"Anyway, Chip's a good guy," she continued, glancing out the window at the snow that tumbled and collided before melting into the mirror-black pavement of the old highway. "He's one of the last of the 'old school' guys. One of those men who still sees everything in black and white and isn't afraid to tell you what he thinks. And in case you haven't noticed, he's still pretty damn quick for his age."

"I've never seen a man his age drink a beer faster," Tom said with a wry smile.

Jeri nodded and opened her book. "So there you have it. Now you know as much about Chip as I do."

"I doubt it, but thanks for the history lesson."

"You're welcome."

"Can I ask you another question?"

"Only if it has nothing to do with the next obvious topic of discussion."

"And what would that be?" Tom asked, feigning ignorance. Jeri shot him a threatening look. "Right, never mind."

Defeated, Tom took a drink of his beer and glanced around the saloon. A few patrons stood in the far corner studying the letters and photos—the "shrine," as Joe the owner called it—pinned to the wall. He watched as they read and laughed, one of them even raising a hand to gently touch a Polaroid photo as if in a strange gesture of affection. Tom himself knew the letters and pictures by heart. He had discreetly taken digital photos of each a few nights earlier and spent the last two days poring over them in his office. Unfortunately, they had given him nothing more to go on, other than the frustrating realization that their composer was a master of revealing just enough information to taunt him. The photos were particularly maddening. Anyone passing by Tom's cramped office as he studied the reproduced images on his laptop would have heard a chorus of expletives and frustrated sighs. This, followed by yet another failed attempt to talk to Jeri, was now turning Tom's mood as dark as the late-autumn sky outside.

Perhaps even worse, the e-mail he had sent to Alex three days ago had still gone unanswered.

Maybe I am going off the deep end, Tom thought bitterly before dismissing the thought with a shrug. "No, no . . . I'm right, and I know it," he muttered under his breath before emptying his beer glass.

"Right about what?" Chip said, suddenly next to Tom as he slid back onto his stool.

"What? Oh, nothing . . . just thinking out loud." Tom fell into silence, visibly brooding as he stared at the empty glass in front of him.

Chip watched him curiously for a moment before looking over at Jeri nestled in her corner behind the bar with her book. "Good lord . . . I leave for two minutes and the mood in the whole bar goes to hell." He leaned toward Tom. "Wait, let me guess," he whispered, nudging him on the shoulder. "You asked Jeri about the letters, didn't you?"

Tom shook his head. "I didn't even get that far."

"Yeah, well, I could have warned you about that."

Tom reached over and grabbed Chip's arm. He was once again surprised by the firmness of Chip's muscles as the older man tensed in alarm.

"Look, Chip, I need to know something. Are you *really* worried about this guy Jeri's getting letters from?"

Chip's eyes quickly lost their glint of humor as he gazed at Tom. "Of course I am. Why are you asking?"

"Because I'm worried about him too. But the difference between you and me is that I'm in a position to do something about it."

Chip looked at him curiously. "What do you mean?"

"Let me show you," Tom said, releasing Chip's arm. He reached into his jacket and pulled out a business card, holding it out for the older man to see.

Chip noted the federal crest emblazoned on the card and raised his eyebrows in surprise. "You're with the Department of Homeland Security?"

"Keep your voice down," Tom hissed as he glanced over his shoulder. "Yes, I'm an investigator with the ICE division of Homeland Security, and before I say anything else, I need your word that everything discussed here stays strictly between the two of us."

Chip furrowed his brow. "Do I strike you as the kind of guy who handles confidential information loosely?"

Tom stared at Chip.

"Yes, you have my word."

"Good," Tom replied. He looked around again to make sure no one else was within earshot before glancing down the bar. Jeri was still coiled in her corner absorbed in the book on her lap. "What I'm about to tell you is highly confidential," he said quietly, still weighing his next words. Ethically speaking, Tom knew he was about to tread on shaky ground, but he didn't have a choice. He needed the older man's help. It was clear that Chip was the only man Jeri appeared to trust—let alone like—which meant he was also Tom's only hope of being an informant. Of course, the best way to control a potential informant was to "amp up" the scale and seriousness of the situation. And as Tom now saw it, exaggerating the level of federal agency involvement was the most convincing way to do this.

"I'm currently heading an investigation of potential terrorism involving the deaths of three individuals that have occurred within the last two months," he said quietly, his voice low and serious. "And here's what I know. Each of these individuals was either murdered or died under suspicious circumstances. Each of them was a researcher with the same large oil company. But what's most interesting of all"—he paused and pointed at the far wall—"is that each of them died at a time and location that exactly matches a letter pinned to that goddamn wall."

Chip looked at Tom disbelievingly. "You can't be serious," he muttered, his blue eyes wide with shock.

"The first incident occurred in India," Tom continued, "in what appears at first glance to have been a freak accident. The second incident involved a terrorist-style explosion inside a luxury hotel in Nigeria. And the third incident, perhaps the craziest one of all, involved the victim falling overboard from a yacht that was cruising off the coast of Venezuela and getting chopped into little pieces. India, Nigeria, Venezuela—all places Jeri's little pen pal has visited, and each at the same time as our victims' deaths. Now, you tell me, Chip . . . would you call that a coincidence?"

Chip shook his head.

"Of course, Homeland Security has limited international resources, at least directly, so the CIA is handling the majority of the on-site investigative work overseas. I'm handling the investigation here." Tom slipped his business card back into his pocket and looked at the older man. "Chip, this situation is as serious as it gets."

Chip narrowed his eyes on Tom, as if sizing up his credibility.

"How long have you been investigating this?" he asked.

"Not long," Tom said, improvising quickly. "Investigations into the deaths obviously started at the time of each incident, but I didn't make the connection to Jeri's mysterious letter writer until the night you and I first met. Immediately after that, I sent a report to my connections at the CIA. It's been a 'highest priority' investigation ever since."

Chip nodded and took a long drink of his beer.

"And why are you telling me all this?"

Tom considered the question carefully. His answer would be critical in getting Chip to cooperate, but it was a delicate task. He needed to play heavily on the older man's emotional attachment to Jeri, but not in a way that sounded dishonest or patronizing. He needed to be persuasive in his conviction, but not in a way that invited more questions about the details. In short, Tom thought morbidly, just as he'd done on that horrific night in Afghanistan, he again had to tell a perfect lie.

"Because I need your help," Tom replied firmly. "Look, you're the reason this investigation is even happening. If you and I hadn't met that night a few weeks back, my team would have never figured out that a rogue terrorist was responsible for murdering scientists in one of the world's largest oil companies. Hell, you were the one who made me think this guy could be a killer in the first place. When this is over, our government and the entire fucking country will owe you a debt of gratitude. But for now, the painful truth is that, like it or not, you're right in the center of this mess, and we need you to be our eyes and ears here as much as possible."

"And by 'we' you mean you and the federal government?" Chip replied, regarding Tom wearily.

Tom nodded. "Think about it, Chip—you're the perfect choice. You know this place as well as anyone, and you know the kind of people who normally hang out here. You'd be the first person to spot something that looked out of the ordinary. Plus, you already spend a lot of time here, so you won't be changing your routine in a way that anyone would notice."

He paused and leaned in closer. "You're also the closest thing to a friend Jeri has around here, which means you'd probably be the first person she'd talk to if anything happened outside of the bar." Tom leaned back and took a sip of his drink. He could tell that his argument was having its intended effect on Chip, who now sat thoughtfully, his hands slowly swirling his beer.

A moment later, Chip turned and fixed his piercing blue eyes on Tom intently. "If I help you, it will only be for the same reason

I've been hanging around here from the start—to make sure no harm comes to Jeri."

"Of course," Tom replied.

"My interest in this situation only goes so far as her safety," the older man continued. "The rest of this matter is in your hands . . . and I sure as hell hope you and your agency friends know what you're doing."

"Trust me . . . we do."

"So what exactly are you expecting me to do?"

Tom shook his head as he reached into his jacket for his pen and notepad. "Nothing more than what you're already doing, Chip. I just want you to keep an eye out." He quickly scribbled his phone number and tore out the page. "If anything happens, just call me at this number. I can be here in ten minutes."

Chip took the note and glanced at it doubtfully before tucking it into the pocket of his jeans. "And what about Jeri?" he asked quietly. "Are you planning to inform her that her pen pal might actually be an international terrorist?"

Tom ignored the sarcasm in the older man's voice. "The less she knows, the better. Telling Jeri the truth would only terrify her, and anyone keeping tabs on her would notice a change in her behavior."

Chip chuckled as he continued worrying the glass in his hands.

"What?" Tom asked.

"That's the unwritten policy of the feds these days, isn't it? Presume that no one is capable of handling the truth and keep them safely locked behind a wall of ignorance. Tell them nothing, even when their safety's on the line."

"Look, Chip, that's not—"

"Or is this about the need to control the one person who can lead this guy into your hands?" Chip continued. "After all, you can't have Jeri just up and leave for fear of her own safety now, can you? If she did, your tenuous little thread to this guy would vanish completely. Better that she doesn't know anything and remain the tantalizing bait you need to catch him with. She's just a lowly expendable bartender anyway, right, Tom?"

Tom started to respond when his cell phone suddenly buzzed to life. He grunted irritably and dug it from his pocket. The screen identified the caller simply as *Private*. After debating for a moment, Tom pressed the "Answer" button. "Tom Coleman."

"Tom, it's Alex."

"Hi, Alex," Tom replied, keeping the surprise from his voice. In the ten years he'd known him, Tom couldn't recall a single time his brother-in-law had actually called him. "How can I help you?"

"You can start by telling me what the fuck you're up to," Alex replied, his voice low and threatening.

Tom shifted uncomfortably on his barstool. "I apologize, Alex . . . would you mind if I called you back in a few minutes? I'm in the middle of something right now."

"Tom, whatever you're in the middle of, you've got exactly ten minutes to get out of it and get your ass downtown. Meet me at Heritage Square by then, or I swear to god I'll put a warrant out for your arrest."

"Wait . . .you're here in Flagstaff?" Tom replied, the shock evident in his voice.

"Ten minutes."

The line went dead the moment Alex finished his sentence. Tom kept the phone to his ear and smiled uneasily as he looked over at Chip. "Sounds good, Alex. I will see you shortly." He slipped the phone back into his pocket, his mind spinning.

Alex is in Flagstaff.

Something serious has happened.

Tom quickly composed himself and turned to Chip.

"Look, Chip, I understand what—"

"Sounds like you're off to handle more important matters," Chip interrupted as he grabbed a handful of peanuts from a bowl on the counter.

"Sorry, but I have to go," Tom said as he stood up from his stool.

"Right, of course. Don't worry, *Agent Coleman* . . . I'll stay here and keep an eye on things," Chip replied, giving Tom a clumsy military salute.

"Please, Chip," Tom said in a low voice, "I just need to know if I can count on you."

The older man drained his glass and placed it gently back on the counter. "You already have my answer," he answered, glancing up at Tom. "I'll do my part in this. Just make sure you don't screw up yours."

Chapter 26

The redbrick pavers of Heritage Square were hidden under a pristine blanket of glittering snow as Tom paced down the wide center path. The large outdoor courtyard, a popular spot for concerts and sunbathing coeds in the summer, was now a cold, deserted landscape of folk-art benches and low fieldstone walls in the center of Flagstaff's old downtown. It was a short walk from Joe's Last Stand Saloon, and just minutes after his brief conversation with Alex, Tom was sitting on one of the frigid steel benches, anxiously tapping his gloved fingers against his crossed arms as he waited for his brother-in-law's arrival.

He was dumbfounded that Alex was in Flagstaff. *What the hell happened that would make him come here?* The question hung in Tom's mind as the wind whistled softly through the leaf-stripped trees around him. *Was it the e-mail?* He knew the e-mail to his brother-in-law had been a gamble, but what did he have to lose? If his theory was wrong, Alex would dismiss it as he always did—as another nonsensical rant by his wife's irritating younger brother.

But what if he was right?

Tom was still mulling over this question when he noticed two men walking north on Leroux Street. Both were ominous-looking figures, dressed in heavy dark overcoats that concealed everything but the bottom hems of dark trousers and black patent leather shoes. They stepped swiftly across the snow-covered intersection of Aspen Avenue directly toward the square.

Tom shifted uneasily as he watched them approach.

The two men stopped at the north end of the street and briefly exchanged words before one of the men nodded and continued north on Leroux. The other turned and walked directly toward Tom. As he passed under the streetlight, Tom immediately recognized the tall, athletic build and blond hair of the approaching figure and stood to greet him.

"Happy holidays, Alex," he said, reaching out his gloved hand.

"Tom," his brother-in-law said coldly, ignoring Tom's hand as he gestured toward the street. "Let's take a walk, shall we?"

"Sure," Tom replied, a nervous weight pulling at his stomach.

The two walked silently along Aspen Avenue toward the populated stretch of bars and restaurants. Tom kept pace next to Alex, trying to sense the nature of the conversation that was about to take place. He glanced casually over his shoulder to see if the other agent was following them, but the sidewalk behind them was empty.

"So, how are Jane and the girls?" Tom asked, trying to ease the tension. "Jessica must be going on, what . . . five now?"

"She's nine, Tom," Alex said coldly as he stared ahead, the steam of his breath trailing behind him. "But I'm not here to talk about the family. I'm here to get some answers from you." He stopped and grabbed Tom's jacket at the center of his chest. "Starting with that fucking e-mail you sent me last week."

Tom swallowed hard as he stared up at his brother-in-law. At six feet four, Alex stood nearly a foot taller than him.

"And since you're family, I'm going to give you the chance to tell me the no-shit truth about everything going on here before I decide whether or not to bring you up on charges."

Tom's eyes went wide. "Charges? For *what?*"

"Withholding critical information in matters of national security," Alex replied matter-of-factly. "In a few minutes we're going to be joined by one of my colleagues, and if you're nervous now, you have no fucking idea what you'll be in for if you don't tell me what the hell this is all about." He released his grip on Tom and continued walking. "I've played along with your game of trying to get into the CIA for the last several years because you're my brother-in-law, but enough is enough. You needed help with knowing the inside workings of agency recruiting—fine. You needed some coaching on the entrance exams—no problem. I gave you every form of help I could possibly give you, Tom, and guess what—you *still* blew it. That's the truth of the matter. Now tell me." Alex stopped again and faced Tom. "After everything I've done for you, are you honestly trying to use some kind of self-discovered intelligence on a possible terrorist as a bargaining chip to get into the agency?"

Tom stared quietly back at his brother-in-law. At just thirty-five years old, Alex embodied everything the CIA looked for in an agent. He'd graduated from Penn State with a degree in criminal psychology before joining the Navy and undertaking the grueling task of becoming a SEAL. Despite the ultra-clandestine nature of the SEALs, Tom knew from his gloating sister that Alex had been a well-liked and highly respected commander of his team.

Now, just four years after leaving the Navy and breezing through the CIA entrance exams, Alex was running ops for the agency's Special Operations Group. He was smart, strong, and, when it came to his career in the agency, unflinchingly driven. He was everything Tom wanted to be, which is exactly why Tom hated him.

"So I take it you *did* read my last e-mail," Tom replied.

"Fuck you, Tom. How did you come into this information?"

Tom shrugged. "I don't get it. Three days ago I sent you an e-mail about a theoretical connection between a series of seemingly unrelated incidents, and you didn't even respond. Now here you are in Flagstaff crawling up my ass and threatening me—your own brother-in-law—with a crime. Why is that?"

"You know why, Tom."

"No I don't," Tom replied, his mouth forming a smug grin. "That is, unless something happened in Kaliningrad."

Alex glanced around warily. Apart from a few young women standing by the door of a nearby restaurant, they were alone on the sidewalk. He looked at Tom and nodded slightly. "Keep walking."

The two men continued down the street.

"All right, Tom, you want the truth? The truth is, you've pretty much blown all credibility with me in the last few years. In fact, I consider you to be about one IQ point above a goddamn idiot. But the information you presented in your e-mail was compelling enough for me to pay attention. Your theory that the three deaths were linked was a stretch, but against my better judgment I put Kaliningrad on my watch list—just in case something happened."

Tom nodded slowly. "And?"

"OREA confirmed an event this morning."

Tom knew that OREA, the Office of Russian and European Analysis, was the CIA's key intelligence arm overseas. Anything of importance that happened in Europe or Russia inevitably came to the attention of that office first.

"A researcher named Tatyana Aleksandrov was found dead at a laboratory in Kaliningrad. She was unfortunate enough to be in the cafeteria when an explosive device in a vending machine detonated. Half of the building's second floor is now a fucking open-air patio. Everyone at OREA is scratching their heads over this one. And now, thanks to the fact that I put Kaliningrad on my watch list just a few hours before the attack on that shithole on the Baltic Sea, my boss is crawling up my ass for answers."

A bolt of electricity shot through Tom as he stared back at Alex. He was *right*! His terrorist was *real*. He'd felt certain of it since uncovering the facts just three nights earlier, but to have the truth confirmed by his brother-in-law made everything now chillingly real. "So what did you tell him?" he asked, forcing the excitement from his voice.

"Not a goddamn thing. Do you think I'm going to tell the director of Special Operations that my brother-in-law in Arizona came up with this information? Which brings us back to the reason I'm here." Alex leaned down toward Tom, his dark brown eyes watering from the cold. "You can imagine my surprise when this incident popped up this morning. But the real surprise came when I got my hands on the OREA report stating that the lab is owned by a Russian oil company called Tyukos."

Alex paused and looked at Tom, waiting for a response. Tom stared back at him blankly.

"For chrissake, Tom, didn't you finish your own fucking research? Tyukos is a wholly owned subsidiary of Petronus." He slapped his hands together and started walking. "Christ, it's cold here."

Tom quickly collected his thoughts as he fell into step next to Alex. At the next intersection, Alex turned north and began marching up the hill toward a quiet neighborhood that bordered the old downtown. Tom followed with his head down, careful to avoid any muddy snow that threatened to stain his shoes. He glanced over his shoulder once again. "Isn't your friend supposed to be joining us?" he asked casually.

Alex grunted as he walked ahead. "That depends entirely on you."

Tom nodded. It was clear that his brother-in-law was using old-school interrogation techniques to try and frighten him into saying everything he knew, but this was just a façade. Tom had simply supplied Alex with a theory based on available information, and that theory had been proven correct. That was it. The only thing Tom had withheld from Alex was the source of the information that produced the theory. But everyone in the intelligence game, certainly

Alex included, knew that sources were not revealed at the risk of losing their trust—and the information that came with it.

The truth, Tom realized as he followed his brother-in-law through the quiet neighborhood, was that Alex was the one under scrutiny. By putting Kaliningrad on his watch list, Alex had inadvertently put himself on the CIA director's radar, and the director was demanding answers. Now Alex was simply trying to apply the same pressure on Tom that he himself was feeling.

The idea of having his oversized brother-in-law by the testicles brought a smile to Tom's face.

"Who's your source, Tom?" Alex demanded, his voice low and insistent.

"Jesus, is that the tone your director used when he asked you that same question?"

"Answer the question."

"Did it happen to occur to you—maybe somewhere between getting your ass chewed out and jumping on a flight to Flagstaff— that I just might have come up with this on my own?"

"Sure it did," Alex replied as he looked over at Tom with a wry expression. "But we both know you're not that smart. Someone must have helped you."

"Well, I'm smart enough to know that you're the one who will get fucked by this if any more Petronus employees meet an early demise, so you might want to check your attitude. As far as you and the CIA know, I *am* the source."

Alex spun around and glared at him. "Listen to yourself, Tom!" His voice trembled with anger. "Do you have any idea how fucking ridiculous that sounds? No one—and I mean *no one*—could have found a link between these deaths without some kind of inside knowledge. I'd give you the benefit of the doubt if this was just putting a few pieces of the puzzle together, but whatever you stumbled upon here is way beyond that . . . and way out of your fucking league." He leaned over and pressed his index finger into Tom's chest. "You're right, my ass is on the line thanks to you, so stop fucking around and tell me what you know. Family or not, I swear to god this is my last offer to make this easy."

Tom took a step back from Alex and sized him up. He had never seen his brother-in-law in this state of panic before. How much of it, he wondered, was real? Was Alex really in jeopardy, or was this just the act of an experienced agent trying to extort information? He didn't know his brother-in-law well enough to know.

"Okay, Alex, I'll tell you what I know. But it's going to come with conditions."

"Start talking."

Tom turned around and started walking back toward the old downtown. "Do you and your invisible friend mind if we start heading back? It's fucking cold out here."

Alex looked around cautiously before nodding. "Fine."

Tom paced quickly a few steps ahead of Alex, his mind racing. If Alex were to find out the truth—that his source was a handful of letters hanging in an old saloon just a short distance from here— he'd probably arrest Tom just for spite. But he didn't know the truth, and Tom would make sure that it stayed that way. This was *his* investigation, his smoking gun, and most important, his chance to prove to the CIA that he was a worthy member of their agency.

Of course, it wasn't going to be easy. Tom needed to give Alex enough information to act on, but not enough to lose his own leverage or value in the investigation. The obvious challenge was deciding exactly what to tell Alex. Lying to his brother-in-law wasn't an option. Alex would have no qualms with throwing him in jail if he suspected Tom of lying or intentionally misleading him—especially if this was going to be a high-priority CIA investigation. Nor was Alex going to settle for too many vagaries or gaps in the intelligence being provided.

For the second time this evening, Tom was faced with the delicate task of delivering the facts of the story in his favor.

"A few weeks ago, an acquaintance of mine mentioned that a friend had been receiving odd letters from an anonymous man traveling abroad, and asked me to take a look at them."

"What's the nature of the correspondence?" Alex asked, walking a few paces behind Tom.

"Well . . . love letters, essentially, although apparently the recipient, a young local woman, has never had prior contact with the author."

Alex chuckled cynically. "I find that hard to believe."

"So do I, but let's put that aside for a moment. The letters seem to be just rambling confessions of love. No apparent substance or meaning beyond that. The only thing I found particularly curious about them was the author's location. Each letter was written from a different country."

"How many letters?"

"Five so far," Tom said as he glanced over his shoulder. "Would you mind walking next to me? I feel like you've got a fucking gun pointed at me back there."

"Who says I don't?"

"Fuck off, Alex. I don't think my sister would appreciate how much of a prick you're being right now. Does she even know you're here?"

"I hate to say this, Tom, but your sister thinks you're a scumbag. If Jane knew I was here right now, she'd probably tell me to pull the trigger."

"Yeah? Well, that's only because I'm holding a secret over that bitch too. Maybe when you get back home you can ask Jane how many months after you two were engaged she was still fucking her ex-boyfriend."

Tom grinned at the sound of cursing behind him as Alex slipped on the icy pavement. He turned to find his brother-in-law sprawled awkwardly on the sidewalk, his jaw clenched tightly in anger. Tom reached his hand out, but Alex roughly slapped it away. He rose to his feet and gestured for Tom to keep moving.

"I won't even justify that with a response," Alex said, the anger evident in his voice. "Now get to the fucking point and tell me why we're talking about love letters."

"We're talking about love letters because they were written by our suspected terrorist."

Alex looked over at Tom incredulously. "And you have proof of this?"

Tom shook his head. "Come on, Alex, you know I don't have any *proof*, but obviously I found enough circumstantial evidence to get your attention. And you sure as fuck wouldn't be in Flagstaff right now if you didn't believe I was right."

"Maybe," Alex replied. "But you haven't explained how you came up with this. How in the hell did you manage to make a connection between a handful of love letters and the actions of a potential international terrorist in the first place?"

Tom considered the question for a moment before shrugging. "You wouldn't believe me if I told you, Alex. The fact that I have good intuition and some serious investigative skills just doesn't fit with your image of me, so why should I try to convince you otherwise?"

"Try me."

"Okay . . . two things. Like I said, everything about the letters is strange, especially their places of origin. India, the Middle East, Africa, South America, Russia . . . that's a pretty odd pattern of travel for most people. Definitely not places for the faint of heart. And then there's the photos," Tom said as he shook his head. "These weird Polaroid pictures of himself that he sends with each letter, standing in the middle of nowhere. I mean, seriously, who the fuck still carries around an old Polaroid camera?"

"Wait a minute." Alex stopped and grabbed Tom's arm. "You're telling me you have photos of this guy?"

"Well, yes and no. The guy was clever enough to conceal his face in every photo. But from what I could tell, he appears to be a taller-than-average, thirty-something Caucasian with dark brown hair and an athletic build."

"I want those photos, Tom," Alex demanded, leaning toward Tom. "Now."

"We'll come back to that," Tom said, waving his hand dismissively. "Anyway, I was about to discard this whole thing as some kind of strange obsession by a typical stalker type when I decided to check the locations and dates of the letters against criminal reports in the same areas, and *bingo*. That's when everything started falling into place."

They descended back into the old downtown and stopped once again when they reached Aspen Avenue. Tom looked at his brother-in-law expectantly. "Where to now?"

Alex nodded toward Heritage Square. "What else?" he asked as they resumed walking.

"That's about it," Tom replied. "I could give you my notes on the homicides prior to Kaliningrad, but you've probably got more information on those than I do."

"To hell with your notes, I want every fucking photo and scrap of paper this bastard has sent to this 'acquaintance' of yours." Alex shot Tom a suspicious look. "And I want to talk to this woman right away."

"Unfortunately, that's not going to happen. My friend is protective of this woman, to say the least. Not that it matters. Even if he wasn't, she has absolutely no desire to speak to anyone about the situation. Believe me, I've tried. The best I can give you for now is information on the terrorist's location the minute she gets another letter."

"You know that's not good enough, Tom. I need access to the evidence—and her."

"And I'm telling you that you're not going to get it." Tom stopped on the sidewalk and rubbed his gloved hands together. Alex spun and faced him.

"Right, of course. This is where your conditions come in." Alex sighed and looked resignedly up at the sky. "So, what do you want?"

Tom looked up at his brother-in-law's imposing figure and smiled. "You know what I want, Alex."

"For fuck's sake," Alex replied, throwing his arms out in frustration. "How long it is going to take to get this through your thick skull? I can't make you a CIA agent."

"No, but you *can* make me the next best thing," Tom replied cheerfully. "You see, Alex, you're looking at this all wrong. You have to stop seeing me as just your wife's tenacious little brother and start seeing me for what I am."

"And what's that?"

"A distinguished colleague from another terrorist-fighting federal agency with critical information to an investigation that could be career-altering at the very least. That is, if you're granted access to it. And let's not forget, time is running out."

"An investigator for ICE hardly qualifies as distinguished. You're two pay grades above the janitor, Tom."

"I'm an investigator for the Department of Homeland Security," Tom replied defensively. "And a Homeland Security agent acting as a formal consultant to the CIA would certainly go a long way in getting a reexamination of his qualifications. Especially one who's been given Level Two information clearance to what's sure to be one of the biggest cases in the agency."

"You can't be serious."

"Of course I am. Think of it, Alex—two brothers working hand in hand in a cross-agency investigation that ends with another rogue terrorist brought to justice. When the smoke clears and the story breaks, they'll be interviewing us on every prime-time news program in the free world. Then afterward, you'll take a nice promotion in the agency and add another medal to your Captain-fucking-America wall, and I'll quietly become part of the club."

Tom paused and pulled a brand-new tube of lip balm from his pocket. As he methodically covered his lips, he noticed that the snow had stopped falling. He then tucked the used tube in his left pocket as a reminder to throw it away before narrowing his eyes on Alex. "Or you can go back to Langley and try to fabricate a good reason as to why you put Kaliningrad on your watch list. Like you said, it's your ass on the line, not mine."

Alex looked at him coldly. He started to reply, then stopped and lifted his head as something caught his attention. Tom turned and looked. Across the street, Alex's colleague stood under the streetlamp, staring back at them, the shoulders of his black overcoat glistening with melted snow.

"Looks like your ride is here," Tom muttered.

Alex shifted his gaze back to Tom. "One week, Tom. You have one week to produce something solid enough to keep this floating. Otherwise I'll make it my mission to end your career with Homeland Security, not to mention any chance with my agency. Do you understand me?"

"I would expect nothing less from family."

Alex raised his index finger to Tom's face. "One week."

"Aye, aye, captain," Tom quipped with a mocking sneer. "I'll do my part . . . as long as you meet my conditions." He leaned toward Alex and smiled smugly. "I look forward to joining the team, brother."

"You're in way over your head, Tom," Alex replied. He gestured to his colleague across the street and began walking back toward Leroux Street. He was nearly a block away when he suddenly spun on his heels and jogged back to the corner where Tom was standing. "What's his name?"

"I have no idea what his name is," Tom replied. "He's never mentioned it in the letters."

"No, not him," Alex replied, shaking his head irritably. "Jane's ex-boyfriend . . . what was his name?"

"Oh, *him*." Tom seemed to think for a moment, giving Alex a wry grin. "Who knows. It was a long time ago, Alex. But I wouldn't worry about it. I just made that up to fuck with you."

Chapter 27

Hotel Keizersgracht
November 21, 1:12 a.m.
Planet Amsterdam

Jeri—

I've found it! The sister bar to Joe's Last Stand has been unquestionably discovered here in the brackish backstreets of my personal mecca of unbridled self-gluttony, which I affectionately call Amsterdam. It was incredible. I was panhandling for peep-show change on the outskirts of the Rosse Buurt when my nose caught the scent of old oak and genever. Before I knew it, my clog-toting feet were standing at the doorway to a wicked little place called Huppel de Pub. Had it not been for the constant sound of slurred Dutch wafting from the interior, I would have sworn I was standing at the entry to your own enchanted tavern. Three hours later I was practically a regular as I swilled Wambrechies with the bartender and snuggled between the heady warmth of Helga from Rotterdam and Nela from Andorra. The only thing missing from this

little taste of Dutch-wrapped nostalgia was you, mijn
liefde.

Our kids will be gorgeous, on that I bet my life.

And don't worry about the ladies, Jeri-girl. I left the
pub with little cash but nearly all my good propriety intact.
This little holiday of mine will soon be over, but I refuse
to let the whims of my own nether regions interfere
with what has clearly grown between us. Not since the
fiery eyes of a woman named Vida gazed down at me
as she tended to my wounds on the cobbled streets of
Pamplona have I allowed this heart of mine to distend so
unnaturally from my chest. If only I'd known then that
Vida was a gunrunner with the mood swings of a Colombian
drug lord and the mouth of an Italian used-car salesman,
but that's neither here nor there. The point is not to
fret the distance . . . this little ticker's in the bag.

In my usual style, I made fast friends with the
bartender at Huppel de Pub, and he absolutely refuses
to let me leave the city without bestowing a certain
type of blue shirt on him and his crew as part of the
official sister-bar christening. Thus, enclosed is the name
and address along with the necessary loot for three Joe's
T-shirts and a box of those goddamn addictive thin-mint
Girl Scout cookies. Yes, the cookies are for me, Jeri.

Speaking of food, the spekdikken are a far cry from
American pancakes, but the biggest culinary calamity of
this half-nude town has to be frikandel. I was halfway
through this hot-dog-mimicking meat stick when the street
peddler I bought it from mentioned something about
the horse he used to make it. I swear I'll never really
understand people, Jeri, just the box they happen to come
in. Don't order dog.

Ta!

Mysterious Joe's Last Stand Guy

P.S.—Don't be jealous of the picture, honey bunny. Helga and Nela refused to let me snap a solo shot.

P.P.S.—Oh yeah, the address of the bar ... Huppel de Pub, Oudesteeg 15, 1012 Amsterdam. Feel free to send it to the attention of my alter ego, Hubbell Gardner.

Chapter 28

Tom Coleman sat in his office and read the one-page letter again, shaking his head at his luck. His eyes paused once more on the final sentence of the last paragraph, the grin on his face deepening as the full meaning of the words soaked in. He then carefully refolded the page along its original crease lines and slipped it back into the certified envelope it was delivered in before gently tucking it into the top drawer of his desk. Satisfied, he quickly grabbed the antibacterial lotion and rubbed it on his hands before closing the drawer.

The grin was still stretched across Tom's face as he stared at the tall stack of case files sitting on his desk. The normal sense of loathing he felt when looking at the files was gone this morning, lifted like a dull weight that had been hanging from his shoulders. He was still enjoying this cathartic feeling of victory when someone knocked on his door.

"Come in," Tom replied as he tidied up the stack in front of him. A handsome, dark-haired man stepped into his office and smiled.

"How's it going, Tom?"

Tom's grin immediately vanished as he glanced up at the handsome face of Agent Rick Martin. He leaned back in his chair and nodded. "Good, Rick. You?"

"Great, man," Rick replied, nodding in return. "Just wanted to stop by. Haven't talked to you in a while."

"Yeah, well, you know how it goes," Tom said, gesturing at the case files on his desk. "Hardly enough time in the day as it is."

"I hear you, man," Rick replied as he glanced around the cramped office with a smug grin. "This undercover ops stuff is just crazy. I'm working with the Tucson agents on some seriously fucked-up shit right now. Drug trafficking, prostitution—fuck, you name it." He sighed and shook his head dramatically.

"Just wrapped up a huge one yesterday. Big weapons-trafficking deal coming out of Nogales. You should have fucking seen it, Tom. We hit this hotel over in Prescott in full ops gear. I'm talking assault rifles, bulletproof vests, helmets—*everything*. Four of us smashed in the door and took down three of those stupid fuckers. It was fucking crazy. These guys must've had two thousand guns cached up in their truck. Guns, ammo . . . fuckers even had a grenade launcher. Can you even believe that? Talk about adrenaline, man. I thought my fucking heart was going to explode! Huge deal, though. Careerwise it's huge too. Heard I might even get a commendation or something, but whatever. It's just good to be doing the *real* work now, you know what I mean?" He paused and looked at Tom. "But enough about me, man . . . how're you doing?"

Tom stared at Agent Martin for a moment before shrugging. "Great . . . just great. Busy with the usual types of cases . . . the *unreal* work, as you might call it."

"Ha! Totally!" Rick replied as he slapped his hands and laughed awkwardly. "But hey, man, somebody's got to do it, you know?"

"Yeah, I know."

"Okay, well, hey . . . I've got to get out of here, but it was great to see you, man."

Tom recoiled in disgust as Agent Martin reached his hand over Tom's desk. "Oh, no . . . trust me . . . you don't want to shake my hand," he replied, shaking his head. "I'm fighting a pretty nasty cold right now."

"Oh, shit, thanks, man," Rick replied, withdrawing his hand. "Yeah, hell no, I don't want to catch something. Got another big op in two days. Should be a good one. All right, Tom, I'll see you, man."

Tom waved a single finger in good-bye as the young agent turned and slipped through the door. *Fucking idiot*, he thought as he shook his head. *And to think he's climbing the promotion ladder faster than me.* Tom grinned as he again thought of the letter in his top drawer. *But not anymore.* He was just beginning to open the drawer to peek at the letter when someone again knocked on the door.

"Who is it?" Tom asked gruffly.

Instead of a response, Tom looked up to see a tall, thin man with a retreating crop of red hair quickly step into his office.

"Mind if I take a few minutes of your time, Agent Coleman?" the man asked as he closed the door behind him. His baritone voice inflected the question in a manner that assumed the answer was "no."

"Oh—no, not at all, Director Preston," Tom stammered as he pointed at the chair across from his small desk. He cleared the surprise from his throat as Division Director Jack Preston sat down and placed the manila folder he was carrying on his lap. He then fixed his dark green eyes on Tom.

"How can I help you, Director?" Tom asked earnestly.

"I'm not entirely sure," Preston replied without smiling. Tom felt his body grow tense as the fifty-two-year-old executive associate director of Homeland Security and head of ICE Western Region Operations opened the folder and briefly scanned the contents before focusing his gaze back on Tom. "I just got out of a briefing with HSI Director Connolly in Washington, and, well, Tom, it seems I'm caught in rather unusual circumstances for my position."

Preston closed the folder and placed it on his lap, then silently examined his hands.

Tom swallowed hard as he stared back at the director. The mention of Connolly and the HSI, short for Homeland Security Investigations, made it clear where the nature of this conversation was heading. The HSI was the primary investigative and intelligence-gathering arm of ICE, and unquestionably the most clandestine. Publicly, the HSI's mission was to investigate everything from smuggling and human rights violations to cybercrime and the security of the nation's infrastructure. Internally, everyone knew that Richard Connolly's appointment as HSI's executive associate director was gained through a fanatical focus on one thing—uncovering and destroying anything that remotely smelled of terrorist activity on American soil. It was widely known that Connolly, a former agent of the NSA, had deep connections with the CIA, the FBI, and of course, the NSA. Connolly also made no attempt to hide the fact he was zealously trying to remold HSI in the image of the NSA— and was stepping heavily on the toes of the other federal agencies in the process. Tom knew it wouldn't take Connolly long to find out if any high-level investigations in the other agencies were linked to his own neck of the woods.

Now, six days after Tom's conversation with his brother-in-law, it seemed Connolly had already caught wind of something connected to Homeland Security's ICE division and sent Preston here to sniff it out.

"I'm not sure I follow you, Director," Tom replied.

Preston narrowed his green eyes on Tom. "I'm actually quite sure you do, Tom," he replied. "You see, Director Connolly just briefed me on a memo he received yesterday from the CIA. The memo stated that someone in our very own Flagstaff Field Office would be immediately receiving investigative privileges and, oh, what was it—"

The director glanced down at the open folder and ran his finger down the page. "Ah, yes, Level Two clearance in a top-priority investigation currently under way." He closed the folder and smiled at Tom. "My oh my, Tom . . . that's pretty serious stuff. Last I heard the CIA doesn't hand out Level Two clearance unless someone has a pretty important role to play, wouldn't you agree?"

Tom shifted uncomfortably in his chair. "Yes sir . . . absolutely."

"I mean, hell," Preston continued, giving Tom the slightest hint of a smile, "I don't think even *I* could get that kind of clearance, and I've been doing this dance for nearly three decades now. So I'm sure you can imagine my surprise when Director Connolly informed me that one of my own was getting special treatment from the boys in Langley." Preston leaned forward in his chair. "And when he told me it was an ICE agent named Tom Coleman, well, I have to admit . . . I just about spit my coffee across the room."

Tom smiled back at the director.

"So," Preston continued, leaning back in his chair, "I figured the best thing to do was to come down here to have a little chat about this unusual situation with the one man who can surely explain it to me. After all, I like to think that the members of this department work together like a family. You know, all of us working for the same cause and watching out for each other's interests. At the end of the day, this department is like any other family—it simply cannot function without trust. Do you see my point, Agent Coleman?"

Tom nodded as he listened to the obvious trap the director was laying for him. "I certainly do, Director," he responded. "And I absolutely agree that trust is a key part of any department or organization." He slowly laid his hands on his desk. "That's why I took the CIA's request very seriously when they approached me and asked me to be a part of this investigation. I knew this would put me in a very difficult position, especially given my loyalty to the Department of Homeland Security, sir."

Tom watched as a brief look of confusion crossed Preston's face. He could see that his statement had just sent a wrecking ball through the director's intended strategy for getting him to talk.

"I'm sorry, Tom," Preston replied as he shifted in his chair. "Did you say the CIA approached *you?*"

"Yes sir. Six days ago, to be exact. Special Agent Alex Murstead, who as you may know also happens to be my brother-in-law, called to inform me he was in Flagstaff and needed to meet with me immediately."

Tom caught a flash of irritation in Preston's eyes at the mention of his brother-in-law. He had little doubt that the director knew of the family connection, and even less doubt that the smug prick was hoping to use it as leverage to get information. Whatever ammunition Preston had brought to use against him, Tom knew the man had very little left.

"And what was the nature of your meeting?" Preston asked.

"We discussed a new case that my brother-in-law is overseeing. Based on some recent information that has come to light, Alex— excuse me—*Special Agent Murstead*—believed I could be very useful in the investigation."

"I see," the director said, his stare fixed menacingly on Tom. "But why would Agent Murstead be under the impression that you could add insight into a high-priority federal investigation that warrants Level Two access? Is it because you were the one who first brought this information to him?"

Tom sat in his chair pretending to consider the questions seriously. His initial apprehension over the director's unexpected visit had now vanished. It was clear that Preston and his counterpart, Connolly, were just fishing for information. And the fact that the executive associate director of Homeland Security was sitting in Tom's cramped, first-floor office was an obvious indication they had almost nothing. Tom gazed back at Preston somberly, wondering if the man had any cards left to play.

"With all due respect, Director, I'm afraid I can't say."

Preston rested his head in his hand and glared at Tom, his index finger tapping a measured rhythm against his freckled temple. After a few moments, a smile slowly stretched across his face. "And why is that, Tom?" he asked plaintively.

"Well, as you said, sir, it's a classified investigation. You of all people understand the need for securing information when it comes to investigating matters of terrorism."

The director's finger abruptly stopped. "And just what the hell do you think *this* agency does, Agent Coleman? Detain a few illegals at the border and call it a day? Are we not as much on the front lines of fighting terrorism as the CIA? Or are you implying that Director Connolly and I are incapable of managing sensitive information in a terrorist investigation that directly deals with the safety and security of this country?"

Tom raised his hands apologetically.

"No sir, I—"

"Don't interrupt me when I'm talking!" Preston shouted. He glared at Tom with an expression of raw anger before leaning back in his chair. "You know, Tom, it's no secret to anyone around here that you've got a hard-on for the CIA. I'm well aware of your recent attempt to join *the Company*, and I have no doubt your brother-in-law has been involved in helping you to do just that." His lips curled upward into a malicious smile. "So why don't you spare us all the normal bullshit and tell me—the regional director of the agency you actually work for—exactly what the hell is going on here?"

Tom smiled meekly at Preston as he opened the top drawer of his desk. "I understand your desire for answers, Director. I sincerely do," he said as he pulled out the letter he'd received earlier that morning and slid it across the desk. "Unfortunately, the CIA doesn't share that opinion."

Preston leaned forward and snatched the letter from Tom's desk. Tom watched as he read, smiling contentedly as the director's expression quickly transformed from curiosity to concealed astonishment. When he was done, Preston tossed the letter back on Tom's desk and locked his hands together thoughtfully.

"Anything else I can do for you, Jack?" Tom asked earnestly.

Preston shook his head as he collected his folder and stood up to leave. "It seems I misjudged you, Agent Coleman," he said quietly. "I thought you were a part of this family, but obviously I was mistaken. I also believed you were a patriot who put his country above all else, but apparently I was mistaken about that as well. I suppose that's just how these things go sometimes . . . we don't know the true mettle of a man until he's faced with tough choices. Oh well." The director walked to the door, then turned and looked at Tom. "Best of luck with your investigation, and be sure to make a good impression with those boys at Langley. After all, I doubt there'll be much use for a man with your *independent mentality* around here when this is done." He was almost through the door when he paused and glared at Tom once more.

"Oh, and Tom . . . don't ever call me Jack again."

Tom ignored the sound of the door slamming shut as it echoed through his small office. He grabbed the letter from his desk and once again smiled at the bright blue crest of the Central Intelligence Agency emblazoned at the top. As he read the crisp official words that had been sent from the office of Agent Alex Murstead, a rush of exhilaration returned once again.

Agent Coleman,

As granted by National Security Directive NSC 32-234, this letter is to inform you that, effective immediately, you are ordered to suspend all activities associated with your current duties within the Office of Immigration and Customs Enforcement in order to assist with a matter of priority with this agency. You are immediately directed to contact the liaison to the Special Activities Division listed below for further instruction and to initiate your participation in this matter.

Furthermore, no information beyond the order of this directive is permitted to be shared with any individual, officer, or agency outside of the Special Activities Division of this agency. Failure to comply with this order is subject to criminal prosecution.

The ring of Tom's cell phone interrupted him. He glanced down at the screen at an unfamiliar number. After a brief hesitation, he grabbed the phone and quickly slapped it to his ear.

"Agent Coleman."

"Tom," a low, gravelly voice replied. "It's your deputy."

"Who is this?" Tom asked impatiently.

"It's Chip, Tom. Chip Shepherd. Christ, didn't they teach you how to recognize a person's voice in that outfit?"

Tom ignored the question as the older man chuckled quietly on the other end of the line. "I'm very busy, Chip. What's up?"

"You asked me to call you if something came up with the . . . well, you know . . . situation. And something's come up."

"What have you got?"

A long pause followed before Chip coughed nervously and spoke quietly into the phone. "Is this really something you want to talk about over the phone?"

Tom realized that at that very moment Jack Preston was storming back to his office to dial up Director Connolly and detail him on their conversation. God only knew what Connolly would ask Preston to do to get information—including a tap on his office phone.

"Good point," Tom answered. "How about I meet you for a drink?"

"Fine," Chip replied. "You know where to find me."

Chapter 29

"What do you mean, 'nonresponsive'?" the gruff, Southern-accented voice of HSI Director Richard Connolly asked angrily.

Jack Preston sat on the large leather couch in the center of his rarely used Flagstaff office with his cell phone pressed to his ear. "I mean he refused to give me anything," he replied defensively.

"Did you threaten him?"

Preston rolled his eyes. "This isn't the NSA, Richard, and it sure as hell isn't like the old days. You and I both know if I even lifted a finger at someone around here, the OPR would be crawling up my ass within twenty-four hours. No, I didn't threaten him. I tried very hard to persuade him."

Connolly sighed loudly into the phone. "Perhaps I haven't properly conveyed the importance of getting that son of a bitch to talk, Jack. If those assholes at Langley circumvent our authority on another investigation, the last thing you're going to be worrying about is the proper treatment of a field agent. Congress is already bleeding us dry with budget cuts, and now the crickets inside the Beltway are beginning to question the very value of the Department of Homeland Security." He paused for a brief bout of coughing before speaking angrily. "It's time for some aggressive tactics, Jack. We need a *win*—but we're never going to get one if our own goddamn agents keep running to the CIA every time they have something, are we?"

"No, Richard, I suppose we aren't."

"Then what are you prepared to do about this situation?"

Preston paused for a moment before responding.

"I'm prepared to go beyond persuasion."

"Then do it," Connolly growled. "And do it soon. Time is running out."

"I'm fully aware of that, Richard."

Preston hung up and cursed under his breath. *Fucking Connolly,* he thought as he grabbed his mug from the table in front of him and threw back the last cold slug of coffee. The HSI director was a cynical relic of the Cold War who still believed covert, aggressive tactics were the best means to solve problems.

Unfortunately, in this case he was probably right.

Preston walked over to the large desk in the corner of his office and once again flipped through the personnel file for Agent Tom Coleman. As before, nothing in the file stood out. The thirty-four-year-old investigative specialist had a fairly typical profile for a Homeland Security agent—military veteran, police veteran, average intelligence, recently divorced. The only noteworthy blemish on Coleman's record was a citation for an off-duty incident that resulted in his voluntary resignation from the Phoenix PD, but even that wasn't uncommon. Otherwise his record indicated nothing more than what Preston had already surmised—Coleman was a competent but entirely mediocre investigator with illusions of CIA grandeur. And yet this mediocre agent had managed to find something that had the CIA's full attention. Something significant enough to give him Level Two clearance on a priority investigation and, perhaps even more infuriating, a smug attitude of secrecy toward his own director.

Preston closed the personnel file and shook his head in anger. There was only one thing left to do. *Aggressive tactics*, he thought irritably as he picked up his cell phone and quickly scrolled through his long list of contacts. When he reached the number of a contact listed simply as "Austin," he immediately hit the "Call" button.

"Hello?" a timid, nasal voice answered.

"Eugene. It's Jack Preston."

"Oh, hey, happy holidays, Jack!" the voice exclaimed cheerfully. "What's up?"

"I've got a new project that requires immediate attention," Preston replied tersely. "I want full collection on this one. Physical, electronic . . . the whole works. How soon can you be available?"

"Um . . . well . . . how about this afternoon?" the voice responded, cracking with enthusiasm.

"Fine," Preston said. "No later than two. The subject will be leaving from this location. I'll e-mail a bio over in a few minutes. Just make sure you call me once you're up and running. I'll want an hourly report on everything that's happening—understood?"

"You got it. Anything else?"

"Yeah," Jack replied, his voice low. "If you fuck this one up, consider it the last paying job you'll ever get from the largest client you'll ever have. Am I clear?"

"Yeah, okay . . . sure," the nasal voice replied with alarm. "I understand. Don't worry, Jack."

"All I do is worry," Preston replied irritably. "Remember . . . hourly reports." He hung up his cell phone and tossed it on his desk before picking up his office phone. He punched the number for his assistant in Phoenix.

"Good morning, Director Preston," an attractive female voice answered.

"Good morning, Amy," Preston replied. "Look, change of plans—I'm not returning to the Phoenix office today after all. Can you arrange for some lunch to be brought up for me here in the Flagstaff office?"

"Of course, sir. I'll call Julie and have her take care of it. Julie is your assistant at the Flagstaff office."

"Julie?" Preston asked. "Is she the heavyset girl with the fake red hair?"

"I'm not sure, sir. I haven't actually met her. Is there anything else I can help you with?"

"Yes, there is. Call Supervisor Michaels in this office and tell him I want two things. First, I want the name of the best field agent in the Flagstaff office. Second, I want to know the exact moment Agent Tom Coleman leaves for the day. Make it clear to him that these requests stay between the two of us, understood?"

"Yes sir. I'll contact him now."

"Thanks, Amy."

Preston opened his briefcase and grabbed his morning security briefing. He flipped through it, absently scanning the latest status updates on pending investigations. A few minutes later his office phone rang.

"Jack Preston."

"Hi, Director," Amy replied. "I spoke to Supervisor Michaels, and he would recommend Agent Rick Martin in Undercover Operations for any special projects you may need assistance with, sir."

"Very good. Anything else?"

"Yes sir. He also asked me to inform you that he just checked, and apparently Agent Coleman has already left for the day."

"Okay, thanks."

Preston barely slammed the phone down before a stream of expletives erupted from his lips.

Chapter 30

"So what are you going to write, Jeri?"

Chip asked the question with an anxious smile on his face as Jeri thumbed through a book at her corner seat behind the bar. She glanced up at him with an annoyed expression.

"What are you talking about, Chip?" she asked.

"Your pen pal. What are you going to write to him? You weren't planning on sending a package without including a letter, were you?"

Jeri stood up and tossed the book on the counter. She looked out the front window of the saloon at the maple trees that stood along the sidewalk. A tattered blanket of snow sat on their stark, gray-brown branches as they swayed against a constant midday wind. Even from the warm interior of Joe's, the view made her shudder with cold.

"I haven't really thought about it," she answered quietly.

Chip raised his eyebrows as his hand stroked the beer in front of him. "Somehow I find that hard to believe."

"Well, if it's that important to you," Jeri said as she turned away from the window, "why don't you just write him for me?"

Chip started to respond when the front door of the saloon groaned open and a short, stocky figure walked in. The man closed the heavy door behind him before pulling a small disposable wipe cloth from his jacket with his gloved hand and meticulously cleaning the tops of his shoes. Satisfied, he stood and carefully dropped the soiled wipe into a nearby wastebasket. As he took off his winter cap, Jeri noticed the buzzed haircut and immediately recognized the man named Tom who'd become something of a regular in the last few weeks. She looked over at Chip and slowly shook her head.

"We'll talk about this later."

Jeri poured a beer from the tap and placed it in front of Tom as he sat down next to Chip. Heading back to her corner, she grabbed her book and slipped quietly onto her stool, pretending to read as the two men exchanged greetings and began talking in low, muted voices. Curious, she glanced repeatedly at Chip, but he was too engaged in the conversation to notice.

A few minutes later, after reading the same page on global supply chain management for a fourth time, Jeri grudgingly accepted that her mind was focused on a different subject. She glanced once again at Chip before flipping through her book to a spot where the pages were separated by a thick object. Jeri gazed at the airmail envelope jammed into the crease of the book, its familiar blue-and-red-striped edges standing out vividly against the black text of the book's pages. The top of the envelope was torn open, revealing the shiny white edge of the Polaroid that had come with the letter.

Jeri slipped the photo from the envelope and discreetly held it against the open page of her book. She studied it closely again.

In the photo were three people sitting in what appeared to be a dimly lit bar. In the center, a familiar figure with short, curly dark hair smiled broadly, his tanned face further darkened by the shadow of a day-old beard. Were she able to see them, Jeri imagined two large intelligent eyes staring back at her. Instead, the man's large hands were pressed playfully over his face, covering everything but his mouth. On each side of him sat two women, both laughing wildly at the camera, one with long brunette hair and the other with short, bright red curls. But what Jeri noticed more was what the two women had in common—both appeared to be at least in their late fifties. She smiled as she once again examined their gestures. The woman on the left sat with her hands cupped over her mouth, the other with a hand over each ear. Together, the threesome completed a clumsy rendition of the age-old proverb—

See no evil, hear no evil, speak no evil.

As she stared at the photo, a single nagging question played repeatedly through Jeri's mind, tugging her mouth into a concentrating frown.

What was she going to write?

===

Tom Coleman could barely contain his anxiety.

Within minutes of getting Chip's call, he'd slipped inconspicuously out of the ICE offices and driven directly to see the older man. Or nearly directly. After his conversation with Jack Preston, he'd taken the extra precaution of turning onto side streets and watching the traffic behind him to make sure he wasn't being followed. Once he was downtown, Tom had parked his car several blocks from the saloon and taken a back-alley route to the entrance. The only mishap during the trip had been at the end, when he'd stepped into an unseen pothole in the alley that had left a disgusting layer of filth on his normally spotless leather shoes. Nevertheless, Tom was in high spirits as he strolled into the dark, warm interior of Joe's Last Stand Saloon. Now, as he sat down at his usual spot next to Chip, Tom suppressed his restlessness and took a quick drink of the beer that Jeri had poured for him.

"You certainly made good time," Chip commented.

"I got the impression this was important," Tom replied. He quickly glanced around the room and noticed that the saloon was practically empty. Only two other men sat at the far end of the bar, both middle-aged professor-types. Jeri, aloof as always, had already settled into her corner and was now engrossed in a thick book.

Chip sat up straight on his barstool and rubbed his eyes with exhaustion, then glanced over at Tom. "Could be," he said with a neutral expression, his blue eyes blinking into focus. "But of course, I'll leave that up to you and your vast expertise."

"Did Jeri get another letter?" Tom asked, ignoring the sarcasm.

Chip nodded slowly. "Came in the mail this morning. Apparently he's in Europe." He paused and took a drink. "Amsterdam, to be specific."

"Is it up yet?" Tom asked, looking toward the far corner of the room where the rest of the letters and pictures were hung.

"Not yet," Chip replied. "Jeri still has it."

Tom glanced briefly over at Jeri before nodding. "So what's in this new letter that was important enough to bring me down here?"

"We'll talk about that in a minute," Chip replied. He rested his elbows on the bar and gazed at Tom with a somber expression, his blue eyes narrowing suspiciously. "But first, I have a few questions of my own."

Tom gave him a blank look. "Questions about what?"

"The investigation," Chip replied.

"The *investigation*?" Tom repeated, chuckling. "What the hell are you talking about, Chip? You know that's not how this works. I'm the one in charge of asking the questions around here—not you." He shook his head irritably and took a long drink of his beer. Between his brother-in-law and Jack Preston, Tom now had two separate agencies breathing down his neck—which meant the clock was ticking. Every hour that passed increased the chances of one if not both of them crawling up his ass and finding the real source of his information. And if that happened, he knew it would spell the end of his career in *any* agency. Whatever had caused the change of heart in the man next to him, Tom didn't have the time or patience to deal with it right now.

"Oh, really?" Chip said, gazing at Tom intently. "Is that how this works? Because I distinctly remember you asking for my help in this matter. But perhaps I was wrong. In fact, perhaps I should just walk over to Jeri and tell her what's going on here."

"Okay, fine . . . fine," Tom conceded, raising his hands in surrender. "What do you want to know?"

"The other day when you showed me your business card, I happened to notice your title—*Investigative Specialist*. I'm not sure why, but I decided to look into it a little bit. No offense, Tom, but that's not exactly a high-level position for a Homeland Security agent, especially for one heading up a terrorist investigation. So it got me to thinking." Chip paused as his face eased into a slight grin. "What's this low-level Homeland Security agent *really* doing here? And if this is such an important investigation, why isn't this place crawling with agents?" He picked up his beer. "So those are my questions, Tom. Would you care to fill me in?"

Tom sat stoically and considered his response. From the corner of his eye, he noticed Jeri glance in their direction.

"All right, you want the truth?" Tom said quietly. "Here's the truth." He took a long drink of his beer and turned toward the older man. "There was no investigation of any kind surrounding these deaths before I walked in here and saw those letters. I pieced this whole thing together on my own. I'm the one who did the research and connected the dots. I'm the one who figured out this guy is some kind of corporate terrorist. And you know what?" Tom leaned in toward the older man. "I was *right*."

"How do you know for sure?" Chip asked.

"I took a gamble," Tom replied. "I told a contact inside the CIA about the first three incidents. I told him what I thought was happening. Then I told him if I was right, something was going to happen in the location of the fourth letter—in Kaliningrad."

"And?"

"A researcher was killed at a Petronus-owned research facility in Kaliningrad eight days ago."

"Good lord," Chip replied, shaking his head. "Okay, so now everyone knows you were right about this guy. But that still doesn't answer my second question. If this is a real investigation, where are all your friends?" He pointed his thumb toward the shrine of letters and photos. "And why are those still hanging on the wall instead of being analyzed in a crime lab somewhere?"

Tom's mouth curled into a slight grin. "Because I haven't told anyone my source for this information."

Chip looked at him curiously. "And why would that be, Tom?"

"Let's just say I have something to prove to a few people," Tom replied. "But that's nothing you need to worry about. The good news is that this place isn't going to be crawling with agents anytime soon—unless you'd prefer otherwise." He narrowed his eyes on Chip. "Would you rather see Joe's Last Stand turned into a federal circus show?"

"No, I wouldn't," the older man replied.

"Good. Neither would I," Tom agreed. "So, have I answered all your questions now?"

Chip nodded slowly. "See, all you had to do was be honest with me," he replied, taking a slug of his beer. He rested his glass on the bar and looked at Tom gloomily. "Actually, I still have one more question, but I don't think you can answer it."

"What is it?" Tom asked.

"Jeri," Chip replied, fidgeting with his beer. "Why her? Of all the places and people this guy could have picked, why did he pick this one? Why did he pick Jeri?"

Tom shrugged. "I'll tell you why. At some point in the recent past, this guy walked in here and noticed the hot bartender serving drinks, and he wanted to get her attention. But of course, being like most terrorists, when it comes down to it he's nothing more than a gutless coward. It's probably easier for this asshole to plant an explosive device in someone's kitchen than it is to speak face-to-face with an attractive woman. So what does he do? He buys one of those ugly goddamn T-shirts and starts writing Jeri when he isn't busy killing Petronus scientists. He probably figures there's nothing to lose. After all, what are the odds that someone's going to take notice of some stupid love letters written to some girl in Flagstaff, right? That's it. End of story. The truth is that shit like this happens all the time, Chip. Not everything is done with a plan. And you and I both know that even smart guys make stupid mistakes. Assuming this guy even *is* smart."

Chip suppressed a sudden laugh. Tom paused and gave him a questioning look. "What . . . are you going to tell me you have a better theory?"

"No, not at all," Chip replied quietly. "If I were a terrorist and wanted a good-looking woman to notice me, I suppose I'd do the same thing. You know . . . buy a T-shirt, fly around the world, and drop her an occasional letter. I'd say that theory is as solid as they come."

Tom nodded impatiently and looked at his watch. "Right, okay. Look, Chip, I don't have much time. Can we get back to the reason you called me down here?"

"Sure." Chip drained the last of his beer and cleared his throat before leaning toward Tom. "Well, as I said earlier, the guy is apparently in Amsterdam right now. He mentioned that he's on a bit of a holiday, and that he's found a bar there that reminds him of this place. Other than that, the rest of the letter was mostly his usual nonsense." Chip paused and shot a quick glance at Jeri, then gave Tom a conspiratorial grin. "But there was one thing unique about this letter."

Tom leaned toward him eagerly. "What?"

"He asked Jeri to send him some Joe's Last Stand Saloon T-shirts for the guys at the bar over there. Which means—"

"Which means he included an address," Tom interjected, a grin slowly growing on his face.

Chip nodded. "It also means he'll be hanging around there for a little while."

"I need that address, Chip," Tom said quietly. His eyes drifted over to Jeri. "We don't have much time."

Chip seemed to ignore him as he stared at the empty beer glass in front of him. A moment later he reached into his shirt pocket and pulled out a small handwritten note. "I figured you would," he muttered, laying it on the counter. "I wrote it down when Jeri wasn't paying attention."

Tom glanced down and read the quickly scrawled text.

Huppel de Pub
Attn: Hubbell Gardner
Oudesteeg 15
1012 PT Amsterdam

Hotel Keizersgracht

"Hubbell Gardner?" Tom mumbled as his brow furrowed in confusion. "What the hell kind of name is that?"

"I hear it's a popular name for terrorists these days," Chip replied sarcastically. "And before you ask, the second name is the hotel he wrote the letter from. I assume he's staying there until he leaves. Either way, that should be more than enough information for a top-notch team of federal agents to find him, right, Tom?"

Tom stared at the address, shaking his head in agreement. He pulled out his notepad and jotted down the information, tucked his pad back into his pocket, and turned to Chip. "This is turning out to be a helluva good day for me," he said, giving him a broad smile. "And it's all thanks to you."

Chip shrugged. "You can thank me later when this mess is done. I've already made it clear why I'm doing this."

Tom nodded and glanced at the far corner behind the counter. There, still perched on top of her barstool, Jeri sat engrossed in her book.

"What the hell is she reading, anyway?" he asked as he stood to leave.

"A book on global trade, I believe," Chip replied dryly without looking over. "In case you didn't notice when you did your extensive background check on her, Jeri has a master's degree in economics."

"Really?" Tom said as he zipped up his jacket. "Beauty and brains, huh? Well, good for her." He put on his gloves and extended his hand to Chip. "I owe you big for this, Chip," he said earnestly.

The older man smiled and shook his hand. "Good luck, Tom. I look forward to hearing how everything turns out in Amsterdam."

"I'm afraid I won't be able to talk about it," Tom replied. "Operational stuff like that is classified. But don't worry, we'll get him."

Chip's pale blue eyes watched him closely as he nodded. "I have no doubt that you will."

———

Agent Rick Martin opened the door of the director's third-floor office and confidently stepped inside. "You wanted to see me, sir?"

Preston looked up from his latest briefing and studied the tall, handsome agent standing in front of him. "Agent Martin?"

"Yes sir."

"Have a seat, Agent," Preston said, pointing at the chair across from his desk. He watched as the young agent swaggered over and sat down. "I understand you're currently working in Undercover Operations. Is that correct?"

"Yes sir," Agent Martin replied.

"That can be pretty risky work at times, can't it?"

"Depends on the assignment, sir," Agent Martin answered matter-of-factly. "Most are pretty low-key. But we do get a good adrenaline rush from time to time."

"And you enjoy that?" Preston asked. "The adrenaline rush?"

Agent Martin eyed the director curiously. "Yes sir, I do."

Preston nodded. "Good." He closed the briefing folder in front of him and leaned back in his chair. "I'm sure an agent working undercover ops like yourself understands that protecting this country can sometimes require unconventional tactics to get the job done."

"Absolutely, sir."

"Tactics an average agent might be unable or even unwilling to use," Preston continued, watching Martin carefully.

Agent Martin shrugged. "Well, I don't consider myself an average agent, sir."

"That's why you're sitting in my office," Preston replied. He spun his chair around and stared absently out the window. "I might have an assignment that would require an agent with exceptional talent to do whatever it takes to get the job done. No paperwork, just my direct orders. That means complete trust on both sides of the table." He turned and fixed his dark green eyes on Martin. "Does that sound like something you'd be interested in, Agent Martin?"

Agent Martin leaned forward in his chair. "Would this assignment have a high probability of adrenaline, sir?"

Preston nodded.

Agent Martin smiled. "Then yes sir. Very much so, sir."

Chapter 31

Eugene Austin sat behind the wheel of his mother's maroon Toyota Corolla and stared out at the quiet neighborhood on the northeast edge of town. The neighborhood, a mixture of duplex homes and small '30s-era bungalows, appeared to be in a state of decline, and Eugene again checked the locks on the doors of the parked sedan before settling back into the seat. He then turned up the volume on the new rap album he was blasting into his headphones.

The clock on his iPhone read 4:23 p.m.—almost six hours since he'd gotten the call from Jack Preston urgently requesting his services on a new case. Preston had given Eugene some "top priority" shadow gigs before, but he'd never sounded as impatient or anxious as he did with this one. Nor had he ever been so threatening. *If you fuck this one up, consider it the last paying job you'll ever get from the largest client you'll ever have.* Eugene shook his head with bewilderment.

The last few rays of winter sun were just beginning to slip behind the rooftops when a car matching the description he'd been given turned onto the street. *Finally*, he thought with a mix of excitement and relief. Preston had called Eugene at noon to tell him that the target had left his office before expected and would have to be acquired at his home. Now, after several hours of mind-numbing boredom, Eugene pulled the long bangs of dark hair away from his acne-blemished face and watched as the vehicle slowly drove up the street and turned into the driveway across from him. He quickly eased his seat back until his body wasn't visible, then reached over and flipped a small electronic switch.

On the backseat, the green power light of the listening device pointed at Tom Coleman's house glowed to life.

=====

Tom stood inside the entryway of his home and patiently removed his gloves, jacket, and shoes. He started to place his shoes in their proper spot on the mat in the entryway, but remembered the mud puddle he had stepped in earlier and realized they needed to be thoroughly cleaned. He walked into the kitchen and grabbed a plastic bucket from under the sink, then unwrapped a new cleaning sponge. He was just starting to put on rubber gloves when his cell phone began to buzz. Tom looked at the caller's name on the screen and smiled as he brought it to his ear.

"Alex," he said warmly. "Thanks for returning my message so promptly."

"Cut the shit, Tom," Alex replied brusquely. "What have you got?"

"Something important," Tom said as he tossed the rubber gloves onto the kitchen counter and walked into his living room. He stopped at the window and briefly scanned the quiet neighborhood.

"Let's hear it."

"I have new information on our guy," Tom said as his eyes narrowed on a maroon sedan parked across the street. He'd never noticed the vehicle parked on his street before, but there was nothing particularly suspicious about it. Plus it looked to be empty. He held his stare for a moment longer then walked over to the couch and sat down.

"Okay then, give it to me," Alex replied tersely.

"I will, but first I want to thank you for the letter. I have to say, that was one helluva way to be recruited into the CIA. I don't think I've ever felt so needed in my entire life."

"I didn't write it, our legal department did. Now please tell me something that will make that letter worth everyone's time."

Tom could hear the irritation rising in his brother-in-law's voice. "Well," he replied, "it was still a great letter. It even left the regional director speechless when he came into my office this morning sniffing around for information." He paused expectantly. "Anyway . . ."

"What the hell are you talking about, Tom?" Alex asked, the alarm apparent in his voice. "Jack Preston came to see you today?"

"Yep, first thing. He walked in and said he and Director Connolly were aware that I was involved in something with the CIA. He said I needed to let them in on it."

"And what did you tell him?" Alex demanded, his voice descending into a low growl.

"Absolutely nothing," Tom replied matter-of-factly. "I handed him your letter, and that was it. He read it and left."

"Good . . . let's keep it that way. And the next time Preston or that goddamn idiot Connolly even so much as sniffs in your direction, you let me know. Do you understand?"

"I understand," Tom responded. "Of course, Preston made it pretty clear that assisting the CIA with this case was seriously jeopardizing my current career with ICE and Homeland Security."

"What's your point?"

"Oh, nothing," Tom said dismissively. "I just hope you've got more than a letter to back me up if this tug-of-war between our two agencies gets ugly."

"I look after the people who look after me, Tom," Alex replied tersely. "Now, what have you got?"

"I have the name of the hotel where our target is currently

staying," Tom replied. "I also have the name and address of the local pub where he's hanging out. Apparently he requested a care package from my source."

"What kind of care package?"

"Nothing you need to worry about. Anyway, assuming a minor condition is agreed upon, I would be happy to share it with you now." Tom listened as his brother-in-law exhaled resignedly on the other end of the line.

"And what condition is that?"

Tom smiled. "You may not believe this, Alex, but I've never actually been to Langley during the holiday season."

"So?"

"So I want to be there when the action happens," Tom replied. "You know, to witness the fruits of my labor. After all, I'm a part of the CIA family now. It just wouldn't make sense for the man responsible for this victory not to be there for the big finale. When this shit goes down, I want to see it."

"I'll give it some serious consideration, Tom," Alex replied derisively. "Now give me the fucking intel."

"That's not how this works, Alex. Give me what I want, and I'll tell you what I know. Otherwise I'd be happy to just call your European field office with this information."

Tom's mouth stretched into a grin as his brother-in-law cursed into the phone and then yelled out for his assistant. A few seconds later Alex was back on the line.

"My assistant, Alycia, will call you back in ten minutes with your flight arrangements. She'll arrange for someone to pick you up and bring you here. I suggest you pack light, because you're not staying long. Got it?"

"Got it."

"Good. Now, for the last time, give me the fucking intel."

=====

Holy shit.

Eugene Austin ripped off his headphones and immediately flipped open his laptop to send the audio file of the phone conversation he'd just captured between Tom Coleman and the CIA agent named Alex. The voice quality wasn't perfect, but certainly good enough to hear exactly what had been said. *Not bad for an eighteen-year-old geek with his own homemade equipment*, he thought smugly as he began preparing the message he would encrypt and e-mail to Preston along with the audio file.

With the message ready to send, Eugene glanced anxiously over at Tom Coleman's house. Just a few minutes earlier Coleman had peered suspiciously out through the blinds of his front window and stared directly at Eugene's car, but the house now stood quiet. He grabbed the headphones to the listening device and pressed them to his ear. The sounds of scrubbing and a running faucet emanated from the interior. Satisfied that he hadn't been noticed, he flipped off the listening device and pressed the "Send" button on his e-mail.

As dusk settled around him, Eugene folded up his laptop and checked the time on his iPhone. *I can still make dinner*, he thought happily as he started his mother's car and drove quickly toward home.

Chapter 32

"You're too late, Jack!"

The raspy Southern voice screamed from the speakerphone and echoed through the office. "The only value in this audio recording is for training other Homeland Security agents to see what happens when you get too goddamn sloppy!"

Jack Preston sat hunched on the leather couch in his Flagstaff field office, saying nothing, as Richard Connolly paused to let him respond. Five minutes earlier he had played for the HSI director the audio file he'd received the night before, between Tom Coleman and Tom's brother-in-law, Alex Murstead. Now, as his intelligence colleague breathed heavily into the phone, he stirred his coffee and waited for Connolly to finish his outburst.

"And thanks to the efforts of this Tom Coleman sonofabitch," Connolly continued, "our modest little department that has been entrusted with the safekeeping of the American people just took one more step toward getting shit-canned by Congress! And just so we're clear, Jack, if that really does happen, I'll blame you and your blatant lack of action in this matter as the reason."

Preston winced as Connolly erupted into a fit of coughing. A moment later his strained voice was back, shouting into the phone.

"Well, Jack—are you going to speak up and say something for yourself?"

"I disagree with your assumption, Richard," Preston replied. "I don't believe we're too late."

"Oh, really?" Connolly retorted, the anger in his voice unmistakable. "Well then, what do you suggest we do, Jack? Should we hop on the plane with your man Coleman and tag along on his tour of CIA headquarters?"

Preston stood up and paced slowly toward the large window in his office.

"Come on, Richard, you've been doing this even longer than I have. You know damn well what we should be doing right now— getting someone we can trust to Amsterdam to immediately begin verifying this information. You also know how the CIA works. Shit, it'll take them two days just to verify the intel and get a team into play. If we act quickly enough, we have a good chance of getting to this guy before they do."

Preston stared out at the morning mist that hung like a veil over the winter landscape outside. He listened patiently to the wheezing rhythm of Connolly's labored breath as the man considered his suggestion. In their years of working together, Preston had grown to admire Richard's intelligence and dogged tenacity, traits he'd no doubt honed from his former life in the NSA. Unfortunately, Richard was also plagued by a common ailment of men who spent too many years analyzing information—a terminal inability to make quick decisions. *Analysis paralysis*, Jack thought scornfully.

"Okay, Jack," Connolly finally replied, his voice hesitant. "Here's what we're going to do. I'm going to make a few calls to some friends within the AIVD. They'll—"

"What's the AIVD?" Preston interrupted.

"The Netherlands General Intelligence and Security Service. It's essentially the equivalent of the CIA, Secret Service, and Homeland Security forces combined into one agency." Connolly paused and coughed roughly. "It's not a big country, Jack. They don't have the budgets for multiple security and intelligence agencies like we do. Nor do they have the need."

"Okay, got it. So what's your plan?"

"There are some men within the AIVD whom I trust. We'll feed them the information and let them do the legwork—assuming you're right and there's still time."

Preston shook his head at the phone. "That's it? That's your plan? Dispatch the Danish secret police and see what they stumble onto?" He spun on his heel and paced quickly toward his desk, glancing at his watch as he walked.

"They're Dutch, Jack, not Danish," Connolly replied.

"Dutch, Danish . . . whatever," Preston muttered. "What happened to your demand for more-aggressive tactics, Richard? Even if your Danish friends did manage to get there before the CIA and nab this guy, what possible benefit would that be to us?"

"What benefit?" Connolly replied angrily. "You mean other than derailing another CIA victory in the war on terror that was made possible by our efforts? Christ, that by itself would make it a win for us, Jack. And I can assure you that my associates in the AIVD will make it clear where this information came from."

Yeah—you, *you power-hungry fuck,* Preston thought irritably as he fell into his chair and opened his laptop. "With all due respect, Richard," Preston said as he brought up an airline website and quickly typed in a flight number, "we need something far more aggressive for this situation than what you're suggesting . . . which is why I've already put some other things into play."

"*Other* things?" Connolly asked skeptically. "Such as what?"

"I've got an agent en route to Amsterdam as we speak," Preston answered as he studied the flight schedule on his screen.

"You're kidding me."

"Arriving at nine twenty-five p.m. Central European Time," Preston replied, looking again at his watch. "He should be on the ground there in approximately two hours." He leaned back in his chair and listened to what sounded like a stifled cough on the other end of the line.

"You actually sent one of your Homeland Security agents to Amsterdam?" Connolly asked in disbelief.

"One of *our* Homeland Security agents, Richard."

"And just what are his qualifications?" Connolly demanded.

"His qualifications are exactly what this assignment requires," Preston responded.

"Goddammit, Jack!" Connolly's Southern drawl cracked with anger. "Is this your way of trying to make up for the colossal mishandling of that Coleman idiot? Because if it is, I can tell you right now you're only setting the stage for a larger catastrophe with a halfbaked idea like this."

Preston brushed off the HSI director's comment. "Richard, if there's one thing we agree on, it's the time-sensitive nature of this situation. I was fortunate enough to receive information on the whereabouts of our terrorist target the same time the CIA did, and I decided to act upon that information. Now correct me if I'm wrong, but I believe stealing headlines from the CIA and gaining the credibility and budgetary backing from Congress that the Department of Homeland Security deserves are still your top priorities, right?"

"Of course they are, Jack, but—"

"Then it's time we implemented the tactics to see this through, Richard—plain and simple. No more kowtowing to the CIA, especially when they're operating on information this department was coerced into providing."

Connolly breathed a heavy sigh into the phone. Preston heard the unmistakable sound of a lighter flint as the HSI director lit a cigarette and inhaled deeply.

"Those things will kill you, Richard."

Connolly grunted exasperatedly. "You're going to kill me first, Jack—and the entire Department of Homeland Security along with me." He coughed again before speaking in a flat, defeated tone. "Let me make myself clear. I don't agree in any way with your decision to send an unqualified, unsupported agent into the field. Nor do I have any intention of backing you up if and when he fails."

"I didn't think you would, Richard," Preston replied. "That's why I didn't ask."

He clicked off the phone before Connolly could respond.

Chapter 33

He shot up from bed, his heart racing.

The dream began to vanish before his waking mind could focus and recapture it. He sat back on his elbows and tried to remember, his mind slowly corralling the disjointed images and shadows.

Then, in a flash, he remembered.

He was sitting in the corner, watching from a table nearly hidden from her view as she drifted behind the counter. She looked up as a patron approached, her fair skin glowing in the murky darkness. A smile grew on her face, a wayward lock of hair quickly tucked behind her ear. She poured the patron a drink. From his table in the corner, he admired her graceful movements, her natural ease. Then more patrons appeared and stepped up to the bar. His view of her was broken. The occasions of her appearance became shorter and less frequent. He waited patiently for another glimpse of her, but it was hopeless. The old saloon was packed. He finished his drink and stood to leave.

The mob turned at once and glowered at him, their cold eyes fixed on his. He froze with uncertainty as the room turned ghostly quiet. Then, without warning, everyone around him collapsed as one, falling to the floor as if connected to a power source that had instantly been cut. He scanned the lifeless bodies, and then looked up at the bar.

Her hazel-brown eyes stared back at him, smoldering with a deep inner fire. He watched as she bent down and collected something behind the bar. She then stood and held it out to him, gesturing him forward before resting it on the countertop.

Even from a distance he could see that the small cardboard box was tattooed with postal stamps and marks, its corners beaten by its journey from some distant place of origin. He stepped forward as requested. The soles of his shoes pressed heavily into the soft bodies that littered the floor. His heartbeat sounded in his ears, rising from a measured whisper to a pounding drum. Finally, he reached the bar.

She stood across from him, silent and still. Then, with sudden unexpected speed, she reached out and began to open the package. Her hands worked quickly at the heavy wrapping, the paper cutting her with the sharpness of razors as her fingers grabbed and pulled. *This isn't right*, he thought with alarm. A wave of panic coursed through him as his heartbeat thundered deafeningly in his ears. He reached out to stop her, to keep the package closed.

No, don't do it! Don't open it! he screamed, grabbing at her arms. She avoided his grasp easily, her bleeding hands pushing him away before continuing to pull and tear, pull and tear.

Stop! Jeri, stop! Jeri . . . please . . . STOP!

And then a blinding flash of light.

That was the last thing he remembered before waking.

He glanced over at his watch on the nightstand: 2:12 a.m. Nearly time to get started anyway. He flipped on the lamp and sat up against the cracked headboard of the bed. On the small desk across from him sat an assortment of small metal canisters and electronic components, each labeled with a small white tag. Next to the desk, several long shipping tubes with red labels warning "Flammable" rested against the wall. *Like a Hollywood movie*, he thought as he shook his head and rose from the stiff, squeaky mattress.

The light in the bathroom flickered erratically as he stood naked before the small sink. He waited patiently for the water to warm, ignoring the large object wrapped in black plastic that lay under a melting mound of ice in the bathtub. A thin cloud of steam finally rose from the faucet. He washed quickly and dried himself with a thin, rough cloth emblazoned with the Hotel Keizersgracht crest before walking over to the wardrobe. Five minutes later, dressed in blue scrubs and a fresh pair of latex gloves, he was finally awake and ready to start working.

===

Two hours later, he stood back from his work and studied it critically. He moved slowly around the room, carefully examining the placement and position of every item one last time before nodding in satisfaction.

Everything was ready.

He ripped the soiled scrubs from his body and carefully stuffed them in the large waste bag he'd placed by the door. His stomach growled with hunger as he then tended to his tools. Fifteen minutes later, with his tools cleaned and neatly packed away, he stripped off his latex gloves and added them to the waste bag. He was just beginning to unwrap a celebratory energy bar when a soft knock sounded from the entry door.

He moved toward the door, listening intently. The knock repeated, louder and more urgent. He glanced at his watch. It was 4:06 a.m. *Too early*, he thought as he rubbed at his forehead, perplexed. At the sound of a third knock he stepped to the side and cautiously cracked open the door.

A timid shudder caught his attention as he peered into the narrow hallway. He looked down and found himself gazing into the frightened eyes of a small, dark-haired young boy. "Hi there," he said softly as he opened the door and scanned the dimly lit hall. The corridor was empty. The child, who appeared no older than six or seven, said nothing as he stared back at him.

"Do you speak English?" he asked as he crouched down in the doorway. The child shyly stepped away and nodded affirmatively.

"Okay. Are you lost?" he asked calmly. The boy considered the question for a moment before shaking his head.

"No? Good, now we're getting somewhere," he said, giving him a grin.

The boy began to smile, then paused as if confused. His face contorted into a frown as his mouth struggled to form the right words. "She . . . she needs . . . help," he said slowly.

"Who needs help?" he asked.

"Mama," the boy replied, his pale face transforming into a pleading, frightened expression. He stepped forward and grabbed his hand tightly, pulling him toward the stairway at the end of the hall. "Please, please," the high-pitched voice cried. "We go now!"

He stood up, resisting the child's surprising strength as he pulled and tugged at him. "Shhhh, hold on," he whispered, holding his finger to his mouth. "I need to get my things. Wait here."

Releasing himself from the boy's grip, he darted back into his room and quickly closed the door behind him to make sure the boy couldn't see inside. He shouldered his backpack and then paused. An odd feeling of foreboding suddenly gripped him as his eyes made their final assessment of the package, sending a sharp chill up his spine. *Relax*, he thought, shaking his head. *What could go wrong?* He turned and grabbed the bag of trash by the door.

He watched the boy fidget eagerly as he stepped into the hallway and locked the door behind him. "Okay," he said, taking the child's outstretched hand. "Let's go."

Chapter 34

Tom marveled at the scene around him.

Less than twenty-four hours after his conversation with Alex, he was standing next to his brother-in-law in the center of a large, state-of-the-art command room deep in the lower levels of the CIA's massive complex in Langley, Virginia, as a team of mission specialists moved purposefully around them. In front of them, a mesmerizing symphony of data and images appeared and shifted on a massive digital display wall that Alex called HUDSON, his team's affectionate term for the Heads-Up Display System that projected an endless stream of critical mission data. From real-time satellite imagery and weather conditions to video feeds of jostling images from head-mounted cameras to even the heart rates of the Special Operations Group team members who were now moving into position on the ground, everything could be seen at a glance.

"Quite a show, isn't it?" Alex said coolly as he watched his SOG team on the screen in front of them. He glanced over at Tom with a smug grin as he chewed on the end of a toothpick.

"Not bad," Tom replied quietly, unable to suppress the awe in his voice.

"It's amazing what you can do with just a few hundred million dollars these days," Alex said as he reached up and clicked a button on the small headset he was wearing. "Forrestal, this is Command. Are we ready?"

The command room's speakers briefly crackled with static and then cleared as the sound of a strong male voice filled the air.

"Command, this is Forrestal. All teams are in first position, sir. Please confirm all feeds are online."

"Affirmative. We've got all feeds," Alex replied into his headset as the data appearing on HUDSON shifted once again. Six high-definition video feeds from the SOG team's headset-mounted cameras were instantly magnified to fill the center of the wall. "Okay, Agent Forrestal . . . what are we working with?"

Tom watched as the SOG team leader appeared on screen. His thirty-something face was framed by short dark hair and a square jaw tightly clenched in concentration. Deep brown eyes stared into the camera with confident intelligence. Mounted to the corner edge of his protective glasses was the same minuscule video camera that one of his team members used to broadcast him. Tom noticed that, unlike a normal military unit, Forrestal and his team wore a minimal amount of tactical gear. A black balaclava rolled down to his brow covered his head, while a black sweater noticeably absent of any rank or agency insignias covered his broad chest. The team leader spoke quietly into the camera.

"We've got exactly what we expected, sir. Target location sits on a very narrow corridor, flanked on the west side by the street and the canal. One narrow alleyway running on the south side of the building. Main entry on the street, ancillary entry from the back garden. In other words, minimal cover and very little room to maneuver, over."

"Looks like you're also working with minimal light."

The video feed from Forrestal's camera quickly nodded. "Affirmative, sir. No streetlights. This guy picked a good location."

"Right," Alex said curtly. "Okay, your local time is four-forty-two a.m. Things will start getting busy around there in less than two hours. Get two pairs of men to positions two and three on the south and northeast ends of the hotel immediately. I want a full recon view of this place with thermals in five minutes."

"Roger that," Agent Forrestal replied.

In the command room, Tom watched the video feeds as four of the SOG team members moved stealthily through the narrow brick-walled alley, the tips of their assault rifles repeatedly popping into view in the lower edge of the screen.

Alex turned and gave him a menacing stare. "Now we'll find out if the intel you provided is worth its weight in shit."

Tom looked at his brother-in-law and smiled confidently. "Don't worry, Alex. You'll have another plaque on that Captain America wall of yours before you know it."

═══

A few blocks from the hotel, the boy looked up at him as they turned into an unlit alley, and tugged impatiently at his hand. "Hurry," he said, his eyes wet and pleading.

"Who are we going to see?" he asked again.

"Mama."

"Can you tell me what's wrong with Mama?" he asked.

"Hurry!"

The alleyway was barely wide enough for his shoulders. The cool air smelled of urine and beer, and his shoes slipped on something unseen in the darkness beneath him. Without warning, the boy released his hand as they came to a small, unmarked door in the wall, produced a key from a thin chain around his neck, and deftly inserted it into the lock. As it opened, a faint glow of light from inside illuminated the door's surface, which he could now see was painted a bright red. The boy grabbed his hand and pulled him inside.

He stepped into the cramped interior as the boy shut the door behind him. They stood in what appeared to be a makeshift kitchen, built from milk crates and stocked with canned foods and parchment-paper-wrapped bread. Next to him, a rusty spigot sticking out from the brick wall dripped rhythmically into a tin bucket beneath it. A cockroach scurried erratically up the deep mortar line of the brick.

"This way," the boy said, tugging impatiently at his hand. He was led toward a recess in the far corner of the room that opened to a short hallway. As they stepped into the narrow corridor, he could see the room that contained the source of the light. The boy sneezed and quickly wiped his hand against his jacket, then looked up at him and smiled.

"Do you like the Brainybuddies?" he asked the boy.

The boy's grin stretched even farther as he nodded his head rapidly.

"Me too," he replied softly.

"Anya!" the boy cried as they entered a narrow, windowless room. He ran to the side of a small bed that nearly filled the tiny space.

He watched as the boy placed his hand on the forehead of the frail-looking young woman tightly curled on her side in the center of the bed. Her long black hair stood out sharply against her sickly, ghost-pale complexion. Beads of perspiration covered her face and neck, and as he stepped closer he could see her lean body shivering beneath the blanket that covered her.

"Anya," the boy whispered, gently stroking her hair, *"megtaláltam."*

The woman shuddered and slowly opened her eyes. "Jakob," she whispered, giving him a weak smile. The boy pointed at the visitor and repeated, *"Megtaláltam."* She turned her head and gazed up at him.

"My son said he would find you," she said with a heavy accent as her dark eyes looked him over. "I'm so happy he did. Thank you for coming."

He slipped his backpack off his shoulder and kneeled down next to the bed. "I take it you're a friend of Anna's?" he asked as he pressed his hand against her forehead.

"Yes, Anna," the woman answered weakly. "She said you helped her when she was sick." She paused and swallowed with a pained grimace before continuing. "When she saw me today she said she knew a man that could help me. She said you always tell her when you are here so that you can help any of us that need help."

He nodded as he took her pulse, remembering the night a few years before when he first met Anna. It had been a cold winter night. He'd been walking along the outer edge of the Rosse Buurt, the red-light district, when he'd heard the unmistakable sound of a woman moaning in pain. She was lying on a park bench when he found her, her body crumpled on the cold steel like a rag doll. Anna had not been sick, but drugged and badly beaten. He'd carried her the short distance back to his hotel and checked her into the room next to his, treating her cuts and contusions and setting a broken wrist and finger with the few supplies he'd had on hand. After three days Anna had recovered enough to walk. She had thanked him, offered her services for free, and stared dumbfounded at him when he graciously declined. "I could use the good karma," he'd said to her as he placed a small vial of painkillers in her unbroken hand. "So I help where I can." She had cried and hugged him tightly, a genuine, surrendering display of raw gratitude that he still vividly remembered.

She had then looked at him with red swollen eyes and told him between sobs that many of her friends, prostitutes like her, were often in need of help. He'd told Anna he would help whenever he was there, and asked for a way to contact her. She had scribbled an e-mail address on a sheet of the hotel stationery and handed it to him. "Use this," she'd said, her eyes looking into his with a mixture of emotions that had made him uncomfortable. "This is how my family contacts me." When he had asked if they knew what she did, she'd smiled with a steely expression and said they had to—prostitution was the only profession that allowed an uneducated woman like her to support them.

"I was happy to help Anna," he said to the woman now lying in front of him. "And I'm happy to help you as well. What's your name?"

"Marika," she replied.

"Nice to meet you, Marika. Now tell me what you're feeling."

He listened as she described her symptoms, checking her pulse and carefully palpating her abdomen. When he pressed against her lower abdomen, she grimaced and cried out in pain.

"What was the last thing you ate?" he asked.

"Jakob brought me special breakfast this morning," she replied, reaching out and placing her hand against her son's cheek. "For my birthday." He smiled back at her with the flushed cheeks and liquid eyes of a frightened, protective son. "*Rullepølse* with *skæreost*," she said, smiling softly at his blank expression. "You Americans would call this pork sausage and toast."

"How long ago was that?"

She looked up at the large wood beams that formed the ceiling of the room. "Many hours ago. Almost a day has passed, I think."

"And your symptoms came on quickly? Within the last few hours?"

"Yes."

He nodded and dug his hands into his backpack. "You're going to be fine, Marika," he said as he pulled out a small bag of clear fluid with a long plastic tube attached to it. He handed the bag to the boy and pointed at a small shelf on the wall beside them. "Hang this up there for me, okay, Jakob?" The boy nodded and jumped up immediately.

"You've most likely got food poisoning . . . an unexpected gift from your birthday breakfast. Probably salmonella." He rubbed her arm with an alcohol pad before squeezing it tightly. A vein rose in her thin arm. "I'm going to give you an IV of sodium chloride to keep you hydrated," he said as he inserted a needle into her vein. "It will take about four hours for this to empty. When it's done, remove the tape and slowly pull the needle out while applying pressure. Then put a bandage over it. Do you understand?"

She nodded weakly as she looked at him with an appreciative grin. "What is your name?" she asked, her dark brown eyes studying his face. "Anna never told me."

He secured the IV line to the needle and started the drip of saline. "My name isn't important. You should just worry about resting right now."

"Such a mysterious man," she said mockingly, her accent dragging over the words. "Perhaps I should make up a name for you."

He gave her a quizzical look. "Marika, where are you from?"

"Hungary."

"And what brought you to Amsterdam?" he asked as he began packing his things.

"What brings every young woman to Amsterdam?" she replied wryly, her thin smile contorting into another pained grimace.

He glanced over at Jakob, who was now sitting on the edge of the bed, mesmerized by the sight of the saline fluid as it slowly made its way down the IV line into his mother's arm. "How old is your son?"

"I am seven," Jakob replied, his eyes never leaving the strange tube.

"He watches out for me, as you can see," Marika said quietly. "We watch out for each other."

"I can see that," he said, placing his hand on the boy's small shoulder. "I need you to take care of your mother now, okay, Jakob?"

Jakob shook his head yes.

"Okay then," the visitor said, standing up to leave. "It was very nice to meet you, Marika. Stay in bed and try to drink as much water as you comfortably can. You should be feeling better by tomorrow."

Marika gave him a weak smile as she reached out her hand to him. "I cannot thank you enough, Tódor."

"Tódor?" he asked, taking her hand and squeezing it gently.

"It is the name I have decided to call you, since you won't tell me your real one. It is a Hungarian name," she said softly, her eyes studying his face again. "It means 'gift of god.'"

He smiled and released her hand. "What's the name for 'average guy'? I think that would be more appropriate."

"No, I like Tódor."

He slung his backpack over his shoulder and stepped into the small hallway. As he turned to say good-bye, Marika looked at her son and quickly said something in Hungarian. The boy immediately stood and walked past him and into the small kitchen. "Jakob will see you out," she said.

"Get some rest, Marika."

"I will." Her fingers waved a quick good-bye. "*Viszontlátásra,* Tódor."

He walked into the kitchen to find Jakob standing quietly by the door. The boy was staring somberly at his hands as he repeatedly intertwined and separated his small fingers. The visitor kneeled down in front of him and playfully ruffled his hair. "Your mother will be just fine, Jakob. She just needs a little rest." He put his finger under the boy's chin and gently raised his head until he looked up at him. "She wouldn't be feeling better if it weren't for you, do you know that?"

Jakob nodded as his eyes filled with tears.

"I need you to take care of her until she feels better," he said as he reached into his pocket. He pulled out a small wad of folded euros and placed them in the boy's hand. "Use this to buy food and anything else you and your mother need."

Jakob stared in shock at the money for a brief moment before quickly stuffing it into his pocket and blurting, "Thank you."

"Don't mention it, kiddo," he said as he opened the door to leave.

"Wait!" Jakob said, grabbing his arm with both hands and staring up at him with pleading eyes. "Are . . . are you a doctor?"

He looked down at the boy's smooth, innocent face as he stood at the doorway. "No, Jakob . . . I'm not a doctor," he replied, giving him a wry grin. "I'm an artist."

He then turned and disappeared into the dark alley before the boy could respond.

"Goddammit," SOG team leader Matt Forrestal hissed as he watched the screen of the small electronic tablet resting on his knee. He was tucked between two vehicles parallel-parked in front of the target location, staring in frustration at the infrared images being fed to him by his teams on the opposite end of the target building. "Team Two, give me another sweep of the second and third floors on the east wall."

"Roger."

Forrestal studied the heat-revealing image for a second time as his team slowly panned the infrared camera across the brick façade. The exterior of the hotel's north-facing rooms was painted in the deep blue-black colors of a cold, lifeless building.

"Doesn't look like there's anyone on this end, sir," the Team Two agent said as he finished his sweep.

"Understood," Forrestal replied. "Team Three?" He patiently watched the thermal image from Team Three as they scanned the southern face of the hotel. When they reached the corner window on the third floor, it glowed with the radiant red-orange color of molten steel.

"That's the manager's room, over," the Team Three agent said over the radio. "Looks like he's got the heat cranked up."

"Roger that," Forrestal replied. The rest of the hotel's thermal scan showed no signs of life. "Command, are you seeing this?"

More than three thousand miles away in the command room in Langley, Alex turned and glared at Tom. "We're seeing it," he replied tersely. "Looks like we might have bad intel on this one after all." Tom shifted uncomfortably next to Alex as Forrestal's voice crackled through the speakers of the large room.

"Roger that, Command. How would you like us to proceed, over?"

Alex held his eyes on Tom as he considered the answer. After a long moment he shook his head irritably and pressed his hand against his headset. "Hold your positions for ten more minutes."

"Roger that."

═══

He walked slowly, enjoying the cold night air. The dark street was deserted, creating the impression that he was the only living being among the procession of old row-house buildings that lined the oil-black water of the canal. He glanced up from the cobblestone sidewalk. The hotel stood just a short distance ahead, its small entry door illuminated by a single incandescent light. An odd feeling came over him as he approached, causing him to slow. He glanced over his shoulder before pausing to study the quiet neighborhood. His eyes caught the movement of a shadow on the street, and he immediately crouched low against the cold cobblestones. The shadow moved closer and halted. A moment later, a familiar sound broke the silence. He smiled with relief as a small house cat slowly meandered along the parked cars that lined the avenue. He was just about to stand when the cat tensed at something tucked between two cars. The animal meowed loudly and walked toward the hidden object. A blunt cry followed as the cat was kicked roughly back into the street. The animal hissed angrily at its hidden assailant before turning and disappearing into the night.

His smile evaporated as he stared at the gap between the cars.

He reached into his pocket. The small device felt cold as he gently wrapped his fingers around it. He stroked the smooth surface with his thumb, feeling the rubbery indent of a small button on one side. He then took a deep breath of the crisp night air and cleared his mind. It was time. He stood and continued walking toward the hotel.

=====

Agent Matt Forrestal spotted the dark-haired man walking toward the target location and instantly froze his position. His hand tightened around the grip of his SIG Sauer sidearm as he whispered into the small microphone attached to his shoulder. "Command . . . be advised, possible target approaching."

In the command room, all eyes immediately focused on the live feed from Forrestal's camera as a figure slowly emerged from the darkness.

"Roger that," Alex said as he stared at the screen. "We see him."

Tom studied the video as a technician quickly adjusted the brightness of the image. Suddenly a tall, dark-haired figure wearing jeans and a jacket materialized into view. He walked calmly, seeming unaware of the nearby SOG agents as he strolled directly toward them.

"Well?" Alex asked as he turned and looked at Tom. "Is that our man?"

"Well, I . . . I'm not sure," Tom mumbled as he squinted at the video image. He couldn't tell Alex the truth—that he'd never actually seen the man's face. All eyes in the command room were now on him, waiting for confirmation as the man moved closer to the SOG team leader's position. Then, as he stared at the light-enhanced video, Tom noticed something.

"Wait," he said excitedly, pointing at the video wall. "Can you get a closer shot of his jacket?"

Alex looked at him suspiciously for a fleeting moment before turning and addressing a technician sitting nearby. "Mike?" he asked sharply.

"I'm on it," the technician replied as his fingers rapidly punched at his keyboard. As they watched, a still frame from the video appeared on the large display. In an instant, the area of the image containing the man's jacket was quickly highlighted and expanded. As the image sharpened, Tom's pulse quickened. The man's jacket was unzipped, revealing a blue shirt underneath. A white logo slowly came into focus.

"That's him!" Tom said as he slapped his hands together excitedly. "That's our target!"

"You're sure?" Alex asked.

Tom turned and smiled at his brother-in-law. "I'm sure of it."

Alex nodded tersely and immediately drew his hand to his headset.

"Forrestal, this is Command. We have confirmation on the target. You are free to engage, over."

"Roger that."

Forrestal gave a quick hand signal to his Team One counterpart crouched behind him, and whispered into his microphone. "All teams, be advised . . . target is approaching on foot from the north.

Hold positions. Team One will engage as target enters the hotel. Be ready for my command."

He held his .40-caliber handgun against his chest and watched as the target moved nonchalantly toward the hotel entrance, clearly oblivious to the world of pain awaiting him. *That's it, keep coming,* he thought as the man turned and walked up to the hotel entrance, his face finally visible in the dim entry light.

It was in that brief instant that Forrestal noticed the target staring directly at his position between the parked cars, a wide grin stretched across his face. Before he could move, a flash of blinding light erupted from the headlights of the vehicle he was crouched against. An instant later, the deafening sound of the vehicle's horn blasted into his ear. Disoriented, he immediately stood and leveled his handgun in front of him. *Goddamn car alarm!* he thought with disbelief as he sprinted half-blind toward the hotel entryway.

"Team Two, breach rear access now!" he screamed into the microphone as he approached the main entrance. "Team Three, take position at the southwest corner and make sure target does not get past you!"

Forrestal paused next to the door, listening intently as his Team One counterpart followed closely behind him, his assault rifle drawn tightly to his chest. "Target must be inside," he said, timing his words with the intermittent blast of the car horn still sounding behind them. As he listened, Forrestal heard the unmistakable echoing rhythm of someone moving quickly up the metallic stairs in the hotel lobby. He signaled to his team member, and both men took positions inside the small room.

"Team Two, report!" Forrestal demanded.

"Team Two is in position inside the rear hallway of the first floor. Area secured, over."

"Maintain your position!" Forrestal ordered as he made his way toward the spiral staircase that led to the two upper floors. "Team One will secure the second floor."

He followed his team member as they twisted up the narrow stairs, shifting his handgun with each changing line of sight. As they reached the second-floor landing, Forrestal heard movement at the far end of the hall. "Team Three, take position at the entry and report."

"Roger that."

Forrestal signaled to his team member to move down the hall. Both men kept close watch on the doors that lined the corridor, guns raised and ready to fire. The sound of movement in the lobby below echoed up as Forrestal's radio crackled to life.

"Team Three in entry, over."

"Roger that. Secure the third floor," Forrestal commanded. The sound of footsteps on the stairwell immediately followed as the two men of Team Three moved up to the third floor. A few seconds later the hotel was quiet.

"Team Three in position."

Forrestal quickly nodded to himself. The three floors of the hotel were now covered. Their target had nowhere to go.

"Okay, Team Three, begin your sweep," he ordered. "Finish with the manager's room."

"Roger that."

Forrestal listened intently as Team Three began to enter and secure the rooms on the floor above him. He easily visualized his men's coordinated actions as they moved down the hall. Less than two minutes later, the two-man team communicated their progress.

"Third-floor sweep nearly completed. Entering manager's room now."

Forrestal flinched as the sound of a large-caliber gun suddenly echoed from upstairs. Almost immediately, the sound was met with the whispered retort of two silenced assault rifles. The team leader grabbed at his headset, resisting the urge to sprint up the stairs and check on his team as he spoke into the microphone. "Team Three!

Team Three, report!" A long moment passed before the radio crackled in his earpiece.

"Team Three here," the SOG team member replied calmly. "Target has been neutralized. No injuries sustained by team, over."

"Roger that. Command, can you confirm with a visual?"

Back in the command room, Tom and Alex watched tensely along with the support team. "This is Command," Alex replied. "Team Three, please give us a visual." The two members of Team Three cautiously entered the manager's room, their gun-mounted flashlights aimed forward. The pale, bullet-torn figure of a middle-aged man lay facedown on the floor. A puddle of crimson blood surrounded the body.

"Team Three, this is Command," Alex said into his headset. "Turn him over so we can see the face."

"Roger that."

The two agents stepped forward and carefully turned the lifeless body over. The weathered, pudgy face of the dead man came into frame, a wide-eyed look of shock frozen on his features. A dark, reptilian tattoo covered his neck and a portion of his left cheek.

Tom shook his head and moaned. "Fuck . . . that's not him," he muttered.

Alex turned and looked at him. "What?" he asked, his voice a high octave of disbelief.

"That's not him."

"That man there," Alex said as he pointed his finger at the video feed. "The one who just shot at my team. You're saying that's not our target?"

Tom shook his head.

"Then who the fuck is he?"

"How the fuck should I know?" Tom shrugged. "But it's not our guy."

"He's right, sir," a young woman seated at a computer nearby said sharply. "I just ran a quick scan. Feature analysis is showing no match with the earlier video images of the target."

Alex's eyes darted wildly around the room as the full weight of the situation struck him. He cursed under his breath and clicked on his headset. "Forrestal, this is Command. Team Three's kill is not . . . repeat . . . not our target. Target is still active."

A moment of silence followed before the SOG team leader replied, "Roger that, Command. Target is still active."

Forrestal exhaled slowly as he crouched against the wall at the front of the second-floor hallway. The words from a training manual he'd read long ago now echoed in his head. *Team leaders must always be ready to accept and adapt to rapidly changing circumstances.* He shook his head in frustration. What was supposed to have been a simple, surgically precise operation was quickly turning into a massive clusterfuck. In less than three minutes, he and his highly trained team of operatives had managed to set off a car alarm before converging on the target as well as find themselves in a shootout with a trigger-happy hotel manager.

And the real target was still active.

Forrestal adjusted his balaclava as he spoke into his headset.

"Team Three, I want you down here now."

"Roger that."

The two men abruptly vacated the manager's room and descended the stairs. With the two teams assembled on the second floor, Forrestal signaled the plan. Each team would sweep the hotel rooms on their respective sides of the hallway. Seconds later, with a brief nod of understanding from his men, Forrestal gave the signal to begin.

Tom, Alex, and the entire mission support team watched anxiously from the command room as the first two rooms were breached. Both teams simultaneously entered with their weapons drawn, scanning the dark interiors with the piercing light of their barrel-mounted flashlights. Tom watched in silence, awed by the efficient bravado of the highly trained men as they methodically searched for the terrorist who was still hiding in one of the rooms. In less than two minutes the teams had completed their sweep of four of the six rooms on the second floor. All four of the rooms were eerily empty.

Outside the last two rooms, Forrestal signaled his men to pause.

"Okay, this is it," he said quietly, clenching his jaw as he stared somberly at the three men. "Our target has now had several minutes to decide how he's going to greet us when we come through his door, and I'm betting he has a flair for the dramatic. We'll do these last rooms one at a time. Two men on each side . . . and I'll be the bell ringer."

Both teams quickly lined up on each side as Forrestal took his position in front of the first door. *I don't get paid enough*, he thought wryly as he mentally prepared himself. Then, with a quick signal to his men, he leaned his muscled, six-foot-two frame forward and drove his right foot squarely into the flimsy door.

The explosion from inside the room seemed surprisingly quiet as Forrestal felt his body launched backward with sickening velocity. The door followed with him as the expanding ball of fire sent man and wood hurtling like weightless projectiles. The SOG team leader felt the brief impact of something slapping against his back as the concentrated energy blew his body through the door on the opposite side of the hall. He was then mercifully dropped in a rain of smoking debris on the hard floor just inches from the room's small window. Seconds later, he felt the hands of his team grabbing at his outstretched body.

"Sir! Sir! Can you hear me, sir? Are you okay, sir?" The screaming voice of one of his men was barely audible over the loud ringing in his ears. Forrestal cautiously wiggled his fingers and toes before slowly shaking his head.

"Well, I guess this room is now clear," he mumbled with a weak smile.

"Sir?"

"Nothing. I'm fine . . . I'm fine," Forrestal replied as he wiped off his face and opened his eyes. He blinked rapidly before fixing his stare on the ceiling. A small access hatch in the ceiling came into focus. The team leader looked at it vacantly for a moment before shaking his head. "Help me get the fuck up."

In the command room, Tom and Alex watched breathlessly as Forrestal's team carefully helped him to his feet. The force of the explosion had destroyed the team leader's camera and microphone, and they now studied the remaining video feeds through a filter of smoke and dust.

"Forrestal, this is Command," Alex said urgently into his headset. "Report on your condition." A moment later the sound of static crackled overhead.

"Command, this is Forrestal," the team leader replied into a borrowed headset. "My team and I are all fine. Entering the room now."

The video images were a nearly indecipherable montage of shadows and flashlight beams as the SOG agents moved back toward the room where the detonation had occurred. They entered slowly, cautiously examining the charred remains of a bed and small desk that appeared to be at the epicenter of the explosion. Strewn around them on the floor and embedded in the walls was a precisely crafted display of annihilation. Everywhere the agents looked, small pieces of molten plastic and fragments of silicon boards were interspersed with smoldering pieces of wood, metal shards, and charred pieces of desiccated flesh.

"Jesus, what a mess," one of the men mumbled in disgust as he pulled his balaclava over his face. "I forgot how bad the stench of exploded terrorist was."

Forrestal nodded wordlessly as he turned to face the small bed across from the desk and stopped. There, illuminated by his flashlights, a grotesquely distorted human body was pressed against the head of the bed, the upper chest and remains of the head driven deep into the plaster wall above the headboard. As Tom watched from the command room, the team leader moved in closer, the video feed from his camera rising and falling rhythmically with his steps.

As the smoke dissipated from view, Tom studied the image on the large screen and gasped. Illuminated by Forrestal's flashlight was the twisted back of the body, still clothed in a torn and burned blue T-shirt that appeared fused with the skin. In the center of the back, a large silk-screened logo was still visible, the words "Last Stand" reflecting in the bright light.

"That's him!" Tom yelled out as he slapped Alex on the shoulder. "That's our guy!"

The loudspeaker crackled overhead as Forrestal's low voice filled the air. "Command . . . looks like we have a self-detonation by the target."

"Roger that, Forrestal," Alex said as he looked over and eyed Tom quizzically. "Okay, finish your sweep and start tagging and bagging the leftovers."

Alex turned his attention to the female technician seated nearby. "Sarah, what kind of feature scan can we get from that wall-mounted piece of toast?"

"Not much, sir," the woman replied as her fingers rapidly punched at her computer keyboard. "We need at least fifty percent of the face intact to draw a conclusive scan from the earlier video, and I'm assuming there'll be nothing even close to that once we pry him from the wall."

"Yeah, no shit," Alex said irritably.

"That's him, Alex. I'm sure of it," Tom replied. "He's wearing the same shirt we saw in the earlier video. Trust me, I know that T-shirt."

"Oh, really?" Alex replied, glaring at Tom intensely. "And why is it that you know this guy's T-shirt so well?"

Tom felt his face flush red as several heads in the command room turned to look at him. He smiled nonchalantly as he looked at his brother-in-law. "I . . . I've seen a partial photo of our target wearing that shirt, Alex. I can assure you that it's him."

"Oh, right," Alex replied, taking an intimidating step closer to Tom. "The photos of the target that you talked about, but never produced. Got it."

Tom swallowed quietly as Alex stood facing him, his tall frame towering over Tom. The two men exchanged stares.

"You know what, Tom?" Alex said, his face relaxing into a smile as he reached out his hand. "That's good enough for me."

Tom stood in shock as Alex grabbed his hand and shook it zealously before turning to the room. "Great job, everyone! We got him!"

An eruption of applause filled the large command room as Alex clicked on his headset and congratulated the SOG team as they quickly collected the morbid evidence in the small hotel room. He then pulled off his headset and turned to Tom. "Well, Tom," he said with a wide grin. "I suppose it's time we go back to my office and talk about your future."

Chapter 35

Tom sat in the austere, colorless office of the CIA's deputy director of Special Operations and stared indifferently at the awards and citations that covered the wall in front of him. On the desk, a picture of his brother-in-law standing in the middle of a team of young, serious-faced commandos stared back at him. Next to it, an autographed photo of Alex standing in the Oval Office shaking the hand of the president sat in a large black frame. Tom shook his head and glanced at his watch. It was 12:37 a.m.

He'd been waiting more than two hours for Alex to finish the string of debriefing meetings that had followed the operation in Amsterdam. Through the narrow window by the office door, Tom could see Alex's assistant, Alycia, sitting quietly at her desk, quickly preparing a small mountain of paperwork that Tom was certain had to do with tonight's lethal little exercise. He stood and stretched the exhaustion from his legs, glancing repeatedly at the small black dome of glass concealing the camera that Alycia was using to monitor him as he waited. A moment after he sat back down, Tom's eyes were just beginning to ease shut when the intercom on Alex's desk crackled to life.

"Can I get you anything, Agent Coleman? Another coffee, perhaps?"

Tom jumped in alarm before looking at the camera. He smiled and nodded. "Sure, Alycia, thanks."

"Sugar and cream, right?" the perky, high-pitched voice asked politely.

"Yes, thank you."

Tom watched through the window as Alycia stood to get his coffee. She paused as an unseen figure approached her. They spoke for several minutes before she nodded and walked out of view. A moment later the door to the office opened, and Alex walked in carrying a thick manila envelope. He looked over at Tom and smiled.

"Sorry to keep you waiting," he said as he dropped into his chair behind the desk. "Those mission debriefings are always a fucking nightmare."

"No problem," Tom said wearily. He sat up in the chair and forced himself awake as his brother-in-law immediately opened the envelope and tossed its contents onto his desk.

"Quite a night, huh?" Alex said as he quickly thumbed through the pages of documents.

"Unbelievable," Tom replied.

"Well, I can tell you everyone around here is very pleased with the outcome of tonight's mission," Alex said as he glanced up from the pages and smiled. "Including me."

Tom nodded and smiled. "I told you I'd help you put another plaque on your wall, Alex. You just needed to believe in me." He leaned forward in his chair expectantly. "So, as you said earlier, let's talk about my future."

"So what do you want to do, Tom?"

"You know what I want," Tom replied earnestly. "I want to join *the Company*. And as of tonight, you and I both know I've earned that right. I've proven that I've got what it takes."

"Okay," Alex said, giving him a curious look. "And what exactly do you think this job takes?"

"Come on, Alex," Tom said, rubbing his eyes wearily. "It's almost one in the morning and I've had about three hours of sleep in the last two days. Are we really going to do a fucking job interview right now?"

A look of irritation passed over Alex's face for a brief instant before he grinned and nodded. He looked down at the documents in front of him and once again started thumbing through the pages. A moment later he paused on a particular document and pulled it from the pile. He studied it carefully for several seconds before looking up at Tom with a distracted stare.

"Sorry, Tom . . . you're right. I just want to make sure you've really thought this through before this goes any further. Are you sure you can just walk away from the Department of Homeland Security? From ICE?"

Tom laughed at the question before realizing his brother-in-law was being serious. "Are you kidding me? Of course I'm sure. For fuck's sake, I was just biding my time there until I got into the CIA. Besides, even if I wanted to go back, Director Preston wouldn't exactly greet me with open arms right now, would he?"

"Yeah, well, you dug your own grave with Jack Preston, Tom."

Tom studied Alex for a moment, trying to understand where his strange line of questioning was going. He pointed his finger at his brother-in-law and glared at him with a threatening intensity.

"Do you know what I did for you tonight, *brother*? Tonight I single-fucking-handedly delivered an international terrorist to your doorstep. How many non-agency personnel can claim that on their résumé? Fuck . . . how many of your own men can claim that? You and I both know I put my ass on the line to live up to my part of our agreement—and I came through. So please understand my position when I say that all I fucking want to hear from you right now is how you're planning to get me in."

Alex looked up from the document in his hand and nodded slowly. "I have just one more question, Tom. Are you really willing to give up everything you have in Flagstaff to make this happen?"

"Yes."

"The mountain air?"

"Yes."

"Your ex-wife?"

"Fuck yes."

"Even Jeri Halston?"

It took a moment for Tom's exhausted mind to fully register the name that echoed in the large office. By the time it did, his brother-in-law was already speaking again.

"Sorry, Tom . . . I should backtrack a bit here. You see, something was nagging at me a little earlier when I was sitting in one of the debriefing meetings. And then it struck me. I remembered that when you were identifying our target in the command room, you weren't interested in his face—you were interested in his T-shirt. I was too caught up in the mission at the time to really give it much thought, but afterwards I started realizing that *that* T-shirt obviously meant something to you. So I had my team do some quick research on it. Of course it only took them about fifteen seconds to figure it out."

He paused and looked at Tom with a conspiratorial grin. "Is Joe's Last Stand Saloon a nice place, Tom?"

"Hold on a second, Alex . . . I—"

"Actually, I already know it's a shitty little dive bar," Alex interrupted as he slid the document he was holding across the desk toward Tom. "Which is surprising, considering how much of a germophobe you are. But I suppose it does have its charms, especially when it comes to Miss Halston."

Tom picked up the thick document and examined it. It appeared to be a hastily crafted field report. He flipped through several of the pages and swallowed nervously. There in black and white were full-page photos of the interior of the saloon. Most of the images were of the "shrine" of letters and Polaroid photos hanging in the corner, the letters captured closely enough to read. On the last page of the report, framed in several discreetly taken photos, Jeri Halston stood casually behind the bar. Tom shook his head slowly and tossed the document back onto the desk.

"Do you remember the agent who was with me the night I dropped by to see you?" Alex asked as a wry smile stretched across his face. "You know, the one you kept looking for over your shoulder. Well, I thought it might be useful to keep him in Flagstaff. So I did. Within five minutes of getting the intel on our dead man's T-shirt, my agent was sitting inside Joe's Last Stand Saloon ordering a drink from that lovely amber-eyed bartender."

Tom watched as his brother-in-law opened another file on his desk. "Let's see . . . twenty-six-year-old Jeri Halston. Grew up in Flagstaff. Has a master's degree in economics from Northern Arizona University. No known affiliations to any groups or organizations. No known religious affiliations. Doesn't own a firearm. Presumed heterosexual. Mother, Catherine, died of breast cancer when Jeri was three years old. Father, James, economist and consultant, also an alumni of NAU. Died a little over a year ago from a brain tumor."

Alex closed the file and looked at Tom. "That's all we've got so far, but I think it's safe to say she's not in league with terrorists. She does have a knack for giving them a hard-on, though, doesn't she?" He opened the field report containing the photos from the saloon and shook his head. "I've gotta tell you, Tom, these letters are really something. I mean, I honestly kind of regret neutralizing this motherfucker tonight. He wrote some really funny shit."

"Yeah, it's a real shame he was killing innocent people in his spare time," Tom replied sarcastically. "Now, would you mind making your point? Because whatever it is, it doesn't change the fact that I handed this guy to you."

Alex's smile evaporated. "You're right, Tom. The fact that I uncovered the source of your information and exposed the manner in which you concealed it from this agency does not change your role in this investigation. But it does confirm something."

"What's that?"

"That you have no business being in the CIA."

Tom stared at his brother-in-law in silence.

"You know," Alex continued, "back in SEAL training we had a name for guys like you. *Individual contributors.* You're only motivated by one thing . . . outcomes that benefit yourself. Honesty and teamwork have no meaning to you, and yet that is exactly what you need if you're going to be a part of this agency. No one is going to deny that you brought a terrorist to our door, Tom. But you did one lousy fucking job of doing it. That's why you'll never be a CIA agent—because you're in it for yourself. Christ, I honestly wonder if you'd let one of your own people take a bullet if it worked to your advantage."

Tom snapped straight up in his chair and glared at Alex, his eyes red and livid. "What did you say?"

"I'm sorry . . . did I hit a nerve?" Alex asked. He quickly gathered the documents on his desk and pressed a button on his desk phone. A moment later the door to his office opened, and a tall, heavyset man in an expensive-looking suit and dark, pomade-slick hair walked in and gave Tom a guarded smile. Behind him, Alycia glided in with Tom's coffee and a stack of documents.

Tom took his coffee from Alycia as he eyed the large man standing in front of him.

"Tom, this is Mike Moretti," Alex said, nodding to his colleague. "Mike's part of our legal team. He's got a few documents for you to sign."

The two men briefly shook hands as Alycia dropped the hefty pile of documents on Alex's desk before exiting the room. Tom turned and looked at his brother-in-law.

"So what exactly are you expecting me to sign?"

"Oh, the typical stuff. Some nondisclosure agreements, a few affidavits confirming the nature of the mission should it ever come under scrutiny by a Congressional ethics investigation." Alex waved his hand at the lawyer slowly settling his corpulent frame into the chair next to Tom. "And a few other things that Mike here can explain."

Tom took a sip of his coffee and turned to face the lawyer. "Well, this ought to be good."

"Tom, first of all I would like to thank you on behalf of the Central Intelligence Agency for assisting Agent Murstead and his team in bringing swift and definitive justice to this terrorist tonight." He smiled at Tom with a flash of smoke-stained teeth before continuing. "While of course your assistance can never be made public, our agency and the American people owe you a debt of gratitude for your service in this investigation."

Tom nodded impatiently.

"Now, Tom, Agent Murstead has informed me that you may have somehow misinterpreted his request for assistance as some form of implied offer to work for our agency. Unfortunately, I'm here to tell you that this is simply not possible. Regardless of the assistance you've provided in this case, we cannot sidestep the existing protocols for recruitment."

"Bullshit. You mean you *will* not sidestep protocols for recruitment," Tom said sharply.

"No, Tom, I mean cannot," the lawyer retorted with a firm, practiced tone. "Despite what you may believe, the rules of this agency don't fall into any gray area of interpretation that we can choose to ignore when it suits us. You don't guard a country by playing fast and loose with the rules that ensure that protection." He shook his head irritably and glanced at Alex, who nodded thoughtfully in agreement.

"So that's it, huh?" Tom said as he stared venomously at the oily, heavyset man sitting next to him. "Captain America here gets a promotion and another plaque on the wall for killing the terrorist I handed to him tonight, and I get the 'thanks for playing' speech from the fat fucking lawyer?"

The lawyer stared back at Tom for a long moment, his eyes watering in anger as his thick jaw clenched and then slowly relaxed. He chuckled quietly, then leaned over and grabbed the stack of papers that Alycia had laid on the desk.

"No, Tom. That's not it," he said matter-of-factly. "You see, I'm actually in a very kind mood tonight." He handed Tom the first of several thick documents before reaching into his tailored pinstriped jacket for a pen.

Tom quickly scanned the document. The content was typical legalese—the same intricate, pedantic nonsense that all lawyers liked to sell by the pound. He flipped to the last page and read the final paragraph before glancing up at Alex. "Are you fucking kidding me?"

"It's all true, Tom," Alex replied, his face strangely serene.

"Really? And how did you come to that conclusion?"

"Agent Coleman, the facts are clear," the lawyer interjected. "You knowingly withheld information regarding a suspected terrorist from agents conducting a federal investigation. That alone is a serious criminal offense."

"Exactly what the fuck did I withhold, asshole?" Tom asked, stabbing his finger at Alex. "I'm the one who made this idiot aware of him!"

"That may be true. But you provided this information only on the condition that you become employed by the agency. That's considered coercion and bribery. That's also a federal crime. But I have good news for you, Agent Coleman." The lawyer paused and handed Tom a second document. "In light of what you've done for our agency and our country tonight, Agent Murstead and I have agreed not to pursue any charges against you. That is, on two conditions."

"And what are those?"

"First, that you never discuss the details of this case or your involvement in it with anyone. Not even senior-level officials back at the Department of Homeland Security—including Director Preston."

"Especially Director Preston," Alex chimed in.

"Second," the lawyer continued, "that you fully agree with the assessment previously provided to you from this agency stating that you do not meet the qualifications for entrance into our recruiting program." He shifted his weight and gave Tom a halfhearted sigh of empathy. "I'm sorry, Tom, but sometimes we just have to accept things and move on."

Tom glowered at the lawyer. A crushing weight suddenly pressed against his chest, a weight he knew all too well. It was the same feeling he'd felt after his wife had told him she was leaving; the same one he'd felt after being suspended from the Phoenix PD; certainly the same one he'd felt the instant everything had turned so completely fucked up in Afghanistan.

It was the oppressive, inescapable feeling of failure.

He nodded slowly and stared at the heavy silver pen in his hand. He signed the two documents in his hands before handing them back to Mike.

"Excellent," the lawyer said as he checked the signatures on the pages and quickly signed and dated beneath them. "I hope you realize this does not diminish the great work you've done for your country tonight. You're a true patriot, Tom. Now go back to your job with Homeland Security. That's where you're supposed to be."

Tom stood from his chair and walked toward the door, tossing the pen onto the lap of the lawyer's pressed pants as he passed. He was just opening the door when Alex spoke.

"You did the right thing tonight, Tom. I know you don't believe it now, but give it time. You will."

Tom turned and looked at his brother-in-law with a murderous stare.

"This isn't over, Alex," he said threateningly before slipping out the door.

The heavyset lawyer adjusted himself in his seat and looked somberly over at Alex. "Well . . . I'd say that went as well as can be expected."

"What else could we do?" Alex asked as a wry grin stretched his face. "Everybody wants to be in the fucking CIA."

The two men exchanged a nod before laughing.

Chapter 36

"They did what?" Jack Preston asked, nearly spilling his glass of scotch as he spun around and stared at the speakerphone.

"They neutralized two targets in Amsterdam less than two hours ago," HSI Director Richard Connolly replied angrily. His raspy voice echoed loudly inside the large upstairs study of Preston's Scottsdale home.

"Two targets?" Preston responded, leaning back in his chair. He looked at the clock on the wall and noted the time as just after ten p.m. "That doesn't make any sense. Christ . . . what else do you know, Richard?"

"A team from Special Operations carried it out this morning," Connolly continued. "Raided a hotel around five a.m. local time. One man was neutralized by the SOG team. The other apparently detonated an explosive charge and killed himself before they could get to him." There was a pause and the sound of a cigarette being lit and inhaled. When Connolly's voice returned, it was low and hostile. "The CIA is going to claim another huge victory in the war on terror, Jack. Which means our cash-strapped Congress is going to be asking once again why they need to fund a Department of Homeland Security when the homeland is being secured just fine by all the other goddamn agencies. And we can all thank your very own Agent Coleman for this one."

Preston ran his hand through his receding wisps of red hair and shook his head in disbelief. He knew the clock had been ticking on this situation—especially when Eugene Austin called to confirm that Agent Coleman had gone to Phoenix and hopped a flight to Washington the day before. He just wasn't expecting things to progress so quickly. Now, for the second time in two days, he was being raked over the coals for underestimating the speed of Coleman and his brother-in-law, Agent Murstead. He pounded his fist on the desk in anger.

"What have you heard from your agent in Amsterdam, Jack?" Connolly asked, his Southern accent thick with sarcasm. "Has he come up with anything of value? Or are he and his penis still making their way through the red-light district?"

Preston cringed at the director's question. Despite several attempts, he'd still not made contact with his field agent, and he was reluctant to share this news with his colleague. "Nothing of value yet," he replied dismissively. "If he's gathered any more intel on this morning's mission, I should know in the next hour."

"Well, I don't know what the hell you're expecting him to find in the ashes of a successful CIA operation, but apparently you handle your intel ops a little differently than I would. I just hope this field agent has a bit more loyalty than Agent Coleman."

Jack considered the comment for a brief moment before responding. "Yes, he does."

"That's good, because you and your field agent have exactly forty-eight hours to come up with something worth my time. Otherwise my next congressional discussion is going to include some painful budgetary cuts for ICE in the Western Region." Connolly muffled a cough and wheezed loudly. "I may not control your ass directly, Jack, but I can still squeeze you where it hurts. Remember that the next time you decide to jeopardize the department by sending another untrained agent into the field."

Preston shook his head and threw back the glass of scotch in his hand. A dull headache began to press against his skull.

"And Jack," Connolly continued, "if I were you, I'd do everything I could to acquire that package Coleman's source sent to that pub in Amsterdam. My gut tells me there's more to this terror network than the guys lying dead in that hotel, and it's a good bet the CIA boys have been too distracted to put men on that little detail. If we have any chance of getting back into this game, it's going to come from that package."

Preston considered the advice for a moment before reluctantly nodding. "I'm on it."

"I hope so, Jack . . . for everyone's sake. Keep me posted."

Preston grunted and hung up the phone. He immediately grabbed the bottle of single-malt scotch and refilled his glass before walking over to the window. The desert landscape appeared barren and lifeless under the black Arizona night. Preston stared at it absently as he drained his glass dry, then pulled out his cell phone and quickly dialed another number.

Chapter 37

Agent Rick Martin sat on the hard wooden stool and focused his attention on sipping his iced tea and looking inconspicuous. From his vantage point in the corner of the dim room, he could easily keep his eyes on the handful of patrons lounging at the bar and sitting at the tables around him. He sucked through his straw and glanced out the large, Romanesque window. Outside, a bone-gray blanket of clouds was releasing a drizzle of late-morning rain that polished the cobblestone streets and foreign street signs that lined the sidewalk.

Rick was hungry, but he was reluctant to order anything from the kitchen. The previous day's lunch and dinner from the bar menu had practically destroyed his stomach, and he knew there was little hope of getting anything that wasn't some variation of the heavy, greasy sausage that made him nauseated at the mere thought. He stirred his muddy brown tea and sipped at it resignedly. He'd been in Amsterdam for a little more than a day, and nearly all of that time had been spent in this strange, dark little bar.

And he didn't even really know why.

Director Preston had clearly not been happy with him when he checked in hours behind schedule upon arriving at the Hotel Keizersgracht, but how was he supposed to know it was going to take that long to find? It wasn't exactly standard procedure to send an ICE field agent to another country, and Agent Martin hadn't had the faintest idea what the cabdriver was saying when the man started yelling at him in the harsh-sounding gibberish of the local language.

He'd been too late anyway. The hotel was crawling with firefighters and police investigators when the cab finally pulled up to it, and he'd quickly motioned to the driver to keep going as the blue-coated *politie* stared at him suspiciously. After a few minutes of screaming at him over the phone, Preston had told him to proceed directly to a bar called Huppel de Pub and call him immediately if any packages showed up that were larger than a matchbox. He'd also made it clear that any fuckups on this part of the assignment were unacceptable if he wanted to continue his career with the Department of Homeland Security. Rick had practically stuttered in fear when he'd assured the director that he indeed wanted to continue his career with the DHS, and that there was no way possible he was going to fuck up anything related to his assignment. The director had merely grunted disparagingly before ending the call.

Rick stirred his tea and stared out the window, brooding about the whole strange situation. Preston had told him nothing more than he needed to know, but Rick was smart enough to know that whatever package he was waiting for must be hugely important. Why else had Preston met with him privately and told him he was being given a high-priority, top-secret assignment that was well above his pay grade? "You talk only to me on this one," Preston had said as he stared at Rick with those cold, menacing green eyes.

"Yes sir," he'd said, practically saluting at the director in terror and excitement. Next thing he knew he was flying to Amsterdam and doing his best to not look like an agent on special assignment. He'd even taken out his contacts and worn his old glasses to avoid being recognized. It wasn't until he was halfway across the Atlantic that it even dawned on him that this was his first trip to Europe.

And now, here he was, working on his fifth iced tea and trying not to think about the fact that he needed to urinate again.

The bartender walked over with an impassive smile and asked him in English if he wanted something else. *At least he speaks fucking English*, Rick thought as he glanced around the room. *Maybe I should order a beer. Nobody drinks iced tea at a bar. No, I need to stay focused. The mail should be arriving soon.*

Rick shifted in his chair again and reluctantly decided his bladder couldn't wait. He glanced out the window to make sure no one was entering the pub before quickly heading off to the restroom.

———

Tom unlocked the door to his bungalow and dragged his suitcase out of the cold Arizona night and into the small entryway. He clicked on the light, removed his shoes, and carried the suitcase into his bedroom. Five minutes later, with everything unpacked and sorted, he returned the suitcase to its proper spot in the closet and walked into the kitchen. He opened the freezer and scanned the neatly stacked rows of frozen dinners that were categorized by date. Seeing nothing that looked appealing, he grabbed a bottle of beer and a clean glass and walked wearily into the living room.

He dropped heavily onto the couch and clicked on the TV. The full weight of his trip to Langley suddenly struck him, forcing an exhausted sigh from his lips as he turned to a twenty-four-hour news channel. He poured the beer into the glass and drank half the contents in a single gulp as a handsome, thirty-something news anchor smiled and rattled off the latest stories. A few minutes later, just as Tom's eyes began to slide closed, the tone of the anchor's voice rose in excitement.

"We have some breaking news from Washington," the anchor said as a large "Breaking News" graphic flew onto the screen. "Sources from the Pentagon have just announced that an active terrorist cell has been infiltrated in Amsterdam, and two men have been killed."

Tom opened his eyes and watched as footage of a familiar hotel filled his TV screen. A large group of police and firemen stood listlessly in the foreground as the camera panned slowly up the Hotel Keizersgracht's narrow façade and paused on the second floor. The camera then zoomed in on a blown-out window that was scarred with the black remnants of a recent fire. The baritone voice of the anchorman continued over the images.

"One of the terrorists, whose identity has not yet been disclosed, is reported to have detonated an explosive device, killing him and destroying what may have been a large cache of weapons-making materials . . ."

A mug-shot photo of a heavyset man appeared on the TV, his neck and the left portion of his face covered by a large, reptilian-looking tattoo. Tom immediately recognized him as the man the SOG team had fired upon in the manager's room of the hotel.

". . . the other, a Hungarian man named András Vida who is pictured here, was already known to Dutch police and international authorities from prior arrests ranging from sex trafficking to child molestation . . ."

The image of the dead man was replaced by that of the handsome news anchor.

". . . while the Pentagon remains tight-lipped on who's responsible for finding the two men and bringing them to justice, some experts are saying this looks like the work of the CIA's Special Operations Group—a covert team of highly trained men that in recent years have played a key role in fighting the war on terror and keeping America safe . . ."

Tom finished his beer with a second quick gulp as the anchorman smiled and moved on to the next story. He gently placed the empty glass on a coaster on the coffee table in front of him before stretching out on the couch. Within seconds he was asleep.

Agent Martin stepped out of the restroom and walked back to his seat in the corner. He was just sitting down when a striking young brunette woman in a bright orange-and-white jacket entered the pub, carrying a large satchel embroidered with a crown and the name "PostNL." She stepped toward the bar and dropped the heavy bag unceremoniously onto the counter as the bartender smiled and walked toward her.

"Hallo, Danielle," the bartender said warmly, eyeing the postal carrier keenly as she opened the satchel and pulled out a handful of bundled letters.

"Hallo, Henrick," she replied, ignoring his stare as she quickly sorted the parcels.

Rick watched as the woman handed a few letters to the bartender before slipping the strap of her satchel back over her shoulder and turning to leave. She was halfway out the door when she stopped and glanced down into the large bag as if remembering something. Rick's pulse quickened as she pulled a shoebox-sized package from her mailbag and walked back to the bar. The bartender glanced at it quizzically when she handed it to him, muttering something incomprehensible as he shook his head. The woman simply shrugged and smiled before walking out into the wet Amsterdam morning. Rick stared at the brown, paper-wrapped package in the bartender's hands and drained the last of his iced tea. *That has to be our package*, he thought excitedly. Luckily he'd already worked out the plan for getting it. He'd simply walk up to the bartender and order another tea. When the bartender turned to refill his drink, he'd snatch up the parcel and make a quick exit. It wasn't elegant, but it would get the job done.

He grabbed his empty glass and stood up.

As he headed toward the bar, a man Rick hadn't noticed suddenly rose from a nearby table and stepped in the aisle in front of him. He was tall and well built, perhaps a few inches taller than Rick's own six-foot frame, with blond hair and stylish new clothes. The man moved purposefully, and Rick realized with a sudden feeling of dread that the man was also heading toward the bartender—and the package on the counter.

Rick followed him to the bar and calmly sat down as the man stepped up to the bartender and smiled.

"Hallo, Henrick," the man said with a friendly voice.

The bartender smiled in response.

"Deed mijn pakket eindelijk aankomen?"

A few barstools away, Rick listened with a growing sense of alarm. *What the hell is he asking?* he wondered as the bartender looked at the newcomer suspiciously. As if reading Rick's mind, the bartender glanced at the package before replying in English.

"This is your package?" he asked with a thick Dutch accent, sliding the small box in front of him.

"Indeed it is," the man responded in perfect, American-sounding English. Rick noticed that the man was extraordinarily handsome. He briefly wondered if Amsterdam attracted a disproportionately high number of people endowed with such good looks.

"So you are"—the bartender glanced at the name on the package—"Hubbell Gardner?"

"In the flesh."

The bartender's friendly smile faded. "May I see some identification?"

The man stared at the bartender for a moment before laughing uncomfortably. His eyes flickered at the package. "Well, that's the funny thing . . . I somehow managed to forget my wallet this morning. But I can assure you that I'm the person this package was intended for."

Rick listened intently as he watched the exchange from the corner of his eye.

"I'm sorry," the bartender replied. "But I can't give you this package without some proof of identification." He laid his hand protectively on top of the box.

"Right, of course," the blond man replied. He glanced embarrassedly over his shoulder at Rick. Rick realized he was staring at the man and smiled. The man studied him briefly before turning and slapping his hand on the bar. "I think I have an idea!" he said excitedly.

"What is that?" the bartender asked.

"How about I tell you exactly what's in the package, and then you open it? If I'm right about the contents, the package must belong to me."

The bartender looked at him with a mixture of suspicion and amusement. "And if you're wrong? What do I tell the person who comes in and finds their package opened?"

The blond man leaned his muscular body against the bar and flashed another smile. "Just cut along the edge and have a peek inside. Assuming I'm wrong, the rightful owner won't even notice. But I'm a betting man, and I'll bet you a few T-shirts and a box of Girl Scout cookies that I'm right."

The bartender tapped his fingers against the package for a moment before finally sighing and nodding. He grabbed a knife from under the counter and carefully sliced open the top edge of the box. From his seat a few feet away, Rick watched, transfixed. His heartbeat pounded loudly in his head as the bartender peered inside and lifted his eyebrows in surprise.

"Well?" the blond man said calmly, leaning in closer.

The bartender shook his head as he closed the package and looked up at him with a smile. "May I have one of the T-shirts?"

Chapter 38

"What the hell do you mean, someone *else* took the package?" Jack Preston screamed into the phone, his voice seething with anger.

"I'm . . . I'm sorry, sir," Agent Martin stammered. "A man walked into the bar just moments after the package was delivered and convinced the bartender it belonged to him."

"And just how did he manage to do that, Agent?"

"Well, he bet the bartender that he could tell him what was in the package. And apparently he was right."

"So?" Preston asked expectantly.

"So *what*, sir?"

"So what the hell did he say was in the package?"

"Oh, right . . . sorry, sir. He said there were a couple of T-shirts and a box of cookies. Girl Scout cookies, to be precise."

"And did you see anything that would confirm this?"

"No sir," Rick replied. "But I have to assume he was right. The bartender gave him the box. He even asked if he could have one of the T-shirts, but the guy wouldn't let him have one. He said it was for his own good."

"So where is this man now?" the director demanded. "Please tell me you didn't just let him walk out."

"Well, yes sir, I did let him walk out. But I'm following him. He's in the taxi ahead of me."

"And where does he appear to be heading?"

"I believe he's heading toward the airport, sir."

"All right," Preston replied, pausing to think. "When you get there, stay on him, but not too closely. Even if he doesn't know he's being followed, he's probably going to take precautions to make sure of it before he gets to his boarding gate. Do you understand me?"

"Yes sir," Agent Martin replied. "I won't let him out of my sight."

"Get your ass on whatever flight he's taking, and call me the moment you know where you're heading. Got it?"

"Yes sir, understood."

"Nice work, Agent Martin. Call me with an update . . . and don't lose him," Preston said brusquely before immediately ending the call.

"Thank you, sir," Rick said into the dead line before tucking his cell phone back into his jacket pocket. He looked over at the taxi driver and spoke with an awkward tone of superiority.

"Stay close, but not too close. Understood?"

"I understand. Not too close," the Dutch driver replied quietly.

Rick nodded smugly and adjusted his position in the passenger seat as the driver gently eased off the gas. Two hundred meters ahead, the blond man's taxi sped down the A4 Motorway toward the airport.

———

Tall Tommy sat in the backseat of the taxi, staring at the package in his hands. Through the knife-torn corner of the box, he could see the blue cloth of a T-shirt and the familiar green color of a box of Girl Scouts Thin Mint cookies. He stuck his finger into the open corner and quickly ripped open the package. The taxi driver glanced up at the sound and eyed him suspiciously through the rearview mirror before returning his attention to the busy motorway. Tall Tommy pulled the T-shirts and the box of cookies from the box and laid them on the seat next to him. He then gently picked up the last item from inside and looked at it closely.

The white envelope was sealed and unmarked. It was thin, making him believe it contained only a single sheet of paper. He held it to his nose and inhaled slowly, glancing up at the taxi driver, who was once again watching him through the mirror. Beyond the faint smell of the sealing adhesive, the envelope held no scent.

"Which terminal, sir?" the taxi driver asked.

"International, please," Tall Tommy replied.

He held the envelope for a moment, hesitating with uncertainty before finally tearing it open. A lone page of stationery fell into his hand. After one last glance at the driver, he unfolded the letter and began reading.

Chapter 39

Dear Mysterious Joe's Last Stand Guy, aka "Hubbell"—

Enclosed, please find more of the Joe's Last Stand T-shirts you're so fond of wearing, along with the money you provided for their purchase. Joe, the bar owner, has found your letters to be entertaining, and given their cult status at the bar, lucrative enough to extend his gratitude in the form of some free shirts. Don't be too overwhelmed with this gesture, as the actual cost to produce these shirts is less than $2 each. To be honest, the fact that you sent more than the long-established price of $12 for each of these shirts leads me to question your intelligence.

On another note, I wish to state for the record that I am breaking all self-imposed codes of conduct by responding to your letter. If you think this is a thinly veiled compliment, don't. But even after six letters, I still find myself believing that you somehow know more about me than I do about you. So I request that we level the proverbial playing field here and shed some light on a topic of mild interest in this quiet little corner of the world—that topic of interest being you.

I'm not requesting anything out of the ordinary; nothing more than what two people would normally know of each other after a quick introduction or perhaps five minutes over coffee. If you could answer three simple questions for me—beginning with what you're up to, continuing with why you're writing me, and concluding with a plausible reason for not revealing your identity— then I believe we'll be on much more equitable terms.

That's all I'm asking. No more, no less. Perhaps your response will get us off to a good start, or maybe just an awkward finish. Either way, reinstating my normal code of conduct now lies entirely in your hands.

You have my attention, so make it count.

Ta-ta.
—Jeri

P.S. Did you honestly think the alias "Hubbell Gardner" was clever? Anyone in the developed world with an iota of interest in movies knows Robert Redford's character from The Way We Were. You're going to have to do better than that.

Chapter 40

"Your time's almost up, Jack." The gruff voice of HSI Director Connolly rang out loudly over the speakerphone in Preston's Phoenix office. "So what have you got?"

"The situation has changed," Preston replied matter-of-factly as he stared at his computer screen and punched at the keys. "My agent in Amsterdam reported in. It appears there's still something in play."

"Give me the details."

"A package arrived today from Coleman's source, as we expected. My agent was waiting there as directed, but someone else claimed the package before he could. Took it and immediately headed for the airport."

"What do we know about him?" Connolly asked.

"Tall, Caucasian man. Presumably American. Well-built with blond hair. No other information on him right now, but according to my agent, the man was clearly expecting the package. My agent followed him from the bar, and within an hour he was boarding a flight to Beijing."

"And where exactly is he now?"

Preston paused briefly at the question as he stared at his computer monitor. "Our agent lost him in Beijing."

"No, you mean *your* agent, Jack," Connolly replied with a disgusted tone. "Good god, it's a miracle your agent managed to follow him as far as China, assuming he's a professional. And I have no doubt we're dealing with a professional here."

Preston nodded. "I'm sure we are. I'm also sure there are a lot more players involved in this than the two lying dead in an Amsterdam morgue."

"Be careful with your assumptions," Connolly retorted. There was a pause as he took a deep drag of his cigarette. "I got a briefing from the National Security Council about an hour ago. If what I'm reading is correct, only one of the men neutralized in the Amsterdam hotel was directly involved in this."

Preston stopped typing and looked over at the speakerphone. "What are you saying?"

"I'm saying the Dutch police had already been monitoring the Hungarian named Vida as part of a large sex-trafficking investigation. They'd had phone taps and surveillance on him for months. Apparently they'd collected more than enough evidence to convict him of trafficking young Hungarian girls into the Netherlands. But what they did not have was a single shred of evidence that suggested he was involved in an international terrorist organization. The report also indicates he was more than a few bricks shy of a full load when it came to intelligence. Not exactly the profile of a rogue terrorist, Jack. As incredible as it may seem, it appears this Vida moron was just a common thug who was unlucky enough to be holed up at the hotel when Murstead's team showed up."

Preston winced as Connolly erupted into a loud fit of coughing. He shook his head in disbelief. "Leave it to the fucking CIA. They kill a guy by accident and he still ends up being a criminal. Jesus, some agencies just get all the luck."

Connolly continued coughing.

"Well, the good news for us is that there's definitely something still in play. And it seems the Langley boys aren't aware of it."

"I haven't heard anything from my channels that suggests otherwise," Connolly replied, his voice weak from coughing. "But we need more information—starting with the goddamn identity of Agent Coleman's source in Flagstaff." He paused and cleared the phlegm from his voice before speaking clearly into the phone.

"It's time to tighten the screws on your boy again, Jack."

Chapter 41

The first muted rays of morning sun filtered through the living room blinds and settled on Tom Coleman's sleeping face. Tom twitched and blinked as he begrudgingly woke up, cursing the beer that was still sloshing in his skull from the night before. A few minutes later he rose from the couch and began picking up the empty glasses neatly arranged on the coffee table. It had been the same routine for the last three mornings, the same routine since he'd returned home from Langley.

He glanced out the living room window and shivered instinctively. A deep frost covered the neighborhood outside. Across the street, his neighbor was carefully shuffling to his car. Tom watched with a pang of envy as the man angrily scraped at the ice on his windshield before jumping into the driver's seat and heading off to work. As the car disappeared from view, Tom noticed the same maroon sedan he'd seen several days before, parked farther down the street. He studied it curiously for a moment, then shook his head and walked into the bedroom. Thirty minutes later he was showered and dressed. He fixed a simple breakfast of scrambled eggs and toast, finished half of it, and spent an hour cleaning and restraightening things around the house before once again facing the stark reality of his situation.

I have nowhere else to go.

Tom stood in his living room, deep in thought. He tried not to think about the meeting with Alex and his shitbag lawyer. His anger was still too intense to evaluate the situation objectively. But one thing was now certain—Alex had been using him from the start. He'd played on Tom's dream of being in the CIA to get exactly what he had needed, then tossed him aside like some nameless fucking informant. Tom balled his hands into tight fists and breathed slowly, forcing himself to remain calm as he began pacing back and forth across the living room floor. He focused his thoughts on what he needed to do now. *The CIA is a closed door*, he told himself, letting the words sink in. *I need to focus on getting my old job back. I need to get back on Jack Preston's good side. I need to convince him this wasn't my idea, that I was used by the CIA. I need to get my life back to normal* . . .

He stopped pacing and took another deep, calming breath.

And then, when everything's done, I'll focus my hatred on Alex.

Tom smiled briefly at the thought before a more somber one came to mind. Standing in his living room, he suddenly realized there was one other thing he needed to do. He strolled into the kitchen, grabbed his car keys, and headed off into the frigid cold morning.

===

"Holy Christ, the prodigal son returns," Chip said as Tom walked into the dark warm interior of the saloon and settled onto the barstool next to him. "What brings you here so early?"

"I was just going to ask you the same question," Tom replied. "Don't you ever take a day off?"

"I take every day off. That's why I'm always here."

Tom nodded as he removed his gloves and carefully arranged them in their usual spot in front of him. "Well, I suppose I'm taking the day off too."

"Well, good for you," Chip responded. "I'm sure Jeri will be happy to set you up."

Tom looked over at the corner behind the counter. Jeri, nestled cozily on her stool with a book in hand, glanced up and gave him the slightest hint of a smile. He smiled awkwardly and gave her a quick nod.

"Haven't seen you for a few days," Chip continued, his blue eyes studying Tom closely. "Everything okay?"

"Yeah, fine," Tom answered dismissively. "Just busy. You know how it goes."

"I believe I do." The old man raised his glass and took a drink. The two men watched as Jeri poured a fresh beer from the tap and walked it over to Tom.

"Thanks, Jeri," Tom said as he pushed a five-dollar bill across the counter. He stared at her until her large amber eyes met his. "It's good to see you again."

"Thanks," Jeri replied coolly. She grabbed the cash and walked over to the register.

"Keep the change," Tom said as she walked away. He watched as she quickly worked the register and tossed the coin change into the tip jar on the counter before slipping back onto her stool. Within seconds she was reabsorbed in her book. The sound of Chip clearing his throat snapped Tom back into reality.

"So," Chip mumbled as he leaned toward Tom. "What's the latest with the investigation?"

Tom pretended to weigh the question for a moment as he took a long sip of his beer. He then rested the glass on the counter and looked somberly at the older man. "It's over."

Chip's eyes widened in surprise. "Are you serious?" He glanced at the wall of letters and photos before turning back to Tom. "So what does that mean?"

"I'm legally obligated not to discuss details about the case," Tom said quietly, his stare wandering back to Jeri's figure nestled catlike on the barstool. "But I can tell you that Jeri is no longer in any danger."

"What makes you so sure of that?" Chip asked skeptically.

Tom's eyes lingered on Jeri for a moment before he turned and narrowed them on Chip. "Because her mystery writer is dead."

———

Eugene Austin parked across the street from the bar he'd watched Agent Coleman walk into and flipped on his homemade listening device in the backseat. He would have been in place sooner, but he'd decided to stop and put the signs from his old pizza delivery job on his mom's car just in case Coleman had noticed it parked in his neighborhood earlier.

From where he sat, Eugene could look directly across old Route 66 into the arched window of Joe's Last Stand Saloon. Unfortunately, he could barely see anything within the dark interior. *Whatever*, he thought irritably as he opened his laptop and put on his headphones. He turned a small dial on the top of the device and immediately heard Coleman speaking to another man. The other man's voice was low and unfamiliar. Satisfied that the listening device was capturing the conversation, he reached over and punched the "Record" button on the laptop next to him.

He pulled off the large headphones and eased the car seat back. *I'll check the recording later*, he thought as he slipped a cool new pair of earbuds into his ears and began listening to a mix of songs he'd just downloaded on his phone.

He stared out at the late-autumn landscape and yawned. A postman paced briskly down the sidewalk on his route, the blue collar of his uniform turned up against the cold as his breath steamed out behind him. Otherwise the old downtown was deserted. After a few minutes of scanning the empty street, Eugene closed his eyes and drifted off to sleep.

══

"I just don't get it," Chip said gruffly. "A few weeks ago you were telling me that I was instrumental in solving this case. Now you're saying the case is solved and I don't have the right to know any details."

Tom shrugged dejectedly. "Look, Chip, it's classified information. I came here to tell you the case was closed. I wasn't under any obligation to do even that, but I thought it was the right thing to do. I understand that you want to know the details, but I'm not in a position to give them. The guy is dead, and that's all that matters. The rest is just so much bullshit in a CIA report." He shook his head and drained the last of his beer.

"I thought you were running this thing," the older man replied as he stared at his beer.

"Well, you were wrong."

The front door of the saloon opened with a groan. Both men turned to watch the postman walk in and give them a half-smile as he strolled toward the bar. He tossed the day's mail on the counter in front of Jeri and flashed another smile before quickly disappearing out the door.

"Hey, Jeri, can I get another one?" Tom asked quietly. Jeri nodded as she stood and began sorting through the mail.

Tom stared at his empty beer glass, his thoughts churning in his head. He still hadn't decided how to tell Jeri the news. *Would it even matter to her?* he wondered. Jeri wasn't exactly the warmest of people, especially when it came to men. Why should some unknown pen pal's death be any different? Considering he was an international terrorist, she should be leaping for joy that the scumbag was no longer walking the earth.

In fact, depending on what he revealed to her, Jeri might even look at Tom as something of a savior. He smiled to himself as he considered that thought.

"So he's dead, huh?" Chip said, interrupting his train of thought. "You're sure of that?"

"For Christ's sake, Chip . . . I saw it myself. Yes, I'm sure of it."

Chip pointed his thumb toward the corner of the bar and gave Tom a wry grin. "Then how do you explain the airmail letter Jeri's holding in her hand?"

PART III

More financially solvent than most economies, more powerful than most governments, and more technologically advanced than most militaries, the mature Corporate State will rapidly outgrow every external threat to its existence, with one notable exception—competing Corporate States.

In order to defend key assets such as intellectual property and vital personnel from competitive threat, the Corporate State will employ the same strategies and tactics of any major government or country. With billions of dollars in revenue at stake, clandestine activities ranging from intelligence gathering and sophisticated electronic warfare to coordinated military-style operations will become an everyday reality in the new business ecology.

Ultimately, the competitive actions of the Corporate States will mimic those of any competing predators in the natural world. Alliances will be made, weakness will be studied, and, when the opportunity to dominate presents itself, power will be exercised with swift and lethal precision.

—James H. Stone, *Predictions in the New Business Ecology*

Chapter 42

Jeri stood behind the counter and vaguely noticed her heart beating faster as she held the red-and-blue-edged airmail envelope. It was thicker than any of the previous, its corner covered with extra airmail stamps and the dull smears of red "RUSH" postmarks. She smiled and began tearing it open excitedly when Tom's voice cried out across from her.

"Don't open that!" he screamed as he leaned across the counter and roughly snatched the envelope from her hand. Jeri stared at him in shock.

"What the hell are you doing?" she asked angrily, holding out her hand. "That belongs to me!"

Tom ignored her as he carefully examined the envelope. He shook his head disbelievingly as he held it up to the overhead light.

"It can't be him," he mumbled. "It just can't be."

Jeri watched him cautiously for a moment before looking over at Chip.

"Do you have any idea what he's talking about?"

Chip nodded slowly. "I'm afraid I do."

"Then please, enlighten me," Jeri demanded.

"Your former pen pal was a terrorist, Jeri," Tom said matter-of-factly as he dropped the envelope onto the counter.

"A what?" Jeri asked, smiling at the absurdity of the comment.

"You heard me," Tom replied gravely. He turned and pointed at the shrine of letters on the far wall. "You see all those letters over there? They weren't written by a doctor, or an art collector, or some freelance journalist out on assignment. They were written by a killer. By an international goddamn *terrorist*. And when he wasn't writing letters and taking silly pictures for you, he was murdering innocent people."

Jeri's smile slowly faded. "You can't be serious."

"I'm absolutely serious," Tom replied.

Jeri looked back and forth at the two men. "Okay, what the hell's going on here? Is this some kind of practical joke?"

"I think it's time Jeri heard the full story," Chip said softly as he stared into his beer. "Wouldn't you agree, Tom?"

Tom narrowed his eyes on Chip. "Sure, why not." He frowned at Jeri and pointed at the barstool next to him. "You may as well come over here and sit down."

"I'll stand right here, thanks," Jeri replied tersely, crossing her arms as she leaned against the counter.

"Suit yourself," Tom countered. "You want the story? Here's the story."

Tom quickly began summarizing his investigation, beginning with his initial discovery of the link between the letters' origins and the deaths of several Petronus Energy researchers. Jeri's eyes widened in surprise as he told her about the death in Kaliningrad that proved his assumption was more than just a theory. He was just about to tell her about Alex and the SOG team raid in Amsterdam when she held up her hand.

"I don't get it," Jeri said, shaking her head. "Even if there was some shred of truth to what you're saying, how could you possibly know all this?"

"It's my business to know all this," Tom replied as he reached into his jacket. He pulled out his ICE badge and briefly showed it to her before returning it to his pocket. "I'm not playing with you,

Jeri. I'm an agent with the Department of Homeland Security. This is what I do. I know everything there is to know about your pen pal." He paused and pointed at the envelope on the counter. "And I'm telling you . . . that letter can't be from him."

Jeri picked up the envelope and held it in front of Tom. "What makes you so sure?"

Tom looked at her with a cautious expression. "Because four nights ago I watched him die in his hotel room in Amsterdam."

Jeri stood frozen for a moment, waiting for the shockwave to pass through her. She squeezed the envelope tightly in her hand before walking over to her barstool and sitting down. A moment later she looked up at Tom with an accusatory stare.

"You used the address he included in the last letter to find him, didn't you?"

"Yes," Tom replied.

Jeri's eyes flashed to Chip. "And you knew about this?"

Chip nodded. "I did, Jeri. I'm sorry. That's why I've been spending more time here lately. I thought if nothing else I could at least . . . well, keep my eye on you."

Jeri glared at him angrily before looking at Tom. "So how did he die?"

"He killed himself," Tom answered unapologetically. "We had him holed up in his hotel room, surrounded by agents. There was no chance of escape, and he knew it. So he detonated a bomb, like any other gutless terrorist would do. Luckily none of the agents involved were killed."

Jeri stared at the envelope in her hand and shook her head. "I don't believe it." She ripped the corner open and looked inside. The folded sheets of hotel stationery were covered in a familiar handwriting. Jeri started to remove them, then stopped and looked at Tom.

"Did you see him do it?" she asked.

Tom looked at her quizzically. "See him do *what*?"

"Did you actually see him detonate the explosive?"

"Yes. Well, I mean . . . I watched it happen over a live video link from the agents conducting the operation. They were just about to enter his room when the explosion happened."

"Was the door closed?"

Tom sighed. "Yes, the door was closed."

"So you did *not* actually see him detonate the device—correct?"

Tom shook his head in frustration. "Look, Jeri, I see where you're going with this, but it's pointless. There were three teams of agents covering the guy when he entered the hotel. They swept the entire place before entering his room. He blew himself to hell, and I saw it happen. Okay?"

"But how did you identify him in the first place?" she asked, her voice holding an edge of doubt. "You can't tell what he looks like from the photos."

"His T-shirt," Tom replied. "He was wearing that same goddamn Joe's Last Stand T-shirt when he walked into the hotel, and part of it was still sticking to what was left of his body after the explosion."

"Jesus Christ, Tom," Chip said quietly.

"Hey, she asked the question, didn't she?" Tom shot back defensively, his eyes still fixed on the envelope in Jeri's hand. "So . . . are you going to open it or what?"

Jeri nodded as she carefully pulled out the letter and unfolded the crisp white pages. She glanced at the top right corner of the first page before again looking over at Tom.

"When did you say you killed him?"

Tom looked at her quizzically. "It was last Saturday . . . the twenty-fourth. Why?"

Jeri ignored his question as she started to read, the slightest trace of a smile pulling at the corners of her mouth.

Chapter 43

847 Jinan Road
No. 1549
November 26, 9:27 a.m.
Planet Dongying
The Galaxy of China

Jeri—

I'm not going to kid you, Jeri-girl, I'm writing this with more than a touch of the melancholy. Maybe it's this country. Don't believe what you've read about China. The only things this country really makes are great walls of concrete and ceilings of smog. Sometimes it's hard to tell one gray mass from the other. All I know is that the image of you curled up warmly behind that magnificent chocolate-colored old bar reading this humble little letter of fanatical obsession and abject devotion is the only thing keeping me going. Well, that, and the definitive collection of Eugene O'Neill I bought online last night in a drunken moment of weakness. Talk about under-celebrated playwrights! Seriously . . . have you ever seen The Iceman Cometh?

Getting your letter was like being the pope after finding the Holy Grail. I've read it no less than sixteen times. Everything that flowed from your pen, from the moment you questioned my intelligence until the final threat of never talking to me again, was nothing short of poetry. I doubt that such a marginally warm letter has ever been so well received.

Our kids will be precocious little buggers, Jeri. I know it.

Of course, this letter isn't intended to be just another long-winded sermon of pharmaceutically enhanced incidents and accidents on my journey toward self-endarkenment. You have questions that need to be answered.

"Beginning with what you're up to" I believe was your first request, though you already know the answer. The tequila, the womanizing, the endless travel through the seedier folds of terra firma . . . isn't it clear that I'm up to no good?

Not that I've had much choice in the matter, Jeri-girl. Spin around this planet as much as I do and you're forced to pack light. I'm toting enough proverbial baggage as it is without the extra weight of a moral compass. And who needs one anyway? Right and wrong are as mythical as true north itself. It's all just a matter of degrees, baby-like points on a map. Some are good, most are bad, but in the end, they're all worth seeing for yourself.

This brings us to your second request—the question of why I'm writing you. Of course, you already know the answer to this one too. You see, from that moment I first laid eyes on the beauty behind the bar at Joe's, I simply and selfishly knew that she was someone worth knowing. I mean, how often does one come across the path of a fair-skinned lass with eyes as deep and turbulent as the spring-fed Amazon, a mind as sharp as a thirty-gauge needle, and looks that would put even the dawn-sky view of Victoria Falls to shame? Not often, Jeri. Have I already mentioned that our kids will be gorgeous?

And then there's your last request . . . the revelation of my identity. I have to say, this one stumps me, Jeri. Not the question, just the value of the answer. A name? Mine is a name you wouldn't know. This face? As common as they come. The rest of me, baby, is just tequila and words. Six feet of random thoughts and a smoking cigarette, wandering the back roads of sanity and society one sinful step at a time. The truth is, Jeri, if you've read my letters carefully, you know me better than anyone.

Was that last paragraph as depressing as it sounds? Christ, I'd better sign off until the lithium kicks in Time to find a cozy communist bar that serves Fortaleza and Chinese-made Camel Lights. I swear, Jeri, fun is harder to find around here than a virgin in East LA.

I'll be glad when all of this is over.

Ta!
Mysterious Joe's Last Stand Guy

P.S. Thanks again for sending the T-shirts, Jeri-girl. Don't tell the boys in Amsterdam, but I ended up keeping a few for myself.

P.P.S. Please tell me you heeded my advice on the Brainybuddies. It's happening NOW. I've nabbed three of them so far, but finding the last is proving to be a real bastard.

P.P.P.S. You can't turn a street corner here without running into a barbecued terrier. Show me canine charcuterie and I'll show you the culinary abyss. Fuck it.

Go ahead, order dog.

Chapter 44

"May I read it, Jeri?"

Tom Coleman stretched his arm across the counter and wiggled his fingers impatiently.

Jeri looked up from the letter. *This can't be happening*, she thought as she stared out the front window at the cold November morning. She shook her head and closed her eyes as a torrent of questions began flooding her mind.

"Jeri . . . *please*?"

Jeri paced down the bar and dropped the letter into Tom's outstretched hand. He grabbed the pages and started reading, his shoulders slumping lower with every sentence.

"Holy shit . . . it's him, isn't it? The son of a bitch is fucking *alive*."

He looked up at Jeri with a disbelieving stare.

"You tell me," she answered sharply. "You're the one claiming to be the expert on this guy."

Tom muttered something under his breath and turned his attention back to the letter. Jeri turned and fixed a venomous stare on Chip.

"I think you have some explaining to do."

In his corner seat, Chip sat up straight and cleared his throat.

"Jeri, I'm as sorry as it gets for keeping this from you, but it wasn't entirely my decision." He pointed his thumb at Tom, who was too absorbed in the letter to notice. "Apparently the current thinking of our country's Homeland Security is that you catch bigger fish with ignorant bait."

Jeri glared at Chip for a moment before turning on Tom.

"Is that true?" she asked.

"What?" Tom asked, absorbed in the letter.

Jeri reached over and snatched the letter from his hands. "If you knew this guy was a terrorist, why didn't you tell me?"

"It's not that simple," Tom replied, reaching his hand out impatiently. "Can I have that back?"

"No, you may not."

Jeri walked to the end of the bar and stood in front of Chip. She laid the letter on the counter and rested her hand on it protectively. "I'll let *you* read it, Chip . . . on one condition."

The older man looked up at Jeri with a pensive stare. He could see the glow of anger beginning to smolder in her eyes. "What condition?" he asked.

"Stop trying to look out for me."

She pushed the pages of the letter toward him and grabbed his empty glass. "I've done just fine on my own," she said as she walked toward the beer tap, her eyes burning into Tom as she walked past. "And I certainly don't need the protection of the Department of Homeland Security. Not that you guys made any effort to provide it anyway."

Tom shrugged and gently waved the air in front of him. "Look, I understand you're upset, Jeri. But once you calm down, we can talk this whole situation out . . . including ways we can ensure your safety, if such a thing is needed." He pushed his empty glass toward her. "Honestly, I don't think you're in any real danger."

"Is that your professional opinion?" Jeri asked.

"Yes, it is."

"Just like it was your professional opinion that this guy was dead, right? Thanks, but your professional opinion means absolutely nothing to me."

The front door of the saloon groaned open, stabbing a long blade of cold light into the dim interior as a short, barrel-chested, bald man walked in and quickly closed the door behind him. He took off his coat and met the three faces staring at him with a wide grin as his stout legs paced toward the bar.

"How's my best bartender doing, Jeri?" Joe Brown asked as he stepped up to the bar next to Tom.

"Just great, Joe," Jeri muttered as she walked a fresh pint of beer over to Chip, his attention still fixed on the letter. "How are you?"

"Goddamn weather's wreaking hell on my joints," Joe replied, shaking his head. "Took me twenty minutes just to get outta the damn bed this morning. Got any hot coffee on?"

"I do," Jeri replied softly. She grabbed the coffeepot and a mug and brought it to him. Joe watched as she filled his cup before turning to the man sitting next to him.

"Having a nice morning so far?" he asked Tom.

"Not exactly," Tom replied, staring at his empty glass. Jeri turned without acknowledging him and returned to her seat. Both men gave her a perplexed look as she opened her book and started to read.

"Jeri," Joe said finally, "I believe our friend here could use another beer."

"I'm sure he could, Joe," Jeri replied without looking up. "But he's not our friend, and he's not going to be served another beer from me."

Joe looked suspiciously at Tom and scratched his chin. His eyes drifted down the bar to Chip, who was still absorbed in the letter. He turned and looked at Jeri with a lost expression. "What the hell's going on, Jeri?"

Jeri gave him a weary frown before closing her book and sitting up straight on her barstool. "Let me give you a brief update, Joe. I got another letter from the postman this morning. Unfortunately, I was accosted by the gentleman sitting next to you before I could read it. His name is Tom, but you and I should probably refer to him as *Agent Coleman*. Agent Coleman works for the Department of Homeland Security. He's also been secretly investigating my mysterious letter writer." She paused and gave Chip a snide look. "With the help of a certain *senior* assistant."

"Is that true?" Joe said, looking at Chip. Chip nodded.

"Agent Coleman was surprised to see a new letter from our mystery writer this morning," Jeri continued. "Especially since a team of commandos raided his hotel a few nights ago in Amsterdam and forced him to blow up everything in his room—including himself." She leaned forward on her stool and whispered mockingly, "You see, Joe, my letter writer was a terrorist."

Joe stared back at Jeri, his eyes wide with shock.

"Or should I say *is* a terrorist?" Jeri said as she stood up and walked toward Chip. "Because if he was dead, I don't think he'd still be writing letters." She glared at Tom as she passed. "Anyway, I just found out a few minutes before you walked in that both Chip and Agent Coleman here have been aware of this fact for some time, but decided it was best to keep it from me."

"You gotta be kidding me," Joe said in a hushed tone of disbelief. He turned and scowled at Chip, sitting quietly. "What the hell were you thinking, Chip? For chrissake . . . I thought you looked after Jeri like she was your own daughter!"

Chip looked up from the letter and narrowed his blue eyes at the bar owner. "Don't start with me, Joe. Why the hell do you think I've spent every single day sitting here? To look after *you*?"

"Go easy on him, Joe," Jeri said as she stopped in front of Chip. She reached out and took the letter from his grasp, squeezing his hand gently before walking back to her corner. "He wasn't the one who decided to keep me in the dark."

"Oh, really?" Joe said as he took a step back from the counter and turned to Tom. "Then I'm starting to understand why Jeri won't serve you that beer after all. In fact, I'm wondering why I shouldn't just throw your ass out of my saloon."

Tom broke his stare from the letter in Jeri's hands and glanced over at the bar owner. He hadn't met Joe before, but he already disliked the heavyset bald man with the shiny head and flashy temper. He gave Joe a smug smile and raised his hands defensively.

"Okay, I think everyone needs to just calm down for a minute. It's not like I made up the rule book for investigating terrorism. I was just following protocol." He turned and looked at Jeri. "Can I at least see the Polaroid, Jeri?" he asked.

Jeri eyed him coldly for a moment before shaking her head. "There wasn't one."

Tom looked at her skeptically. "Are you sure? I swear I felt a Polaroid in the envelope before you opened it."

Jeri returned his stare with a contemptuous smile. "Well, it looks like you were wrong once again, Agent Coleman."

Tom slammed his fist onto the counter. "Jesus Christ! How do you expect me to do my job when you won't even share the fucking evidence with me?"

"She just told you there wasn't a photo," Joe replied, his voice low and threatening. "And around here, Jeri's word is a helluva lot stronger than that of some goddamn federal agent. So unless you have a warrant to search my establishment, I suggest you drop the subject."

Tom nodded and looked up at Jeri with a piercing stare. "You know what's funny, Jeri? The reason I came down here this morning was to tell you the truth about all this . . . to explain everything and tell you that your anonymous pen pal was dead. There's no rule in the handbook for *that*, no rule that says we have to tell you anything about the murderers and terrorists we protect you from. I just thought you deserved to know."

"But he's not dead, is he, Tom?" Jeri replied angrily, holding up the letter. "He's alive and well . . . and apparently in China now." She shook her head. "Which means he's also going to kill again, doesn't it?"

Tom glanced at the letter before nodding.

"Excuse me for a moment," Jeri said, slipping from her barstool. She ducked under the counter and headed toward the restroom. Joe waited until she was gone, then walked behind the bar and grabbed the letter.

"Joe, are you sure there isn't a Polaroid sitting inside the envelope over there?" Tom asked.

Joe looked around and shrugged. "I don't even see the envelope."

Tom nodded and looked off toward the restroom. "Right."

Both Tom and Chip sat quietly as Joe stood behind the bar and read the letter. When he was done, he tossed the pages on the counter and scratched his head.

"Shoulda known this guy was a damn lunatic from the start," he said as he poured himself another coffee. "What with all that romantic nonsense and those ridiculous coded messages."

Tom grabbed the letter and began to pull out his notepad when he paused and looked at Joe.

"What do you mean, *coded messages?*"

Joe rolled his eyes at Tom from behind his coffee cup. "Are you kidding me? You really think he's collecting some damn toys called *Brainybuddies?* Give me a fuckin' break. Whatever he's collecting, it ain't toys. And look at the way he always ends each letter with that 'don't order dog' statement. That didn't strike you as odd?"

Tom looked again at the letter. His eyes widened in shock.

"Jesus Christ," Joe said, shaking his head at the Homeland Security agent. "It's a wonder you ever found him in the first place."

"He didn't find him," Chip muttered, his hands wiping the sweat from his beer glass. "The guy gave Jeri his hotel address in the last letter."

Joe chuckled cynically. "Man, I've heard some crazy shit in my days, but this one beats 'em all."

Jeri emerged from the restroom and walked back to the bar, an odd, distant expression on her face.

"You okay, Jeri?" Joe asked as she ducked under the counter and emerged next to him.

"Yeah, I'm fine," she replied. "But I need to ask a favor. Can you have Owen fill in for me for a few days, starting this afternoon? I could really use a break from this whole situation."

"You got it," Joe replied, squeezing her shoulder. "Between Owen and me, we've got this place covered. Get outta here."

Jeri gave him a weak smile before gathering her things. She was about to leave when she glanced at the letter and paused. Joe knew what she was thinking.

"I won't put it up, Jeri," he said quietly. "Hell, maybe it's time to just rip the whole goddamn shrine down. Hasn't been getting much attention lately anyway."

Jeri stared at the letter for a moment, deep in thought, before turning and looking at him with an expression that bordered on fright. "No, don't do that. Put the letter up, Joe. Put it up and just pretend like nothing has changed. After all, nothing *has* changed."

Joe looked at her curiously and nodded. "Okay, Jeri . . . if you're sure that's what you want me to do."

"I'm sure." She turned and waved to Chip. "Maybe you should take a few days off from this place too, old man. There's not going to be anyone around to look out for."

Chip looked up at her with a solemn smile. "There's always some-one to look out for, Jeri. Just make sure you stay safe for the next few days." His blue eyes narrowed. "Whatever it is you're planning to do."

"I will."

"Need a ride, Jeri?" Tom asked. "I can drive you home if you'd like."

Jeri didn't bother to make eye contact with him as she pulled on her coat and grabbed her bag. "No thanks, Agent Coleman. In fact, if I see you so much as turn onto my street, I'll have you arrested for stalking. Do you understand?"

"Got it," Tom replied. He finished scribbling something in his notepad and returned it to his pocket.

"Thanks again, Joe," Jeri said over her shoulder as she walked out the door. Joe nodded.

Tom watched through the arched windows at the front of the saloon as Jeri stepped outside and crossed the street before disap-pearing from view. He was about to turn away when a maroon sedan parked at the corner caught his attention. He looked closer at the familiar car now covered with pizza delivery signs. Someone appeared to be stretched out asleep in the driver's seat.

"Hey, would there happen to be another exit in this place?" Tom asked Joe, who was now busying himself behind the counter.

Joe glared at him before pointing toward an unmarked door next to the bathroom. "That'll take you to the back alley," he mum-bled. "And I won't even ask why you need to use it. I'm just happy you're leaving."

———

Eugene Austin was standing outside of Melissa Carson's window in his dream. A warm soft light was on inside her bedroom, cast-ing provocative shadows as someone moved around the room. He stood still as a statue as he watched, crouched in the shadows of a manicured row of shrubs that lined the edge of her parents' large home. He took a deep breath and exhaled slowly, listening intently as the smoke of his breath curled around the features of his young face. He could hear her moving around the room, the soft purr of her voice warm and inviting as she spoke to some unseen person.

And then she appeared.

The most beautiful girl in his trigonometry class, Melissa stood centered in the window, her unblemished face gazing quizzically out at the black night. She leaned forward as if seeing something, forcing Eugene to shrink farther into the shadows before he realized she was simply admiring her own reflection in the window. She was distracted, her hand pressed tightly to her ear as she spoke into her cell phone. Her free hand moved up along the large, loose-fitting T-shirt that covered her body, pulling at the material until the pale white skin of her stomach appeared underneath. Eugene let out a quick breath of air as a sudden shiver of excitement moved quickly up his spine. He was just getting comfortable when, strangely, the ground beneath him began to shake. He glanced around anxiously as the slow, swaying movement turned to a violent jolt. It was then that his conscious mind suddenly registered what was happening.

Eugene snapped upright in his seat as the back door of his mother's car slammed shut. "What the fuck!" he screamed, tearing the earbuds from his ears as he frantically spun around to face the intruder in the backseat.

Tom Coleman looked at him and smiled.

"What the fuck do you want?" Eugene stammered, his nasally voice cracking with mock courage. He instinctively reached for the small asthma inhaler lying on the seat next to him.

"I'll take a large pepperoni pizza and a good reason for why I'm being followed by a fucking pizza delivery driver," Tom said matter-of-factly.

"Oh, fuck, it's *you*," Eugene replied, recognizing the face of the man sitting in the back of his mother's car. He instinctively covered his face with his hands and shook his head.

"What do you mean, 'it's you'?" Tom asked as he glanced around at the car's interior. His eyes paused on a large black box sitting on the seat next to him. "Who sent you to watch me? Alex?" he asked threateningly.

Eugene groaned loudly.

"Hey, I'm asking you a question. Did my fucking brother-in-law hire you?" He slapped Eugene's headrest hard with his hand, causing the teenager's head to snap forward. "Answer me!"

"Ouch! No . . . I mean . . . I don't know! Fuck, dude—chill out!"

Tom paused and studied Eugene closely. "Jesus Christ. What are you . . . sixteen?"

"Eighteen," Eugene replied flatly, slumping lower into the front seat. "I'll be nineteen next month."

"What's your name?"

Eugene shrugged at Tom's question before mumbling one of his favorite quotes from an old spy movie: "You're on a need-to-know basis, and you don't need to know."

Tom slapped the headrest again, causing the boy's head to once more snap forward. "Don't get smart with me, shithead. I could arrest you right now if I wanted to."

"I doubt that," Eugene replied sulkily.

Tom sat in the backseat, his mind spinning. He realized there was only one reasonable explanation for his being under surveillance. "It's Preston, isn't it?" he asked, watching Eugene through the rearview mirror.

The teenager's eyes nervously flickered up at him.

"Fuck, I knew it!" Tom said angrily as he slapped the headrest again. He leaned forward and glared menacingly at the eighteen-year-old. "How long have you been sitting out here?"

Eugene hesitated before answering. "For as long as you've been in that bar over there," he said dejectedly as he gestured toward the saloon.

"Right," Tom replied, throwing his arm over the front seat and placing his gloved hand firmly on Eugene's shoulder. He was surprised at how thin and bony the kid was. "And were you recording the conversation that just took place?" he asked, squeezing his shoulder persuasively.

"That's . . . that's none of your business," Eugene answered defiantly. Tom could hear an unmistakable crack of fear in the kid's voice.

"I'll take that as a 'yes,'" Tom responded. "Has it been sent to Preston?"

"I report immediately after each contact," Eugene replied, grimacing at the fact that he'd just confirmed he was working for the director. He cursed and shook his head.

"You didn't answer my question," Tom replied, tightening his grip.

"No, I haven't. I should be reporting in right now."

"Good," Tom said, releasing his grip. He thought quietly for a moment before smiling and gently patting Eugene on the shoulder. "Okay, change of plans."

"What do you mean?"

"You're not going to send that recording to Jack."

"The fuck I'm not," Eugene responded, spinning around in the front seat. "Look, dude, I'm not about to take orders from the guy I'm supposed to be monitoring. I'm sending my report to Director Preston with that file just like I'm supposed to."

Tom smiled and again rested his hand on the teenager's shoulder. "You like your job, don't you?" he asked in a friendly tone.

"Yes."

"Probably pays pretty well too, huh?"

Eugene gave him a smug smile. "Better than what you make."

"Sure, of course," Tom replied, smiling back at him. "Which is exactly why you wouldn't want Preston to find out I just blew your cover." He leaned closer, squeezing the boy's shoulder firmly. "Think about it, kid. All I have to do is make one phone call to Preston, and it's over—and I'm betting that the Department of Homeland Security is the only paying gig you've got right now, correct?"

Eugene stared at him glumly.

"I'd hate to see you lose your paycheck right before Christmas," Tom continued. "You've probably still got gifts to buy for your girlfriend, not to mention all those new games and gadgets that geeks—I mean *guys*—like you are so fond of."

Eugene shrugged Tom's hand off his shoulder. "So what do you want me to do? I can't *not* report to Jack. He knows I'm watching you. I have to send him something."

"Of course you do," Tom replied. "So here's what you're going to do. First, you're going to erase everything you just recorded. Then you're going to follow me home."

"Dude, why should I do that?"

"Because when I get home, I'm going to make a call on my landline, which I'm guessing you've already tapped. I want you to record *that* conversation and send it to Preston. I guarantee what I say on that call will make him so happy he'll have no choice but to renew your contract for another year . . . or semester."

Tom reached over and playfully slapped Eugene on the cheek. "So, do we have a deal, kiddo?"

Eugene sat rigidly for a moment before slowly nodding. "Deal."

Chapter 45

"For god's sake, Allie, just say it."

Jeri continued walking along the trail, her arms raised in front of her to keep the branches of scrub brush from whipping at her face. Behind her, Allie followed in her footsteps and quietly cursed her decision to come along.

"Say *what*?" Allie replied, her voice thick with sarcasm.

"Whatever it is you're dying to say. I can practically hear it spinning around in your head right now." Jeri looked up and quickly noted the direction of the trail before refocusing her attention on the dense barrage of branches.

"You mean besides 'where in the hell are we going?' Because that's what I was thinking at the moment."

"You'll find out soon enough where we're going," Jeri responded. She turned and faced her best friend. Allie stopped and looked at Jeri from under the brim of her wool cap as the withered remains of a leaf fell between them.

"You don't need to hear me say it, Jer."

"Actually, I do."

"Okay, fine." Allie stepped back and gave her an appraising stare. "I told you so."

Jeri beamed a wide smile before turning and immediately marching forward up the trail. "Thank you. That was all I needed to hear."

Allie sighed as Jeri vanished into the underbrush. She shook her head in frustration and trudged after her. "Jer . . . wait up!" She swatted at the thick tangle around her and quickened her pace. "Dammit, Jeri . . . *wait up!*"

A few minutes later Jeri broke through the last of the thick brush and stared up at the late-autumn landscape around her. The wide profile of Agassiz Peak stood stoically in front of her, its lower face softened by golden grasses and green armies of spruce. Above her, the sky was swept with thin, wispy strands of cirrus clouds that appeared frozen against a crystal-blue backdrop.

Beneath her feet, the trail rose upward in a long, serpentine line toward the snow-tipped summit. It was a steep, unrelenting climb that even now, years later, she still remembered vividly. Her eyes clouded with tears as they followed the long empty path toward the sky.

I miss you, Dad.

She blinked back the tears as Allie stumbled through the brush behind her, muttering an angry cascade of curses. Her best friend slapped her gloved hands together and paced back and forth.

"Jesus Christ, it's cold!" Allie said dramatically as she wrapped her arms around herself. She shot Jeri a scornful look. "I must be one great goddamn friend to follow you up here, do you realize that? I gave up a happy-hour date with that new guy in my office for this, so will you please tell me exactly why we're standing here freezing our asses off?"

Jeri looked at her friend with a plaintive expression before slowly reaching into her pocket. "I haven't told you everything, Allie," she said as she pulled out a small square photo and held it out to her friend. "This came in the last letter."

Allie took the Polaroid photo and stared at it intently. She was just about to ask Jeri who or what the object in the photo was when the meaning struck her. "Oh, fuck, Jeri. Is that who I think it is?"

Jeri nodded. "Now turn it over."

Allie turned the photo and read the sharp, precise handwriting that she'd seen in the letters. She exhaled a frightened sigh and handed the photo back to Jeri. "Has anyone else seen this?" she asked, her face pale white.

Jeri shook her head.

"I don't understand, Jeri." Allie's voice was high with panic. "Why is this guy doing this? What does he want from you?"

"I don't know for sure, Allie, but I have an idea." She turned and stared up the mountain. "And if I'm right, the answer is buried somewhere up there."

===

Jack Preston was sitting in his Phoenix office, thumbing through a newly released psychological profile for domestic terrorists, when his cell phone buzzed. He picked it up and quickly tapped the screen to view the waiting message.

Contact w/ subject. Audio file attached in e-mail.

The director spun around to his laptop and brought up the e-mail address to which Eugene was directed to send all correspondence. Sitting at the top of the list was a new e-mail titled "13:32_11.28." He glanced at his watch. Based on the name, the file had been recorded that afternoon, just eleven minutes earlier. *An eighteen-year-old kid is a more competent spy than most of my field agents*, he thought cynically as he clicked on the e-mail. A brief summary was written inside.

Subject made call at 13:29 (MST) to Alex Murstead from landline.
Recorded audio attached. Duration: 3 minutes.

Preston grunted irritably and opened the attached audio file. A few seconds into playing it, his eyes widened in surprise. Three minutes later, he was frantically calling HSI Director Richard Connolly.

=====

"What am I even looking for?" Allie asked as she walked aimlessly through the tall grass. "A treasure chest? A shoe box? A sign that says 'Big secrets buried here'?"

A few feet away, Jeri shook her head. "I don't know. Keep looking." She glanced out at the wide valley known as the Inner Basin, which ran northeast through the vast Coconino National Forest. They were nearly halfway up the mountain, standing in a wide meadow that skirted the trail. Jeri knew the moment they'd stopped that it was the same meadow where she and her father had rested when they'd come here to hike. Even now, more than a decade later, it looked exactly as she remembered.

As she gazed out at Sunset Crater lying placidly in the distance, Jeri could almost hear her father's laughter echoing through the valley. Her thoughts turned again to the last night in the hospital with her father, just minutes before his death. She had never known if their cryptic conversation about the secrets he'd hidden away was the truth or simply hallucinations brought on by the tumor, and the truth was that Jeri was afraid to know the answer. She had tucked it deeply away in her mind, the memory resurfacing only in brief moments or the occasional nightmare. Since then, it had been an easily dismissible idea—until she'd looked at the Polaroid from the latest letter.

Jeri wasn't even sure why she had hidden the photo from Agent Coleman. Perhaps it was because of the way he'd abruptly thrown her whole world upside down with the story of her mysterious letter writer. *International terrorist? Corporate killer?* It all seemed so absurd. She still wanted to believe her writer was just another harmless, misdirected romantic, a man whose only link to her was simply stumbling into the saloon in the recent past and deciding to send a few letters from around the world.

But the photo had instantly destroyed that hope.

She had tucked it into her back pocket when Coleman and Chip weren't watching before slipping into the bathroom to have a look. Like Allie, it had taken Jeri a moment to understand the object in the picture, but when she finally did it was unmistakable. Her heart had nearly stopped when she realized what it was—and what it meant. Suddenly it was clear that her unknown writer knew more about her past than she could have ever imagined.

Perhaps even more than Jeri herself knew.

Now, as she walked through the sun-swept mountain meadow she last hiked with her father more than a decade ago, Jeri wondered what other painful secrets she was about to uncover.

"So we don't even know what we're looking for, huh? That's great . . . that's very helpful." Allie threw her arms up in the air. "I'm sure we'll find it before any serious hypothermia sets in."

"I don't know exactly what it is, Allie, but I'm sure it's here. My dad wasn't an idiot, and he never left anything to chance. He must have left a clue around here somewhere that he was sure I'd find."

"Well, let me know when it comes to you," Allie replied. "In the meantime, I'm going to warm up my ass on that nice cozy rock."

Jeri paused and watched her friend as she climbed up onto the broad, smooth rock in the center of the meadow and lay down on its sunbathed surface. The image triggered a memory she couldn't quite capture. Was it something her father had said that final night? She glanced around at the otherwise featureless meadow of grasses and sighed.

"Come up and join me," Allie said as she stretched out across the top of the boulder. "It's almost comfortable up here."

Jeri paced forward as her eyes searched earnestly for a sign from her father. She climbed onto the boulder next to Allie and slowly surveyed the area around them. A minute later she shook her head in frustration. "Nothing. I don't see a single damn thing."

Allie looked up at her and shrugged. "At least there's no snow on the ground. If there was, you'd be shit out of luck. Thank god for global warming, you know?"

Jeri smiled somberly. "Yeah, I suppose you're right. Maybe I'm—" She paused and stared at Allie intently.

"Maybe you're what?" Allie replied.

"Allie, move your head."

"What?"

Jeri stepped closer and kneeled down. "Move your head!"

Allie sat up and spun around in a panic. She expected to find a snake or other slithering creature, but nothing was there. "Jesus Christ, Jeri, you scared the hell out of me! What are you doing?"

Jeri ignored her as she reached out and gently touched the rock where her friend's head had been lying. "Allie, look."

Allie looked closer and finally saw what Jeri was looking at. A small symbol was carved into the surface of the stone. "It's a heart," she said irritably. "Big deal."

Jeri gave her a sharp look. "Yes, it's a heart with an arrow through it . . . but look at the initials inside." She stood up and walked to the edge of the boulder as Allie read the initials.

"J.H."

"That's right," Jeri said as she peered over the edge. She glanced back at Allie. "Is the arrow of the heart pointing at me?"

Allie looked up from the carving and nodded. "Yeah, right at you."

Jeri smiled before turning and jumping off the edge of the boulder.

Allie waited a moment and then sat up in curiosity. "Hello? Are you down there?" she asked as she stood up and walked to the edge of the rock. Several feet beneath her, Jeri was hunched on her knees digging frantically at the rocky soil around a large, pillar-shaped stone. "What the hell are you doing?" she asked.

Jeri paused and looked up at her impatiently.

"Will you please just get your ass down here and help me?"

——

Go fuck yourself, Alex.

Tom Coleman sat at his small kitchen table and threw back another beer. In front of him, his cordless phone lay shattered on the table, the pieces swept loosely into a pile. *I really need to learn to control my temper*, he thought sarcastically as he reflected on his conversation with his brother-in-law. He decided it had been perfect. Just the right mix of raw emotion and attention-getting information. All in all, an Oscar-worthy performance. Tom smiled contentedly. He briefly considered getting a copy of the conversation from the nerdy teenager sitting in his car outside, but decided against it. It was better for both of them to avoid any further contact or communication.

He gathered up the empty beer bottles and the pieces of the phone and tossed them in the trash before methodically washing his hands in the kitchen sink. He grabbed two more beers from the fridge and trudged listlessly into the living room. At the window he paused, resisting the urge to see if Eugene's sedan was still parked across the street, before dropping onto the couch. It didn't matter anyway. By now Jack Preston was no doubt scrambling to decide what to make of Tom's call to Alex—if not already discussing this turn of events with HSI Director Connolly. Either way, the groundwork was laid. The only thing left to do was walk into the director's office tomorrow morning and lay out the details.

And then they'll welcome me back with open arms, he thought contentedly as he drank half of his beer.

His thoughts drifted back to that morning at the saloon and the appearance of the latest letter. *How in the hell had that son of a bitch survived the raid on his hotel in Amsterdam?* Tom shook his head incredulously. He still couldn't believe that Jeri's letter-writing terrorist was alive. But the facts were hard to deny. The handwriting matched the earlier letters, and the tone was the same rambling nonsense as before.

But assuming he was still alive—and there was little doubt he wasn't—the next question was obvious: Who was it they'd found burned and half blown to hell inside the hotel room? Tom shuddered as the image of the charred and twisted body came rushing back to him.

He wondered again about the possibility of Joe's claim. Was Jeri's admirer actually sending coded messages to someone through his letters? There was no question they were cryptic, if not downright psychotic. But what possible benefit would there be in sending messages through such a slow, archaic form of communication in an age of e-mail, cell phones, and instant text messages? It just didn't make any sense. But then again, nothing in this case made any sense.

The more Tom thought about it, the more convinced he was that he was missing something. It was something important, something deeper that connected the dots. Unfortunately, he was now too buzzed to figure it out.

He placed the beers on two coasters on the coffee table and picked up his laptop. There was only one more thing he needed to do before his meeting with Director Preston. He brought up a search engine and typed a simple, two-word string:

Petronus Dongying

He leaned forward expectantly as the results flashed onto his screen. Tom scanned them anxiously, then nodded as the result he was looking for finally scrolled into view. "Gotcha," he murmured as a smile stretched across his face.

=====

"For Christ's sake . . . did he have to pick such a heavy rock?" Allie looked up at Jeri with a red-flushed face as she grunted in exertion.

"Just keep pulling, Allie," Jeri snapped as she pressed her shoulder hard against the weight of the stone. "It's going to roll over . . . we just have to lean on it a bit more."

The two women continued to muscle the stone from its partially buried position next to the boulder. Finally, after a few coordinated pushes, the ground yielded in submission as the smooth block of granite heaved onto its side.

"Please tell me there's something under there," Allie said as she fell backward, panting heavily.

Jeri let go of the rock and looked into the void left in the ground. She stared transfixed for a moment before responding. "There is."

Allie sat up excitedly as Jeri reached down into the hole. An odd metallic sound echoed out as she pulled on a thick leather handle attached to a wide rectangular lid that was flush with the compacted earth. After a second hard pull, the object was yanked free. Jeri lifted the heavy steel container out of the hole and dropped it onto the ground. She sat back and sighed with nervous exhaustion as her eyes scanned the container's dark, weathered surface.

"What the hell?" Allie whispered as she stared at the box. "Who put this here, Jeri?"

Jeri looked over at her friend and gave her a faint smile. "My father."

Allie's eyes widened in disbelief as Jeri pulled the container closer and pried at the heavy latch. A cloud of dirt and rust erupted from its surface as it finally released. Allie leaned forward inquisitively as she opened the lid, but Jeri raised her hand to stop.

"Give me a second, Allie . . . please?"

Allie nodded apologetically and smiled. "Sure. I'll go take a walk." She stood and looked out at the sharp undulating backs of the mountains in the distance. Beyond them, an ominous wall of curling, blue-gray storm clouds was slowly moving in their direction. "We shouldn't stay too long, though. The weather up here isn't going to stay nice for much longer."

"Just give me five minutes."

Jeri watched her friend disappear into the meadow before returning her attention to the container. She could feel her pulse rising as she tilted it forward and peered inside. A stack of leather-bound journals was packed tightly within the container, their spines labeled with dates written in heavy black ink. *I know that handwriting*, she thought wistfully as she pulled out the thick journals and carefully piled them on the ground next to her.

Next in the container was a silver case Jeri vaguely recognized, its intricately etched surface tarnished with age. She noticed it was heavy as she pulled it from the box. Placing it on her lap, she released the small clasp and opened the top, then gasped in surprise.

Resting inside the felt-lined interior was a small handgun, its black metal surface gleaming in the sun. Jeri glanced around nervously to make sure she wasn't being watched. She stared at the gun apprehensively for a moment before carefully lifting it from the case and tucking it into the inner pocket of her jacket. She then reached into the container and held her breath anxiously as her fingers grasped the last item inside. Although she knew it was the object she'd expected to find, Jeri still felt a surreal sense of disbelief that it existed at all. She pulled it from the box, her eyes already knowing what to expect.

The cover of the thick hardback book was simple in style, as if intended for an academic audience. Its title, *Predictions in the New Business Ecology*, was written in a simple, understated type across the front. Beneath it, the author's name was etched in small print.

JAMES H. STONE

Jeri stared curiously at the author's name before steeling herself and flipping the book over. Her breath caught the instant she saw it. On the back was a black-and-white picture of the author sitting at a desk stacked with papers and books. A typewriter was wedged tightly into the space in front of him. He was leaning toward the camera, his young, handsome face flanked by long dark hair as his large, curious eyes smiled from behind a pair of tortoiseshell glasses. Jeri stared into the eyes in the picture as her hand absently traced the outline of his thin form. Until this morning, she had never seen this picture of her father. Until this morning, she didn't know he had ever written a book.

A feeling of anger coursed through her as she stared at the picture of her young father. Why hadn't he told her? What possible reason would he have for keeping a secret like this from the one person in the whole world she thought he told everything? A flood of questions flowed through her, but a single nagging question loomed larger than the rest.

If I didn't know about this, what else didn't I know about him?

Jeri fought back the urge to cry as she turned the book over and opened the front cover. As she did, a folded piece of paper slipped out from between the pages and fell onto her lap. She set the book aside and slowly opened it, immediately recognizing her father's handwriting.

Dear Jeri,

I've spent my life pursuing my passion, and that passion has always been to truly understand this world. Of course, it has never been an easy pursuit, and I'm painfully aware of the sacrifices others have made—perhaps none more than you—to allow me to do this. For this, Jeri, I am unendingly sorry. I've often wondered how different our two lives would have been had my passion been something else. But this is irrelevant. We don't get to choose our passions, my dear. Our passions choose us.

The journals in this container are a collection of what I've learned in this pursuit. By no means is it any Shakespeare, just quickly scrawled discoveries and revelations I've made along the way. But beneath it all lies something significant, a trail I spent most of my early years trying to follow.

A trail to a very dangerous truth.

That truth is the core theme of the book you're now holding. Next to you, it is undoubtedly my greatest achievement. And yet, only you and a handful of others even know it exists. Once you read it, you will understand why.

My passion chose the first path of my life, but the truth chose the rest. I had to bury that early life, including my own name, to protect both of us. Trust me when I tell you that the information and ideas inside the book and journals are tremendously important. But for now, for your own safety, tell no one they exist.

I'm sorry, Jeri. I'm sorry for the sacrifices and the secrets. I kept all of this from you for one simple reason—to protect you from the burden that the truth may now bring. In time, I promise everything will become clear.

But for now, just remember. Great truths are like great treasures.
Sometimes you must keep them buried deep.

I love you,
Dad

P.S. Leave the journals. Take the gun.

Jeri slowly folded the note and tucked it back inside the book. For the second time that day a powerful feeling of nausea overwhelmed her. She rolled forward onto her hands and knees, waiting for it to pass. A cold wind raced up the mountainside and swept through the meadow, bending the dried blades of field grass into rolling waves of shimmering gold. Jeri tried not to think, tried not to feel anything but the wind as it whipped at her face and hair. A torrent of thoughts and emotions swirled behind some deep inner floodgate, but she calmly forced it to remain shut. After a few minutes the feeling of sickness had subsided. She sat up and focused on repacking the container, careful to return the empty silver case and journals in the same order they were found. When she was done, she closed and latched the heavy top and lowered the container gently back into the hole. Working quickly, Jeri filled in the loose dirt around the top, then once more leveraged herself against the large rock and rolled it back into position. A final sweep of the area with her hands left the ground looking as it had when they arrived. Satisfied, she turned and gazed across the valley at the approaching storm.

Fresh snow on the ground by tonight, she thought. *By tomorrow, no one will know we were ever here.*

Jeri picked up her father's book and climbed back onto the large boulder. Allie was at the far edge of the meadow, walking aimlessly through the tall grass as the wind tossed her short blonde hair.

Jeri raised a hand to wave and immediately felt the weight of the handgun pressed against her chest. After getting her friend's attention, she sat down and waited under the waning rays of sunlight. Next to her, the carving her father made years ago pointed silently toward the buried box.

You always were a clever man, Dad.

She glanced down again at her father's image on the back cover of the book. A sudden curiosity gripped her. She pulled the Polaroid from the latest letter from her pocket and studied it carefully. The photo appeared to have been taken in a narrow corridor between two stark, featureless concrete buildings. Daylight fell bleakly into the corridor, painting everything in a palette of dull, muted colors. In the center of the photo, Jeri's letter writer stood alive and well— his slim, muscled physique clad in a crisp new Joe's Last Stand T-shirt. As always, his face was hidden, this time by an object he held out in front of him. Jeri stared at the object, keenly aware that it was meant to be the focus of her attention.

It was an open copy of her father's book.

She flipped the Polaroid over and again read the precisely scribed note written on the back.

> I read your father's book, Jeri. Brilliant guy. I guess the apple doesn't fall far from the tree after all, though I admit I have no idea what that saying really means.
>
> By the way, I'm coming to Flagstaff. You'd better be there when I arrive, or there will be blood on the ceiling and skin on the walls.
>
> Don't say it, Jeri. I already know.

"So what was inside?"

Jeri jumped at the sound of Allie's voice. Her friend stood staring up at her from the base of the rock. She quickly tucked the

Polaroid into her jacket pocket and held up the book. "Exactly what I expected."

Allie glanced at the book and nodded. "Anything else?"

Jeri stood on the boulder and looked out at the view. Sunset Crater stood placidly in the distance, its disfigured peak exactly as she remembered from the day she'd sat in this same spot with her father. Above it, storm clouds rolled and darkened, dwarfing the mountain as they moved ominously closer. She watched them approach for a moment, then jumped off the rock and smiled somberly at Allie.

"Nope. Let's go home."

Chapter 46

"Have you read it, Richard?"

The earnest voice of Jack Preston echoed hollowly from the speakerphone in Richard Connolly's office. Next to the phone, a lit cigarette dangled on the edge of a large crystal ashtray.

"I have," Connolly mumbled. He pressed his yellow-stained fingers against the two-page transcript on his desk and slid it toward his thin body, slumped forward in the chair. "It's rather interesting."

"Interesting?" Preston replied, his voice incredulous. "It's a goddamn miracle."

Connolly grunted skeptically. "Let's not get ahead of ourselves, Jack."

He took a deep drag of his cigarette and looked over the transcript again.

Murstead: Agent Murstead.

Coleman: Alex, it's Tom.

Murstead: Happy holidays, Tom.

Coleman: Right. Hey, look, we need to talk.

Murstead: About what?

Coleman: I want to let Jack Preston and the department in on the investigation.

Murstead: What investigation is that?

Coleman: Don't be a prick, Alex.

Murstead: Now why in the hell would you want to do that? The case is closed. You know that as well as I do.

Coleman: I have reason to believe that it isn't. In fact, I have reason to believe our terrorist is still alive.

Murstead: (Laughter) Jesus Christ, Tom! I knew you were gonna pull something like this again. Some new conspiracy theory, some new bullshit angle to try and get back into the agency. I just didn't think you were stupid enough to try again so soon.

Coleman: No offense, Alex, but after seeing firsthand how sloppy the CIA is at running a fucking investigation, not to mention a covert mission that kills two innocent people and lets the real target get away, I think I'm much better off staying with the team I started with.

Murstead: (Pause) What possible reason could you have for believing our target got away? You saw what was left of him in that hotel room, just like the rest of us. For fuck's sake, you were the one who identified him, Tom! If that wasn't him, then who the fuck was it?

Coleman: I have no idea, but I'm now sure it wasn't him, Alex. Our terrorist is still alive, which means we're dealing with a killer who's a hell of a lot smarter than either one of us. It also means you need to reopen the investigation immediately, but this time you need to open it to Preston and the Department of Homeland Security. This thing is too big for one agency.

Murstead: Tell me, what are you after this time, Tom? If it's not a spot in the agency, what could you possibly hope to accomplish with this fucking story?

Coleman: Fuck you, Alex. For once, could you try to see past your own ego and admit you might have made a mistake? Our friend is still out there, and he's going to continue to kill off Petronus employees and god knows who else until he's stopped. Reopen the fucking investigation!

Murstead: No, Tom, I won't. This investigation, like this conversation, is

over. Furthermore, let me remind you of the
documents you signed the night this case came
to an end. You say one word to Jack Preston
about the details of the investigation, and
I promise you that my agents will be picking
little pieces of you out of a burned-out
hotel room too.

Coleman: He's not dead, Alex.

Murstead: No? Then tell me—where is he going
to kill next?

Coleman: China.

Murstead: (Pause) Where in China?

Coleman: Reopen the investigation and I'll
tell you.

Murstead: Go fuck yourself, Tom. Where in
China?

Coleman: Fuck you, *brother-in-law*. You heard
my conditions. Of course, I suppose you could
show up here and put a gun to my back like
last time and force the information from me.

Murstead: You're unbelievable, Tom. I never
realized just how much of a low-life conniving
scumbag you really are. You've got nothing—
absolutely nothing—and yet you're still

369

trying to pull yourself out of the giant
shithole you've created for yourself. Family
or not, I'm done with you. I've heard your
conditions. Now you're gonna hear mine. If you
call here again, I'll have you arrested and
invent enough charges to keep you locked away
until you can't remember what a shower feels
like without being sodomized. If you talk to
Preston about the investigation, don't even
bother listening for the knock on the door.
Do you understand me?

Coleman: You can't be serious.

Murstead: Good-bye, Tom.

(Phone disconnects)

Coleman: Alex? (Pause) Alex? Fuck!

(Loud banging noise.)

----- **END OF TRANSCRIPT** -----

Director Connolly snuffed out his cigarette and eased back into
the soft leather of his chair. He glanced casually at the numerous
framed photos of himself and various celebrities and heads of state
hanging on the wall across from him. When he spoke, his gravelly,
Southern-accented voice was slow and deliberate.

"So how do you intend to handle this, Jack?"

"I intend to drag Agent Coleman into my office tomorrow and

find out what he knows," Preston replied earnestly. "If he knows what I think he knows, then we're back in the game."

Connolly looked impatiently at the speakerphone. "He obviously knows something. He wouldn't have mentioned China if he didn't. Whether or not it's of any value to us is the real question. Either way, you won't need to drag him into your office to find out. I suspect he'll be waiting for you bright and early tomorrow morning."

"What makes you think he would do that?" Preston asked, his tone skeptical.

"Because he has nowhere else to go," Connolly replied, pausing to light another cigarette. "And if I were you, Jack, I'd call attention to that fact when you talk to him. Coleman needs to realize we're the only family he has left."

"Right."

"How's your man in Beijing?" Connolly asked.

Preston hesitated briefly before answering. "He's fine. Focused on finding these guys, like the rest of us."

"I'm sure he is. Just make sure he doesn't do anything stupid. If he's anything like Coleman, who knows what could happen. Reconnaissance only, correct?"

Preston nodded. "Correct."

Connolly stared thoughtfully at the thin trail of smoke curling from the tip of his cigarette. He shook his head and took another deep drag. "Call me immediately after your conversation with Agent Coleman."

"Will do," Preston replied.

"And Jack, don't fuck this up."

Connolly clicked off the speakerphone before Preston could respond. He pushed the transcript into a thin folder titled "Coleman, Tom/ICE-West" and turned his attention to another document lying on his desk. Embossed at the top of the page was a familiar seal. Connolly sighed exhaustedly as he looked it over. In three days he would be speaking to the House regarding budget appropriations and the future role of the HSI—the intelligence and investigations arm of Homeland Security that he effectively commanded. Of course, he knew he'd have no problem winning over the Congressional members he'd be appearing before. All it took was the right mix of humble intelligence and passion for the cause—served up in his charming Southern accent. A few hours of political wrangling, followed by some easily deflectable questions, and a large chunk of ICE's more than seven-billion-dollar annual budget would once again be secured.

But behind his outward appearance of absolute confidence, Connolly was feeling increasingly nervous.

He knew this terrorist situation had the potential to be a huge victory for the department, as well as a political windfall for himself once knowledge of his deft handling of the incident was circulated through the appropriate channels. The fallout from the CIA's presumed mishandling of the investigation would be just more icing on the cake. *Christ, I could have the pick of the litter in intelligence appointments when this is all done*, Connolly thought smugly as he smiled and took a deep drag of his cigarette.

But his smile quickly faded as his nagging sense of nervousness returned. There was another possible outcome to consider as well—one that ended in disaster if the situation were left solely in the hands of Preston and his rogue idiot in China. Connolly grunted irritably at the thought. He couldn't allow that to happen.

A contingency plan is always required.

Connolly produced a small key from the inside pocket of his suit jacket and unlocked the bottom drawer of his desk. There, lying by itself, was a small Moleskine notebook. He removed it and flipped through the thick pages, pausing on a page containing a long sequence of numbers. A fleeting feeling of nostalgia from his days with the National Security Agency passed through him as he scanned the numbers, his mind decoding the embedded pattern to the information. He jotted down a number as he read. When he was finished, he returned the notebook to its drawer and immediately relocked it. Grabbing the phone, he punched in a code for a secure line and entered the string of numbers he'd written down. He took a patient drag of his cigarette as a series of authentication clicks echoed in the handset. A few seconds later, a deep, authoritative voice answered on the other end.

"Code in, please," the voice demanded bluntly.

Connolly tapped the ash from his cigarette and spoke slowly into the phone.

"Connolly 209-4736-07913."

"Hold, please."

Connolly again felt a twinge of nostalgia as he waited. It had been a long time since he'd "coded in," and he briefly wondered if his clearance still held. He thought the feeling was oddly similar to calling one's bank to find out if anything was left in a long-forgotten account.

The line echoed with a second series of clicks, followed by the same male voice. "Code-in verified. How may I help you, sir?"

Connolly took a final drag of his cigarette and smiled into the phone.

"Korean Field Office, please."

Chapter 47

He was done.

He stripped off his latex gloves and stepped out onto the balcony. The sky above him was a featureless dome of ash-colored clouds. A short distance away, dark smudges of rain fell onto the endless rows of concrete apartment buildings and stained them in deeper tones of gray. He stretched his arms and took a deep breath. The acrid air of the city filled his lungs like an unwelcome drug. He let the morning chill wake him before stepping back inside.

The only empty piece of furniture in the dingy one-room apartment was a bright red futon made of imitation leather. He sat down and lit a cigarette as his eyes fell back to his work. Sitting opposite the futon on a matching red chair, the package stared lifelessly back at him. He studied it carefully, examining it with a critical eye before nodding to himself. He then pulled out his phone and sent a brief message. A few seconds later his phone buzzed in response.

I'll be there in five minutes.

He read the message from Tall Tommy, then yawned and shoved his phone into his pocket. As he did, his hand met the sharp edge of a folded piece of paper. His fingers stroked it curiously for a moment before he remembered what it was and pulled it out with a knowing sigh. The single sheet of stationery seemed to glow in the soft light as he unfolded it. He looked at it closely, admiring the sweeping feminine curves of handwriting that covered both sides as he slowly read it again. Once again his mouth formed into a grin. When he was finished, he refolded the letter and returned it to his pocket.

The fake-leather futon felt cold against his neck as he sat back and stared contentedly at the package. His stomach groaned with hunger, but he ignored it. His thoughts were still on her as he sat in the small, strange apartment, waiting for a knock on the door. He wondered what she would think of him when it was over. He wondered if she would accept what had been done.

More than anything, he wondered if she would forgive him for what he was about to do.

Chapter 48

Tom Coleman marched through the Immigration and Customs Enforcement office, nodding curtly to the few familiar faces that looked up as he passed. He strolled by the door to his office without so much as a glance and stepped into the elevator. Once on the executive floor, he walked directly to the corner office of the Western Division director and stopped at the desk of his assistant. A plump, middle-aged woman with short red hair and thick mascara turned and stared at him dully.

"Is the director going to be in today?" Tom asked, nodding at Preston's door.

"He's actually in now," the assistant answered. "Do you have an appointment with him?"

"Yes. Well, no. Just tell him Agent Coleman is here to see him," Tom replied. He waited as the assistant finished typing on her computer and picked up the phone. A moment later she hung up and gave him a surprised nod.

"You're in luck, Agent Coleman. The director says he can see you now. Please go on in."

Tom thanked her as he passed, certain that luck had nothing to do with being granted his unannounced meeting. He opened the door to Preston's office and immediately grimaced. A nauseating mixture of stale cigar smoke and expensive cologne hung in the air.

He glanced around at the lavishly furnished office before noticing the large antique-looking desk in the corner. There, hunched in his dark leather chair, the director stared back at him with a grim face.

"Agent Coleman," Preston said coldly without moving. "What brings you back to your old employer?"

Tom approached Preston's desk with a calm, plaintive expression. "Information, Director," he replied earnestly. "And also an apology."

Preston leaned back in his chair and motioned Tom to take a seat. "What kind of information?" he asked, an obvious tone of skepticism in his voice.

Tom sat down, quietly thankful the director didn't want to shake hands. He hated the physical contact of such useless formalities, especially this time of year. The human hand was a fucking petri dish of cold and flu viruses. He pulled out a thick folder, took a deep breath, and focused on the speech he'd practiced the night before and during the drive over.

"I'll get to that in a moment, sir, but first of all I want to apologize for the way I acted the last time we talked. As you know, for legal reasons I'm not able to discuss my assistance with the investigation that Agent Murstead and his team were carrying out. But let me be clear about one thing—it was never my intention to keep you or anyone in this team in the dark. I was simply following strict orders from the CIA not to discuss it, and they made it very clear what would happen to me if I didn't comply." He paused and pretended to search for the right words. "I only hope that this situation hasn't destroyed my opportunity to continue working with you and the department, sir."

Jack Preston looked at Tom with a somber expression before spinning his chair toward the window and gazing at the frozen landscape outside. When he finally spoke, his voice was low and soft. "When you've been in the Department of Homeland Security as long as I have, you come to accept a few things. One of the first is the fact that every agency but ours seems to have the upper hand when it comes to recruiting the best and brightest talent. Most days, the same rule seems to apply to our luck. And if you haven't figured out by now that luck plays a huge part in any agency's success . . . well then you're just a total goddamn idiot."

He spun and fixed his dark green eyes on Tom.

"So what do you do with an agency like ours? You accept that there's still a job to do. You accept that the only way to defend our little patch of democracy against a fanatical fucked-up world is by putting your trust in the team of people you *have*—regardless of the team you *want*. Around here, trust trumps ability, Agent Coleman, and up until recently I thought you might have both. But your recent side job with the CIA has forced me to reevaluate your loyalties, and it's gonna take a helluva lot more than an apology to make me think otherwise. Do you understand?"

"I do, sir," Tom answered.

"You're a damn good investigator, Tom. Certainly much better than your pay grade might suggest. But I'll be damned if you don't keep stepping on your own dick with this fucking dream of being a CIA agent." Preston leaned forward and pointed his freckled hand at Tom. "I only hope this last little taste finally set you straight, because truth be told, your brother-in-law royally fucked you. Not that I'm surprised. That's the way they do things at Langley. Christ, just imagine what he might have done if you two weren't actually family." He waved his hands dismissively and sat back in his chair. "Anyway, I'm not here to give you a fucking sermon. But if you still want to be a part of this team, you've got a shitload of rebuilding to do."

Tom looked at Preston thoughtfully and nodded.

"I intend to do just that, sir."

Preston eyed him keenly. "And how do you intend to start?"

Tom leaned forward and tossed the thick manila folder onto Preston's desk.

"By giving you full disclosure."

The director looked at him suspiciously before opening the folder. "What's this?"

"As I said, sir, for legal reasons, I can't verbally discuss the details of the investigation I assisted Agent Murstead with. But that doesn't mean you don't have the right to see the personal notes I might have left lying around my office while assisting his agency, correct?" He looked up and gave Preston a conspiratorial grin. "After all, anything I placed in my ICE files, regardless of the materials, would technically be the legal property of the department, if I'm not mistaken."

Preston smiled back. "That would be correct . . . *technically*."

Tom stood and walked toward the window. The director's corner vantage looked out over the large parking lot of the Flagstaff field office, its black pavement now covered in a thin blanket of white snow. Out of habit, he scanned the parked cars for a maroon sedan. *This shit can drive you fucking crazy*, he thought as he shook his head and faced Preston.

"What you're holding in your hands is a summary of a terrorist investigation that Agent Murstead and the CIA now consider closed. *Corporate terrorism*, to be precise." Tom reached forward and grabbed the folder from the director's hands. "However, as of yesterday, I have new evidence that strongly suggests the terrorist at the center of this investigation is not dead. Furthermore, if this man's pattern holds true, an employee of the Petronus Energy Corporation is in imminent danger of being murdered—and I mean *today*."

Tom quickly summarized the murders of the previous four Petronus employees to the director as he pulled their incident reports from the folder and tossed them on his desk. He then pulled out a printed copy of one of the Polaroid photos from the letters and laid it on top of the pile.

"Now, I don't pretend to have your level of expertise in how to deal with matters of international terrorism, Director. But I can only imagine how grateful our government and the international community would be, not to mention one of the world's largest corporations, if the Department of Homeland Security managed to finish what the CIA started. Or should I say *corrected their mistake*?" He dropped the entire folder back onto Preston's desk. "But we don't have much time."

Jack Preston studied the obscured image of the man in the photo for a moment before looking up at Tom with a solemn expression. "So where is he now?"

"China," Tom replied without hesitation. "A coastal city in the north called Dongying. Petronus has a major oil refinery there, as well as a research facility." He pulled a small notebook from his pocket, flipped to a page, and tossed it onto Preston's desk. "That's his last known address."

The director glanced at the notepad for a moment before glancing up at Tom. "And the CIA doesn't have this information?"

"No sir."

A grin parted Preston's thin lips as he spoke. "Well, then . . . welcome back to the team, Agent Coleman."

＝＝

"I thought you were staying clear of this place for a few days," Chip said as Jeri strolled through the door of Joe's Last Stand Saloon.

"I thought you were going to do the same," Jeri replied as she stepped up to the bar and dropped a sealed envelope onto the counter.

Chip shrugged. "Old habits die hard," he muttered, pointing at the envelope. "What have you got there?"

Jeri ignored his question and glanced around the bar. "Where's Joe?"

"He just left to grab some lunch. I told him I'd stay here and tend the bar in the rare event that someone else needed a midday drink. He'll be back in a few minutes. Sit down and keep me company."

Jeri shook her head and smiled softly, her brown eyes hinting sadness. "Maybe another time."

The older man narrowed his eyes suspiciously. "What's this about, Jeri?"

"This is about you winning, Chip," she answered matter-of-factly. "I'm finally taking your advice. All this time you've been telling me I need to move on. Well, I woke up this morning and realized you were right." She tapped her finger on the envelope. "I know a formal letter of resignation is a little overkill for a bartending job, but I thought Joe deserved it."

Chip stared at the envelope with shock. "Well, I'll be damned," he muttered, his face slowly composing into a smile. "Are you serious?"

"Serious as a heart attack," Jeri replied as she turned and headed for the door.

"Don't you want to wait for Joe?" Chip asked, watching her leave.

"I think it's better if he hears it from you. Just make sure he gets my letter."

"I will. So, Jeri—" Chip said earnestly, forcing her to stop and look back. "When's your last day?"

"Tomorrow," Jeri replied. "Just enough time for everyone to say their good-byes and for Joe to work out the schedule." She glanced over at the shrine of letters and photos still hanging on the wall and shrugged. "And who knows . . . maybe he'll just keep writing letters to the next bartender?" She gave him a quick wave before slipping through the doorway and into the wintry Flagstaff morning.

As he watched her disappear, Chip sipped his beer in the empty saloon and softly whispered an answer to her question.

"I don't think so."

======

Jack Preston finished reading the five-page investigation summary Tom had given him and dropped it on his desk. His eyes lingered on it for a long moment before staring dumbfounded at Tom. "This is unbelievable, Agent Coleman," he said quietly. "I mean un-*fucking*-believable."

From his chair across from the director, Tom smiled and nodded. "Yes sir, it is unbelievable. But it's all true."

Preston picked up the thick stack of supporting documents Tom had included with his summary and thumbed through the pages. He flipped past the photocopies of the letters and Polaroid pictures and stopped when he came to a photo of Jeri that Tom had taken at the bar. "So this is her, huh?" he asked as he pulled it out and studied it. "Our pretty little bartender at the center of this mess?"

"Yes sir," Tom replied. "Her name is Jeri Halston. Twenty-six years old . . . single . . . a graduate of the university. I've included a brief bio and background summary in the file. But honestly, I don't think it's worth your time to read it."

"And why would you say that?"

"Because we have more important information to act upon, sir," Tom replied, surprised that he needed to spell out this fact to the director. "We have the location of the man—the *terrorist*—who's killing these researchers, and we have a legitimate opportunity to stop him." He leaned forward and gave the director an emphatic look. "But as I've already said, sir, we need to act quickly."

"I understand that," Preston replied irritably. He wasn't about to reveal that he'd already sent another agent—Coleman's own colleague, no less—to handle the situation in China. That would only lead to questions, and the last thing Preston needed right now was for Coleman to find out his conversations with Murstead had been recorded. If nearly three decades of intelligence work had taught him anything, it was that full disclosure worked only when it flowed *up* the chain of command, not down.

"I'll handle getting resources to Dongying," the director said as he shoved the photo back into the file and closed it. "You focus on figuring out what Miss Halston is really up to."

Tom gave the director a surprised look. "I beg your pardon, sir?" he replied.

"I may be coming into this investigation a little late, Agent Coleman, but of all the implausible pieces to this situation—and god knows there are plenty of them—the most implausible of all would be to think that the person receiving these letters isn't somehow involved. You even speculated in your summary that the letters may contain coded messages for someone in Flagstaff who's affiliated with this terrorist group, correct?"

"Yes sir."

"So isn't it reasonable to assume that those messages were intended for the recipient of the letters herself?"

"Perhaps," Tom replied reluctantly. "But I don't believe that's true in this case."

The director's green eyes narrowed. "I've already said you're a good investigator, Tom. But you need to understand that sometimes the answers are right in front of you. This Halston woman is involved in this. I have no doubt in my mind. Your job is to find out how."

"I understand, sir," Tom said as he stood to leave. "I'll get started immediately."

"Good," Preston replied, his tone pleasant. "I have every confidence that together we can resolve this situation before another innocent Petronus employee dies at the hand of this madman . . . or madmen."

Tom paused and gave the director a puzzled look. "I hope so, sir."

He turned and walked to the door.

"Oh, and Agent Coleman," Preston said as Tom reached the door, his expression severe. "Not a word of this to anyone else, understood? This one stays between you and me for now."

Tom gave the director a brief nod. "Understood."

The moment the door closed behind him, Preston reached for his cell phone and quickly dialed a number. A few seconds later, the raspy voice of Richard Connolly answered.

"Hello, Jack," Connolly answered, his Southern drawl guarded. "Have you got something for me?"

"I have more than something, Richard," Preston replied eagerly. "I have *everything*."

"What does that mean?"

"Coleman just left my office," Preston said, a smug smile curling his lips. "You were right. The prodigal son has returned."

Chapter 49

Agent Rick Martin glanced around at his surroundings and cursed under his breath.

This was not going to be easy.

Around him, rows of dilapidated dormitory buildings seemed to stretch out in every direction. He studied their gray forms carefully as he marched through the narrow maze of corridors and courtyards that connected them to the massive industrial complex nearby. A mosaic of hanging laundry and piled rubbish cluttered nearly every one of the small balconies. Faded newspaper covered the few windows that punctured the tall façades of reinforced concrete. Above him, the upper floors disappeared into the ash-colored smog that hung incessantly over the city. Other than a few subtle variations in their states of decay, the buildings all looked identical.

He quickened his pace with a renewed sense of urgency. The phone call from Director Preston in the middle of the night had stirred him from yet another restless sleep in his tiny Beijing hotel room. But this time the news had been good. Very good. Thanks to some recent intelligence, the details of which the director wouldn't disclose, Rick now had a possible location on the blond man he'd lost three days earlier at the Beijing airport after arriving from Amsterdam. He was still scolding himself for the fuckup. He'd been certain he was following the right taxi from the airport, but the person who'd stepped out at their downtown destination had been neither tall nor blond. Three days of nearly nonstop searching through the dense sprawl of downtown Beijing had been Rick's self-imposed punishment. His conversation with the director had been even more painful. Even now, the words Preston had whispered over the phone upon hearing of his mistake still echoed in his head.

Find him, Agent Martin.

Or don't bother coming home.

But Rick knew his luck had changed with this morning's call. Even more so when he'd been told his target was believed to be in Dongying. Trains to the large industrial city on the coast ran hourly, and Dongying was less than 350 kilometers away. Within thirty minutes of receiving his new assignment, Rick had made his way to the massive main hall of the Beijing West Railway Station and purchased his ticket.

Now, as he walked in the dim light of dawn on the northeast side of the city, he wondered exactly how long it was going to take to find his fucking target.

Rick glanced around warily. The large dorms were already beginning to stir with activity. A cacophony of footsteps and human voices filled the cold morning air as young men and women dressed in simple, monochromatic uniforms suddenly filled the corridors and courtyards. They eyed the tall, dark-haired American curiously as they made their way toward the nearby factories for another grueling sixteen-hour shift. Rick ignored them as they passed. His attention was instead focused on the large three-digit numbers painted on the corners of each building. He continued to thread his way through the labyrinth of dorms for another twenty minutes, barely noticing the quickly thinning crowd. When the number of the building he was searching for finally appeared before him, Rick realized he was once again walking alone.

Building 847 stood at the southeast corner of dormitories that bordered the colossal factories within the complex. He stopped next to it and stared up at the grim façade. The lifeless building looked like something out of a bad horror film, and a sense of foreboding briefly stirred in Rick's stomach. He shook his head and stepped into the corridor that led to the elevators. Almost immediately he was struck by the smell of rotting waste.

Of the four elevators located in the corridor, three stood open and useless. Their cramped interiors were filled ceiling-high with layers of decomposing trash. The fourth hummed noisily as Rick stepped up to its closed doors. He watched with growing impatience as the floor indicator light hovered, unmoving, on the sixth floor. A young girl in a factory uniform marched past him, watching him with a wry grin as she headed toward one of the large open stairwells. A few minutes later, Rick sighed in frustration and begrudgingly followed after her up the stairs.

═══

Inside his small ICE office, Tom leaned back from his laptop and stared at copies of the letters spread across his desk, each of them marked heavily with red ink. Normally such messiness would have caused something of a panic attack in him. The random arrangement of pages and thick scratches of ink was a picture of disorder and chaos. And yet, at this moment, the disorder didn't bother him at all. In fact, as he looked at the landscape of paperwork, Tom felt something else entirely.

Validation.

Despite their conversation earlier that morning, Tom had ignored the director's instructions to focus his attention on Jeri Halston. As far as he saw it, there simply wasn't any point. It wasn't that he failed to see Preston's logic. After all, the letters were addressed to her. And even if she wasn't the person the messages were intended for, she almost certainly knew that person. *But a terrorist?* Not a chance. Jeri might be a cold, introverted bitch who didn't like men, but she wasn't a terrorist. Tom was sure of it. Which meant there was only one real question worth asking.

Who were the letters really meant for?

It was that question that led Tom back to his cramped office following his meeting with Preston. He'd immediately pulled out his own copies of the letters and investigation summary that had been handed over to the director. It had taken several hours to painstakingly analyze the details of each murder and look for statements in the corresponding letter that matched those details. But now, as he stared at the summary of what he'd found, Tom was certain he was on to something.

Letter #1 / Assam, India:
Corresponding Incident: Marcello Avogadro / killed in vehicle collision / subject was driving in a tuk-tuk / flammable materials in one of the vehicles caught fire and quickly consumed the body.

Statements made in letter: *took my last tuk-tuk ride to the market last night, which means this assignment is done / I'm burned out, baby*

Letter #2 / Al Jubail, Saudi Arabia:
Corresponding Incident: No known incident

Statements made in letter: *I am in Al Jubail / waiting for a new assignment*

Letter #3 / Port Harcourt, Nigeria:
Corresponding Incident: Director of Research Shahid Al Dossari killed / explosive device in his hotel room

Statements made in letter: *don't blow up at me / it's going to go off / one in four*

Letter #4 / Puerto La Cruz, Venezuela:
Corresponding Incident: Derrick Birch killed / falls overboard on a private yacht

Statements made in letter: *Brainybuddies / there are four of these little bastards / cash cow / drowning in charm / I've nabbed one of these little bastards, and the other three are practically in the bag*

Letter #5 / Kaliningrad, Russia:
Corresponding Incident: Researcher Tatyana Aleksandrov killed in a laboratory cafeteria / explosive device in vending machine

Statements made in letter: *a lowly vending machine in the loathsome global cafeteria*

Letter #6 / Amsterdam, The Netherlands:
Corresponding Incident: CIA raid on target's hotel room / death of target

Statements made in letter: *were planning to throw me off course*

Letter #7 / Dongying, China:
Corresponding incident: —unknown—

Statements made in letter: *—unknown—*

Tom leaned back in his chair and shook his head in frustration. The messages had been staring out at him from the beginning, hidden in plain sight within the words of the letters. *Why had he not seen it sooner?* He silently chastised himself for a moment before realizing there was no point in questioning his competence at this stage in the investigation. Regardless of whatever mistakes he had made, he was still the only one who had managed to follow the terrorist's trail. And now he finally knew what the man was up to.

Or at least *nearly* knew.

He leaned forward and quickly typed a brief summary beneath the notes.

Death of Marcello Avogadro in Assam marked the completion of a previous assignment by target.

Target traveled to Al Jubail, where he obtained current assignment.

Current assignment involves the assassination of four Petronus Energy researchers.

Target successfully carried out three of the four assassinations prior to trip to Amsterdam.

Amsterdam trip was designed to throw investigating agencies from target's trail.

Target is currently in China to complete the fourth and final assassination of assignment.

Tom looked at the summary, confident in his conclusions. He was now certain that the statements in the letters were in fact status updates on the murders and were intended for someone here in Flagstaff. Unfortunately, they didn't reveal any clue who that person might be. And trying to find them without something to go on would be next to impossible. He couldn't very well detain every person who walked into the bar and glanced at the shrine of letters. Even if he did, what then? What would he be looking for?

Only one other piece of evidence remained that Tom hadn't fully examined—the letter that arrived yesterday morning. Between Joe's aggravated state and the unexpected discovery of being followed, Tom had failed to take a photo of it when he was at the saloon. Considering what he'd just uncovered in the first six letters, there was little doubt something useful was hidden in this latest letter as well. Perhaps it might reveal something about the final assassination in China. But there wasn't much time. He needed to get to Joe's and examine that letter immediately.

Tom glanced at his watch and was shocked to see that it was already after four p.m. He quickly saved the document on his laptop and refiled his written notes before grabbing his coat and heading out the door. Halfway through the first-floor corridor of the ICE offices, the same colleague who was always asking Tom to lunch suddenly appeared in the hallway before him.

"Hey, Tommy-boy," his coworker said with a sarcastic grin. "What's the rush? Getting ready to raid Taco Bell for illegals again?"

"It's classified," Tom said tersely as he brushed past him.

"All right . . . all right," his coworker replied as he raised his hands defensively. "Jesus, man, what's going on around here? First you disappear for a while, then Rick Martin disappears, and now you're running around all serious and secretive. It's like we're becoming the CIA or something."

Tom shrugged dismissively as he walked toward the exit, mumbling a response under his breath.

"Fuck the CIA."

═══

Rick trudged up the last flight of stairs of building 847 and stepped cautiously onto the dormitory's top floor. Despite being in decent shape, he felt winded and slightly dizzy. He briefly wondered if he was coming down with some form of Chinese flu as he turned up the collar of his jacket and studied his surroundings. On his right, through a thinning veil of fog, the open corridor offered a panoramic view of the dorms and factory buildings that formed the vast industrial complex. In front of him, interrupted in regular intervals by the recessed entryways of apartments, the fifteenth floor stretched for several hundred yards before terminating at another large stairway. Rick stared down the empty walkway and tried to ignore the nervous excitement that now gripped his stomach. The director's final words from their conversation that morning once again echoed in his head.

For better or worse, the fate of this investigation once again rests in your hands, Agent Martin. So let me make one thing clear—this is your last chance. I strongly suggest you make the most of it.

"I'll make the most of it, motherfucker," Rick mumbled to himself as he shrugged at the cold, damp air. He shoved his hands into his jacket pockets and shot a furtive glance at the stairwell behind him before heading down the walkway.

Apartment 1549 stood near the center of the long, open corridor. Rick glanced around nervously as he moved toward it. He was now dangerously exposed to anyone who might appear from one of the apartments or stairwells. His footsteps echoed against the cold concrete, forcing him to slow his pace. As he neared the apartment, he wondered if someone might be lurking unseen in the recess. He braced for the possibility and glanced quickly at the rusty steel door as he passed. He then nearly stopped in surprise.

The apartment door was slightly open.

Rick continued down the corridor, his eyes darting rapidly as he replayed the image of door 1549 in his mind. *Were there lights on inside?* No. Any light coming from inside the apartment would have stood out against the dark recess of the entryway. He stopped and glanced around. The walkway and stairwells were still empty. Before fully knowing what he was planning to do, Rick turned and paced back to the apartment. Without hesitating he pressed against the door and stepped inside. His heart punched against his chest as he closed the door and immediately spun around to face whoever might be waiting. He stared nervously into the dark room, senses on full alert, then slowly exhaled with relief.

Apartment 1549 was empty.

———

"Oh, Christ, not you again," Joe Brown moaned as the old saloon door opened and Tom appeared in the entryway. "Haven't you done enough damage already?"

Tom ignored the bar owner as he quickly stomped the wet snow from his black leather shoes.

"Don't even think of asking for a drink, agent-man," Joe growled. "I only serve people who aren't trying to fuck over their own fellow Americans. Understood?"

"Got it," Tom said as he marched past the bar toward the far corner of the saloon. "I'll only be a minute."

A handful of young coeds seated at the bar watched with interest as the heavyset bar owner grunted with irritation. Sitting nearby on his usual stool, Chip observed silently. His piercing blue eyes followed Tom across the room.

"Good," Joe muttered. "Go look at the letters, write down your little investigation notes—then get the hell out of here."

Tom stopped at the shrine of letters and immediately focused on the one from China that had arrived the day before. He scanned the all-too-familiar handwriting, looking for anything that stood out as particularly odd or suspiciously phrased. *There has to be something here*, he thought, reading it again. Then something caught his eye. His eyes narrowed on the first paragraph. When he got to the final sentence, he read it carefully and stopped.

Seriously . . . have you ever seen The Iceman Cometh?

Tom took a step back as his lips slowly mouthed the words. His eyes widened as a new meaning began to reveal itself.

. . . *ever seen* The Iceman Cometh?

. . . The Iceman *cometh?*

. . . *The ICE man cometh.*

"Oh fuck."

Tom ripped the letter from the wall and ran toward the door, his wet shoes slipping noisily on the old hardwood floor.

"What the *fuck* are you doing?" Joe yelled as he watched Tom sprint past the bar with the letter clutched in his hand. "Stop right there, you little flat-headed piece of shit!" The bar owner ducked under the counter and popped up on the other side, his thick hands curled into fists, but it was too late. Tom had already darted out the door. Joe turned and slammed his fist against the bar top before glancing over at Chip. "Can you fucking *believe* that guy?"

Chip calmly shook his head at Joe before staring out the frost-framed window at the front of the saloon. His eyes followed the running figure of Tom Coleman as he crossed the street and quickly vanished behind a white cloak of falling snow.

=

Rick Martin stood in the entry of apartment 1549 and carefully examined his surroundings. The single-room dwelling, no more than ten feet wide and perhaps twice that in length, was dark and unfurnished. A stale mixture of cigarette smoke and mildew hung heavily in the air. On the floor in front of him, a rectangular patch of relatively clean concrete revealed the spot where a rug once lay. Other than that, the only sign of recent occupation was a cook pot left on the small stove in the far corner of the room. A flimsy-looking door leading to the apartment's balcony stood next to the stove, the small pane of glass in its center covered with torn, age-yellowed newspaper. Rick walked toward it, pausing at the stove and laying his hand on its surface. As expected, it was cold.

I'm too late, he thought as he ripped the newspaper from the window and peered out at the balcony. A large black plastic bag sat in the corner, filled to the top with what appeared to be trash. Rick opened the door and gingerly grabbed the bag, tossing it inside before kicking it over with his shoe and scattering the contents across the floor. He pulled a pen from his pocket and began carefully poking through the rubbish, wincing at the smell. Nearly all of the items seemed to fall into two categories—empty packs of cigarettes, mostly Camel Lights, and leftover containers of street-bought food. A few pages of newspaper were also mixed in, printed in unintelligible Chinese. He studied them closely for a date but couldn't find anything even remotely decipherable.

After five minutes of fruitlessly picking through the trash, Rick stood up in frustration. He walked over, picked up the empty trash bag, and roughly snapped it in the air to see if anything was left inside. As he did, a flat, white-framed object flew out and twirled gently in the air before settling facedown on the floor.

He bent down to examine it.

Looking closer, Rick realized it was a Polaroid photograph like the ones his parents had taken when he was a kid. He flipped it over with his pen and gazed at the smiling face of a middle-aged Chinese man dressed in a white lab coat. The man's dark eyes stared out with intelligence as he stood in a large room surrounded by scientific-looking instruments. Along the bottom edge of the photo, "1556" was written in heavy black ink. Rick picked up the Polaroid and studied it intently until the meaning of the photo and number struck him.

This man is the target. He's in apartment 1556.

I'm in the wrong goddamn apartment.

He stuffed the Polaroid into his pocket and raced to the front door of the apartment. He started to open the door and then paused, his heart pounding loudly in his chest. He reached into his jacket and pulled out the "gift" the director had given him before leaving for Amsterdam—a small .22-caliber pistol. Until that morning, it had traveled in disassembled pieces, all of them concealed within various areas of his laptop, cell phone, and backpack. Rick stared down at the ugly, dull-gray plastic weapon, which looked more like a child's toy than something that could deliver lethal power. A bead of sweat ran down his forehead as he pulled the slide back and checked to make sure the gun was loaded. Satisfied, he tucked it back into his pocket and readied himself by the entryway. As he grabbed the door to leave, Preston's voice sounded once again in his head.

For better or worse, the fate of this investigation once again rests in your hands . . .

Rick shook the words from his head as he opened the door. The cold, chemical-laced air of the factories filled his lungs as he peered down the deserted corridor. *This is it*, he thought as he stepped cautiously out into the gray morning light. No more searching. No more instructions. He closed the door and focused his eyes on the dark entryway of apartment 1556, several doors down. A sudden surge of energy washed over him as he marched forward. He thought of the phone call he'd make to Director Preston when this was over. With any luck, he'd be calling with the confident voice of a freshly minted hero.

=====

"Agent Coleman, the director is in a meeting right now, but I'll be sure to—"

"You don't understand!" Tom screamed into his cell phone at Preston's assistant as he sped back toward the ICE offices. "I need to speak to the director *now*! Tell him it's Agent Coleman. Tell him I have information that requires his immediate attention!"

The assistant exhaled haughtily. "One moment, Agent Coleman."

A few seconds later, the director's low voice broke the silence.

"What have you got?" he asked curtly.

"Director, I've been digging a little deeper into the letters, and I believe I've found something. It's not good. *Jesus*—" Tom dropped the phone and gripped the steering wheel with both hands as the car began sliding on the icy pavement toward an oncoming vehicle. The director's voice shouted from the phone on the seat next to him as he nudged the car back into the lane.

"Agent Coleman? Hello? What the hell's going on?"

Tom kept his viselike grip on the wheel as the oncoming vehicle miraculously slipped past him by just inches. He cursed under his breath and grabbed the phone off the seat. "I'm on my way to the office, sir, and I have the last letter with me—the one that just arrived yesterday. As I said, I think I've found something. A message in the letter."

"What message?" the director demanded.

Tom paused briefly, weighing the absurdity of his conclusion. He knew if he was wrong, Jack Preston would be merciless on him, but he also knew the stakes were much higher if he was right. He shook the doubts from his head and spoke slowly into the phone.

"His message to us, sir. He knows we're coming for him."

———

Rick stepped down the walkway and quietly counted off the apartment numbers as he went.

1552 . . . 1553 . . . 1554 . . . 1555 . . .

He paused outside the next entryway and reached into his pocket. His fingers wrapped reassuringly around the grip of his pistol. Unlike before, the door to apartment 1556 was closed. Rick glanced over his shoulder to see if anyone was approaching, but the corridor still stood empty. A cold gust of wind swirled around him, leaving a fresh mix of nauseating chemicals in its wake.

He moved cautiously into the entryway and placed his ear against the door. The low murmur of a male voice could be heard speaking inside the apartment, followed by another higher-pitched response.

He's still alive, Rick thought with relief.

He stepped back and pulled the handgun from his pocket. His heartbeat was a pounding drum in his ear as he leveled his leg against the door and kicked hard. The heavy steel door snapped inward and slammed against the wall with a resounding *CRACK!*

"Department of Homeland Security! Don't move!" Rick screamed as he pointed his pistol into the dark interior and took a step closer. Staring into the small apartment, he could barely make out the rough silhouette of a man sitting in an armchair. He aimed at the man and stepped inside.

"Identify yourself!"

The man didn't respond.

"I said identify yourself!"

"I'm afraid you're in the wrong homeland," a low voice responded from the nearest corner of the room.

"Don't move!" Rick replied, immediately swinging his gun toward the voice. He then froze, staring in confusion. Instead of a human target, a tiny black speaker rested on a wooden table in the corner. He glanced nervously around the room. "What did you say?" he demanded.

"I said you're in the wrong homeland," the voice replied from the speaker on the table. "I don't recall the US Department of Homeland Security including China as part of its jurisdiction."

Rick again aimed at the man in the chair. "Tell me who you are, or I swear to god I'll put a bullet in your fucking chest!"

"I'm afraid he can't help you," the speaker said calmly.

Rick stepped farther into the dimly lit apartment and studied his seated target. He appeared to be a slightly built Asian man, with thick features and a wide, oval-shaped face. He was wearing glasses and dressed in beige slacks and a simple button-up shirt. His arms hung loosely off the chair, and Rick thought something appeared odd about his hands.

"Can you speak English?" he asked.

"He can't speak at all," the speaker crackled. "By the way, is that a real gun?"

Rick looked more closely at the man's face. He couldn't tell if it was the man in the photo. The pale tint of his skin seemed unnaturally gray, and behind the lenses of glasses, his eyes appeared waxy and dull.

"Wait, what's wrong with—"

The tap on Rick's back was soft and nearly imperceptible, like the finger of a child wanting attention. The sound that followed was equally soft and gentle—a fleeting breath of wind that seemed to rush past him through the narrow interior of the apartment. He immediately turned and pointed the handgun at the empty doorway, ignoring the odd, warm wetness that was now soaking into his shirt. Confused, his eyes searched the façade of the dormitory building that stood just opposite of the courtyard.

There, hunched low atop the edge of the roof, a dark figure lifted his head and briefly looked at him before settling back into position.

Rick saw a brief flash of light appear from beneath the man's head at the same instant he felt another gentle tap on his chest. He stood quietly for a moment, staring across the courtyard at the anonymous figure with a mixture of shock and terror before turning and stumbling back into the apartment. A few steps in, he dropped to his knees on the concrete floor and leaned heavily against the wall. The only sound he could hear was the sickening gurgle of air and blood rushing from his chest. He looked up at the man sitting placidly in the chair and slowly raised his small plastic handgun toward him.

"This is your last chance to talk."

The tap against the base of his neck pushed Rick's body violently forward. He gasped reflexively as the last bubbles of breath poured from his chest. A second later, his twisted body slumped lifelessly onto the floor.

═══

Sergeant Andrew Kearney scanned the top-floor corridor of building 847 one final time before engaging the safety on his sniper rifle and rolling quickly out of view. The body of his target, lying conspicuously in the entryway of the apartment, would have to be dealt with, but that wasn't what concerned him at the moment. He reached into his tactical vest and pulled out the small satellite phone that had been provided to him for the assignment. After tapping in the phone's security code, the sergeant immediately opened the COMLINK application that enabled real-time communication between field grunts like himself operating anywhere in the world and the tactical commanders who authorized their missions. *It's like the text-messaging god himself,* Kearney thought morosely as his fingers navigated through another authentication screen and punched in his message.

Identify Kearney 50473095

First target NEUTRALIZED at site

NO VISUAL on second target

> CONFIRM SITE INSPECTION

Less than a minute later, the response flashed onto his screen.

Kearney 50473095 confirmed

AFFIRMATIVE on request for site inspection

Proceed with caution

Assume second target in area

KILL ORDER STILL IN EFFECT

Authenticated 0091245

Kearney stared at the authentication code in the last line of the response and raised his wide brow in surprise. A four-month assignment as a liaison for a colonel in Army Intelligence two years earlier had required him to be intimately familiar with authentication codes—particularly the first three digits that indicated the military division or government agency providing the order. Kearney knew that a directive from authentication code 009 could have come from only one source—but this was the first time he'd seen one from this agency. *And a kill order, no less.*

He shook his head at the strangeness of it.

The sergeant returned the phone to his vest and rolled his muscular, five-foot-ten-inch frame back into position. Looking through his binoculars, he briefly noted the unchanged position of his first target, the body lying unceremoniously against the entryway wall. He'd been a far easier target than Kearney was expecting, especially considering the intelligence briefing that warned him of a highly trained terrorist.

In truth, the man had looked more like a rank amateur, wandering the corridor of the target location in plain sight and hardly studying his surroundings before pulling out that tiny pistol—*what the hell* was *that thing?*—and kicking in the door of his intended victim. Kearney could still see the look on the man's face after the first fatal shot, the way he had turned around and stared across the distance at him with that look of utter shock and . . . innocence? It was almost convincing.

Almost.

But again, that wasn't what concerned him. As the intel briefing and the last COMLINK message confirmed, the man wasn't working alone. Somewhere in the area, if not quietly hidden away in the apartment across from him, was the second target—a tall, blond man who by all accounts should stick out like a sore thumb in this miserable complex full of underpaid Chinese workers. Sergeant Kearney hadn't seen anyone even remotely matching that description since arriving on-scene an hour earlier. As he scanned the building through the magnified field of his binoculars, the obvious question was repeating in his head.

Where the fuck is he?

Certain that his second target wasn't going to make the same mistake as the first, the sergeant dismantled his sniper rifle, packed it in a small nylon case, and tucked it beneath an air vent on the roof of the building before quietly crouch-walking to the stairway access door. Once in the stairwell, he paused briefly to make sure the magazine of his .40-caliber handgun was full before moving down the stairs. Time was now a serious factor. He needed to secure the body of the first target before it was noticed by a passing tenant, while also staying fully alert for the second target. This, plus the fact that he didn't have a teammate to act as a spotter while he was "moving blind," meant he needed to haul his ass up to the fifteenth floor of building 847 as quickly as possible. All while drawing as little attention to himself as possible.

He arrived at the ground floor and stepped purposefully out through the central corridor and across the small courtyard toward building 847. Luckily, with the factories' morning work shift now well under way, the massive compound of dormitories appeared as deserted as a ghost town. Seeing no one, Kearney double-timed it through the lower corridor of building 847 before heading up the stairs.

———

"You'd better start making some goddamn sense, Agent Coleman," Director Preston said indignantly, dismissing with an impatient wave the redheaded assistant who escorted Tom into his office.

Tom nodded as he stepped forward with the letter he'd ripped from the wall of the saloon and slapped it onto the desk in front of Preston.

"I think this guy has been playing us all along, sir," he said as he reached down and pointed to the reference that had made him drive so recklessly back to the ICE offices. As the director studied the page, Tom shoved his hands into his pockets and paced anxiously. His right hand found the small bottle of antibacterial lotion he kept in his pocket, and he could barely resist the urge to use it.

Preston looked up and fixed his green eyes on Tom, his freckled face flushed with anger. "So this guy makes a reference to a fucking movie with the words 'iceman cometh' in the title, and you take that to mean he knows we're after him?"

"Yes sir. It's the title of a play, sir."

"Jesus Christ," Preston replied angrily as he shoved the letter back at Tom. "I don't care if it's a verse from the Koran. Your directive was to investigate the bartender, not the letters. Your first day back in the department and you're already ignoring my orders?"

"The bartender is nothing but a dead end!" Tom shouted, snatching the letter from Preston's desk. "Look, Director, if there's anything I can say with confidence after studying these letters, it's that this guy isn't just writing love letters to a bartender in Flagstaff—he's sending messages to someone inside his team!" He held the letter in the air and slapped it irritably. "And as of right now, I'm absolutely convinced they know we're after them!"

Preston spun his chair around and gazed through the window at the landscape of snow-covered cars in the parking lot. "That's ridiculous," he exclaimed.

"What makes you so sure?"

Preston ignored the question as he stared out the window, the corners of his mouth twitching. Watching him, Tom had the growing sense the director had information he was keeping from him. He decided to test his hunch.

"With all due respect, I've been doing this long enough to know when someone is withholding information from me, Director. Is there something you need to tell me, sir?"

Preston spun around and faced Tom with a cold stare.

"All right, Tom. You want full disclosure? How about this—we've been following a member of this terrorist organization since your brother-in-law's little operation in Amsterdam."

"Wait . . . *what?*"

"Did you really think I was just going to sit back and watch while one of my own agents helped the Langley boys win another victory? Not a chance, Tom. I placed an agent at the bar where your friend Jeri sent her package in the hopes that someone just might show up to claim it." He paused and folded his arms. "And guess what? Someone did."

Tom blinked at the director in confusion. "But how did you know about that package in the first place?"

Preston's mouth curled into a tight frown. "I had you under surveillance," he replied matter-of-factly. "Of course, that was several days ago when I was convinced you'd forsaken this department for the CIA. I'm sure you can understand."

Tom held the director's stare. *Of course!* he thought angrily. *You clever son of a bitch. You had that little teenage fucker following me from the moment I stonewalled you in my office.* He had the sudden urge to reach across the desk and punch Preston in the jaw. Then the full weight of the information struck him.

"Wait . . . someone picked up the package? Who was it?"

The director glanced up at Tom with a fleeting look of relief before grabbing a folder on his desk and flipping it open. "A tall, blond man—presumably American—between twenty-five and thirty years old. We have almost no information on him . . . not even a photo. Apparently he walked right up to the bar in Amsterdam just after the package arrived and told the bartender every item that was inside the box. The bartender handed it over, and moments later he was out the door."

"Then what happened?" Tom asked.

"My agent tailed him to the airport and managed to follow him onto a plane to China. Unfortunately, we lost him in Beijing. I was just about to give up on this whole fucking mess until you walked into my office this morning with that address. And now you want me to believe they know we're after them?"

Tom walked over to the chair in front of Preston's desk and sat down wearily. "Five nights ago, I watched a man run into a hotel in Amsterdam that was surrounded by the best-trained men in the CIA and blow himself into a million little pieces—only to find out a few days later he's alive and well in China. Alex Murstead refused to believe me when I called him last night and told him. But of course you already knew this, since you were listening to my phone conversations, correct?"

Jack Preston shifted uncomfortably in his chair before nodding.

"Whoever this guy is—*whoever these guys are*—they're unlike anything we've ever seen or gone up against." Tom leaned forward and looked at Preston with a thin smile. "I don't know who you sent to find these guys, but unless he's one brilliant fucking agent, my guess is that he has no chance."

Preston flipped the folder closed and leaned back in his chair. "And what do you suggest I do, Tom? Pull him out? Let these guys kill another Petronus employee and then walk off into the sunset? This is probably the *only* chance we're going to get, for chrissake! Besides, he checked in from Dongying more than an hour ago. He's already on-site."

Tom nodded reluctantly. "Which is all the more reason to give your agent a heads-up. It wouldn't hurt for him to take extra precautions, would it, sir?"

"Perhaps," Preston replied. "Assuming he hasn't found them already."

Tom stood up to leave. "Don't take this the wrong way, Director, but I hope for his sake he hasn't. Now, if you'll excuse me, I've got some more letter reading to do." He was nearly to the door when he paused and looked back. "By the way, sir—do I know the agent you sent?"

Preston looked at him thoughtfully for a moment before shaking his head. "I can't say that you would, Tom."

Tom nodded. "Right. Good afternoon, Director."

Jack Preston waited for Tom to leave before grabbing his cell phone. He quickly scrolled through his recent call list and selected the number for R Martin.

"You'd better answer your goddamn phone," he hissed, pressing the phone to his ear.

Chapter 50

Sergeant Kearney moved cautiously down the fifteenth-floor corridor of building 847, the pistol in his right hand concealed under his tactical vest. Like the courtyard below, the building was eerily quiet, its tenants now absorbed by the surrounding factories. Reaching apartment 1556, the sergeant paused next to the open door and brought his handgun to his chest. He stood silently, listening for any noise within the dark interior. Hearing nothing, he stepped back, raised his handgun into position, and stepped inside.

As a trained sniper with more than forty successful special-ops missions under his belt and twenty-eight confirmed kills, Sergeant Kearney was familiar with nearly every form of tactical situation imaginable. His résumé contained a wide range of expertly neutralized targets—a political figure enjoying his final course at a fine Italian restaurant, a vacationing drug czar playing on a jet ski with his boyfriend in Thailand, a Congolese warlord raping a young girl in central Africa—all of them completed without so much as a scratch or a close call. The nearest he had ever come to a mission failure was an assignment two years earlier to neutralize an informant for a terrorist cell operating in the Philippines. The informant had been a beautiful twenty-something girl. Upon targeting her in his rifle scope, Kearney had made a brief but nearly disastrous error—he'd looked at her as human. Had it been a short target window, he would have likely blown the mission. Luckily he'd had just enough time to regain his composure and complete the shot. Regardless of the diversity among them, the sergeant's victims had one thing in common:

None of them ever saw him coming.

But as he stepped inside the dark interior of apartment 1556 with his handgun raised in front of him, Sergeant Kearney's gut instinct told him that his luck was about to change.

He had barely leveled his gun on a man seated in front of him when a piercing, high-pitched scream erupted from the nearby corner of the room. Kearney instinctively turned to his right, his eyes straining to see clearly in the dim light. A small black box that appeared to be a speaker stood on a table. Kearney began to move toward it when a sudden flicker of light coming from the seated man caught his attention. Unable to hear and barely able to see, the sergeant dropped to one knee and aimed his gun at the man's chest. The muzzle of the handgun flashed to life as he placed four rounds through the man's heart with lethal precision before rising to his feet and retreating backward toward the safety of the door. Once there, he slowly swept the room with his handgun.

At that same moment, the high-pitched tone stopped.

Disoriented and nearly deaf from the noise, Kearney crouched in the entry of the apartment, watching intently for any other signs of movement. The body of the first target lay motionless next to him, a pool of dark blood collecting around the man's ash-colored face. Even without clearly seeing the damage he'd inflicted, the sergeant knew the silhouetted man seated in front of him must also be dead.

So who was controlling the speaker?

Kearney had barely considered the question when a blow to the back of his head sent him tumbling forward into the apartment. An explosion of light filled his vision as his left temple slammed violently against an unseen object in front of him. Stunned, the sergeant dropped his handgun and threw out his arms as he fell heavily to the floor. At that moment his training took over. Kearney rolled onto his side and quickly scrambled to his knees just as another direct blow—this time to his forehead—spun him painfully onto his back. As he struggled to get up, his assailant dropped his foot onto Kearney's chest and pressed him hard against the ground. He groaned and opened his eyes to see a smiling, dark-haired man standing over him.

"Lie still," the man said calmly in a clear American accent. He kneeled down and wrapped a small plastic strap around the sergeant's wrists and bound them tightly together, then fastened the strap to the Kevlar collar of Kearney's tactical vest.

"Who the fuck are you?" Kearney replied, straining angrily against his bindings. Every movement of his body caused an explosion of pain in his head, and he could feel the warmth of his own blood running in a thick stream down his temple. The man leaned forward and pressed his foot harder against his chest until Kearney was unable to breathe.

"I said lie still."

Realizing there was no chance of escape, Kearney finally conceded and dropped his head exhaustedly to the floor. He gasped for breath as the man finally removed his foot from his chest.

"That's better," the man responded. He pulled a small, pen-sized flashlight from his pocket and shined the light alternately into each of Kearney's eyes. "I'm afraid I'm not in a position to answer your question right now, but I doubt it even matters. You've suffered enough blows to your skull to produce a really nice concussion. You'll be lucky to remember anything I say."

He put the flashlight away and leaned over the sergeant with a curious stare. "However, we do have some questions for you."

Kearney watched in surprise as another man appeared from behind the man's shoulder and flashed him a wide grin. Even in the dim light he could see that the second man was tall and muscular, with bright blue eyes and a tousle of short, blond hair. As the two men gazed down at him, Kearney realized with a dreaded sense of certainty that his smiling captors were his two intended targets.

The blond man looked over at the body slumped against the wall next to him. "God, what a bloody mess," he said with an Australian accent as he turned and walked to the entry. Kearney listened as the front door was closed and locked. A second later the sergeant heard the click of a light switch and winced in agony as the room was flooded with light.

The dark-haired American removed a backpack from his shoulder and sat down next to him on the floor. The sergeant tried once again to rise up, but the attempt brought on a nauseating wave of disorientation. He laid his head back onto the cold concrete as the Australian walked past him and sat down on what Kearney could now see was a bright red couch in the center of the room. The man ignored the chair next to him where the body of Kearney's second victim still sat.

"Why are you here?" the American asked him as he reached into his backpack.

"Do you really expect me to answer that?" Kearney replied.

"Eventually, yes." The American paused and smiled at something concealed in his bag. "Ah, here it is."

"Fuck you. I'm not giving you *anything* . . . no matter what you have tucked away in that fucking backpack."

"They always say that," the Australian man said in a flat, weary tone. "They always say 'I'm not going to talk.' And then, about two minutes after the injection, they start weeping and carrying on as if you were their mother and they hadn't seen you in twenty years."

He looked at Sergeant Kearney and gave him a doleful grin. "But who knows? Maybe this one will go differently."

"No," his colleague replied. "It won't."

The sergeant barely had time to notice the small syringe in the American's hand before its needle was slipped into his neck. The American watched Kearney with a cold, detached stare as he depressed the plunger.

"I admit, I've never tried this on a person suffering from a concussion or brain trauma, so it'll be interesting to see what we end up with." He removed the needle and pressed his finger firmly against the sergeant's skin.

"Seriously, go fuck yourself," Kearney sneered as he looked up at the American. Almost immediately a calming sensation began to ripple outward from his neck to his head and chest.

"Eyes dilating," the American said, checking his watch. "Right on schedule."

Kearney closed his eyes as the sensation continued flowing through his body, erasing all pain in its wake. His breath grew shallow; his heartbeat began to slow. Somewhere in the vicinity of his left hand, he felt a vague sensation of being pinched.

"Reflexive reaction diminishing."

I have to fight this! Kearney's mind screamed, struggling to remain lucid. *I have to fight!* His skin tingled; his body began to drift with his thoughts. The sergeant dimly realized the sensation he was now experiencing was not unlike floating on a warm, still lake.

"Sergeant Kearney?" a friendly voice asked.

Kearney opened his eyes and glanced around as if waking from a deep sleep. *I have to . . . what?* he asked himself, trying to recall.

"Hey," the man sitting next to him said, snapping his fingers. "How are we doing?"

The sergeant gazed slowly up at the dark-haired American and smiled.

Chilly glanced again at his watch. "Two minutes."

"How does he look?" Tall Tommy asked halfheartedly.

"Clinically speaking, he looks highly chemically induced."

Tall Tommy leaned over and glanced at the serene face of the sergeant sprawled across the floor. "Nice work. I think you may have just discovered the cure for the common assassin."

"You might be right," Chilly replied, looking down at the sergeant. "Okay, are we ready to play?"

The sergeant gazed up at him with glassy, dilated eyes. "What are we playing?" he asked slowly.

"Twenty questions—starting with your name."

"Okay."

"No, that was the first question. What is your name?"

"Oh," the sergeant responded, blinking. "My name is Sergeant Andrew Kearney. United States Army, Second Division."

"And why are you here, Sergeant Kearney?"

"My assignment was to . . . to neutralize two terrorists believed to be operating in this location."

"Did you kill that man?" Chilly asked, pointing toward the body slumped against the wall.

"Yes," the sergeant replied.

"So he was one of your targets?"

"I thought he was, but . . . but now I'm not so sure. I think . . . I think *you* might be the intended target. You both look somewhat alike, and I didn't have any . . . any pictures, you know?" The sergeant turned his head toward the couch and pointed his finger at Tall Tommy. "That man is definitely the second target. I was looking for him when I entered the apartment."

Chilly grabbed the sergeant's face and twisted it roughly toward the body on the floor. Kearney winced in pain.

"Did you know that man was an agent for the US Department of Homeland Security?"

"No . . . of course not," Kearney replied, his face contorting into a strange grimace. "I didn't have any idea."

From his seat on the couch, Tall Tommy leaned forward and let out a low whistle. "Now it's getting interesting."

Chilly nodded. "Sergeant, I want to know who—"

The ring of a cell phone interrupted him. Chilly gave the sergeant an inquiring look before realizing the sound was coming from somewhere else. Both he and Tall Tommy glanced at the body by the entry.

The cell phone rang again.

Chilly moved over to the body of the slain agent and began feeling along his chest and legs. He found the phone inside the man's heavy jacket and pulled it free as it rang again. The small screen illuminated a single word as the caller's identity.

DIRECTOR

"Who is it?" Tall Tommy asked.

He turned and looked at his colleague, a slight grin on his face.

"What?" Tall Tommy asked.

"I have an idea."

"All right, let's hear it."

Chilly held a finger to his lips for silence before clicking the "Answer" button on the phone.

Chapter 51

Jack Preston was about to hang up when a sudden click on the line made him stop and bring the cell phone back to his ear. Annoyed, he didn't wait for a response before speaking.

"In case I didn't make myself clear before, Agent Martin, I expect a goddamn progress report every fifteen minutes here forward. Now give me the status on the situation—starting with your exact location."

"I'm afraid the situation isn't as expected," an unfamiliar male voice replied coolly into the phone. "Agent Martin is dead."

"Who the hell is this?" Preston demanded.

"Agent Martin has just suffered three shots from a high-powered rifle," the man continued. "From what I can tell, the first two shots collapsed his left lung but were nonlethal. Unfortunately, the third shot shattered his fourth thoracic vertebrae and severed his spinal cord before destroying his heart. I'm quite certain the third shot killed him instantly. Please give his family my sincere condolences."

Preston sat speechless in his chair as the unknown man paused and waited for his response.

"Are you still there?" the man asked.

"I'm . . . yes, I'm still here," Preston stammered. "And who am I speaking to?" he asked as he rose from his desk and rushed toward the door.

"I happened to be nearby when this whole horrible *situation*, as you call it, occurred. Unfortunately I wasn't able to offer any useful assistance to Agent Martin after he was shot. His injuries simply were not survivable."

The director threw open the door to his office and looked anxiously down the hallway toward the elevators. *Dammit!* Tom Coleman was already gone. He turned to Julie, his assistant, and irritably motioned for something to write with. She pushed a notepad across her desk and handed him a pen.

"I'm . . . I'm very sorry to hear that," Preston replied as he scribbled down a single underlined word and held it out to her.

Trace!

Julie nodded and immediately picked up the phone to initiate a trace of the call as the director paced back into his office and quietly shut the door. "I'm sure you did everything you could. I apologize, but I didn't catch your name."

"I didn't provide it," the man replied matter-of-factly. "My employer has a rather strict policy against the use of real names while on assignment. Of course, I might be persuaded to bend the rules a little if you were to tell me *your* name."

Preston stood by the window in his office and considered his reply. The voice on the other end of the line almost certainly belonged to the man—the *terrorist*—they were after, and yet nothing about this call made any sense. *Agent Martin dead?* It didn't seem likely. But then why had this man just described his injuries in grisly detail? Even more perplexing was the call itself. If this truly was their terrorist—the man who'd murdered four Petronus Energy employees and miraculously evaded the CIA—why had he answered the call? The only chance of getting an answer and maintaining a traceable thread to the man at the other end of the line hinged upon keeping him on the phone long enough to gain some information. But the director had to play it smart. Under no circumstances could he provide any useful information in return.

"I wish I could," he responded. "Unfortunately my employer follows the same policy."

"That's too bad," the man replied. "I was hoping we could speak under a greater sense of mutual trust, *Director*."

A cold chill ran up Preston's spine. *How in the hell did he know this? Christ, what other information had Agent Martin given him?* He ran his hand through his receding crop of red hair and started pacing the floor. "I was hoping for the same, but it seems you already know a lot more about me than I know about you."

Preston heard a brief click on the line. The signal trace had started. If his surveillance team in Phoenix was doing its job, they'd also started recording the conversation and initiating a voice analysis on his unidentified caller.

"On the contrary, I know almost nothing about you, Director," the man replied. "My knowledge is limited to two simple facts— you sent a US Homeland Security Agent named Martin to China on an assignment, and Agent Martin is now dead."

The remark sent a bolt of anger through the director. "You forgot one important fact," he replied slowly, any trace of politeness now stripped from his voice. "*You* killed Agent Martin."

"No, Director, that's not a fact. That's an assumption . . . and an incorrect one as well. But this must be your lucky day, because the man who *did* kill Agent Martin is here next to me, and I would be delighted to introduce you. Please hold for just a moment."

"What?" Preston replied. "I don't understand. Who—" He paused at the muffled sound of someone speaking in the background. A moment later, another male voice spoke languidly into the phone.

"Hello?"

"Who is this?" Preston demanded.

"This is Sergeant Andrew Kearney. United States Army . . . Second Division."

The director stopped pacing and stood rigidly next to his desk. Did he just hear this man correctly? "Sergeant, what's your involvement in this situation?"

The sergeant hesitated for a moment before speaking. When he did, his baritone voice came across the phone line in a soft, faintly slurred whisper.

"At twenty-one hundred hours last night I received eyes-only orders to neutralize two terrorist targets believed to be operating at this location. I arrived on-site at zero four hundred hours this morning and set up my primary position on the roof of the building directly south of this location. Shortly after zero seven hundred hours, I observed a tall Caucasian male with brown hair who I believed to be the first of my two targets walking into the apartment number I was provided. Upon exiting the apartment, the target proceeded to enter another apartment with a weapon drawn, and it was at that time that I decided to engage. I then neutralized the target with three shots from my rifle."

Preston listened without saying a word as he walked around his desk and sank dumbfounded into his chair. The sergeant continued in a slow, droning monotone.

"After neutralizing the first target, I received permission via COMLINK to investigate the target site and neutralize the second target if encountered. Upon entering the apartment . . . I mean the target site . . . I was confronted with a man sitting in a chair and was immediately disoriented by a loud noise and a bright flash of light. At that time I determined the man sitting in the chair was an aggressor and engaged him with my handgun. I fired several shots before I was subdued by the man who is now holding the phone. That . . . that pretty much summarizes my involvement in this situation."

Jack Preston sat in stunned silence. He couldn't believe what he was hearing. An American army sergeant had just admitted to killing a federal agent and god knows who else. The reason his elusive terrorist had taken his call to Agent Martin was now clear—he wanted to make sure that Preston and everyone listening knew exactly what had transpired. *He didn't just know the call was being traced and recorded,* Preston thought incredulously. *He was fucking counting on it.* Right now his team of technicians was analyzing the voice on the other end of the call, and the worst possible outcome would be what he already knew to be true. Agent Rick Martin's death, through some unfathomable mistake, had come at the hands of another American soldier.

You clever son of a bitch.

Preston checked his watch. The trace had started just over one minute earlier. He knew he needed to keep the call active for at least another two minutes to give his team enough time to complete the signal trace. There was only one question left to ask, and the director had no intention of ending the conversation without getting the answer.

"Sergeant," he said with a steady tone of authority. "Who gave you those orders?"

The sergeant let out a sudden breath before responding. Preston had the odd impression that he had woken the man up from a deep sleep.

"The . . . the orders came directly from my CO, sir," he replied, reflexively adding the "sir" in response to Preston's tone. "But that doesn't mean anything. I knew the minute I was given the mission that it was just another charter."

"Another *charter*?"

"Yes sir, that's our name for any special-ops assignments that come from other agencies. You know, like a contract. Nobody does their own dirty work anymore. Too fucking messy." The sergeant laughed softly at his own remark. "Excuse my French, sir."

"So you're saying you don't have any idea who requested your assignment?" the director pressed.

"No sir, I'm not saying that. I mean, yes sir, I *do* know. In fact, I'm absolutely sure I know who requested it."

Preston hesitated before responding, faced with yet another dilemma. He needed to know who was responsible for the sergeant's kill-order assignment, but asking the question meant allowing the man sitting next to the sergeant to hear what was essentially highly classified information regarding military operations and protocols. And yet what other option was there? The entire investigation was now a complete and utter clusterfuck. The only hope of salvaging anything—including his own career—was to finish the location trace and find out who in the hell had authorized this idiot sergeant to go on a killing spree.

"Then tell me, Sergeant," he said firmly. "Who ordered it?"

"The COMLINK response I received before entering the target location had an authentication code that started with zero zero nine," the sergeant said matter-of-factly, his voice low and dull. "And the only agency that uses that code is the National Security Agency."

Preston spun his chair around to the window and looked up at the dull, featureless sky. The NSA? How could they have gotten tangled in this? Even if they were monitoring a suspected terrorist, the NSA would rarely if ever initiate a kill-order directive unless they were absolutely certain of their information. He gazed out at the unbroken gray, puzzling over the information and beginning to doubt the likelihood of the sergeant's assertion. Then it hit him.

Connolly.

It made perfect sense. The HSI director had made it abundantly clear he didn't approve of the way Preston was handling the investigation—demanding to know everything that was happening with Agents Coleman and Martin under the threat of carving Jack's divisional budget into pieces if he wasn't forthright about every new development. He was also the only person with whom Preston had shared the Dongying intelligence. And of course, Connolly was ex-NSA. He could have easily used his knowledge and connections within the government's most clandestine organization to submit a kill-order request, and then concealed his tracks beneath the agency's thick layer of surreptitious protocols.

Richard, you conniving old prick, Preston thought as he shook his head in anger. A heavy sigh on the other end of the line brought his attention back to the call. He checked his watch again. It had been nearly two minutes since his team had started the trace.

"You're certain of this, Sergeant?" he asked sternly, choosing his words carefully in light of the fact that every word was now being recorded. "You're certain your orders, including the authorization to use lethal force, came from a source within the NSA?"

"Yes, sir. I'm certain of it."

Preston turned back to his desk and grabbed the case file Coleman had given him earlier that morning. He flipped to the copies of the Polaroid photos from the letters and immediately examined the obscured figure standing in each. "Sergeant, the man holding the phone . . . is he Caucasian, maybe six feet tall, with short, curly brown hair?"

"Yes sir."

Preston nodded. "By any chance is he wearing a blue T-shirt with a logo on it?"

The sergeant hesitated for a moment. "Uh . . . yes sir. It looks like it's a T-shirt from a bar. It says 'Joe's Last Stand Saloon' on it."

So much for discretion, Preston thought as he slapped the manila folder closed and leaned back in his chair. "Okay, thank you, Sergeant. I would now like to speak to the man holding the phone, but I want you to know I will do everything in my power to get you safely back to your unit. Do you understand?"

"Yes sir," the sergeant replied, a slight slur still evident in his voice. "Thank you, sir."

"Good luck, Sergeant," the director replied, rubbing his fingers deep into his temples. He knew Sergeant Kearney would likely be killed within seconds of ending the call, but he had to present an illusion of hope.

The voice of the man returned to the line. "It seems you know practically everything about me now, wouldn't you agree, Director?" he asked in a cheerful tone.

"The only thing I know is what you've done . . . and what you're capable of," Preston replied contemptuously.

"Be careful of what you believe to be the truth, Director. The only thing I've *done* is expose the fact that you sent an innocent man to his death this morning. If there's anyone you should be pursuing right now, it's the person who initiated the murder of your agent. As far as what I'm *capable of*, well . . . do any of us really know our full potential?"

Preston looked again at his watch. Almost three minutes on the signal trace; certainly his team had pinpointed the exact location by now. They should have also collected enough audio to run a full vocal analysis. Within the hour they could have a voiceprint of the man distributed to every governmental agency in the free world, if necessary. Preston knew it probably wouldn't be enough to catch him, at least not in the short run, but that hardly mattered right now.

Solving the case was no longer his primary objective.

The only thing that now mattered was pinning all responsibility for this atrocious situation on HSI Director Connolly and, with any luck, saving his own ass. Preston considered this as he spoke into the phone.

"I can assure you that whoever is responsible for the actions leading to Agent Martin's death will face justice," he replied. "I can also assure you if you kill that American soldier or the Petronus employee we both know you're there to execute, there will be no limit to the resources brought forth by the American government to bring you to justice. Do I make myself clear?"

"I'm afraid you're operating under the wrong assumptions once again, Director," the man replied. "Unfortunately, I don't have time to discuss those details right now. The Chinese authorities will be here soon, and I want to make sure that Sergeant Kearney is appropriately prepared for their arrival. Personally, I don't think they'll be too upset over the death of Agent Martin. But the man sitting here with four of the sergeant's bullets in his chest is another matter entirely."

Preston paused. He'd assumed the second man the sergeant had shot was the tall blond man Agent Martin had lost in Beijing. But if not him, then who was he? Another wave of dread washed over him as he considered the next logical possibility.

"Who is he?" he asked.

"I believe the authorities here will identify him as one Dr. Chung Zhu, a highly regarded forty-seven-year-old chemical engineer who, until being abducted from his home two nights ago, was the head of research for Petronus Energy's operations in northern China. Unfortunately, it appears Dr. Zhu has suffered from a fair amount of torture over these last few days. Both of his hands have been horribly smashed, his fingers mutilated. Even the poor man's teeth have been pulled out, no doubt in some sadistic way designed to force him to talk. We can only hope the sergeant's well-placed shots to the doctor's chest brought a quick end to his misery."

The director dropped his elbows onto the desk and rested his head dejectedly in his hands, the cell phone still pressed against his ear. *This can't get any worse*, he thought as his office door opened and the round face of his assistant Julie appeared in the entryway. He gave her a wary stare as she shuffled toward his desk, a piece of notepaper poised in her plump hand. He snatched it from her and quickly read the brief message.

Signal trace attempts failed—cannot establish or confirm coordinates of location.

Preston pressed his hand over the mouthpiece of his cell phone and screamed out loud.

"Jesus fucking Christ! Is there *anyone* on this goddamn team who can do their fucking job?"

He waved an angry hand, and Julie abruptly turned and marched out of his office, her head hung in a submissive bow as she closed the door behind her. Preston jumped up from his chair and loosened his tie. The air in his office suddenly felt stifling. He moved to the window and rested his pale, freckled head against the cold pane of glass. He then closed his eyes and took a slow, deep breath.

"Are you still there?" the man asked.

"I'm here," Preston replied, fighting an overwhelming urge to end the call. What else was there to discuss? In just a few short minutes, the man on the other end of the line had managed to effectively destroy his career. In the next few hours, the United States would become embroiled in a diplomatic shitstorm involving two American operatives and a murdered Chinese scientist—and he'd be squarely stuck in the middle of it. For the first time in his thirty-plus years of service, Preston felt utterly and hopelessly outmatched. He spoke slowly into the phone.

"Why are you doing this?"

"You see, Director, therein lies the problem. You ask me *why* I'm doing this, but you don't even know what I'm doing."

"Then what exactly are you doing?"

"Exposing weakness."

"In what?"

"In you," the man replied. "But anyway, by now I'm sure you've been told the trace on this call was unsuccessful. Unfortunately, the recording of my voice won't be of much use either. I only wish things had ended differently this morning, Director. I'm sure Agent Martin didn't deserve his punishment. As for the rest of you, I doubt it will be enough."

"I don't understand."

"Of course you don't. Good-bye, Director. And good luck."

The line went dead. Preston cursed softly and turned from the window, tossing his phone onto the desk before collapsing into his chair. He sat quietly, replaying fragments of the conversation in his mind. A few minutes later, he sat up and carefully straightened his tie.

There was only one thing left to do. He picked up the phone and dialed Julie.

"Yes, Director?" his assistant answered timidly.

"Julie, I'd like to apologize for my outburst a few minutes ago."

"It's fine, sir."

"No, it's not. Luckily for you, you probably won't have to put up with me for much longer."

"Sir?"

"Never mind." The director sighed. "Please get me the State Department immediately."

Chapter 52

Alex Murstead barely noticed the cold morning wind that blew along C Street as he stepped from his car and glanced up at his destination. The exterior of the Harry S Truman Building stood ominously under a gray Washington sky. He crossed the intersection at the building's south entrance and presented his credentials to the guard. The guard studied his solemn face and quickly checked his credentials against a computer screen before waving him through. Alex marched past the guard station toward the entrance, staring once more at the massive limestone-clad façade that housed some of the country's most powerful offices. Waiting just a few steps inside the large entryway, an attractive thirty-something woman in a tailored gray suit smiled and walked over to him.

"Agent Murstead?"

"Yes."

"Good morning," the woman replied, shaking his hand firmly. "I'm Susan Baker, Deputy Secretary McCarthy's assistant. Would you follow me, please?"

Alex glanced apprehensively at the large seal of the United States State Department that hung in the center of the lobby as they walked toward a waiting elevator. Once on the third floor, the deputy secretary's assistant led him through another security checkpoint. A badge with Alex's name and clearance level was pinned to his shirt by a guard before the two continued via a second secured elevator to the seventh floor. Once there, he followed her down a long hallway of closed-door offices and meeting rooms. At the end of the hallway, the assistant paused and pointed to a small waiting room.

"If you don't mind waiting in there, the deputy secretary should be with you shortly."

"Thank you," Alex replied, glancing around apprehensively. The woman gave him a thin, practiced smile as she turned and disappeared down the hallway.

Alex stepped into the waiting room and absently noted the antique furnishings and a large, expensive-looking oil painting of old ships battling at sea. The other walls were covered with the décor de rigueur of Washington—pictures of powerful people shaking hands with other powerful people. He was just starting to sit down when a door adjoining the room opened and a slight woman with short gray hair and a severe expression appeared.

"Agent Murstead?" Deputy Secretary Rose McCarthy asked curtly.

"Yes ma'am."

"Let's talk," McCarthy replied as she turned and walked back into her office.

"Happy holidays, Deputy Secretary," Alex said warmly as he followed her into the large room. McCarthy pointed him to the chair opposite her desk as she settled back into her own chair. She stared across the desk at him with a serious, calculating look.

"I wish that were true, Agent."

"I'm sorry to hear that it isn't, ma'am," Alex replied as he sat down across from her. His fear that this unscheduled and highly urgent meeting with the deputy secretary wasn't going to be pleasant seemed to be coming true. Even more alarming was the fact that Alex didn't know what he was here to discuss. He decided to tread lightly until McCarthy explained herself.

"How may I be of service to you?" he asked earnestly.

McCarthy seemed to consider his question for a moment as her small, hawkish eyes studied his face. "Do you know anything about the history of the deputy secretary's role at the State Department, Agent Murstead?" she asked with an aloof tone.

"No ma'am, I'm afraid I do not," Alex replied. "Please, call me Alex."

"The position, Agent Murstead, didn't exist until the Nixon administration. Before then, most daily matters of the State Department were handled by the undersecretary. But by the early 1970s the rest of the world had started to grow up. And as most parents will tell you, the path to any child's adulthood is usually marked by a long and troubled adolescence. Our government found itself ever more embroiled in the growing complexities of international affairs—the Cold War, Vietnam, stirrings of unrest in the Middle East. Places most Americans couldn't even find on a map were suddenly demanding ever more attention and persuasion. So our government did what all governments do best. We created yet another layer of bureaucracy to deal with it. And with that"—McCarthy snapped her fingers—"the role of deputy secretary of state was born."

She paused and gave him a cynical smile.

"Of course, in this town, those of us who sit behind desks with midlevel titles on them know damn well that any new layer of bureaucracy isn't created to solve problems. It's created to provide a political scapegoat for the top brass when the shit hits the fan." McCarthy leaned forward and narrowed her dark eyes at Alex. "And let me just tell you, Agent Murstead—a *lot* of shit hits the fan around here."

"I imagine it does, Deputy Secretary."

"Twenty-four months. That's the average term of anyone who's ever sat in this chair. Certainly some have been here longer when matters of diplomacy were relatively easy, just as some have been here less when matters of diplomacy required something . . . well, something less than diplomatic. Do I make myself clear, Agent Murstead?"

"By all means, Deputy Secretary," Alex replied.

"Good. Then you understand I have no intention of allowing poorly handled affairs by our country's security agencies to jeopardize my stay in this chair."

"Yes ma'am."

McCarthy gave Alex a cold stare. "We have a situation in China," she said wearily, slipping on a pair of reading glasses. She opened a thick file emblazoned with the State Department seal. The word "Classified" was stamped across the front in bold red letters. "Our Beijing Embassy was provided this information a few hours ago." McCarthy pulled out the first page and began reading.

"Approximately twelve hours ago, gunfire was reported at a workers dormitory in the city of Dongying's industrial district. When authorities arrived at the scene, they found an armed and incoherent US military sergeant by the name of Andrew Kearney standing over the bodies of two men. One of the bodies is believed to be that of a Chinese scientist named Chung Zhu, who had been reported missing a few days prior. His body indicates evidence of brutal torture, including several gunshots to the chest that, while not confirmed, Chinese authorities believe match our military officer's handgun."

McCarthy quickly flipped to the next page of the report.

"The second body is believed to be that of an American named Rick Martin. Martin was found with three bullet wounds from a high-powered rifle. An examination of Martin's body produced two items worthy of mention—a compact .22-caliber handgun in his right hand, and a Polaroid photo of the slain Zhu in his coat pocket. Chinese authorities also found a high-powered military sniper rifle on the rooftop of the nearest dormitory building in the compound. The fingerprints on the rifle match those of Sergeant Kearney."

McCarthy dropped the report and gazed over her reading glasses at Alex. "Martin was an agent for the Department of Homeland Security."

Alex's eyes widened in alarm. "With all due respect, ma'am, that sounds rather unbelievable."

The deputy secretary raised her index finger. "Ah, but this story gets even better, Agent Murstead. You see, last night I received a call from Jack Preston, the Department of Homeland Security's Western Divisional Director. After a few minutes of awkward conversation, Director Preston dropped something of a bombshell on me. He admitted to grossly violating protocol and sending one of his agents—Agent Martin, as it turns out—on a little field trip to Dongying. Apparently he'd been sent to monitor one or possibly two men Preston believed were part of a terrorist cell that, according to him, has been assassinating employees of the Petronus Energy Corporation."

The mention of Petronus Energy brought Alex to full alert. He nervously adjusted himself in his chair as the deputy secretary continued.

"Preston told me he had just attempted to call Agent Martin for a progress report when an unknown man answered Martin's phone. Now, I could attempt to explain the nature of that conversation, but I think it would be much better if you just listened to it yourself."

"It was recorded?" Alex asked, his apprehension growing.

She nodded. "Preston at least had the presence of mind to have his team record the call," she replied dryly as she opened the audio file on her laptop. "We've determined that the recording began approximately thirty seconds into the call. Other than that, there's nothing I can tell you that you won't hear for yourself." She punched a key and started the audio file.

Alex listened in stunned silence to Preston's recorded call with the unknown man and US Army Sergeant Kearney. *How is this possible?* he wondered. How could the same terrorist target that his SOG agents had supposedly neutralized in Amsterdam still be alive? His men were the best-trained team in the world. They'd made visual contact of him going into the hotel. They'd swept the entire building. For god's sake, they'd sifted through what was left of him in his hotel room!

When it was over, McCarthy closed the audio file and stared at him expectantly. "Are you starting to get a sense of the scale of this problem, Agent?"

Alex nodded.

"Our own analysis of the audio file confirms that Sergeant Kearney is indeed who he says he is," McCarthy continued. "Vocal analysis also leads us to believe that he was under the influence of some form of truth-inducing agent, most likely given to him by this other man who, as of now, still remains a mystery. Of course, diplomatically speaking, he's a nonentity. As far as the Chinese are concerned, this mystery man doesn't exist. All evidence in the killings of both men points directly to Sergeant Kearney. Unfortunately, whatever that poor bastard was given must have done the trick, because according to the interrogation report, he doesn't remember a goddamn thing." She shrugged in exasperation.

"This situation is truly incredible, Deputy Secretary," Alex replied, quickly composing himself. "Unfortunately, I don't see how this matter pertains to me."

McCarthy stared at him for a long moment. "I had a feeling you might say that, Agent Murstead," she replied in a disappointed tone. "There was another piece of evidence discovered in the apartment that Chinese authorities found rather peculiar. It may in fact be the only reason they've chosen to share this information with us at all." She removed a photo from the file before closing it and returning it to a drawer in her desk.

"What evidence is that?" Alex asked, an edge of apprehension in his voice.

"A small box was found in the lap of Zhu's body," the deputy secretary answered as she studied the photo. "We assume it was placed there by the unknown man who spoke to Preston. Of course, we can't verify that." McCarthy slid the photo across her desk. "This is what was found when they opened it."

Alex could feel her eyes on him as he picked up the photo. The image showed a small cardboard box with the top removed. Inside was a neatly pressed and folded blue T-shirt, a familiar logo printed across the front. Lying on top of the shirt was a small piece of note-paper with a precisely written message clearly visible in the photo.

For Agent Alex Murstead—
Sorry we missed each other in Amsterdam.

McCarthy lifted her small frame from the chair and walked slowly over to the window. In the distance, the Lincoln Memorial stood somberly against the lifeless winter landscape of the National Mall. She spoke quietly as she stared out at the view. "Now, before you start piecing together your bullshit defense, let me just assure you that I have no interest in hearing your side of the story. At least not now." She turned and looked at him coldly. "There's one more wrinkle in this situation you may or may not be aware of. Jack Preston is convinced that the supposed NSA source who initiated Sergeant Kearney's mission was none other than Homeland Security's own intelligence director."

Alex looked at her in a daze of disbelief. "You mean Richard Connolly?"

McCarthy nodded. "Preston said he'd kept Connolly apprised of this situation from the beginning and that he was the only other person who'd been told the terrorist's location in Dongying. Given Connolly's awareness and access to NSA resources, it doesn't seem to be much of a stretch to draw the same conclusion."

Alex placed the photo back on McCarthy's desk and rubbed his hands. "Deputy Secretary, I'm afraid I have absolutely no explanation for that photo."

"Don't insult my intelligence," McCarthy snapped. "You're as involved in this mess as the rest of them. Even if Director Preston hadn't told me about the CIA's recent investigation of these same terrorists, it wouldn't have been difficult to connect the dots. We'll discuss your activities in Amsterdam at another time. Right now I have enough to worry about. I don't have time to turn this situation into some kind of interagency witch hunt."

"Yes ma'am."

McCarthy walked over and pointed a menacing finger at Alex. "So you're going to do it for me."

Alex looked up at the deputy director in confusion. "Excuse me?"

"Make no mistake, Agent—the fallout from this crisis is going to be severe. Careers will be destroyed. Lives will be ruined. But I will tell you right now that mine won't be among them. I've spent far too long in the political trenches to let some power play between agencies pull me out of this office . . . which means we've finally come to the reason I've called you here."

McCarthy returned to her seat.

"Whatever you thought you'd accomplished with these miraculously elusive terrorists obviously failed. So as I see it, Agent Murstead, you have two choices. Either immediately reopen your investigation and make sure it is *properly* concluded this time, or end up on the sacrificial altar along with Preston and whoever else is responsible for this catastrophe."

Alex considered McCarthy's humorless expression for a moment before responding. "You make a persuasive argument, Deputy

Secretary," he replied. "May I get a copy of the Dongying file and Preston's phone conversation?"

"Yes you may," McCarthy answered, her tone now genial. "Susan will have both for you on your way out."

"Then I'll get started immediately."

"Excellent. I believe you've made the right decision, *Alex*."

"I'm sure I have, ma'am."

"I'll expect regular updates on your actions, starting with your first one."

"And just what would you expect that to be, Deputy Secretary?"

McCarthy gave him a hint of a smile. "Richard Connolly has a congressional hearing in less than an hour. I suggest you reschedule that meeting for him."

Chapter 53

Jeri awoke with a start. Her heart was racing, her breath coming in quick gasps, as if she'd just been running a sprint. The remnants of her dream were already beginning to fade.

She had felt him standing there, his face hovering over hers, his dark eyes examining her in the dim light. She opened her eyes and stared up at him, but he gave no indication of noticing. His eyes were focused on something else, something deeper, as if he were watching the very thoughts in her head. She reached out, her long fingers moving slowly toward him. He continued watching her until she'd nearly touched him, then smiled and stepped away.

Jeri sat up and looked out the window. A clear, orange-tinted sky hinted at the coming dawn. The long boughs of nearby ponderosa pines hung low under the weight of a fresh layer of glistening snow. She quietly admired the beauty of it all before finally pulling back the sheets to get out of bed. As she did, an object lying at the foot of the bed fell loudly to the floor. She hopped out and walked over to the object, its cover staring plainly up at her.

Predictions in the New Business Ecology

Jeri picked up her father's book and held it curiously. She was certain she'd left it on the coffee table in the living room the night before. She shrugged at her own forgetfulness and laid it on the nightstand, then headed off to shower and dress.

The rising sun painted the early December sky a pale blue, illuminating the white trunks of aspens standing stoically outside her patio window. For the first time in ages, Jeri sipped her coffee and quietly watched the beautiful procession of morning. A nervous excitement grew in her stomach.

It was her last day at Joe's Last Stand Saloon.

The thought brought a smile to her face. She knew it was time to move on. In fact, it was long overdue. The full weight of that fact had struck Jeri the instant she'd found her father's buried case. It was at that moment, as she'd held his notebooks and read his letter, that she realized the truth. She'd been holding on to her father's ghost for the past year, fighting a feeling of guilt for not being enough, not giving enough, not saying enough to the man who had shaped her world.

The irony that her own sense of guilt had been preventing the very thing her father had wanted most for her—a life spent pursuing her passions—wasn't lost on Jeri. She'd simply never stopped to consider it before now.

She glanced at the coffee table. The plane ticket to India she'd purchased on impulse the night before stared back at her, prompting a fresh wave of excitement. In two days she'd be arriving in Mumbai to begin exploring a corner of the world she'd always wanted to see. An image of busy streets and exotic colors suddenly filled her mind. It would be the first time she had traveled since her father's death.

The ring of her cell phone abruptly ended the daydream. Jeri looked at the caller ID and smiled.

"So, today's the day, huh?" Allie asked excitedly.

"Today's the day," Jeri replied. "The official end of my bartending career. I assume you'll be stopping by. After all, it's your last chance to get free drinks."

Allie laughed. "Girl, I have enough guys knocking on the door to keep me in free drinks for the next ten years. But yes, I'll plan on stopping by after work, okay?"

"I'll have a glass of wine ready for you."

"Make it two. Are you packed yet?"

Jeri looked over at the open suitcase lying empty on her living room floor. "Almost."

"Good. Of course, I still don't understand why, of all the places in the world you could've picked to disappear, you chose *India*." Allie moaned.

"Can you think of a better place?"

"A better place? Sweetie, *anywhere* is a better place. How about Italy, or the Bahamas, or a nice little ride on a cruise ship?"

"Those aren't places, Allie . . . they're tourist traps."

"Well, just remember . . . tourist traps don't have rats. Or slums."

Jeri smiled into the phone. "Exactly. That's why I'm going to India."

Allie sighed resignedly. "Well, just make sure you take plenty of antibiotics. God knows what you might pick up over there."

"Consider them packed," Jeri replied. "Anything else?"

"No. Just that I love you, and that I'm completely pissed that my best friend is leaving me for a third-world country."

"You could come too."

"No, I couldn't."

"Why not?"

"Because I'm not like you. I'm not fearless."

"Allie, I'm anything but fearless."

Allie sighed into the phone. "Look, I know you better than anyone, and all I can say is that whatever your father buried in that box must have worked, because you're *back* . . . back to being the Jeri I knew before he died. And the Jeri I knew then was definitely fearless. So stop arguing with me and take it as a goddamn compliment."

Jeri laughed out loud. "Okay, I'm fearless. But I hate the idea of leaving my best friend just as much as you do. So stop by tonight and we'll toast a proper send-off, okay?"

"I'll see what I can do," Allie replied softly. "Bye, sweetie."

Jeri sat the phone down and stared out the window as the first golden rays of sunlight slipped over the hillside. She closed her eyes and smiled, a single word floating through her mind.

Fearless.

———

HSI Director Richard Connolly took his seat beneath the high, vaulted ceiling of hearing room 311 and quietly busied himself with organizing his notes. Around him, the level of noise and activity within the historic Cannon House hearing room seemed to be rising in anticipation of the next proceeding. A young, pimple-blemished page walked over and placed a fresh bottle of water on the table next to him as another young man adjusted his microphone. Connolly checked his watch.

The hearing would begin in three minutes.

The hearing on Homeland Intelligence Spending and Risk Assessment wasn't an official budgetary hearing, but Connolly knew it might as well be. It would be in this hearing that he would once again have the stage to outline the critical work his intelligence team was conducting against the ever-growing threats of foreign and domestic terror. Within minutes he'd have the committee's chairman and eighteen congressional members riveted. First, he'd lead off with a brief summation of the complex operational and tactical intelligence-gathering procedures being used. He'd then conclude with a list of fear-inducing threats that had been detected and catastrophic disasters averted thanks to the HSI's diligent efforts. After that, the questions that followed would be where the department's true budgetary needs would be defined and, under Connolly's masterful guidance, quickly sold. For Connolly, the only discomfort he'd have to endure for the next ninety minutes would be the absence of a cigarette.

The noise level in the room abruptly dropped as the chairman and members of the committee slowly shuffled into the room. The congressman from Connolly's home state of Georgia gave him a friendly nod as he took his seat behind the rostrum. The room grew quiet. Connolly adjusted his tie and took a quick sip of his water in preparation for the chairman's opening remarks.

"Excuse me, Director Connolly?"

Connolly looked up to see a broad-shouldered man in a suit standing next to him. "Yes."

The man opened his jacket and flashed Connolly his CIA credentials. "Would you please come with me, sir?"

"What's this about?" Connolly asked quietly, feeling the eyes in the room now on him.

The agent nodded toward the front of the room. "That gentleman there will be able to answer your questions, sir."

Connolly turned and saw a tall, muscular man in a dark suit standing before the chairman. As he watched, the man looked up and gestured toward him.

"I'll need you to follow me, sir," the agent standing next to him said firmly as he placed a hand on his shoulder. Connolly forced a casual smile and stood up from his chair. He nodded briefly to the members of the committee before turning and allowing the agent to escort him down the aisle of the hearing room toward the exit. As they walked, Connolly could hear the second agent, who was apparently in charge, following directly behind. The instant they exited the room, he turned and confronted both men.

"What in the hell is the meaning of this?" Connolly demanded angrily.

Alex smiled as he pulled out his CIA identification and flashed it at the director.

"I apologize for interrupting the hearing, Director Connolly, but there's an urgent matter that requires your attention."

A fleeting look of concern crossed Connolly's face before his scowl returned. "What could possibly require my time more than this Congressional hearing, Agent Murstead?"

Alex studied the weathered face of the HSI director. His smile vanished. "Two dead men in China, Director. Ordered through a directive that came from the National Security Agency. Am I correct in understanding that *you* used to work for the NSA, Director?"

Connolly took a step back from the two agents, his face pale.

"I'll take that as a yes," Alex replied softly. He tucked his ID back into his jacket pocket and gently took hold of Connolly's arm. "Please come with us, Director."

===

"He's not going to be in today, Agent Coleman," Jack Preston's assistant said to Tom as he stood in front of the director's office. "The director had an urgent matter to attend to."

"What was the urgent matter?" Tom asked.

Preston's assistant gave him a surprised look. "I'm afraid I don't have that information."

"Is he in Phoenix?" Tom pressed.

"I don't know that either, Agent Coleman. I'm sure the director will contact you if he needs to speak with you. Or I can take a message, if you'd like."

Tom shook his head impatiently. "Do you at least know when he's expected back?"

"No, I do not."

"Fine," Tom replied abruptly. He turned and paced to the elevator. *What the hell is going on?* he wondered. This wasn't a good time for Preston to be out of touch—not with everything that was happening right now. He took the elevator to the first floor and started walking to his office. Halfway there, a thought made him suddenly change direction, and he turned down a side corridor that led to the Undercover Operations area. He walked over to Rick Martin's closed office door and knocked loudly. There was no answer.

"If you're looking for Rick, he's out on some assignment," a voice from the adjacent office called out. Tom walked over and looked in the open door.

"Do you know where he is?" he asked.

"No idea," the agent said with a shrug. "All I know is that he said he'd be unreachable until he was back in the office, which means all the shit happening with his pending cases is ending up on my desk."

"I know how that goes," Tom replied empathetically. "When's he getting back?"

"Should've been back already. He told me he'd probably only be gone for a few days, but it's been at least seven days now." The man looked harder at Tom. "Don't tell me—did he leave you hanging with a case too?"

"No, just curious," Tom answered. "Thanks."

He walked back to his office as he mulled over the facts. Preston had told Tom he'd dropped an agent in Amsterdam the same night as the CIA raid on the terrorist's hotel—exactly six nights ago. Rick Martin had now been gone for more than a week on an assignment where he was "unreachable." In Tom's mind, there was only one reasonable conclusion.

Rick Martin was Preston's agent in China.

Tom marched into his office and glanced around at the cramped room. On the corner of his desk, a tall stack of unopened new case files waited patiently for him. The Landscapes of Sedona calendar pinned on the wall looked dull and lifeless under the fluorescent lights that twitched overhead. He walked over to his chair with its torn upholstery and stopped. A sudden rush of anger swept over him.

This was *his* fucking case to solve. It *belonged* to him—not Alex Murstead, not Jack Preston, and certainly not Rick Martin. Tom turned around and walked out of his office, the steel door shutting loudly behind him.

As he walked down the long corridor toward the exit, Tom realized Preston was right. Whether she was in league with the terrorists or not, the case still revolved around Jeri. There was nothing else he could solve from inside the ICE office, which meant there was only one place left to go.

=====

Alex paused in the corner of the small soundproof room inside the Central Intelligence Agency's Langley complex and stared intently at the two Homeland Security directors seated at the table in front of him. Neither of the men returned his stare as he once again paced the length of the interrogation room's bright white interior. Sitting nearby, the agent who had helped Alex apprehend Connolly earlier that morning was now hovering behind a laptop and a small microphone, recording the conversation.

Alex studied both men as he considered his next line of questioning. His interview of Preston and Connolly was still in its first hour, and already it was clear that the careers—if not the lives—of both were effectively ruined. Once the transcripts of the interview were delivered to Deputy Secretary of State McCarthy, their fates would be sealed.

The first sacrifices for the altar, Alex thought somberly.

Of course, their fate was irrelevant to Alex. Preston and Connolly had knowingly exercised the powers of their offices well beyond their moral and legal limits. In doing so, they had become accountable for the deaths of Agent Martin and the Chinese scientist, Zhu. Whatever consequences they faced—most likely charges from the Department of Justice—would be, in his opinion, fully deserved. The only interest Alex had in these men now was finding out how they'd come by their information.

He turned and faced Jack Preston.

"Help me understand something, Director Preston. You sent Agent Martin to Amsterdam based on the belief that a suspected terrorist was located there. But exactly how did you acquire this information in the first place?"

Jack Preston glared at Alex before responding. "That information was obtained from Agent Coleman."

Alex stopped and looked at him. "So Agent Coleman—who, as you knew, was working with our agency on this investigation— revealed classified information to you?"

Preston shifted uncomfortably in his chair. "Not directly, no."

"Then how were you informed, Director?" Alex pressed.

Preston stared back at him venomously. "Agent Coleman was under surveillance during the time he was assisting your agency with our . . . my apologies . . . *your* investigation," he replied flatly. "Given the strange circumstances forced upon me by the CIA, I thought it only appropriate to keep tabs on any and all conversations *my* agent was having."

Alex's eyes widened in surprise. "So you intentionally eavesdropped on a priority CIA investigation for the purpose of attempting to solve the case yourself? Is that what you're saying?"

Preston looked at Alex and smiled. "On the contrary. I was simply staying aware of my agent's activities in case more of my department's services were needed. With so much going on, I was afraid your team might leave some loose ends that required attention. As it turned out, I was right."

"Don't try to spin this in your favor, Jack," Alex countered. "The only thing you accomplished in all of this was sending an unprepared agent to his death."

Preston slammed his fist on the table in front of him. "Agent Martin's trip to Amsterdam uncovered what everyone in this room knows to be true, *Alex*—that your team missed their fucking target. So don't stand there and pretend to be absolved of your own mistakes in this matter." He looked over and pointed at Richard Connolly seated next to him. "And for the record, *his* actions killed Martin, not mine."

Connolly's calm face contorted in anger. "You spineless son of a bitch!"

Alex ignored the volatile exchange between the two men and continued pacing the floor. Preston's admission of placing Tom under surveillance had come as a complete shock—both in its arrogant stupidity and its deeper meaning. Was it possible that Tom had actually held true to their agreement? After swiftly destroying his brother-in-law's dream of being in the CIA, Alex had been certain Tom's first act of survival would be to go crawling back to Preston and offer anything—including knowledge of the investigation—in exchange for his job. And yet that apparently wasn't the case. He suddenly recalled his heated phone call with Tom just a few days earlier. *He'd tried to tell me the target was still alive, and I ignored him.* He pushed the thought from his mind and raised his hand.

"Enough," he snapped loudly, ending the argument between Preston and Connolly. "We'll get to the details of Agent Martin's death soon enough." Alex walked over to a briefcase lying on the table. He reached in and picked up a thick file, tossing it on the table in front of Preston. "Right now I want to know how you managed to obtain *this*."

Preston stared down at the file of investigation notes Tom Coleman had handed to him in his Flagstaff office the previous morning. In his conversation with Rose McCarthy that same afternoon, the deputy secretary of state had made it clear that Preston would immediately report to Washington with all materials associated with the investigation leading up to the events in Dongying. He opened the file and quickly thumbed through the contents. "This material was located inside Agent Coleman's case files in our Flagstaff office, which makes it the legal property of Department of Homeland Security."

"The hell it does," Alex replied angrily. He pulled the open file away from Preston and grabbed the document on top. "Did Tom Coleman give you this file?"

Preston crossed his arms. "I believe I've already answered your question."

Alex glanced at the document in his hand. The content on the page was broken into two columns. On the left, the page contained a list of highlighted words and statements from the letters the terrorist had written. On the right, the details of the letter's corresponding murder were summarized. Alex read the comparisons and immediately grasped what Tom had uncovered.

Messages within the letters . . . of course!

He slapped the document onto the table in front of Preston and Connolly. "What else can you tell me about the messages in the letters?" he asked excitedly. Both Preston and Connolly looked at him with a blank expression.

"For god's sake, it's right here in the file! Don't you read your own intel?"

Connolly picked up the document and examined it carefully. "I've never seen this document . . . or anything else in this file, for that matter. So I can't even begin to know what you're talking about." He turned and glared at Preston with contempt. "Apparently my colleague chose to keep this information from me."

Alex leaned his muscular frame over the table and fixed his stare on Preston. "So what do you know about this?"

Preston shrugged. "Nothing more than what's written on that page. As you can see, Agent Coleman believes there are messages hidden within the letters. But I don't believe he has any more information, or any *proof* beyond that. Personally, I wouldn't give it too much credence."

Connolly looked up from the notes and gave Preston an incredulous expression. "Am I correct in understanding that the primary suspect in this investigation has been sending letters to Agent Coleman's source?"

"Yes."

"And that source is a . . . a bartender in Flagstaff?"

"Correct."

"How long have you had this information?"

"Less than twenty-four hours, Richard," Preston replied dismissively. "Hardly enough time to fully absorb everything."

Alex looked over at Connolly. He could immediately tell something was wrong. "Why do you ask?"

Connolly spun the page toward Alex and pointed to a list of statements that were repeated in the letter. "Do you notice how this man uses the phrase 'don't order dog' in almost all of the letters?"

"Yes," Alex replied curiously, wondering what the frail-looking intelligence director was getting at. "He ends every letter with that statement."

Connolly shook his head. "No, he ends *almost* every letter with that statement." He slid his nicotine-stained index finger down the column to the last entry on the page. "In his last letter, he says 'go ahead, order dog.'"

Alex ran a quick hand through his hair. His patience was coming to an end. "Yeah, so . . . does that *mean* something to you?"

Connolly considered the question for a moment before finally nodding. "I'm afraid it does." He sat back in his chair and rubbed his eyes as if suddenly exhausted. When he looked up at Alex, his expression was grave. "But what I'm going to tell you is not to be repeated . . . and for purposes of national security, I don't want this recorded."

Alex looked at his agent sitting in the corner. "Stop recording, and give us a few minutes."

Connolly waited until the agent was gone before leaning forward and speaking in a low voice. "I'm sure you're aware that I spent more than twenty years with the National Security Agency before taking my position with the Department of Homeland Security. But I doubt you have the faintest clue what I did for the majority of my early life in that agency. You would probably assume I was a code breaker. After all, that's what everyone believes you do when you're in the NSA, correct?"

Alex grinned slightly at Connolly's sarcastic remark.

"Well, let me tell you . . . with enough patience and determination, nearly *anyone* can break codes. There's no magic to cryptology. It's all just protocols and formulas. Once you understand that, defeating codes simply becomes a matter of resources. But for the NSA—the agency designed to be the cornerstone of US intelligence gathering—that ability in itself isn't enough. Not by any stretch of the imagination. You can't just spend your time scribbling down conversations of interest and deciphering their meaning." Connolly paused to release a deep, wheezing cough. "No . . . you've got to be more proactive than that."

"So . . ." Alex said, prodding him along.

"So you take the next step, of course," Connolly replied with a smug grin. "You start focusing less on breaking your adversary's codes, and more on *making their codes for them.*"

Both Alex and Jack Preston looked at Connolly quizzically.

"I don't think I follow you," Alex replied.

"Of course you do," Connolly responded. "Your own CIA has deep-cover operatives in the field who exist to provide your team with intelligence on the groups or governments they're entrenched in. And I have no doubt those operatives *seed* just as much information as they *harvest*—correct?"

"Perhaps, but—"

"The thinking of the NSA was no different," Connolly continued. "We began creating cryptographic protocols—basically, encrypted language formats—that were then fed to our operatives in the field. The operatives would then introduce these formats to their various contacts, and, with any luck, they'd begin using them."

"So . . . *did* they use them?" Preston asked.

"Let's just say that our success rate was quite high."

Alex nodded. "This is all very interesting, Director, but what does this have to do with our letter-writing terrorist?"

"I'm getting to that," Connolly replied as he raised his hand. "You see, back in the early days, it was my responsibility to oversee one of the teams tasked with creating these cryptographic protocols. As you can probably imagine, managing a large group of geniuses developing new encryption methods had its share of challenges . . . especially when you consider that this was the agency's most covert project. It may sound ridiculous, but communication was our single biggest obstacle. There was so much sensitive information, so many goddamn procedures to deal with. Christ, you could barely assemble a handful of people without violating some mandate or risking corrupting a new protocol. But then, out of the blue one day, a young mathematician on my team came to me with a rather brilliant solution. He'd developed a completely new cryptographic protocol for the project—a new *language* that could be used for all internal communication amongst the teams. The protocol itself was quite simple, made up largely of acronyms and analogous associations that could easily be remembered and modified by the team members themselves. But perhaps the most ingenious aspect of it was that it didn't appear to be a form of encryption at all. It looked and read like any normal message."

Connolly paused and looked up at Alex as if snapping out of a trance. He smiled and laid his hand on the folder in front of him. "That was a long damn time ago—more years than I care to count—but I can tell you with absolute certainty that the creation of that single protocol made the NSA program a success. I can also tell you with the same amount of certainty that these letters are written in that protocol."

Alex stood quietly for a moment, assessing the sincerity on Connolly's face before speaking. "How can you be sure?"

"I used that protocol every day for years, Agent Murstead. Few people could have known it better. Trust me, I'm sure."

"Okay then, what does it mean?" Alex asked as he flipped the page of notes around and pointed at the last entry. Connolly looked at it and shrugged.

"Well, again, the protocol was designed to be adaptable. Without thoroughly analyzing all of the letters, I'd only be able to guess."

"But you *do* have a guess, don't you?" Alex asked.

"Yes, I have a guess."

"Then tell me."

Connolly glanced down at the page of notes. "The same man who invented this protocol once delivered a message to my office regarding his suspicion of an operative assigned to a post in East Germany during the Cold War. I don't recall the exact words of the entire message, but I clearly remember the last sentence. It simply read, 'If you have any interest in a pet, I'd definitely recommend a dog.' I agreed with his assessment, and within twenty-four hours that East German operative was dead."

"Why?" Alex asked impatiently.

"Because Agent Murstead, as these letters so eloquently say, he *ordered DOG,* and as everyone within the NSA understood back then, when you ordered the *Destruction of Goods,* it was time for someone to die." Connolly turned and looked at Preston. "You should have told me about this sooner, Jack. We might have saved her life."

"Whose life?" Preston asked.

"The bartender, of course," Connolly replied matter-of-factly. "I think he means to kill her."

Alex looked sharply at Connolly. "Are you telling me that you think this man—who's already been hunted by the CIA, the Department of Homeland Security, and thanks to you, a US military-tary sniper—is now planning to go to Flagstaff and kill the woman he's been writing love letters to?"

"They're not love letters," Connolly said pointedly. "They're coded messages regarding terrorist activities. Which makes the woman who's been receiving them a loose end. Of course he plans to kill her. And he's got a head start on you if you're planning to catch him. Or should I say, planning to catch him *again?*"

Alex considered the director's response for a moment before walking to the door and waving his colleague back into the interrogation room. The two men talked briefly before Alex nodded and addressed Preston and Connolly. "Gentlemen, Agent Davis will be conducting the rest of this interview. I'm sure you'll give him your full cooperation. Afterward, you will be escorted to a secure hotel for the evening. Please make yourself as comfortable as possible until I get back."

He turned to leave, then paused and looked curiously back at Connolly. "Your man in the NSA . . . the one who invented this protocol. What was his name?"

Connolly tensed noticeably at the question. "You don't have the authorization to know that information."

Alex smiled. "Oh no? I'll bet you a short call to the deputy secretary of state says that I do."

Connolly glared at Alex before twisting his mouth into a frown. "Shafer . . . Robert Shafer," he replied quietly. "But back then everyone called him by his code name."

"Which was?"

"Shepherd."

"And where can I find this Shepherd?" Alex demanded.

"You can't," Connolly answered, shaking his head. "He's dead. He was killed in a car accident nearly thirty years ago."

Chapter 54

Tom Coleman parked along the side street outside of Joe's Last Stand Saloon and quickly paced the empty sidewalk along Historic Route 66 toward the entrance. He shoved his hands into his pockets and shivered at the cold. It was just before noon, and a cloudless, sapphire-blue sky stretched overhead, creating a false impression of warmth. Tom noticed a heavily dressed utility worker preparing to check the power lines on the electrical pole in front of him. A second worker, broad shouldered and much taller than his colleague, stepped out from the side door of the utility van parked in front of the saloon. The worker glanced at him and nodded, his face hidden behind a thick scarf. Tom nodded in return as he reached the door, barely noticing the man's blue eyes as he ducked inside.

As he had expected, the saloon was nearly empty. Chip sat in his regular spot at the bar, quietly talking with another man. He noticed Tom and gave him a friendly wave. Tucked in her corner behind the counter, Jeri glanced up and shot Tom a brief look of annoyance before returning her attention to the book cradled in her hands. Tom walked toward the two men sitting at the bar, noting with a sense of relief that Joe the owner wasn't around.

"Well, speak of the devil. I was just talking about you," Chip said warmly with a wide smile as he walked up to the bar. "Tom, say hello to my new friend, Max . . . a kindred spirit who likes drinking as often and as early as I do."

Tom grimaced at the smell of Chip's breath. He'd never seen the older man this drunk before. He gave him a weak smile before extending his gloved hand to the man sitting next to him. "Tom Coleman."

"Hi, I'm Max Delaney," the man replied politely. "Here, take my seat." Tom couldn't help but notice Max's sheer size as he rose to move to the next barstool.

Tom thanked him and sat down between the two. He methodically removed and folded his gloves before tucking them into his coat pockets, then carefully laid a few clean napkins on the bar to rest his hands on. Next to him, Chip watched with a mocking grin.

"You'll have to forgive ol' Tom here, Max. He's a bit of a germophobe."

The large man shrugged his broad, muscled shoulders. "That's just fine by me," he said quietly. "You never know what you might come in contact with these days."

"Good point," Chip conceded. He peered down the bar at Jeri. "Jeri, can I buy a round of drinks for my two friends?"

Jeri nodded without taking her eyes off her book.

Tom looked at the older man with surprise. "You want to buy me a beer? This must be a special occasion."

Chip patted him on the shoulder. "Oh, that's right, you didn't hear the news, did you?"

"What news?"

"I meant to tell you yesterday, but you snatched that letter from the wall and flew out of here before I could even turn around and say hi. By the way, why were you in such a damn hurry?"

"I don't want to talk about that right now," Tom said with a dismissive shake of his head. "What news?"

"It's a good thing Joe isn't here," Chip continued, a wide grin stretched across his face. "Christ, he'd probably hang you from the rafters."

"For fuck's sake, Chip—what's going on around here?"

"Oh, that . . . yeah. Well, you see, it's Jeri's last day."

"What?" Tom said, glancing over at Jeri as she stood pouring their beers from the tap. "Is that really true? Today's your last day working here?"

"Yep," Jeri replied. She walked the beers over to the three men and placed them on the counter, her amber-brown eyes locked coldly on Tom. "Anything else you'd like to ask me?"

"Well . . . well, yeah," Tom stammered, caught off guard by the news. "I mean, what are you planning to do?"

"I'm planning to get out of here for a while," Jeri answered, narrowing her eyes at him. "There's just a little too much attention being focused on me right now."

"So where are you gonna go?"

"Somewhere far away from here," she replied as she turned and walked back to her seat in the corner.

"Wait, Jeri . . . can I please—" Tom stopped at the rough nudge of Chip's elbow.

"Let it go," Chip slurred, waving his hand. "You're not going to get anything else from her. If there's anything I can tell about Jeri, it's when she's made up her mind. Hell, look at her . . . she's practically gone already."

Tom nodded reluctantly and took a sip of his beer. He could feel Chip leaning closer to him.

"So tell me, what was that whole letter-stealing drama all about yesterday?"

"I told you, Chip, I don't want to talk about it."

"Of course, it's *classified information* now, right?" Chip said mockingly. "Come on, Tom, what the hell could be so top secret, anyway? Have you already forgotten that I was the one who helped you with this whole ridiculous investigation? Does it really even matter now? After all, our little letter-writing terrorist has already killed his last target, and Jeri's getting the hell out of here tomorrow. What else could you possibly expect to accomplish?"

"It's not about her, Chip. It's about the person this guy's sending mess—" Tom paused and looked over his shoulder at the large man seated next to him. Max appeared to be ignoring their conversation as he quietly drank his beer. Tom turned and grabbed Chip's arm. "Just drop it, okay?"

Chip raised his eyebrows innocently. "Okay, fine . . . fine. I was just asking."

The three men sat quietly for a few minutes before Chip took a long drink of his beer and sighed loudly. "Well, anyway . . . it's a damn bittersweet day for this forgotten old saloon," he said, raising his beer glass toward Jeri. "Jeri, there isn't a soul around here who won't miss you pouring their beer, but we both know this day is long overdue. It took the love letters of a terrorist to make it happen, but I'm damn happy to see you finally going back out in the world where you belong. Here's to you, my beautiful, intelligent friend. Cheers."

Tom and Max raised their glasses with Chip. At the other end of the bar, Jeri bowed her head and smiled.

"Thanks, Chip. I'm going to miss you too."

Chip nodded and quickly tossed back a good half of his beer. "Oh, and one more thing," he said, his face breaking into a wide grin. "Make sure you leave me a forwarding address. No matter where you end up, I at least want to know I can write you."

Jeri shook her head. "No promises, old man."

Tom took a sip of his beer, his mind spinning. *What was he going to do now?* Suddenly every piece of the investigation seemed to be dissolving and scattering around him. Jack Preston was strangely unreachable. Rick Martin was somewhere in China chasing their terrorist—if he wasn't dead already. And now Jeri herself was leaving for god-knows-where before . . . before what, exactly? Even that wasn't clear. For the last few months he'd been poring over letters full of obscured messages and photos of an obscured face, all in the hopes of catching a man who was killing for an unknown purpose. This wasn't how investigations were supposed to happen. You were supposed to draw closer to the answers, not drift further away. As he now considered everything around him, Tom realized the facts of this case were like so many grains of sand slipping maddeningly through his fingers. Chip was right. What could he possibly expect to accomplish now? There was nothing—

Tom turned and looked at Chip.

"How did you know that?"

Chip glanced up from his beer, a look of confusion on his face. "How did I know *what*?"

"How did you know that Jeri's letter-writing terrorist has already killed his last target?"

Chip gazed at Tom with a blank stare for a moment. "Oh, that . . . well, from the letters, of course. He must have said something about it in the last letter." He paused and glanced over at the shrine on the far wall. "I don't remember exactly where, but I'm sure that's where I saw it."

Tom shook his head slowly. "That doesn't make any sense."

"What do you mean, it 'doesn't make any sense'?" Chip said defensively. "How else would I know that?"

"I don't know, but I've spent hours studying those damn letters, and I can say with absolute certainty that you didn't learn that from them. Our terrorist refers to his victims as the 'Brainybuddies,' and in the last letter he says he's nabbed three of them, but not the last one." Tom leaned closer. "So I'll ask you again, Chip. How did you know that the last target was already dead?"

Chip rolled his eyes at him. "What are you saying, Tom? Do you actually think *I'm* the letter-writing terrorist?"

"No, but I'm beginning to believe you're the person he's been sending the messages to." He stared at the older man intently. "Those letters have been meant for you all along, haven't they?"

Chip laughed. "Listen to yourself! A minute ago you were sitting here drinking a beer with me, and now you're accusing me of being a terrorist? An old man who spends his day drinking at the bar . . . is that Homeland Security's new profile for bad guys, Tom?"

"You didn't answer my question."

Chip took a swallow of his beer and ran a hand through his salt-and-pepper hair in agitation. "Put yourself in my position, Tom. If you were innocent of these accusations, what would you say?"

"First I'd say I was innocent," Tom replied. "Then I'd explain how I managed to have information that only our terrorist would know."

"And if you were guilty?"

Tom leaned back and studied Chip suspiciously.

"I'd kill my accuser and immediately flee the scene."

"I'm an old man, Tom. Do you really think I'd try that on my own?"

Tom shook his head. "No, I suppose not."

Chip smiled and nudged him playfully with his elbow. "Of course I wouldn't." He glanced over at the large man seated next to Tom.

"Max, would you do me the honors?"

Tom looked curiously at Chip before the meaning of his remark struck him, but by then it was too late. Before he could turn, Max stood and wrapped his massive arm around Tom's neck. Pinned from behind against his attacker's chest, Tom frantically tried to punch at Max's face but was quickly subdued in the viselike grip of the larger man's free hand. Max then tightened his grip. Tom's eyes searched around wildly as he fought for breath, straining to free himself from the pillar of muscle now suffocating him. His eyes locked on Jeri, who stood in her corner behind the counter staring back at him, too shocked to move. He tried calling out to her but produced only a muffled gasp.

"Don't fight it, Tom," Chip said calmly. "It's much better if you don't fight."

From her corner behind the counter, Jeri watched in horror as Tom's eyes slowly glazed over and his body went limp. A moment later, at the command of a brief nod from Chip, Max unwrapped his arm from Tom's neck and gently laid his lifeless body on the floor. The two men spoke briefly before Max spun and marched out the front door.

Chip turned and gazed at Jeri, his blue eyes studying her with lucid intensity.

"I'm sorry, Jeri, but I think I just ruined your last day at Joe's."

Chapter 55

Alex Murstead ran through the private hangar inside Reagan National Airport toward the sleek white Bombardier Challenger powering up outside. Waiting for him at the doorway to the tarmac were two of his SOG operatives, both powerfully built men dressed in plainclothes. Like Alex, the only indication of their paramilitary status was the handgun holstered to their belts.

"Let's go. I'll explain on the way," he said as they marched out across the tarmac and boarded the eight-seater jet. A few minutes later, as the plane's wheels lifted off the runway, Alex excused himself and called the office of the deputy secretary.

"What have you got?" McCarthy asked impatiently.

"I'm en route to Flagstaff."

"And why would you be doing that?"

Alex quickly explained the letters to Jeri Halston and summarized his conversation with Preston and Connolly earlier that morning. "Based on Connolly's interpretation of the statements in the letters," he concluded, "I believe our terrorist is on his way to Flagstaff to kill the woman he's been writing. I intend to be there when he arrives."

"So after killing several top scientists employed by a major energy company, you actually believe this man is going to fly onto US soil and risk his life to kill a bartender?" McCarthy asked skeptically.

"Yes ma'am."

"And just what exactly has this young woman done to deserve that kind of attention?"

Alex hesitated before speaking. "I don't know, Deputy Secretary, but you're presuming this guy needs a reason in the first place."

"He didn't just pick that girl out of the blue, Agent Murstead," McCarthy replied reproachfully. "Nothing this man has done so far appears to be random. I doubt his choice with this bartender is any different. What time will you be landing in Flagstaff?"

"My team and I will be on the ground in four hours, ma'am."

"How many men do you have with you?"

"Two."

"And how many men were in Amsterdam when you lost him?" McCarthy asked matter-of-factly.

"Six," Alex replied.

"Then I suggest you get more men."

"I have four more agents en route from San Diego, Deputy Secretary," Alex replied tersely. "If he or any of his friends shows up, we'll get them."

"I'm sure you will," McCarthy said earnestly. "You know what's at stake if you don't."

Alex didn't respond to the threat.

"Call me when you're on-site, Agent."

"Yes ma'am." Alex hung up the phone and peered out the window at the snow-covered landscape falling away beneath him.

═══

Jeri stared at Chip in shock. "What the hell is going on, Chip?" she asked breathlessly from behind the counter. "Why . . . why did he do that?"

Chip drained his beer and sat back down at the bar, his eyes fixed on the empty pint glass in front of him as he collected his thoughts. A moment later he looked up and gave Jeri a weak smile. "I suppose all this calls for an explanation," he replied. "But first I could use a drink."

Jeri picked up a clean pint glass and started toward the beer tap.

"I'll take a scotch instead," Chip said quietly. "Neat, if you don't mind."

Jeri nodded and grabbed a bottle of their best single-malt scotch. Her hands shook nervously as she poured. When she was done, she placed the glass and the bottle of scotch on the counter in front of him.

Chip picked up the drink and threw back most of it in a single gulp. "Thank you," he said, his voice raspy from the strong liquor. "All right, time for a story." He leaned forward against the bar and leveled his ice-blue eyes on Jeri. "As you've probably started to realize, I haven't been entirely forthcoming about my background. The truth is, I *am* a retired archeology professor. But that wasn't my only profession. My earlier profession was a bit more covert than that, though no doubt far less appealing. You see, a long time ago, long before you were even crawling around in your diaper, I was an agent for the National Security Agency."

He paused and threw back the rest of his scotch.

"They recruited me my final year at Princeton. Not that I required any hard sell. After all, it was the *NSA*—the most respected intelligence-gathering agency in the world. For a patriotic young math nerd who'd grown up with a healthy fear of nuclear war and communism, joining the NSA was the opportunity of a lifetime. I walked in on my first day full of naïve ideals and grand delusions of fixing the world. But then, ideals are like everything else, Jeri. They evolve with time.

"In my first year of service I was a code breaker. Almost everyone started out as a code breaker. But I had certain abilities that were quickly recognized, and over the next three years, I was promoted steadily up the chain of command. Along the way, I came to realize that the agency I admired so much was built largely on two unspoken principles—the first being that if the truth, once discovered, wasn't advantageous, it could be *altered*. The second was an even more dangerous derivative of the first . . . the principle that enemies of the state were not defined by any moral rule, but simply by the report your superiors chose to write." He gave her a wide smile. "For the few of us lucky enough to work there, it was, in almost every way, the perfect place to play god.

"But then something happened," Chip continued, his expression turning serious. "One day I was given a new assignment. Nothing out of the ordinary, just a standard domestic infiltration assignment. A creep-and-sweep job, as we called it back then. The target was a young journalist with the *Washington Post*. Of course, that wasn't unusual either. Journalists were a common target for agencies like the NSA back then. They still are. In many ways they're the private-sector equivalent of government agents—they investigate problems, they thread together facts, and, of course, they have confidential sources.

"I didn't think twice about the assignment before undertaking it. Nor was I surprised when, as was usually the case with reporters, the target came up clean. The only thing even remotely suspicious was a file full of financial statements I found in his apartment that showed large amounts of money inside coded client accounts. But when I had them analyzed by our financial specialists, they also came out clean. Several weeks of wiretaps, records reviews, background checks, and even me personally shadowing the target, and nothing. And trust me . . . I knew what I was doing back then. If my target came out clean, the target *was* clean."

"So what did you do?" Jeri asked, watching him carefully. She slowly edged her way back toward her corner behind the counter.

"I submitted my report," Chip replied with a shrug as he stared at his drink. "And assumed that was the end of it. But it wasn't. Two days later I was sitting in my office when a messenger clerk dropped a file on my desk from my supervisor. I read it and immediately realized it wasn't intended for me but for the director of the NSA himself. You see, back then *everything* was encrypted, even the communication protocols for delivering files by the messenger clerks. Apparently the messenger had read the delivery protocol wrong and mistakenly sent the file back to me, its original author. But when I opened the file and examined it, it was obvious the report inside wasn't mine. Someone had completely rewritten it. But in this version, my target wasn't clean. In fact, in this new fictionalized report, my young *Washington Post* journalist was as dirty as they come."

Chip grabbed the bottle of scotch and refilled his glass.

"Espionage, coercion, subterfuge . . . there were enough fabricated accusations in the report to convict him ten times over. And in case you weren't aware, Jeri, agencies like the NSA effectively operate outside of the law. I knew once that damn document landed on the desk of the director, my journalist was a dead man. Regardless of what three years in the agency had taught me, I just couldn't live with that. So I made what you might call a *career-altering decision*. I placed a copy of my original report in the messenger's file and destroyed the false version." He stared solemnly at Jeri. "Then I walked out the front door of the agency to find the man I'd just risked my career saving."

"Who was he?" Jeri asked as she slipped onto her stool in the corner. She waited for Chip to look away before discreetly reaching into her bag hanging from the counter behind her.

"His name was James H. Stone," Chip replied as he picked up his glass and threw back another slug of scotch.

"Wait . . . what?" Jeri replied, recognizing the name that was written on her father's book. "That doesn't make any sense. That's the name—"

"The name of your father, Jeri," Chip said calmly. "His *original* name, at least."

Jeri froze and looked at him suspiciously. "You knew my father?"

Chip nodded. "I did."

"But that doesn't make any sense. My father was an economist, not a reporter."

"I'm sorry to be the one telling you this, Jeri, but your father had a life you and your mother were never told about," Chip replied bluntly. "And for good reason. The night I walked out of the agency, I went straight to his apartment in Georgetown and knocked on his door. When your father unlocked the door, I stormed in, pointed my gun at him, and asked why the NSA wanted him killed. He looked at me calmly and said, 'I take it you're not here to kill me.' Then he walked into the kitchen and poured me a drink." He paused and looked at the bottle of scotch sitting in front of him. "A nice scotch like this, if I recall. Anyway . . . after that, your father and I had a long chat."

"What did you two talk about?" Jeri asked.

"The truth."

"And what exactly *is* the truth, Chip?"

Chip picked up the bottle and waved it at Jeri. "Care for a drink first?"

Jeri looked at him for a moment before shrugging. "Sure, why not."

She stood up from her stool, quickly hiding the item from her bag behind her apron as Chip refilled the glass. She moved slowly to his end of the counter, watching him warily before picking up the scotch and draining it in a single gulp. Chip observed her with a sympathetic smile.

"Sorry . . . I know this is more than you were expecting to deal with today."

Jeri slapped the empty glass onto the bar and shook her head. "Continue your story."

"Oh, yes . . . the truth," Chip said, running his hand through his hair. "Your father was a brilliant man, Jeri. I don't think I've ever met anyone who understood the way the world works as well as he did. When I first told him I was an NSA agent and revealed that I'd been assigned to keep him under surveillance for nearly a month, he wasn't at all surprised by the agency's interest in him. Nor was he surprised when I told him about the falsified intelligence file that accused him of being a spy."

"If you really knew my father, then you know he was a good man," Jeri replied defensively. "So why would anyone want to destroy him?"

"That's exactly what I asked him," Chip replied as he refilled his glass. "And his answer changed my life."

A cell phone rang.

"Excuse me for a moment." Chip said as he pulled out his phone. "Are we ready?" he asked impatiently. A moment later he nodded. "Okay, tell him five more minutes. We're going to have guests soon." He clicked off the phone and dropped it back into his pocket.

"Who was that?" Jeri asked nervously.

"Max," he replied. "He'll be back in a few minutes."

"I'm guessing he won't be alone."

Chip smiled. "Probably not."

Jeri stepped back from the counter. "Okay, Chip . . . enough. I need to know what the hell's going on here. There's a dead federal agent on the ground next to your chair, and you just told me you've spent the last year lying to me about who you really are." She reached beneath her apron and pulled out the handgun she'd taken from her father's buried container. "I'm sorry, but lately I've lost trust in just about everyone—including you. So here's the deal." She raised the handgun and pointed it at his chest. "You've got whatever time is left before that giant murdering muscle-head and whoever else walks through that door to finish your story and get to the truth. Or we're going to have a very awkward situation to sort out."

Chip looked at the gun with a slight grin before continuing.

"The night I confronted your father and asked him why the NSA wanted to destroy him, he gave me a very direct answer. He told me he was wrapping up a corruption story he'd spent the better part of two years investigating. A *big* corruption story. Your father was about to expose widespread misconduct within a large American investment firm that went all the way to the top—executives and board members alike—and, once published, would most likely prompt a full federal investigation. But there was a complication. One of your father's sources inside the firm revealed that the company was managing several large pension funds for the federal government, including agencies like the FBI and the NSA. We're talking hundreds of millions of dollars. Now this by itself was entirely legal, but as your father's inside source revealed, those funds were also getting special attention in the form of *privileged information*, which definitely was not legal. Of course, the people overseeing these pension funds on the government side knew all about this, but they weren't going to say a thing. On the contrary; they were making far too much money to ruin the arrangement—or take any chances. When they found out your father was nosing around, they immediately got nervous. That's when they decided to find out just how much he knew."

"So they sent you after my father to find out," Jeri whispered, still pointing the gun at him.

"That's right," Chip replied. "They asked my superiors at the NSA to put me on his trail, and I unknowingly confirmed everything they feared when I brought those coded financial statements in for analysis." He shook his head in disgust. "After that, the two principles of the agency were immediately implemented. The truth, not being advantageous, was altered, and a new enemy of the state was created with a few adjustments to my report."

Jeri lowered the gun slightly as Chip looked up at her. His pale blue eyes seemed to glow in the dim light of the saloon.

"Your father helped me realize a very unpleasant but necessary truth that night," he continued, his voice now sharp and commanding. "A government is really no different than any other business, Jeri. It exists to serve a purpose, to fulfill its responsibilities, and to regulate itself in a way that is self-sustaining. In most ways a business is like any living organism. It has a natural urge to grow and become more complex. But as any good biology professor will tell you, as organisms grow and evolve, their interests naturally tend to become more self-serving. Eventually this self-serving behavior determines its actions, even when those actions are in direct violation of their very reason for being."

Chip picked up the glass of scotch and slowly swirled it in his hand.

"The NSA was going to kill your father because he was about to expose our government's very nasty little self-serving secret. Your father didn't want to die any more than I wanted to be a part of his killing, which meant our lives as we knew them were both over. I knew we probably had less than twenty-four hours before we were both deemed enemies of the state and hunted down by every agency in Washington."

"So what did you do?" Jeri asked. She realized the pistol was beginning to feel heavy and shifted it to her other hand.

"You should always hold your gun in the hand you plan to shoot with," Chip replied matter-of-factly. "You'll have much better accuracy."

Jeri shifted the gun back to her other hand and pointed it at his chest. "Answer my question."

"We came up with a rather unique idea for getting unwanted attention off both of us . . . and it worked. After that, your father and I decided to relocate someplace where no one would be looking for us. Flagstaff seemed as good a choice as any. I used my skills to create new identities for the two of us, and we entered the university as graduate students. It didn't take long for us to blend in and become forgettable. I studied archeology and eventually became a professor, and James *Stone* the reporter became James *Halston* the economist and writer. The rest, as they say, is history."

Jeri looked at him skeptically. "Okay, but even if you're telling the truth, you still haven't explained everything." She pointed the pistol at the letters on the wall. "If you're really just an old NSA agent turned archeologist, what are you doing with a letter-writing terrorist and that giant thug outside? And if my father was so worried about his identity, why did he publish a book under the name James Stone? And most important"—Jeri swung the gun back at Chip—"what does any of this have to do with me?"

Chip took another drink.

"Well, we don't have much time, so I'll be brief. The truth is, Jeri, old habits die hard. A few years after settling into our new lives, your father and I were both getting a little bored. Your father missed being an investigative reporter, and I missed being an agent. So we both decided to get back into the game again . . . at least in some way. Your father decided to prepare for his master's degree dissertation in macroeconomics by investigating the behaviors of large corporations.

"He spent several years doing what he did best—interviewing sources inside large multinational companies and learning everything about their inner workings. Your father was a genius at uncovering information and getting people to talk. Eventually all of that work culminated in the writing of his dissertation, and a year later he wrote *Predictions in the New Business Ecology*." He smiled and shook his head. "Your father considered his book to be the conclusion and greatest achievement of his 'former' life, so he decided to publish it under the name James Stone. I have no doubts that his book would have been a bestseller too, if he had printed more than a handful of copies. Luckily, I persuaded him not to do that."

"Why did you do that?" Jeri asked.

"As I said, your father was brilliant. I don't think even *he* realized how prophetic his book was when he first asked me to read it. But I did. I also knew it contained the kind of information that could be very useful in the right hands, and very dangerous in the wrong ones. So I convinced him there were better uses for it than sharing it with the world."

"Like what?"

Chip looked back at her with a stoic face. "Like using it as the blueprint for a new kind of agency."

Jeri studied his expression, trying to interpret its meaning. "And what kind of an agency is that?"

The old man's lips curled into a smile. "My kind," he said before throwing back the last of the scotch. He then pointed at his watch. "I'm afraid my time is up."

A bright shaft of sunlight stabbed the room as the front door of the saloon groaned open. Jeri turned and pointed the pistol at the door as a hooded man wearing dark sunglasses and a heavy winter jacket appeared in the entryway. He immediately stopped and raised his gloved hands. "It's okay . . . I'm not armed."

Jeri looked at the man warily before waving him toward the bar. "Have a seat."

The man nodded and walked toward the bar. When he reached the body of Tom Coleman, he dropped to his knees and quickly stripped off his gloves before checking for vital signs.

"He's dead," Jeri said as the man disappeared from her view.

"I'll be the judge of that," the man replied.

Chip turned on his barstool and watched as the man worked, an odd look of admiration on his face. Jeri shook her head in frustration.

"Chip, who the hell is—" A violent fit of coughing echoed through the saloon. Jeri leaned over the counter and stared incredulously as Tom Coleman began retching on the floor. Hovering over him, the new arrival held his shoulder until the coughing subsided. He then produced a small syringe from his pocket and stabbed it into Tom's shoulder.

"What are you giving him?" Jeri asked.

"A mild sedative," the man replied as he tucked the empty syringe back into his pocket. "It'll keep him asleep and allow his throat to rest. Some things heal better when the mind isn't in a state of panic."

"Are you a doctor?"

"Could I have a glass of water, please?" the man asked.

Jeri lowered the pistol and filled a glass with water before pushing it across the bar toward Chip, who handed it to the man.

"Thank you," he replied as he placed the glass on the floor next to Tom.

"No . . . thank *you*," Jeri replied, shaking her head. "I thought for sure he was dead."

"Yeah, well, you'd be amazed how many times I hear that one." The man stood and faced Jeri, his handsome, friendly face stretched with a smile. He pulled back the hood of his jacket and ran a hand through his short, curly black hair before leaning against the counter. His dark eyes crinkled with amusement as they stared into hers. "But then, nothing is ever what it seems, is it?"

Jeri stepped back from the counter, too stunned to speak. She immediately knew the face staring back at her. It was the face that had been maddeningly hidden from view since the first letter and Polaroid photo arrived more than two months ago. "It's you," she whispered, gazing at her Mysterious Joe's Last Stand Guy in disbelief. "You're . . . you're *here*."

"That's right . . . I'm here," he replied, glancing at Chip. "I just hope I'm not interrupting something."

"Not at all," Chip replied, patting him affectionately on the shoulder. "We were just having a little chat. But where are my manners?" He turned and grinned at Jeri. "Jeri, I'd like to finally introduce you to the handsome young man standing next to me. Jeri, this is Chilly. Chilly, this lovely young woman is of course Jeri."

"It's nice to meet you, Jeri," Chilly said, extending his hand.

Jeri stared back at the man's outstretched hand barely an arm's length away and smiled. "It's nice to meet you too, Chilly," she replied, slowly raising the pistol and pointing it at his chest.

"Now have a seat."

Chapter 56

"I hope I didn't travel all this way just to get shot," Chilly said evenly, glancing at the barrel of the pistol. "Do you have any idea how hard it is to field dress your own bullet wounds?"

"No, I don't," Jeri replied, waving the gun at the barstool. "Now sit down."

Chilly sat and looked over at Chip. "I thought you were going to explain everything to her before I got here."

"Well, I told her most of it," Chip replied with a defensive shrugging. "Just not the last part. I'm an old man now . . . my timing isn't what it used to be."

"Right, sorry." Chilly patted him on the arm. "How about I tell her?"

"Tell me what?" Jeri interjected angrily.

"The best part, of course," Chilly answered, reaching out his hand. "But first I'm going to need that gun."

"No chance."

"Those are my terms. Give me the gun, or we can all just sit here patiently until our other guests arrive. And I can promise you one thing—they'll have much bigger guns than yours."

Jeri glanced over at Chip. He nodded.

"You can trust him, Jeri. He's with me."

"That's exactly why I *don't* trust him."

"Jeri, listen to me," Chip said, his tone earnest. "I realize none of this makes any sense right now. But if you believe what I've already told you, then you know you can trust me. I once gave up everything I had to save your father's life. I would hope that's enough reason to trust me now."

"You could've made that story up, for all I know," Jeri snapped.

"Perhaps," the older man responded. "But what if I could prove it? Would you trust me then?"

Jeri looked at him skeptically. "It depends. Where's your proof?"

Chip pointed at her gun. "You're holding it."

Jeri glanced at the gun in her hand before narrowing her eyes on Chip. "What are you talking about?"

"I gave your father that gun shortly after we arrived in Flagstaff. It was my service arm when I was in the NSA. I was required to know everything about that damn gun, including the serial number. There's no way for me to see it from here, but if you look on the right-hand side you'll find it just above the trigger."

Jeri turned the pistol toward the light. To her surprise, a seven-digit number was etched into the dark steel where Chip had predicted. She studied it closely before flashing her eyes at him. "Okay . . . what's the number?"

"If I tell you the number correctly, will you give the gun to Chilly?"

She considered the question for a moment before nodding. "Sure."

"The serial number is 1136087."

Jeri read the numbers as they were spoken before looking at Chip with astonishment.

"You see," he replied. "Everything I've said to you is true, Jeri. Your father was my friend. He trusted me with his life." Chip gestured for the gun. "And now I'm asking you to do the same."

Jeri swallowed nervously as she looked at both men. She leaned forward and placed the gun on the counter. Her hand had barely let go before Chilly picked up the pistol and ejected the magazine in one practiced stroke. He looked up at her with surprise.

"It wasn't even loaded."

Jeri locked eyes with the handsome, thirty-something man she'd wondered about for the last several months and shook her head. "No, it wasn't," she replied.

"Impressive bluff," he said, looking over at Chip. "I'd say she's ready."

The older man nodded in agreement. "Me too."

"Ready for what?" Jeri demanded.

"To meet the others," Chip answered.

As if on cue, the front door opened, and two men wearing the uniforms of the local power company appeared in the doorway. Behind them, the massive Max followed them into the saloon before closing and locking the door. He then reached over and switched off the hanging neon sign in the window that read "Open" before snapping the wooden blinds shut.

"Allow me to introduce everyone," Chip said cheerfully as the three newcomers walked over to the bar and sat down. "This is Dublin," he said, gesturing to a short, pudgy man with a patchy beard sitting next to Chilly. Dublin smiled and nodded. "This is Tall Tommy," Chip continued, pointing to a tall, physically perfect blond man next to Dublin. Tall Tommy pulled a pair of small earphones from his ears and mumbled a quick greeting. "Of course, you've already met Max," Chip said, pointing to the huge man sitting at the end. Max smiled warmly and waved a large, paw-like hand at Jeri.

Jeri nodded at the three men before turning to Chilly. "So . . . what were you going to tell me?"

Chilly leaned forward against the bar and gave her a smile. "Before I tell you, would you mind pouring me a shot of tequila? It's been a long week."

Jeri looked at him warily before tilting her head. "Let me guess. Fortaleza?"

"Perfect."

She turned to pour his drink. "By the way," she said as she grabbed the bottle of tequila, "I'm curious to know something. Why did you always end your letters with the statement 'don't order do—'"

Jeri gasped at a sharp sting in her shoulder. She looked back to find a small cylindrical object sticking out from the skin. Confused, she pulled it out and examined it briefly before spinning around to see Chilly tucking a small pistol back into his pocket.

"What did you just give me?" she demanded, flinging the tranquilizer dart at him.

"A paralyzing agent," Chilly answered somberly. "I'm sorry, Jeri. I promise to never do this to you again."

"Again?" Jeri said, her voice a horrified whisper. "Why did you do it in the first place?"

"You have something we need," Chilly replied. "Just as we have something you need." He glanced over at Max. "Max, would you please help Jeri before she falls and hurts herself?"

Jeri watched as the huge man quickly rose from his stool and started walking toward her. She could already feel a strange numbness trickling through her body. *Stay calm*, she told herself, looking around wildly. A few yards away, Max ducked under the counter and emerged on her side, his massive frame barely fitting within the cramped space. Jeri knew that even under the best circumstances, she wouldn't be able to get past him. She stepped forward and feigned an attempt to go around him before throwing herself clumsily onto the bar next to Chip. Evading the older man's grasp, Jeri then slipped over the counter and fell hard onto the floor. She tried desperately to make her now lifeless legs respond to her command to stand and run, but it was useless. Not about to give up, she flung herself forward onto her elbows and began crawling toward the door. Behind her, Chip's voice called out plaintively.

"Jeri, please . . . don't fight it."

She ignored him, grunting with effort as she slowly dragged herself forward. Seconds later, the numbness swept through her shoulders and crept mercilessly down her arms. She tried doubling her efforts, but her body simply stalled and stopped. After one last desperate try, she sighed loudly and collapsed onto the floor.

Behind her, the old wooden floor creaked softly as someone walked toward her. She felt him kneel down beside her, his hand gently brushing away the hair on her neck before checking her pulse. "It's going to be okay, Jeri," Chilly's baritone voice said calmly. Out of the corner of her eye, Jeri saw the flash of a small syringe and needle. A moment later, a calming warmth began to circulate through her body. Her panic evaporated as an overpowering drowsiness blurred her senses. As she drifted out of consciousness, Chilly's final words echoed through her mind.

"The first act of your new life, Jeri, is to completely kill your old one."

Chapter 57

"How much longer?" Alex asked impatiently as he leaned into the open cockpit of the jet.

"About two more hours, sir," the pilot replied matter-of-factly. "Maybe a little less. We'll be over Kansas in a few minutes."

"Can we go any faster?"

The pilot shook his head. "No sir. We're already at maximum cruising speed."

Alex grunted in response and sat back down in the soft leather seat at the front of the passenger cabin. He reached into his thin briefcase and pulled out the case file given to him by the deputy secretary. Once again he was gripped by the growing sense of apprehension that had haunted him since their meeting that morning. He quickly thumbed through the pages he'd already read, pausing briefly on the photograph of the box with the Joe's Last Stand Saloon T-shirt and the note addressed to him.

> *For Agent Alex Murstead—*
> *Sorry we missed each other in Amsterdam.*

Alex shook his head and slapped the file closed before angrily tossing it on the seat next to him. The reason for his uneasiness was obvious. His career now depended on solving this case, and yet nothing about it seemed to make any sense. *Just who were these terrorists? What was their reason for the Petronus killings? And what did a goddamn bartender in Flagstaff have to do with any of this?*

Alex grabbed the small MP3 player containing the recording of Preston's conversation with their terrorist from his briefcase and put on his headphones before hitting the "Play" button. He listened carefully to the low, calm voice of his target as he deftly picked away at the director's composure. Sergeant Kearney's slow, slurred description of Agent Martin's death only worsened matters. Two minutes into the recording, it was clear that Preston was painfully outmatched. The certainty of it brought a fleeting smile to Alex's face—until the thought of his failed operation in Amsterdam led him to wonder if the same was true for him. He shook the thought from his mind as the audio recording continued.

"Why are you doing this?"

"You see, director, therein lies the problem. You ask me why I'm doing this, and you don't even know what I'm doing."

"Then what exactly are you doing?"

"Exposing weaknesses."

"In what?"

"In you."

Alex yanked out the earbud and tossed the MP3 player back into his briefcase. Across from him, his two SOG team members sat patiently, both staring out at the monotonous, snow-covered landscape beneath them. One of the men reached down and pulled his .40-caliber Glock from his belt holster, quickly inspecting it before glancing up at Alex.

"Think we'll bag some terrorists today, sir?"

Alex stared at the lethal weapon in his colleague's hand and shrugged. "We'll know soon enough."

He pulled another folder from his briefcase and opened it. After reading the brief summary on deceased former NSA Agent Robert Shafer, Alex turned to the accident report. He flipped through a series of black-and-white photos, all of them gruesomely depicting the charred remains of two men sitting in the front seat of a burned-out sedan. He then turned to the coroner's report. As expected, the cause of death listed on the official autopsy report for Robert Shafer read "thermal burns due to fire." Alex was about to close the report when he noticed something strange. In the box under "Identified by," the coroner had simply typed "n/a."

Not available.

The small jet banked gently south toward the mountains as Alex sighed and closed the file. He stared out at the thin, crystalline air, his uneasiness growing.

═══

Tom Coleman sat up from the floor and gently felt his head.

What just happened?

The pounding in his head was almost unbearable, causing even the slight noise of the voices around him to echo painfully inside his skull. A strange metallic taste filled his mouth, and his throat was dry to the point of burning. He opened his eyes and, as if his wish had instantly been granted, noticed a tall glass of water sitting next to him on the floor. He picked it up and drank greedily, ignoring the pain that came with each swallow. Feeling better, Tom placed the empty glass on the floor and blinked the blurriness from his vision. For some unknown reason, he was sitting in the middle of the saloon. He looked over at the bar and, to his surprise, noticed four men sitting with Chip. Tom could hear Chip talking with the man next to him in a low tone, but he couldn't make out what they were saying.

He needed to get closer.

Tom leaned forward and rose shakily to his feet. He was nearly standing when a sudden wave of dizziness struck him. Losing his balance, he staggered and fell heavily onto his back. Chip and the other men turned at the sound of the commotion to find him sprawled across the old wooden floor.

"Glad you could join us again, Tom," Chip said cheerfully, his blue eyes staring down at him. The other men watched with an undisguised look of pity.

Tom propped himself up on one arm and rubbed his head. "What the fuck happened to me?" he asked, his voice a hoarse whisper.

"You were subjected to a form of compressive asphyxia that, pathologically speaking, brought on a state of generalized hypoxia," the dark-haired man sitting next to Chip replied. "Said a simpler way, you were strangled."

Tom gazed up at the man with a puzzled expression. *What the hell did he just say? And why does he look so familiar?* He looked over at the man named Max sitting at the far end of the bar and suddenly remembered what had happened.

"You motherfucker . . . you tried to kill me!" He rose from the floor again before hurling himself clumsily toward Max. As he did, the blond man sitting next to Max stood and intercepted him, pinning Tom's arms behind his back.

"All right, all right . . . settle down," the man commanded in an Australian accent. He pushed Tom back and deposited him once again onto the floor. "Just settle down now," he continued, pointing at something behind Tom. "Or else you're going to end up like that."

Tom shook his arms free and glared at the Australian before turning to see what he was talking about. When his eyes finally focused on the object, his expression turned to shock. A few yards away, Jeri's lifeless body was stretched across the floor.

"Is she dead?" he asked.

"Don't worry about Jeri, Tom," Chip replied as he swung around on his barstool and faced him. "I'd rather talk about you."

Tom studied the faces at the bar before fixing his eyes on Chip. "What the fuck's going on, Chip? Who are these guys?"

"Who do you think?" Chip said, looking over and giving the men a brief nod. At his cue, Max, the Australian, and a short, pudgy man all stood and walked over to Jeri's body. Max gently lifted her off the floor as the other two opened the door to the back alley and escorted him out.

"Where are they taking her?" Tom demanded.

"That's not your concern now," the dark-haired man replied.

Tom looked at the man more closely. "Wait—you're . . . you're *him*."

"Him who?" the man asked.

"The man in the photos." Tom gestured at the shrine on the wall. "You wrote those letters, didn't you?"

"Indeed I did."

Tom's eyes darted to Chip. "Jesus . . . I was right. It *was* you, wasn't it?" he asked, shaking his head in disbelief. "All those messages within the letters. They weren't meant for Jeri; they were meant for *you*."

From his seat at the bar, Chip smiled and nodded.

"That's right, Tom. You see, the truth is, the first time you walked in here and started asking about the letters, I thought you were just some local idiot passing the time. Imagine my surprise when you began connecting the dots." He paused and shook his head. "You impressed me, *Agent Coleman*. Of course, you also forced me to find out just what the hell you were up to. When I discovered you were a low-level agent for the Department of Homeland Security, I figured I could relax a bit. But when I realized your real motivation for solving the case was to get the CIA's attention, I knew we could use you to our advantage."

"Use me?" Tom replied. "How so?"

"Amsterdam," Chip said, pointing to his colleague. "The operation on Chilly's hotel."

Tom glanced at the dark-haired man. "*Chilly?* That's your name?"

Chilly grimaced. "More of a nickname."

"So tell me, Chilly, how in the fuck did you survive that raid in Amsterdam, anyhow?"

"You already know the answer to that, Tom," Chilly replied. He dragged his index finger across his neck like a knife and smiled. "I killed myself."

Tom looked at Chip. "What do you mean, you *used* me in Amsterdam? Are you saying you actually wanted that raid to happen?"

"Absolutely."

"But why?"

"For two reasons," Chip replied. "The first was to know how many agencies were in play. As expected, your brother-in-law's team took the bait at the hotel. But we were somewhat surprised to find Agent Martin from your own Department of Homeland Security waiting for us at the bar where Jeri sent her gift package. The second re—"

"Wait a minute," Tom interrupted. "Rick Martin was in Amsterdam?"

Chip nodded. "Agent Martin tried to intercept the package when we went in to pick it up. He followed Tall Tommy—that's the Australian gentleman you just met—all the way to China before Tommy cut him loose. Hell, Martin would probably still be wandering in Beijing if Chilly's last letter hadn't tipped you off to Dongying."

Tom shook his head. His suspicion was right—the agent Director Preston had sent into the field was none other than his own idiotic colleague. He still couldn't understand why Preston had chosen Rick Martin. "Where's Agent Martin now?" he asked.

Chip raised his eyebrows in surprise. "He's dead, Tom."

Tom glanced at Chilly, who nodded solemnly. The two men locked eyes for a long moment before Tom returned his attention to Chip. "What was the second reason?" he asked.

"András Vida," Chip replied.

Tom vaguely recalled the name. "Wait . . . you mean the first man killed at the hotel? The Bulgarian?"

"He was Hungarian, actually," Chilly replied.

"I don't care if he was French fucking Canadian. What did he have to do with any of this?"

Chilly narrowed his stare on him. "András Vida was a major trafficker of young Eastern European women in the region's sex trade. I was fortunate enough to have seen the consequences of his work firsthand. He was a bad man . . . and he needed to die."

Tom leaned forward and pointed his finger at Chilly. "You knew he was staying at that hotel, didn't you? That's why you picked it. Then you used yourself as bait and got the SOG agents to storm in there and carry out your personal vendetta, is that it?"

"I'd say that about sums it up," Chilly replied.

Tom looked at Chip with disgust. "And you authorized that?"

"Yes."

"Then you're as much of a goddamn terrorist as he is."

Chip shrugged. "Well, Tom, I suppose that depends on your definition of a terrorist."

"How about someone who terrorizes or kills for their own political or personal gain? That's my definition of a terrorist, you old fuck." Tom glared at Chip, his face red with anger. "And you're guilty of both."

"Or neither," Chilly replied. He stood and walked over to Tom before kneeling next to him.

"What? Are you going to kill *me* now, asshole?" Tom growled. "I'd love to see you try to—" He didn't have time to react before Chilly's left hand swung out and connected with his jaw. Tom fell back, his head once again slamming hard into the floor. In an instant Chilly was on top of him, his right hand gripping Tom's neck. In his left hand was a small syringe, its needle pressed gently against the jugular vein.

"Do you have any idea how predictable you are, Tom? Do any of you people? No, of course you don't. Despite all the evidence against it, you're still operating under the delusion that you guys— you *governmental agency* guys—are somehow more competent than anyone else. Even now, you're failing to realize that we could have destroyed you, or your brother-in-law, Alex, or that smug idiot Jack Preston at any time during this assignment. Hell, killing any one of you would have been a vacation next to the work we do."

Tom forced his eyes from the hand holding the syringe and stared up at him. "So why didn't you?"

Chilly leaned in closer and smiled. "Because we're not terrorists," he said as he pushed the needle into Tom's neck and emptied the contents of the syringe. He then removed the needle and stood.

Tom groaned and put his hand over his neck. "What the fuck did you just give me?"

"Don't worry . . . it's not going to kill you. In fact, it might just do the opposite."

Tom sat up from the floor, the pounding in his skull now subsiding. He looked up at the man he'd been chasing all this time and shook his head. "I don't understand."

"Of course you don't. That's been the problem with you all along, Tom. You and the rest of the idiots you've managed to pull into this . . . all of you scrambling around, trying to insert your egos and authority in a matter that you couldn't possibly begin to understand. It would be comical if it weren't so pathetic."

"But how can you not consider yourselves terrorists?" Tom asked. Despite his anger, a calming sensation was beginning to flow through his body.

"You said it yourself. A *terrorist* terrifies or kills for political or personal gain. And yet we've never terrified anyone—at least not with those goals in mind. Perhaps we've scared the hell out of a few bystanders at times, but that's just the unfortunate reality of our work. I can also assure you that we have no collective affiliation with any government or political organization. Nor are we religious fanatics." He paused and shook his head. "Christ, I can't even tell you the last time I was in a church."

"Fine," Tom replied. "So you're not terrorists . . . you're *mercenaries*. That still makes you just a bunch of hired killers."

"You're half right . . . we were hired."

"So you're not killers, huh?" Tom asked sarcastically. Chilly shook his head.

"Then how do you explain five dead Petronus researchers?"

Chilly looked over at Chip and smiled. "Should I tell him?"

Chip nodded. "Sure, why not. He's not going to remember any of this anyway."

"Tell me what?" Tom demanded. "And what"—he paused to shake the sudden lightness from his head—"what do you mean I'm not going to . . . to remember any of this?"

"They're not dead, Tom."

"Bullshit."

Chilly shrugged. "They're not dead."

"How do you expect me to believe that?"

"Because you've already seen it for yourself. After all, Alex's men killed me in Amsterdam, and I'm not dead."

Tom started to respond when a knock on the door leading to the alley interrupted him. Chilly looked down at him and smiled. "I think this will help clarify everything," he said, turning and opening the door. The short, pudgy man who had left just minutes earlier shuffled back into the saloon, a large backpack slung over his shoulder. Behind him, Max and Tall Tommy carried in a long, heavy object sealed in a black plastic bag.

Tom noticed white wisps of smoke-like frost rising from the bag's surface and realized it must have come from a freezer. He leaned back as they laid it on the floor in front of him.

"That . . . that's a body bag."

"Yes it is," Chilly replied. He raised his hand and his colleague tossed him the backpack. He opened it and pulled out a pair of latex gloves.

Tom watched with detached curiosity as Chilly slapped on the gloves and then handed out pairs to the other men. Whatever had been injected into him was now having its intended effect. Despite what was happening, an overwhelming feeling of euphoria now gripped him. A smile slowly stretched across his face as he glanced at the men standing around him. "So who's in the bag?" he asked dully.

"The package."

"The *package*? What does that mean?"

"Dublin?" Chilly said as he began to unzip the bag. His pudgy colleague stepped forward.

"The package is a twenty-six-year-old female from Phoenix," Dublin said impassively in a thick Irish accent. "Died from a stab wound to the liver by her boyfriend last night. Her family has requested a cremation . . . and that's what they're gonna get."

Tom gasped as the body bag fell open. The pale, thin body of the deceased young woman was eerily calm and serene. Her fair, unblemished face looked even younger than the age the Irishman had stated. He found it difficult to look away from her large dark eyes as they stared lifelessly up at the ceiling. Then he noticed her long, copper-brown hair. "She . . . she looks like Jeri," he said quietly, watching as Chilly examined her.

"Precisely."

"So what . . . what are you going to do with her?"

Chilly gave him a strange smile before glancing at his watch. "It's been two minutes," he said, looking at Chip. "He's ready."

Tom blinked with unfocused eyes. "What? What am I ready for?"

"Our talk, Tom," Chip said as he rose from his stool. "You see, even by *your* definition, none of us here are really terrorists." He walked over and kneeled in front of him. "Except perhaps for you."

"What do you mean by that?" Tom asked slowly, a slight slur in his voice.

"I've done a fair amount of digging into your background, Tom, and there's something that seems rather peculiar to me." Chip paused as his pale blue eyes studied Tom closely. "Not the trivial stuff—your bad relationship with your sister, your failed marriage, your refusal to accept the fact that you suffer from impulse control disorders. None of that really interests me in the least. No, what I'm interested in is an entry in your military records that dates back to your second tour in Afghanistan. Do you remember what I'm talking about?"

Tom nodded. His feelings of anger and betrayal toward the man kneeling in front of him were now gone, evaporated by the wonderful drug now coursing through his body. "Sure, Chip," he replied. "What would you like to know?"

"Tell me about Arghandab, Tom. Tell me about that night on patrol. I want to know what really happened." Chip leaned in closer, his weathered face easing into a wide, friendly smile. "I want to know why everyone in your patrol died but you."

Chapter 58

Alex stepped off the jet under a clear high-noon sky and walked directly toward the large hangar next to the tarmac. His two SOG agents fell in step behind him, both warily scanning the area. As expected, a large group of men were already collected in the empty hangar, all watching him with anticipation as their cups of coffee steamed in the wintry Flagstaff air. Once inside, Alex nodded to the four SOG agents who had just arrived from San Diego. He then turned to the other men in uniform.

"I'm Alex Murstead with the CIA," he said with an impatient tone of authority. "If I got what I asked for, I'm now speaking to the most experienced patrolmen and police officers ever to serve this fine town. Did I get what I asked for, gentlemen?"

"Yes sir," the group said collectively, all of them fully aware that the tall, muscular man standing in front of them was now in command.

"Very good," Alex replied. "I'll make this as brief as possible. Please gather around the table."

The officers and agents formed a circle around a small folding table as Alex pulled out a Flagstaff street map and slapped it down on the flimsy tabletop.

"Gentlemen, I have reason to believe a terrorist or group of terrorists is currently in Flagstaff. While I can't discuss the details of why they're here, I can say without hesitation that, if this is the case, this person or group represents a threat unlike anything you've ever dealt with before."

The police officers glanced nervously at each other as Alex took a pen and circled a small area on the map.

"The good news is that we believe we know exactly what they're targeting and where they'll be located. My team and I will be handling all activities associated with containing and neutralizing this threat. Your job, gentlemen, is crowd control. I want four plainclothes officers to discreetly empty every business and restaurant within a two-block area around the target area. Tell people there's a possible gas leak. Tell them there's a big sale at Walmart. I don't give a shit what you tell them. Just make sure you don't cause a panic.

"Start with the businesses closest to the target and work your way out, then stay the hell out of my target area. The rest of you will redirect traffic and make sure no one gets in or out of the area without my direct authorization." He stared at the officers sternly. "You will do this quickly, and you will do this quietly. No sirens, no flashing lights, and nothing that would indicate anything out of the ordinary. If you see something suspicious, contact me immediately. Do not—repeat—do not attempt to engage anyone without consulting with me first. Is that understood?"

"Yes sir," the officers replied in unison.

Alex detailed the target location and the position each of the officers would take around the area. After answering a few questions, he glanced at his watch and slapped his hands impatiently. "All right, that's it," he said. "Our target location is less than five miles from here. I want it empty in thirty minutes."

As the local officers shuffled out of the hangar toward their patrol cars, Alex addressed the six SOG team members now standing around him. "You've all had time to review the brief, correct?" he asked.

The men nodded.

"Then you know as much as I do . . . which means none of us knows what the fuck we're about to walk into here. Make no mistake, gentlemen—these guys aren't amateurs. Our primary target managed to outmaneuver six of our colleagues in Amsterdam last week, and I still can't explain how he did it. But I can tell you this—I will not accept any such fuckups here today." He pointed at the map. "The saloon is located here on Route 66. I want three two-man teams. Teams One and Two will take flanking positions on the street one block from the entrance. Team Three will cover the back alley. I'll take position across the street in the café on the southwest corner. Got it?"

"Yes sir," his men replied.

Alex paused and looked at his six agents. "There are two ways this could go down today, gentlemen," he said matter-of-factly. "If our terrorists haven't arrived yet, we get Halston and everyone else out of that fucking saloon and set up camp for their arrival. But if they are here, you know the protocol. We'll do everything we can for hostages, but not at the expense of allowing a single one of these motherfuckers to walk out alive. Either way, no one makes any decisions without my say-so. Is that understood?"

The men nodded in unison.

"Okay then, let's go."

=====

Chilly stepped back and took one final look at the body of the young woman in front of him before nodding. "The package is ready," he said casually, shoving his small toolkit into his backpack. He glanced over at Tall Tommy. "You almost ready?"

"Done," the Australian replied, throwing his satchel over his shoulder. The two men looked expectantly at Chip.

"All right, all right . . . I'm almost ready," Chip said with a gruff tone. "God, I'm getting too old for this shit." He stood up and looked around the room curiously. "Where's Dublin?"

"Left a half hour ago," Tall Tommy said with a slight grin. "What else is new?"

"That's fine," Chip replied as he dialed a number on his cell phone. "As long as he isn't passed out drunk behind the bar." He walked over to the window and pressed the speaker button on his phone. "Max, are you in position?"

"In position and ready."

"Good. Let me know what's happening out there." Chip pocketed the phone and turned back to Chilly and Tall Tommy. "Okay, it's about that time. Are you two appropriately dressed for the occasion?" he asked wryly. Both men shrugged before taking off their sweaters. Chip examined their shirts with a critical eye. "Those should work just fine," he said with a slight grin. "You'd better get into position."

Chilly looked at the older man somberly. "Don't stay too long."

Chip nodded. "I'll be right behind you." He watched the two men exit through the back alley before rubbing his eyes tiredly. *I really am getting too old for this shit,* he thought. Luckily there was just one last detail to attend to before the show started. He walked over to the front door and sorted through a large bag of items Max had brought in from the van. Satisfied everything was there, he grabbed the bag and walked over to where Tom Coleman was seated on the floor.

Tom looked up with a dazed, quizzical stare. "What's in there?" he asked.

Chip dropped the bag down in front of Tom and reached inside. "Happy holidays, Tom," he said as he pulled out a heavy red coat and smiled. "Would you like to take a walk?"

Officer Damien Parker parked his patrol car at the center of the intersection of Humphreys Street and Historic Route 66 and quietly listened to the chatter of the radio. He and the other officers had finished clearing and barricading the area around Joe's Last Stand Saloon as ordered. Now it was up to the feds to find out if all this nonsense was really worth the trouble.

He glanced in his rearview mirror at the sound of approaching vehicles. The two Suburbans carrying Agent Murstead and his team of SOG agents were heading toward him at high speed. He watched as the shiny black vehicles swerved around his patrol car toward the target zone. As they passed, Murstead's commanding voice crackled over the radio.

"This is Agent Murstead. My team and I are now approaching the target location. Any officers within two blocks of the area are ordered to evacuate immediately."

Officer Parker picked up his radio handset from the center console and joined the other officers in responding. "Roger that," he said evenly, clicking off the radio before muttering the rest of his response. "You arrogant agency asshole."

He dropped the handset back onto the console and watched the two oversized vehicles as they sped toward the old saloon four blocks ahead. *Well, I guess my work here is done*, Parker thought as he reached for his thermos and poured a fresh cup of coffee. As he did, he noticed the half-eaten cinnamon bun from earlier that morning still sitting in its wrapper. After a moment of deliberation, he shrugged and picked it up. *Why not?* he thought defiantly. *I can always drop the weight after the holidays.* He took a large bite and leaned back contentedly in his seat. He was just about to wash the mouthful of pastry down with a sip of coffee when he glanced out his side window and paused.

Two men were walking toward him.

"What the hell is this?" Officer Parker muttered to himself. He watched as the two men strolled casually down Humphreys Street, both of them noticeably underdressed for the weather. The taller of the two had blond hair and was clad in jeans and a tight-fitting black T-shirt. The other man was slightly shorter, with dark hair and a thin, athletic build. As they drew nearer, Parker noticed the second man was also wearing a T-shirt, a large rainbow stitched across the chest. The meaning of the symbol was just beginning to sink in when the man reached over and grabbed his companion's hand.

"Oh, Jesus . . . you've got to be kidding me," Parker whispered to himself. *So much for fucking terrorists*, he thought as he rested his coffee mug on the center console and lowered his window. He irritably waved the two men over as they reached the intersection.

"Hellooo, Officer," the tall blond man cooed flirtatiously as they walked up to the patrol car.

Officer Parker gave him a stern look. "You two need to evacuate this area immediately," he said coldly, pointing back toward the edge of the barricade area a few blocks west.

"Oh my god, what's going on?" the dark-haired man asked dramatically, flashing an anxious frown as he stepped closer.

"Nothing you need to worry about," Parker replied, again pointing. "Just keep walking in that direction and go about your business."

The dark-haired man sprang forward and pressed something hard and cold firmly against his shoulder. Before Parker knew what was happening, a paralyzing charge of electricity coursed through his limbs, twisting his overweight body into a contorted arc. Within seconds it was over. The dark-haired man released the trigger and quickly checked his pulse as Parker slumped forward against the steering wheel of the patrol car. A long string of drool slowly fell from his mouth.

The blond man walked around the patrol car and quickly slipped into the passenger seat. As he did, his partner leaned forward and whispered softly into Parker's ear.

"I'm sorry, Officer, but this *is* our business."

===

"What the fuck is that man doing up there?"

Alex leaned over the dash of the Suburban and looked up at the utility pole that stood less than ten yards away from the entrance of Joe's Last Stand Saloon. Thirty feet up, a serviceman was hanging from a harness, apparently oblivious to his surroundings as he worked on the large transformer suspended above him.

"Goddammit!" Alex hissed. He clicked on his radio and spoke angrily into the small headset attached to his ear. "This is Agent Murstead. Can anyone tell me why there's a man hanging from the utility pole in front of the target location?"

"Yes sir," the radio crackled in response. "This is Lieutenant Mason. We couldn't get his attention, sir. He must be wearing earplugs or something. I tried waving to get his attention, but he didn't seem to notice. We did call the power company, sir, and they confirmed that they sent someone to that location. So I think he's all right. I mean, I don't think he's up to something, sir."

Alex shook his head in disbelief before responding. "Thank you, Lieutenant. Would anyone else like to communicate some important information to me regarding the target area before my team and I begin?"

The radio remained silent.

"That's what I thought," Alex grumbled as he clicked off his radio and stopped the Suburban a block from the target location. The second vehicle stopped behind him. He quickly scanned the area before focusing on the narrow front façade of Joe's. From the outside, the saloon appeared lifeless. The neon "Open" sign that hung at the top of the window was off, and the wooden blinds were turned down, concealing any view. As Alex expected, the entrance door was closed. He studied the building a moment longer before lowering his binoculars.

"Okay, guys, let's go."

The men stepped from the vehicles and rechecked their weapons. Alex cocked his sidearm and holstered it before addressing his three two-man teams.

"Team One has the west position one block from target location. Team Three has the back alley. Team Two, you'll take the east position one block from target, but first, you're going to help me get that idiot down from the utility pole."

"Yes sir."

As the two other teams moved into position, Alex and his two SOG agents crossed over to the north end of the street and jogged toward the utility pole. A half block farther, Alex paused and turned to one of his men.

"Get his attention."

The agent nodded and raised his assault rifle, painting the shimmering red dot of the gun's laser sight on the utility worker's arm. Thirty feet above them, the man glanced curiously at his arm before looking around. He visibly recoiled in surprise at the sight of the three armed, plainly clothed men beneath him. Alex gestured for the man to come down.

"Keep your gun on him," Alex said to his agent as the utility worker quickly descended in front of them. It wasn't until the man stepped from the utility pole onto the sidewalk that Alex got a true sense of the worker's size. The man was enormous, standing at least a few inches taller than Alex. Even though he was wearing heavy coveralls, it was clear his broad frame was well fitted with muscle. As he stepped forward, the two men exchanged tense looks and briefly sized each other up before Alex flashed his CIA credentials.

"Can I help you gentlemen?" the worker asked guardedly.

Alex reached out and removed the ID badge that was clipped to the man's coveralls. "Your name is George Bissinger?" he asked, reading the ID badge.

"Yes."

"You don't notice much around you when you're working, do you, George?" Alex asked bluntly, watching the man's expression. "Like the policemen that were clearing this area about twenty minutes ago."

The worker glanced at the agent holding the assault rifle and shook his head. "No sir, I guess I don't. There's enough high voltage in those lines up there to kill a man a couple hundred times over. I tend to stay focused when I'm working on 'em."

Alex held his stare for a moment before gazing up at the power lines. "What seems to be the problem?"

The large man removed his hard hat and scratched at his short blond hair. "Pretty odd, actually. Looks like someone tampered with the line and killed the power in this area. A bunch of lines were torn out of the transformer."

"Kind of hard to do something like that without the right tools, wouldn't you agree?" Alex asked.

"Nah, not really. You'd be surprised. People screw with this stuff all the time. Mostly teenagers. Luckily, most of the time they don't kill themselves in the process."

"Is it fixed?"

"Almost," the man replied. "I was just about to repair the last line when you guys pointed your guns at me."

Alex nodded. Despite the man's enormous size, his instincts told him to believe the thick-headed utility worker standing in front of him. And yet something about the situation made him uneasy.

He glanced over at the service van parked next to them. The back door of the van was open.

Alex gestured to the other SOG agent as he spoke.

"Mr. Bissinger, my agent is going to briefly search you and your vehicle as a precaution. Would you mind placing your hands on top of your head?"

The man shrugged and complied with Alex's request as the agent quickly patted him down. A moment later the agent looked at Alex and nodded.

"Is there anything dangerous or illegal in the van that we need to know about before we begin our search?" Alex asked.

"No sir."

"Very well." Alex walked over to the vehicle with his agent while their colleague kept his assault rifle trained on the man. He clicked on his radio and spoke quietly into his headset. "This is Murstead. Lieutenant Mason, I have a question for you."

"Yes sir," the lieutenant replied.

"You said you called to confirm that a serviceman had been sent to this location."

"Affirmative, sir."

"Did you get the serviceman's name?"

"I . . . uh, no sir."

"Lieutenant, you have exactly one minute to get me a name and physical description of the man who was sent down here," Alex hissed. "Do you understand me?"

"Yes sir," the lieutenant replied sharply. "Right away, sir."

Alex walked over to the service van and poked his head inside. A narrow channel of open space ran through the center of the cramped interior, flanked on both sides by spools of wire and large toolboxes. His agent was crouched inside, carefully opening one of the toolboxes.

"Anything?" Alex asked.

"No sir," the agent replied. "But with all this equipment and wiring, he could have ten bombs in here and I might miss them."

Alex nodded. He glanced at the floor of the van and noticed a long compartment that ran the length of the back. He was just about to ask the agent if he'd checked it when his radio crackled to life.

"Agent Murstead, this is Lieutenant Mason."

"What did you find out?" Alex asked as he stepped around the van and stared at the massive man standing on the sidewalk, his hands still resting on his head. The man stared back at him nervously.

"His name should be George Bissinger, sir. He should be a large man, approximately six feet seven inches tall, with hazel eyes and short, blond hair."

"Very good. Thank you, Lieutenant." Alex ordered his agent to exit the van, and the two walked back over to the detained utility worker.

"Sorry to take your time, Mr. Bissinger," Alex replied as he handed back the man's ID. "My men and I have some other business to attend to here. For your safety, I'm going to need you to get into your vehicle and drive to the police officer parked just a few blocks west of here. He'll have further instructions for you."

The large man clipped his ID back onto his chest and picked up his bag of tools. He gave Alex a brief nod before stepping into the van. As the vehicle pulled away, Alex clicked on his radio. "Attention, all units, this is Agent Murstead. I'm routing a utility van west on Route 66 from the target location. I want the first officer this vehicle arrives at to detain the driver until he's been officially cleared. Is that understood?"

A baritone voice responded. "Agent Murstead, this is Officer Parker. Subject is heading toward me now. I'll take care of him, sir."

Alex nodded and looked up at his Team Two agents. "Okay, guys, you know what to do." As his men moved into position, Alex turned and paced a half block west before making his way across the street. A minute later, positioned inside the empty café opposite the saloon, he sat and watched patiently.

===

The officer stepped out of his patrol car and raised his hand commandingly at the approaching service vehicle. He leveled his stare on the driver as the van slowed and stopped just inches from where he stood. The officer then moved cautiously toward the driver's door, his hand resting noticeably on the handle of his holstered weapon. A few feet from the driver's door, he stopped and gestured for the large man to lower his window.

The two men stared wordlessly at each other for a moment before the officer's stern expression eased into a smile.

"How'd it go, Max?"

The driver smiled back at him. "Just fine, Officer *Chilly*."

"Are our new friends in a pleasant mood today?"

"As pleasant as I expected."

"Good," Chilly replied. He glanced down the empty stretch of old Route 66 that led to the saloon before leaning toward the van with a mischievous grin. "Now let's see how they like act two."

Chapter 59

Alex broke his stare from the front entrance of Joe's Last Stand Saloon and anxiously glanced at his watch. It was 1:13 p.m. He and his men had been in position around the target area for nearly thirty minutes, quietly waiting for activity. So far, nothing around them had moved.

He looked again at Teams One and Two positioned on the empty street in front of him before clicking on the radio. "Team Three, are you seeing anything back there?"

From their position in the alley behind the saloon, Team Three radioed in. "Not really, sir."

Alex furrowed his brow. "Say again?"

"No activity, sir," the team leader answered. "All we've got is an old homeless guy passed out in the alley."

"How old?" Alex asked.

"Hard to say, sir. Subject's probably in his midsixties."

Alex thought for a moment before responding. "Okay . . . Team Three, pull him out and question him."

"Command, would you repeat?" the team leader asked.

"You heard me," Alex replied. "Pull him out and question him. And report in when you're done." He'd barely finished speaking when the radio crackled to life.

"Command, this is Team Two. Be advised, we have movement at the front door."

Alex immediately raised his binoculars and focused on the front door of the saloon. As he watched, the dark wooden door slowly eased open. "Team Two, this is Command," he said firmly. "Hold position and do not engage until subject has been identified."

"Roger that."

The front door of the bar was half open when a stout, white-bearded man stepped into view. Alex zoomed in on the unknown subject and groaned. "Jesus Christ . . . are you fucking kidding me?" he mumbled to himself, watching the subject through his binoculars. The man stood stiffly in the entryway of the saloon, seemingly oblivious to the two SOG teams in position nearby. Alex watched him for a few more seconds before speaking into his headset.

"All teams, be advised, we have a lone unidentified subject exiting through the front door of the target location. Subject is wearing sunglasses and a white beard." He paused for a moment, dismayed by what he was about to say next. "Subject is also dressed in a Santa costume."

"Command, be advised," Team Two replied. "Subject's also carrying a large duffel bag. Possibly an explosive device."

The man stepped onto the sidewalk and began walking west toward Alex in a slow, uneven gait.

"Command, subject is on the move," the Team Two leader announced.

"Copy that," Alex replied as he studied the man intently through his binoculars. Despite his ridiculous disguise, there was something strangely familiar about the man. Nevertheless, there was protocol to follow. Alex followed the subject's movements for a few more seconds before acknowledging what he had to do next.

"Team Two, on my command, I want a nonlethal drop of the subject," he said firmly into the radio. "I repeat—a *nonlethal* drop of the subject. Team One, hold your current position on the northwest corner until the subject is down."

"Roger that."

The man slowly continued west toward the intersection where the Team One SOG agents were concealed. When he finally reached the corner, Alex took a quick breath and spoke calmly into his headset.

"Okay, drop him."

A moment later, Alex watched anxiously through his binoculars as the muted report of an assault rifle echoed down the street. At the same instant, their unidentified subject cried out in pain and fell forward onto the sidewalk, dropping the duffel bag that was slung over his shoulder.

"Team One, take him!"

As ordered, Alex's Team One agents immediately rushed forward and pressed the wounded man hard against the concrete, securing his wrists in handcuffs before rolling him onto his back. They then grabbed his arms and quickly dragged him around the corner and out of view of the saloon. Through his headset, Alex could hear the man's loud moans as he lay sprawled on the sidewalk.

"Team One, report in," he demanded.

"Command, subject is secured," Team One replied.

"Weapons?"

"Negative, Command . . . no weapons on him. Be advised, we have not checked the bag the subject was carrying."

"Roger that. Do not touch the bag," Alex replied, his stare shifting from the saloon to the nearby corner where his team had the unknown man secured. "Any identification on the subject?"

"Negative, no formal identification," the agent responded. "But there's a note pinned to his chest under his coat."

Alex furrowed his brow as he spoke into the radio. "What does it say?"

A long pause followed before the agent replied, "It appears to be a confession, sir."

Alex glanced curiously at the entrance to the saloon. *What the fuck are you up to?* he wondered as he clicked on his microphone. "All right. All teams, hold positions. Team One, I'm coming to you."

Alex holstered his gun and jogged down the sidewalk toward Team One. When he arrived at the corner, he moved cautiously around the large duffel bag still lying on the sidewalk before shaking his head at the strangeness of the scene. Kneeling next to the wounded Santa-masked subject, both agents looked up and gave him a brief nod.

"He's unconscious," the nearest agent said as Alex kneeled down beside him. "Probably passed out from the pain."

Alex knelt down and quickly inspected the man's leg. A steady flow of blood was oozing from the bullet's exit wound a few inches above the knee, but nothing appeared immediately serious or life-threatening. He glanced at the man's face. Even though he could barely see any features past the thick white beard and sunglasses, there was something oddly familiar about him.

"Where's the note?" he demanded.

The agent next to him reached over and opened the red, fur-lined Santa jacket. Alex immediately recognized the blue Joe's Last Stand Saloon T-shirt underneath. A small piece of stationery was pinned to the center. He leaned closer and read the shakily scribbled handwriting.

To whom it may concern—

Allow me to introduce myself. I am a terrorist. I say this with complete candor because of the incident that occurred on the clear night of May 21 during my second tour of duty in Afghanistan It was on that night that I led eight men including myself on a night patrol through the poppy fields of the Arghandab river valley. Normally this would have been a routine patrol. But on this particular night, my patrol and I were attacked by a group of Taliban rebels of superior numbers and firepower. Within less than an hour, my patrol was reduced to just three men—myself and two fellow Marines, PFC Grant Matthison and Michael Callahan.

Surrounded and exhausted of ammunition, I told my men that we would have to accept the possibility of capture. Within minutes, that possibility became a reality. Unfortunately, our captors were not kind, and they quickly made it clear that the three of us would be killed if we failed to comply with their demands. After realizing I was the acting commander of the patrol, the rebels singled me out and handed me a loaded handgun. I was then given two options—I could use the handgun to kill myself, or I could use it to kill my two fellow Marines. Of course, there was a catch. If I killed myself, the rebels would immediately kill the other two soldiers. But if I chose to kill the other two soldiers, I would be set free.

Since you already know the outcome of this story, it would be irrelevant to mention that the rebels kept their word. As for me, well, there are few things I can be certain of or clear about, perhaps with one exception—my definition of a terrorist is any individual who kills or terrorizes for personal or political gain.

And there you have it. By my own definition, and by my own actions, on that May night in Afghanistan I became a terrorist.

Sincerely,
Thomas R. Coleman

"It can't be," Alex whispered as he looked again at the covered face of the man in front of him. He reached up and ripped the beard away from his chin.

"Oh, *fuck—Tom!*"

Alex cursed again as he grabbed his radio and switched it to the police channel. "This is Agent Murstead . . . I need the hazmat team and an ambulance at the corner of 66 and Leroux immediately! We've got a man down and a duffel bag that may contain an explosive device. Make sure all drivers approach from Aspen Avenue—and tell them to keep their sirens off!"

"Roger that," came the quick reply.

Alex leaned over and roughly slapped his brother-in-law's face. "Tom! Wake up, Tom! Can you hear me? Why are you here, Tom?" He pulled off his gloves and gently opened Tom's eyes. His pupils were dilated and fixed. He cursed and turned to the agent next to him. "Keep pressure on that leg wound and hold your position until the ambulance arrives." He reached down and angrily tore the note from Tom's chest, shoving it into his vest. Alex then stood up and pointed at the other SOG agent. "You're coming with me."

"Yes sir."

The two men headed back down the street toward the saloon. Halfway there, the radio crackled to life in Alex's ear.

"Command, this is Team Two. We're picking up sounds from inside the target location."

Alex gestured for the agent next to him to hold position as he kneeled down and aimed his handgun at the front of the saloon. Farther down the street, he could see the two agents from Team Two crouched low against a parked car, their assault rifles pointed at the saloon's entrance.

"This is Command. What are you hearing?"

"Command, it's too muffled to be certain, but it sounds like a man's voice."

"Roger that," Alex replied. "Team Three, are you seeing or hearing anything from your position?" He waited several seconds for a response before asking again. "Team Three, this is Command. Say again . . . are you seeing anything back there?"

The radio remained silent.

A cold chill ran up Alex's spine as he looked again at the entrance to the saloon. He knew Team Three's radio silence couldn't be a glitch. Like every other piece of equipment, radios were checked and rechecked before each mission. And both men had one. The chance of both radios now failing was practically nonexistent, which meant only one thing—the old homeless man Team Three had encountered was someone else entirely. *It's fucking Amsterdam all over again*, he thought angrily. Only instead of simply being misdirected as they were in Amsterdam, Alex realized his highly trained SOG team was now being quietly picked apart.

He stared down the street at Team Two and spoke into his headset. "Team Two, this is Command. Be advised, Team Three may be down. I am now leading Team One and approaching your position from the west."

"Roger that."

Alex switched his radio once again to the police channel. "This is Agent Murstead. Be advised, we may have a target on foot who's dressed as a homeless man. Possibly senior-aged or appearing to be older. Anyone who even remotely matches that description needs to be communicated to me immediately."

A chorus of affirmatives crackled over the radio. Alex started to switch the channel but paused as another thought came to mind. He glanced over his shoulder in the direction the utility worker had been ordered to drive a few minutes earlier. Neither the service van nor a police unit was in site. He clicked on his radio. "This is Murstead. Can the officer in charge of detaining the service van hear me?"

"Roger that," a baritone male voice replied a moment later.

"What's your status?" Alex demanded.

"I'm at the north corner of Humphreys and the 66. The service van is parked in front of my vehicle, and I am standing next to the driver's door with a visual on the subject."

"Very good. Now listen, I'm beginning to believe the driver of that van may be involved in this after all. Do not under any circumstances let that man out of his vehicle . . . is that understood?"

"Absolutely," the officer replied calmly. "You can be sure I won't let him out of my sight, Agent Murstead."

"If your detainee attempts to start his vehicle or open the door, shoot him. That's an order, Officer. And make sure you shoot to kill."

"That sounds a bit extreme, wouldn't you agree, sir?" the officer asked.

"Say again?" Alex replied sharply.

"My apologies, sir. I guess I'm just not used to dealing with terrorists."

"That's why you leave the goddamn orders to me, Officer. Now stand by that fucking van with your gun cocked and make sure that man doesn't move!"

"Understood. Like I said, I won't let him out of my sight."

Alex switched channels and shook his head. *What kind of local idiots am I working with?* he thought as he stood and motioned for his Team One agent to follow him. The two moved quickly along the row of empty storefronts until they reached the corner of Joe's Last Stand Saloon. Once there, Alex crouched low and pressed himself against the brick façade beneath the saloon's arched window. He looked at the two men across from him and whispered into the radio.

"Team Two, this is Command. I've got the front entrance of the location. Secure the back alley and give me a status on Team Three."

"Roger that."

Alex watched anxiously as his SOG team abruptly pulled back toward the opposite corner of the building and disappeared into the alley. A moment later, he ripped the earbud for his radio from his ear and cocked his head. Through the window above him, he could just make out the muffled sound his men had heard earlier. He listened for several seconds before shaking his head in bewilderment. There was no mistaking the origin of the sound—it was the low, gravelly voice of a man speaking quietly. He tensed as the earbud for his radio crackled in his hand.

"Command, this is Team Two. We found Team Three."

Alex shoved the earbud back into place. "What's their status?"

"Alive but unconscious," the agent replied. "From the looks of it, I'd guess they were either Tasered or drugged. Their weapons are still on them, but there's no sign of anyone else."

"Roger that," Alex replied. "Anything else?"

"Negative. We're not . . . wait . . . yes, there's something else. Command, their radios are missing."

Alex cursed under his breath. *The terrorists have our radios. They've heard every fucking thing we've said*, he thought as he scanned the street around him. He took a deep breath and spoke calmly into his headset. "All teams, this is Command. Switch your radios to the alternate channel immediately." He then switched his own radio to the alternate channel. "Team Two, are you there?" he asked.

"Yes sir."

"Hold your position, and make sure you maintain a minimum of three meters between each other."

"Roger that."

"Agent Pearson, are you still waiting for that ambulance?"

"Negative, Command. The ambulance is here. They're taking him now, sir."

"Has the hazmat unit arrived yet?"

"Affirmative."

"All right, hold your position and tell me exactly what they find in that bag." Alex checked his watch and rubbed his eyes in frustration. *Sixteen minutes.* Sixteen minutes since his team had arrived. Sixteen minutes since their well-orchestrated operation had started. *Sixteen minutes since everything had begun to completely fucking unravel.* He swept the thought from his mind and waited for Agent Pearson to respond.

"Command, this is Pearson."

"What have you got?"

"Hazmat checked the duffel bag, sir. No weapons or explosives."

"Then what's in the bag?"

"Toys, sir."

Alex shook his head in confusion. "Say again?"

"The bag has toys in it, sir. Boxes of some little weird-looking things called *Brainybuddies.* They kind of look like stuffed animals."

Alex leaned his head against the cold brick exterior of the saloon and took another deep breath. *Was this really happening?* Was it possible that everything he and his team were doing had somehow, once again, been anticipated? He scanned the stretch of old Route 66 in front of him, looking in the vacant storefronts for the hidden face he was certain was now watching him.

"Copy that, Pearson. Regroup with Team Two on the southwest corner of the target location."

"Roger."

Alex turned and reached his hand out to the agent leaning against the wall next to him. "Give me your weapon." The agent gave him a fleeting look of surprise before handing over his assault rifle and pulling out his sidearm. Alex quickly inspected the weapon before moving toward the entrance of the saloon.

"All teams, this is Command. It's safe to assume we've lost the element of surprise with this mission . . . if there ever was any to begin with. Maintain your positions and stay alert. I'm going into the target location."

Alex paused outside the door and quickly rechecked his weapon. Christ, how long had it been since he'd actually been on a field mission? *Too long*, he thought as he took a deep breath. He raised his rifle and kicked hard against the heavy wooden door. As the door swung open he took two quick steps inside before dropping low against the wall. From there, he slowly swept the room with his assault rifle as his eyes adjusted to the dim light. Around him, the saloon felt empty and still. Then, as he drew his gun toward the bar, something caught his attention.

A lone woman sat at the bar.

Alex leveled his rifle on the woman and stood. "Turn around!" he commanded loudly. The woman didn't move.

"Federal agent! I said turn around!"

Again his demand was ignored. He raised his head from the sights of his assault rifle and looked closer. The woman's upper body was slumped forward on the counter, her head cradled in her arms as if she were sleeping. Even with her back to him, Alex recognized the woman's slender build and long, copper-brown hair from the photos in his file. He stepped forward cautiously. "Miss Halston?" he asked, his tone less threatening. "Jeri Halston, are you okay?"

"Good afternoon, Agent Murstead." The voice he'd heard earlier echoed cheerfully through the saloon. "I'm glad you could make it."

Alex swept the bar with his weapon. "Show yourself!"

"I can't," the voice replied. "I'm not in the room."

Alex kept the rifle pinned to his shoulder and moved toward the voice. As he neared Jeri Halston, he paused. Resting on the counter in front of her were an open laptop computer and a small two-way radio. Alex immediately recognized the radio as one of the two that had been taken from his men.

"My apologies for borrowing this," the voice crackled from the radio. "But I thought you and I should talk."

Alex scanned the area once more before easing his grip on his rifle. "All right," he replied. "Let's talk. Who am I speaking to?"

"Call me Shepherd," the voice answered.

"Shepherd, huh?" Alex replied as he studied the laptop. He had no doubt the man he was speaking to was now watching him through the small video camera mounted to the top of the screen.

"You know, it's funny," Alex said, taking another step closer. "I was just reading up on another man who went by the name of Shepherd on my way out here. A rather impressive guy, from what I can tell. His real name was Robert Shafer. He was a former agent of the National Security Agency . . . perhaps one of the most gifted cryptographers the NSA has ever seen. But of course, you couldn't be Robert Shafer."

"Why is that?" the voice asked earnestly.

"Because Robert Shafer died more than thirty years ago," Alex replied. "He was killed in a car accident. Big fire . . . body burned badly. So badly, in fact, that the coroner wasn't even able to determine for certain if it was him." He paused and stared directly at the small camera. "But then, who else could it have been?"

"Good question," the voice answered. "Unfortunately, I haven't read enough autopsy reports on ex-NSA agents to be of much help."

"No, I didn't think you would be," Alex responded. He looked again at the woman slumped on a barstool at the bar. "Miss Halston, are you okay?" he asked, taking a step toward her.

"I'd leave Miss Halston alone for now," the voice said politely. "She's not in a position to respond."

"Why is that?"

"She's been injected with a sleep agent."

"And why would she need a sleep agent?" Alex demanded.

"As a safety precaution," the voice replied. "I didn't want her to accidentally detonate the explosives on her chair."

Alex turned and looked closely at Jeri's barstool. Taped to each of the four legs just beneath the seat was a small cylindrical canister. A wire lead ran from each of the canisters to a black box located on the floor.

"C-four explosive," the voice continued. "There's three ounces loaded into each of the four cylindrical housings you see taped to her chair. Do you know what happens to a human body sitting inside a tightly arranged field of explosives, Agent Murstead?"

"I have a pretty good idea," Alex said dryly.

"It's quite amazing, actually. The compressive energy of the charges turns liquids into gas and bones into powder. In a mere instant the body is reshaped and reconstituted into a perfectly combustible fuel source—like paper waiting for a lighted match. And then, in the next instant, every ounce of that body is consumed . . . literally *vaporized* into nothing. By the time it's over, it's as if they never existed in the first place."

Alex looked again at Jeri Halston's sleeping figure and nodded grimly. "So tell me, Shepherd . . . what turns a former NSA agent into a rogue terrorist and killer?"

"I wouldn't know," the voice answered. "Perhaps you should direct that question to Richard Connolly."

Alex looked at the laptop. "Maybe I should. Of course, Director Connolly already knows he's about to spend the rest of his short, emphysema-filled life in a minimum-security penitentiary when all this is over."

"What a pity," the voice replied tersely.

"So I *am* speaking to Robert Shafer."

"Only if dead NSA agents can speak from the grave, Agent Murstead."

Alex shook his head irritably. "Okay, fine. You're not Robert Shafer. So tell me . . . why are we here?"

"You're here because I'd like to ask you for a favor," the voice answered.

"What favor is that?"

"That you suspend your investigation of this matter immediately."

Alex grinned at the laptop. "You've got to be fucking kidding me."

"No, I'm not."

"And why should I do that?" Alex asked.

"Because as of today, this project is finished," the voice replied. "We have what we came for, and now we'll be on our way."

"Oh, really?" Alex asked, pointing his rifle at Jeri. "And what about her? Did you get what you wanted from her too?"

"In a manner of speaking, yes."

"And if I say no to your request?"

"Then good luck, Agent Murstead. Good luck sifting through the ashes of Jeri Halston. Good luck trying to find me or a single trace of evidence that can save you from the merciless desk of the deputy secretary of state."

Alex watched as the screen on the laptop flickered to life. A large stopwatch display appeared, its numbers set at 00:00.

"You can't see it," the voice continued, "but there's enough C-four in this place to ensure that any evidence of our time here today will be permanently erased." On the laptop screen, the stopwatch display changed to 00:06. "I'm giving you six seconds to make your exit from Joe's Last Stand Saloon from the moment I say 'go.' I suggest you run, Agent Murstead. I also suggest not trying to be a hero."

Alex glanced around at the dark interior, trying to make sense of what was happening. His eyes paused on the wall where the letters and photos were hung. He stared at them grimly before shouldering his rifle and pointing it at the laptop.

"Goddammit, Shepherd, I know who you are! You were an agency man once just like me. You know how this shit works . . . cases like this one don't end until there's an arrest or a fucking body!"

A long pause followed before the radio crackled.

"Then give them a body," the voice replied.

"Shepherd, wait! Let's—"

"Go!"

Alex watched with horror as the stopwatch on the laptop began counting down. He glanced at the lifeless figure of Jeri Halston with a sickening sense of helplessness. There was no way he could disable the charges and grab her before time ran out. He spun and sprinted toward the door, screaming into his headset as he ran.

"All teams evacuate the area immediately! I repeat . . . evac immediately!"

Alex threw open the entry door as a sudden wave of pressure lifted him from the ground and launched him like a projectile onto the street. He landed hard on his side as a massive ball of flames passed just inches overhead, the intense heat scalding his shoulder. A pelting rain of debris fell upon him as he rolled onto his stomach and inched his way across the cold black pavement of old Route 66. When he finally reached the opposite side of the street, Alex dragged himself up onto the sidewalk and collapsed. He lay there, exhausted, for several minutes before rolling onto his back. He then sat up slowly and assessed the damage.

"Oh, fuck," he muttered, surveying the scene in front of him.

The explosives had been expertly placed. Upon detonation, every load-bearing column inside the old building was shattered in an instant, causing the heavy brick structure to collapse under its own weight. The outcome of such precision was total. The old building wasn't just ruined—it was annihilated. And yet, miraculously, none of the surrounding buildings appeared to have been touched.

As he sat on the sidewalk staring at the burned and shattered remains, Alex shook his head at the simple, horrible truth. Jeri Halston and Joe's Last Stand Saloon now shared one thing in common.

Both no longer existed.

Chapter 60

Jeri opened her eyes to darkness.

The rattling noise of an engine had pulled her from a deep sleep. She slowly realized she was in a moving vehicle. Disoriented, she started to sit up—and immediately smashed her forehead against an unseen object. "What the hell?" she mumbled, reaching out cautiously to her pitch-black surroundings. To her surprise, a ceiling of cold steel hovered just inches in front of her. She ran her fingers along its smooth surface and found corners and walls on both sides. She kicked her feet and found the same unyielding walls and ceiling. The more she felt around, the more Jeri realized with a growing sense of panic that she wasn't just tucked into a tight corner of a moving vehicle—

She was locked inside a narrow metal cell.

She pushed the panic from her mind and focused on how she'd ended up here. The last thing she could recall was being in the saloon with Chip and . . . *Chilly* . . . her mysterious letter writer. Everything had happened so quickly. The injection Chilly had given her was obviously some form of sedative, but just how long had she been asleep? And where in the hell were they now taking her? As if in response to her question, the noise of the engine deepened.

They were climbing a hill.

Jeri felt around in the darkness for anything else that might be inside the container. The floor of her cell was covered by something soft and yielding like a thin mattress. She swept her hands back and forth and bumped against a small, heavy object. She wrapped her fingers around it, recognizing its shape. *A flashlight!* Jeri clicked on the flashlight and winced as the blackness was suddenly replaced by a bright beam of light. She waved the light around and examined her surroundings. The container was nothing more than a rectangular steel box, slightly longer than her body, with dents and scratches that suggested it was normally used to contain tools or heavy equipment. The padding beneath her was a thin sleeping pad, folded to fit within the small space. She aimed the flashlight at the opposite end of the container. Three small holes were cut in the metal near her feet, and Jeri could feel a cool rush of fresh air flowing from each. She swept the flashlight along the length of each wall before dropping it hopelessly next to her. The light revealed nothing more than what Jeri had already suspected—there was no chance for escape.

So why had they left it for her?

Jeri was considering this question when she realized her head was raised higher than the rest of her body. She reached beneath the sleeping pad and felt a thick object under her head. She pulled it out and held it in the light. The plain cover of the thick book was all too familiar.

Predictions in the New Business Ecology

Jeri could tell by its worn edges that it wasn't just a copy of her father's book—it was *her* copy. She opened it and slowly turned the thin, crisp pages to the first chapter. There, a sheet of stationery from the Flagstaff Motel 6 was pressed inside. A brief note in a familiar, precise handwriting was written across it.

> Something to pass the time,
> and answer some questions.
> We'll be arriving soon.

Jeri crumpled the note and tossed it angrily at her feet. A sudden rush of rage filled her. She dropped the book and slapped her hands against the ceiling of her steel cell.

"Let me out of here!" she screamed, ignoring the loud echo of her voice in the cramped space. "Goddammit, Chip . . . let me out of here! I know you can hear me! Get me out of this fucking box right now!"

After pounding at the cold metal for what felt like an eternity, Jeri lay back, breathless from exertion, and listened. To her frustration, she could hear nothing more than the steady sound of the engine as the vehicle sped onward toward their destination. Gathering another burst of energy, she pressed her hands and knees against the ceiling of the container and pushed with what remained of her strength.

But it was no use.

Exhausted, Jeri fell back against the thin sleeping pad beneath her and started crying. She wanted to tear through the steel cell around her and rip the heads off Chip and the men who had taken her. She wanted to be free of this madness. She wanted to be on her flight to India. She wanted to be starting a new life. She wanted all of these things. But as she lay there in the light of the flashlight and slowly calmed down, Jeri quietly accepted an inescapable fact. None of these things was possible until she knew exactly what all of this was about.

She picked up her father's book and held it in the bright beam of the flashlight. It felt heavy in her hands. She turned it over and looked at the young smiling face on the back cover. As she looked into the eyes of her father, Chip's words echoed in her mind.

"Your father considered his book to be the conclusion and greatest achievement of his 'former' life, so he decided to publish it under the name James Stone."

Jeri opened the book and flipped to the first chapter. Soon enough she would have the opportunity to confront Chip and her captors. First she needed some answers. First she needed to meet *James Stone*. She took a deep breath and started to read.

=====

Tom opened his eyes and glanced drowsily at his surroundings. He was lying on his back in a strange, unfamiliar room. A noticeable smell of rubbing alcohol and sterilized bandages hung in the air. He moved his arm and winced at a sudden, wakening sting. To his surprise, two IV tubes now ran from large needles in his wrist. He then noticed the heart monitor beeping quietly over his shoulder.

What the hell was going on?

Tom had no memory of arriving at the hospital. And yet here he was, lying under the sterile white sheets of a bed, wrapped in the ridiculous light-blue gown of a patient. He started to sit up—and immediately cried out at the searing pain in his leg. Confused, he threw back the sheets to find his leg heavily wrapped above his knee. The bandage was stained with a small round patch of dark blood. Even without remembering what had occurred, Tom had seen enough wounds like his own in the line of duty to know what it meant.

He'd been shot.

He reached over and angrily pressed the large call button tethered to the bed. A moment later a voice sounded over the speaker.

"Can I help you, Mr. Coleman?"

"I'd like to know what the fuck happened to me."

"Okay, sir," the voice replied tersely. "Someone will be there in a moment."

Tom sat quietly, staring at his wounded leg. Why couldn't he remember what had happened? The last thing he could recall was walking into the saloon and speaking to Chip and another man, but his memory was hazy at best. He sat gloomily, gingerly feeling for any other wounds on his body when a tall figure suddenly appeared in the doorway. He looked up and shook his head.

"Alex?" Tom muttered, surprised at the sudden appearance of his brother-in-law. "What are you doing here?"

Alex said nothing as he closed the door and moved stiffly over to the chair next to Tom's bed. His left arm was bandaged and hung awkwardly in a sling. A large bandage covered most of his forehead.

"Jesus Christ," Tom said as he watched his brother-in-law slowly lower himself into the chair. "What the hell happened to you?"

Alex eyed Tom for a long moment before speaking. "Let me guess . . . you don't remember anything."

Tom gave his brother-in-law a grim look before shaking his head. "No . . . nothing."

Alex smiled back at him pensively. "Well, isn't that extraordinarily convenient."

"Convenient? Hey, fuck you!" Tom said angrily, pointing at his bandaged leg. "In case you didn't notice, I've been shot."

"Of course I know you were shot. I was the one who ordered it."

Tom looked at Alex with a blank stare of shock. "What are you talking about?"

Alex leaned back and rubbed at his eyes. "God, I am . . . I am fucking exhausted." He sighed, his mouth curling into a thin smile. "And this day is still a long way from being over." He looked up at Tom, his smile vanishing behind a tired, somber stare. "You know, your sister and I have barely said two words to each other in the last year or so," he said in a slow, matter-of-fact tone. "The funny thing is, I couldn't even tell you why. Maybe it's because I work all the time. Maybe it's the stress of raising kids. Who the fuck knows. All I know is that whatever we used to have between us is now gone." Alex paused and waved his good arm dismissively through the air. "Not that you give a shit. But the point I'm trying to make is this—no one outside of our perfect little home has the slightest clue that anything is wrong. You know why, Tom?"

Tom shook his head.

"Because, as the old saying goes, we do a good job of *keeping up appearances*. You know what I'm talking about. Smiling and waving to the neighbors, holding hands at parties, taking the girls to soccer practice together on the weekends. All the little shit that other people tend to notice, or at least notice when you stop doing them." Alex leaned forward, the grin returning to his face. "But that's just the way it goes. You wake up one day and realize the things you believed in have all disappeared. Or maybe they never really existed in the first place. Love . . . trust . . . *truth* . . . they're all just fleeting, fictitious characters. They don't stay around long. And once they're gone, they rarely if ever come back. The only thing you can do is pretend they're still around. But whatever. At the end of the day, most of us don't give a shit just how bad things are on the *inside*, do we, Tom? It's all about wearing that fucking mask of lies. It's all about keeping up appearances."

Tom stared wide-eyed at Alex. What in the hell was his brother-in-law talking about? Was the stress of the case finally causing him to crack? The thought of Alex being anything less than infallible seemed almost unimaginable. And yet here he was, confessing all his sins. His marriage was in shambles, his career on the brink of ruin. *Captain fucking America was suddenly imploding*. The thought gave Tom an instant feeling of satisfaction.

"What's this all about?" he asked cautiously.

Alex stood up from the chair and limped slowly over to the bed.

"Do you have any idea how many times I've regretted my decision to put Kaliningrad on my terrorist watch list?" he asked as he rested his wounded arm on top of the bed rail and looked wearily down at Tom. "Imagine if I'd just ignored your e-mail, Tom. Kaliningrad would have been just another random incident. Amsterdam would have never happened. Dongying would have been an isolated diplomatic affair. And that clever old cunt at the State Department wouldn't be crawling up my ass right now, demanding justice and her pound of flesh. If it weren't for that one stupid act, I'd be free and clear of this whole fucking mess. But then, hindsight is always twenty-twenty, isn't it?"

"You need some clarity, Alex? How about this . . . I laid this whole investigation in your lap, and you fucked it up," Tom replied angrily. "Don't even try to say otherwise. Christ, I practically put that fucking terrorist in front of you and your men, and you still couldn't catch him."

Alex leaned forward and stared at Tom coldly. "You want to hear a confession, Tom? How about this . . . you're *right*. In fact, you've been right all along."

"Excuse me?"

"It's true," Alex replied. "I was wrong. All this time I've been saying you were in over your head on this one. But I had it all backward, didn't I? The letters, the terrorists, the point of all this nonsense. I admit, Tom, I didn't have a clue what the hell any of it meant. No one did. No one, that is, except you."

"So," Tom said, shaking his head. "Why are you saying this now?"

"I'm saying this because any chance of resolving this situation quietly died three hours ago in an explosion that nearly killed me and my men. I'm saying this because there's a burning crater in downtown Flagstaff that your fire department is still trying to extinguish." Alex noticed Tom's blank stare and gave him a sarcastic frown. "What . . . didn't anyone tell you? Oh, wait . . . of course not, you've been in surgery getting that bullet out of your leg. Well, let me take a second and get you up to speed. Joe's Last Stand Saloon has been removed from the map. I mean *gone*. Jeri Halston is dead. Your terrorists have miraculously vanished into the cold thin air. And to top it all off, nearly every shred of usable evidence is now a useless pile of ashes."

Tom reached up and grabbed his brother-in-law's injured arm. "Jeri's dead?" he asked, squeezing Alex's wrist.

Alex moaned in pain and slowly nodded.

"How did she die?" Tom demanded.

"Let go of my fucking arm!" Alex exclaimed, grabbing at Tom's hand.

Tom ignored his brother-in-law's request and tightened his grip. He watched Alex's face turn white as the tendons and bones in his injured wrist shifted sickeningly under the pressure. "Answer my question."

Alex stifled another moan and glared at Tom with an expression of pure agony. "She was in the fucking saloon when it exploded!"

Tom shook his head doubtfully. "And how would you know that?"

"Because I was in there with her!" Alex screamed. "I barely made it out myself!"

Tom studied his brother-in-law closely as he fought to maintain consciousness. As hard as it was to accept, he knew Alex was telling the truth. He nodded and slowly released his grip.

"Goddammit!" Alex muttered as he pulled free of Tom's grip and stepped back from the bed. "You stupid son of a bitch."

"Don't act like you didn't deserve that, *brother*," Tom replied bitterly. "Now tell me . . . how the fuck did I end up with a bullet in my leg?"

Alex spoke quietly as he carefully rewrapped his injured arm. "I'm sorry, Tom. I really am. I had no idea you were this fucked up.

I should have read your psych evaluation more carefully." He turned and looked at Tom with a mixture of sympathy and disgust. "Christ, you don't even have the faintest clue why I'm here, do you?"

"Of course I do," Tom replied matter-of-factly. "You already told me. You're here because you need my help again. You need me to help find our letter-writing terrorist *once again* because you and your highly trained team of agents fucked up *once again* and managed to destroy nothing but innocent lives." He smiled and shook his head. "Things aren't looking so good for you, are they, Alex? I'm sure your superiors in Washington can't be happy with the score right now—the terrorist, two . . . the CIA, zero. Amsterdam alone might have just been a manageable embarrassment, but this Flagstaff thing is going to draw all kinds of heat. Especially when they find out I told you our terrorist wasn't dead. I hate to say it, but you're going to need a fucking miracle to save you this time." Tom pulled back the bed sheet to expose his bandaged leg. "Maybe you should have thought of that before shooting the only guy who can help you. Now, I'm going to ask you one more time . . . why did you shoot me?"

Alex looked at Tom for a moment before reaching into his jacket pocket and pulling out a small plastic bag, its top edge folded and sealed with tape that was stamped with the CIA's insignia.

"You're wrong, Tom. You may not remember, but you've already helped me. In fact, you've already given me the key piece of evidence I need to finally solve this fucking case."

Tom watched with sudden interest as Alex held the evidence bag up in front of him. Inside appeared to be a handwritten note. "What is that?" he asked.

"This?" Alex replied, dangling the note playfully. "This is my miracle, Tom. The *holy grail* of evidence if ever one existed. It's a confession of guilt, found on the body of the last person trying to flee from Joe's Last Stand Saloon before all hell broke loose."

Tom abruptly sat up in his bed. "Wait—you're telling me you actually got him?"

"That's right, Tom. We got him."

"So where is he now?"

Alex placed the evidence bag on top of his slung arm and pulled back his jacket until Tom could see his holstered gun. "In the hospital," he said casually as he rested his hand on the gun and smiled. "Recovering from a bullet wound."

PART IV

In contrast to its civil or international counterparts, direct warfare between competing Corporate States will not be driven—nor judged—by such complex factors as ideology, culture, or religion, but by the sole factor of economic gain. Consequently, any and all actions designed to achieve economic advantage will be considered morally and ethically justified by the Corporate State. This new "economic morality" will usher in a highly volatile code of behavior in the new business ecology.

However, while it may operate with relative impunity from governmental oversight, any hostile action taken directly by the Corporate State will not be without risk. Regardless of its size and power, the Corporate State ultimately serves, and thus answers to, its customers and shareholders, all of whom hold an expectation of ethical conduct that is core to the Corporate State's public image and, largely, its success. For this reason, the Corporate State will take significant precaution to ensure any objectionable actions do not elicit the unfavorable attention of media agencies or rights advocacy groups—at least those that it does not own or influence—that could damage this public image.

The logical expression of this precaution will be the use of clandestine teams to carry out the Corporate State's more egregious initiatives. These teams, comprised most likely of top minds from both the public and private sectors as well as selected military personnel, will act as the lethal claw of the Corporate State and the hidden face of intercorporate terrorism.

—James H. Stone, *Predictions in the New Business Ecology*

Chapter 61

Jeri closed her father's book and laid it on the sleeping pad next to her. Her body ached from lying in the same position for what was now several hours, but she quickly put it out of mind. There was too much else to think about. She clicked off the flashlight and focused her thoughts within the darkness of her cramped metal cell. As the drone of the engine echoed steadily beneath her, the fragments of an explanation slowly began to come together.

It was all beginning to make sense.

Jeri was so engrossed in her thoughts that she barely noticed as the vehicle began to slow. A sudden bump in the road jolted her back to reality. She braced her hands against the sides of her small cell as the vehicle abruptly rolled to a stop. A moment later the sound of footsteps echoed above her, followed by the metallic click of a key entering a lock. Suddenly the ceiling above her swung open, and the darkness inside her tiny cell was replaced by the blinding light of day. Jeri covered her face with her hands and squinted up at the harsh light. Through her fingers she could make out a lone figure kneeling over her, his silhouette all too familiar.

"Take my hand."

Jeri reached up and grabbed Chip's large hand, surprised by the old man's strength as he pulled her gently to her feet. She stepped out of the small container and stood up stiffly as her eyes darted apprehensively around at her surroundings. They were standing in the back of a large service van, the interior stripped nearly bare. On both sides, a collection of old hand tools hung from the walls. Looking down, Jeri could see that the cell she'd been locked inside was nothing more than a large tool compartment concealed within the floor. She then looked out the open back doors and gasped. The van was parked near the edge of a high bluff. Outside, a stark landscape of mountains and desert spread out before her, filled by a wide lake of placid, cerulean-blue water. Looking closer, Jeri realized the lake was in fact a bay, its calm surface punctured in the center by a handful of small, desolate-looking islands.

"I apologize for the accommodations," Chip said quietly. "We didn't have any identification for you, so we had to improvise." He handed her a cold bottle of water. "Here, drink that. It'll help with the soreness."

Jeri looked at the bottle suspiciously before twisting off the cap and taking a quick taste. She realized as the water touched her lips that she was ravenously thirsty. A gust of hot, dry wind blew into the van as she drank the bottle. "Where are we?" she asked, tossing the empty bottle onto the floor of the van.

"Mexico," Chip replied, admiring the view below them. "That down there is Bahia de los Angeles, and that beautiful body of water is the Sea of Cortés."

"Okay, great," Jeri replied as she gazed out at the view. She then turned and stared at him coldly. "So is this where you're going to kill me if I don't give you what you want?"

Chip looked at her with a remorseful expression. "I know what happened at the saloon seemed a little extreme, but you needed to experience it firsthand. It's standard procedure for everyone we bring in."

"Bring in? Bring *in*?" Jeri shouted. She reached out and pushed him roughly against the side of the van. "Bring into *what*? Your *agency*?"

Chip caught himself before slamming against the wall and looked at her in surprise. "Look, I know this is all very confusing, and I'm sorry. I wish we could have done this differently, but we simply ran out of time. Let me finish explaining."

"There's nothing left to explain, Chip. I've already figured it out. Tom Coleman was right—you and your code-named team of freaks are nothing more than mercenaries. You're the 'hidden face of intercorporate terrorism' hired by large companies to do their dirty work. You and your men are responsible for the deaths of innocent people . . . including five researchers whose only mistake was working for Petronus Energy. Am I correct so far?"

Chip nodded slowly. "Mostly."

Jeri reached down into the compartment she'd been trapped in and grabbed her father's book. "You were right, my dad was brilliant," she continued, pointing the book at him threateningly. "He predicted thirty years ago what the world was going to become, and he was *right*. No wonder you didn't want him to publish his book! You wanted it all for yourself, didn't you? After all, you were *bored*. It wasn't easy for a big-time secret agent like yourself to just give up everything and go into hiding in a quiet little place like Flagstaff. And I'm sure your new career of digging up fossils wasn't cutting it. When my father handed you a blueprint of the future, you immediately saw an opportunity to get 'back in the game,' as you put it. That, and a two-decade jump on the competition."

Chip looked at her without responding.

"It suddenly dawned on me as I was lying there, locked in that little metal box, that all of this was planned years ago. You didn't walk into the saloon by accident a year ago, did you, Chip? It was no coincidence that you first appeared just weeks after my father died. You knew my father was dead. But there was something else of my father's—something perhaps even more important than this book—you still wanted. So you came up with this elaborate idea of getting close to me in the hopes I could help you get it. How am I doing so far?"

"Quite well," he replied.

Jeri tossed her father's book at Chip and glanced around the van. She noticed a rusty utility knife lying on the floor and picked it up. Chip watched her curiously as she quickly assessed the blade before gripping it tightly in her hand. She then looked at him with a menacing smile.

"I have to say, though, the letters were brilliant. What better way to arouse my curiosity than with some handsome, mysterious world traveler? Of course, I now know they weren't intended just for me. All those ridiculously written letters were nothing more than Chilly's cryptic progress reports to you . . . updates on where he was and how he was planning to kill his next victim. You obviously knew when the letters were arriving, just as you knew that with enough prodding I'd share them with you. No texts or e-mails that might be traceable by others—just simple, old-school pen and paper. Once Chilly had my interest, you had him hit me with the Polaroid of my father's book. After that, you waited to see what I did. Or perhaps I should say you waited to see what I *uncovered*."

Chip looked at her quizzically.

"The only thing I haven't figured out yet is Tom Coleman," Jeri continued, taking a step toward him. "Was he part of your plan too?"

"No," Chip replied. "At least not initially. But after I realized who he was and what he was up to, I figured out a way to put him to use. In the end, he turned out to be quite handy." He briefly admired the book in his hands before fixing his eyes on Jeri. "So where *did* you find the book?"

Jeri pointed the knife at him threateningly. "You've spent more than a year of your life sitting on a barstool to get that answer—to get your hands on everything my father had hidden away, haven't you? Well, tough shit, old man. I'm not telling you."

Chip shrugged in confusion. "What are you talking about?"

Jeri narrowed her eyes at him. "Don't try to play me, Chip. You know I have it."

"Have what?"

"My father's research. Everything he collected from those years preparing for his book. Journals . . . field notes . . . boxes of recorded interviews. God knows how many sellable secrets are collecting dust on those pages. But then, that was your plan all along, wasn't it? Manipulate me into giving it to you, and then auction it to the highest bidder." Jeri took another step forward. "I even have documents surrounding the government pension plans that nearly got him killed. Financial statements, transaction logs, internal memos—enough evidence to send everyone responsible to jail." Jeri paused and looked at Chip with disgust. "Or, in your case, bribe them for your silence."

Chip stared at her for a long moment before a small grin appeared on his face. He stepped back and erupted in laughter.

"What the hell is so funny?" Jeri demanded. She watched as Chip tried to speak but was seized by another fit of laughter. Nearly a minute passed as he leaned against the side of the van trembling uncontrollably. When he was finally able to compose himself, he wiped the tears from his handsome, weathered face and looked apologetically at Jeri.

"I'm sorry, Jeri . . . I don't mean to be rude. It's just . . . well . . . is that really what you thought we were after? Some buried old lockbox of your father's?"

"Of course I did," Jeri replied cautiously. "What else could it be?"

Chip stepped toward her, his expression again serious. "You're right . . . you did figure it out. Almost everything you said was true,

Jeri—with a few notable exceptions. We'll talk about those later. But what I can tell you right now is that we were never after your father's journals."

Jeri shook her head in confusion. "Then what were you after?" she demanded.

A hot, arid gust of wind whipped through the van as Chip ran a hand through his hair. "What we've always been after, Jeri," he said as he pointed his finger and grinned.

"You."

Chapter 62

Tom sat up in his hospital bed and glared at his brother-in-law.

"Are you insane, Alex? *Me—a terrorist*? That's fucking ridiculous!"

"It's not ridiculous at all," Alex replied as he took his hand off his holstered gun and reached into his jacket. "Here," he said, pulling out a folded piece of paper and tossing it on the bed. "See for yourself."

Tom picked it up and looked at Alex inquiringly.

"A copy of the confession," Alex said, tapping on the evidence bag he was holding. "I found it pinned to your chest after I ordered my men to take you down."

"Bullshit . . . I didn't write any fucking confession note."

"Initial analysis of the handwriting says you did," Alex responded.

Tom started to unfold the note and then paused. "So that's why you had your men shoot me? Because I had a note pinned to my chest?"

"No, Tom," Alex replied, shaking his head. "You were shot because you walked out of a suspected terrorist location wearing a fucking Santa Claus costume, complete with a big bag of god-knew-what slung over your shoulder."

Tom stared at him with a blank expression. "You're kidding me."

"I've got the Santa suit with your blood all over it sealed up in another evidence bag," Alex replied as he pointed at the door. "Want me to go get it?"

Tom looked down at the note in his hand and shook his head.

"Read it," Alex demanded impatiently.

Tom gave him a venomous glance before unfolding the note and starting to read. Alex watched quietly as a look of anguish grew on Tom's face. When he was done reading, Tom slowly laid the note on the bedside table and fell back despairingly.

"It's true, isn't it?" Alex asked. "You killed two of your fellow Marines to save your own ass, then fabricated a very plausible lie for your superiors."

Tom glanced around the hospital room, admiring the white, minimalistic simplicity of the space. He imagined the cleaning staff carefully scrubbing every surface of the room, killing the endless onslaught of germs that infested it. The thought gave him a strange feeling of comfort.

"You tell me," he replied hollowly. "You're the fucking CIA agent."

Alex shook his head. "I can't believe I didn't see it sooner. For god's sake, even your rejection letter spelled it out, and I didn't see it."

Tom glanced over at him. "See what?"

"Your *illness*, Tom," Alex replied solemnly, tapping his index finger against his temple. "When you got rejected by the CIA, something up here snapped. That's when this all started. You didn't just happen to walk into a bar where an anonymous man was sending letters and photos to the bartender. Those letters and photos came from *you*, didn't they?"

Tom looked at him curiously for a moment before laughing. "Fuck you, Alex."

"You created a fictitious character, took pictures of someone wearing a Joe's Last Stand Saloon T-shirt, linked his locations and actions to some random Petronus deaths, and boom . . . instant terrorist. I haven't had a chance to look into it yet, but I assume you stole the Kaliningrad tip from a Homeland Security colleague in order to complete the illusion. Before you knew it, you had a story with just the right blend of legitimate field intel and complete bullshit. Then you packaged it up and sold it to the last person on earth who should have believed you—me." Alex paused and shook his head. "You did a helluva good job convincing me it was real, Tom. Of course, I don't have all the details yet. Like the identity of that dumb, T-shirt-wearing bastard you sent the care package to in Amsterdam, or how he managed to blow himself up in the hotel room. But I can guarantee you one thing—you'll be the one who hangs for it, not me."

Alex turned and began slowly pacing the floor.

"Two dead bodies in Amsterdam, Tom," he said bitterly. "And for what? To prove you were *worthy* of the CIA? That's it, isn't it? That's why your elaborate little plan seemed to fall apart when I told you there was no place for you in our agency. Most people would have given up at that point, but not you. You did exactly what any obsessive psychopath would do—you brought your dead terrorist *back to life* and dangled him in front of Jack Preston and Richard Connolly."

Alex glanced over at Tom with a crooked smile. "And who better to dangle him in front of? Those dumb sons of bitches were practically falling on top of each other to take a victory from the CIA. And what did they end up with?" he asked rhetorically, holding up two fingers. "Two more dead bodies, including one of your fellow ICE agents." He stopped pacing and looked coldly at Tom. "By the way, how would you describe your relationship with Agent Martin, Tom?"

Tom grabbed the steel rail that ran along the side of the bed and pulled himself upright. "Stop fucking around, Alex!" he shouted angrily. "Right now the people responsible for all this are getting farther and farther away, and you're standing here wasting time with these bullshit accusations! You want to catch the *real* terrorists, you stupid fuck? Start with the man at the center of this! Start with *Chip Shepherd!*"

A brief flicker of uncertainty crossed Alex's face. "Who?" he asked, raising his hand at Tom in a calm-down gesture. "Chip *who?*"

"Chip Shepherd," Tom replied irritably. "An old regular at the bar. He's the one behind all of this—the killings, the letters . . . everything.

He was there when I walked into the saloon this morning, but he wasn't alone." Tom paused and slowly rubbed his forehead, trying to coax the vague threads of memory back into focus. "There was another man—a huge, muscular guy. I think . . . I'm pretty sure he was the one who attacked me."

Alex shuffled his feet uncomfortably. He knew the man Tom was describing. It was the man he and his men had pulled from the utility pole on the street in front of the saloon—the same man who'd overpowered the officer assigned to guard him before escaping. Now, hours later, an ever-expanding search for the man and his service van had turned up nothing. Even roadblocks on Interstates 40 and 17 had failed to produce a single lead. It was as if the giant man had disappeared into the thin Flagstaff air. Of course, Alex had no intention of divulging this information to Tom. Nor did he have any intention of telling Tom, or anyone else, about the conversation he'd had with the anonymous man on the other end of the laptop inside the saloon just moments before it was blown to hell. Such things would only complicate matters further, and additional complications were the last thing this investigation needed right now.

"So we should immediately drop all charges against you and start looking for an old drunk named Chip Shepherd, is that what you're saying?" Alex asked sarcastically.

Tom nodded. "We were sitting at the bar, talking," he replied. "And that's when I figured it out."

Alex looked at him curiously. "What?"

"He mentioned that the terrorist had already killed his last target, but there was no way he could have known that from the letters."

"Are you sure about that?"

"Jesus Christ, am I the only one who read the fucking letters?" Tom replied, shaking his head in frustration. "Yes, I'm sure. The terrorist referred to his victims by the name of some stupid toys, and in his last letter he said he still had one more to collect."

Alex's stern look slowly eased into a sarcastic grin. "You mean the Brainybuddies?" He laughed and again started pacing the small room.

"Yeah, that's right," Tom said cautiously. "What's so fucking funny?"

"A terrorist who collects toys, Tom. That strikes me as very funny. Especially those particular toys. Do you know how many times my girls have pleaded with me to get them one of the Brainy-buddies for Christmas?"

"It's a fucking code word, Alex. He wasn't actually collecting the damn toys."

Alex reached into his pocket. "Oh, but our terrorist *was* collecting them," he said as he pulled out a photo and tossed it on the bed. "We found them in his Santa bag. Congratulations, Tom . . . you managed to get all four."

Tom picked up the photo and studied it carefully. The photo showed four small stuffed animals packaged in new, brightly colored boxes lying on a sidewalk next to a red Santa bag, a large evidence tag tied to each. He shook his head in disbelief.

"This can't be happening."

"Of course it's happening," Alex replied matter-of-factly. "You *made it* happen." He stared at Tom with a detached look of disgust. "This whole situation is just Afghanistan all over again, isn't it? You'll do whatever it takes to get what you want, regardless of who has to die for it."

He limped closer to the bed.

"You have two options, Tom. You can either accept the pile of evidence against you, admit to conceiving an imaginary terrorist, and face a list of felonies that include falsifying evidence, misleading federal agents, and two counts of voluntary manslaughter for your fallen Marines. Or you can deny everything, pursue this ridiculous fantasy story of 'corporate terrorists' who miraculously evade capture when they're not killing international scientists, and spend the rest of your miserable life in the psych ward at Belmont. Either way your life is over. Either way you're going to be locked up for good."

Tom looked at his brother-in-law with a lethal stare. "That would be the perfect ending for you, wouldn't it, Alex? Cover up the real evidence, save your ass with a simple 'lone madman' story, and get rid of your annoying brother-in-law—all in one single step. Talk about keeping up appearances. I can't imagine a better Christmas gift for Captain fucking America than a storybook ending like that." He shook his head and stared at the floor. "Congratulations, brother. You've managed to fuck this investigation as badly as anyone possibly could and still find a way to come out on top. You've had it all wrong from the start . . . except for one thing."

"What's that?" Alex asked indifferently, turning his back on Tom as he continued to pace the floor.

"I've got nothing left to lose."

Alex paused in surprise as a thin plastic tube suddenly dropped over his head. Before he realized what was happening, the tube was drawn tightly around his neck, pulling him violently backward. An instant later he fell hard against the steel railing of the bed.

"What the *fu*—"

The words were choked from Alex's throat as Tom tightened the IV tube around his neck with crushing force. Alex gasped for breath as a sudden surge of panic rose within him. He swung frantically back at Tom with his good arm, but it was useless. With his back pinned against the railing, he growled in fury as Tom grabbed his arm and tied it tightly to the bed rail with his second IV tube.

"That should do it," Tom muttered as he leaned over and playfully slapped Alex on the face. He then reached down and took the handgun from his holster.

"Wha . . . what the fuck are you doing?" Alex gasped between breaths.

"Shut up," Tom said abruptly as he pulled Alex's head back and secured the tube around his neck to the bed rail. He then lowered the railing on the opposite side of the bed and slowly lowered his feet to the ground. Alex listened as Tom tried to put his weight on his wounded leg and groaned in agony. A moment later, Tom hopped around the bed on his good leg and stopped in front of Alex.

"Do you honestly think you can escape?" Alex asked, looking at him with astonishment.

"What other choice do I have?" Tom replied, waving Alex's handgun angrily. "You've made it clear what'll happen if I stay. My only chance out of this fucking nightmare is to find Chip, and I sure as hell can't count on any of you fuckers to do it." He leaned forward and shoved his hand into Alex's pocket. "If you don't mind, I'll take that confession note with me."

"You're out of your mind, Tom. Just think about what you're doing."

Tom grabbed the evidence bag containing the note from Alex's pocket and then gently pressed the barrel of the gun against his forehead.

"Tell me the truth, Alex. Do you really think I did this, or was this just the easiest answer?"

Alex looked at Tom with a thin smile. "You see, that's why you never would've made a good agent, Tom. You never learned that the truth *is* the easiest answer."

Tom studied his brother-in-law's face before nodding. "Well, no matter what happens to me, I'll at least take some comfort in knowing this little predicament isn't going to help your career. Good luck explaining how a wounded terrorist managed to tie you up and take your gun."

"You're insane, Tom."

Tom smiled and raised the handgun over Alex's head. "Good night, Captain America," he said quietly before swinging the gun hard against his temple. Alex recoiled in pain, his dark brown eyes staring at Tom in surprise before slowly dilating into unconsciousness. A moment later his muscular body collapsed limply against the side of the bed.

Tom quickly glanced around the room. He needed to go—*now*. As expected, his clothes were gone. Probably collected and stuffed into an evidence bag along with everything else when he was admitted to the hospital. He briefly considered taking Alex's clothes, but they wouldn't fit. And there wasn't enough time. At any moment a nurse could walk in and see what had just happened. Tom grabbed the IV stand next to the bed and, using it as a crutch, shuffled toward the door. Once there, he cracked the door open and peered down the hallway. A nurse in blue scrubs was walking in the opposite direction. He opened the door farther and noticed a chair across from his door. A folded newspaper rested on the seat, a steaming cup of coffee next to it on the floor. Tom realized with a sudden feeling of dread that he was staring at the empty chair of a police officer stationed outside his hospital room. *Standard procedure for any hospitalized criminal . . . or terrorist*, he thought angrily as he scanned the hallway again. Luckily, the officer must have decided to take a quick break after Alex had entered his room.

But he would be back any minute.

Tom started through the doorway when he suddenly remembered the gun in his hand. As much as he wanted to take it with him, there was no way to conceal it under his gown, and he wasn't about to try shooting his way out of the hospital. After a brief hesitation, he tossed it into the wastebasket inside the room and shut the door behind him.

He paced quickly down the hallway, grimacing with each step at the pain of his gunshot wound as he pushed the IV stand toward the elevator. A young female nurse appeared from a doorway in front of him. Tom looked up in surprise and gave her a pale smile.

The nurse barely glanced in his direction before disappearing into another patient's room. Tom sighed with relief and continued walking. Had the nurse looked more closely, she might have noticed he was dragging an IV stand that was missing its tubes.

He reached the elevator and hurriedly punched the button for the first floor. The pain in his leg was now nearly unbearable, and a wave of nausea swept over him. Tom closed his eyes and grasped the IV stand tightly. *Keep it together*, he commanded himself, forcing his body to remain standing. The silence in the hallway was finally broken by the sound of the arriving elevator. Tom opened his eyes as the elevator doors opened—and suddenly found himself staring into the eyes of a uniformed police officer.

The returning officer on duty stepped off the elevator and glanced at Tom. "How you doin'?" he asked.

Tom stared back at him in shock for a moment. "Me? Oh . . . I . . . I'm fine," he stammered. The officer nodded calmly. It was clear from his reaction that he didn't know who Tom was.

"You looking for the nurse?" the officer asked as he glanced down the hallway.

"No, I'm . . . I'm just stretching my legs a bit," Tom replied, glancing over the officer's shoulder at the open elevator.

"Yeah, well, don't overdo it," the officer said as he turned and started walking down the hallway. "You don't want *another* hospital bill, do you?"

Tom watched anxiously as he walked away. "No, I guess not," he replied as he stepped closer to the elevator. The doors began to close, and he quickly threw his arm out to stop them. As he glanced down the hallway one last time, Tom noticed the officer had paused and gripped his sidearm. He then saw what the officer was staring at.

Oh, fuck.

Tom watched as his brother-in-law stumbled into the hallway, the IV tube he'd used to tie Alex to the bed rail still wrapped around his neck. Alex then pointed past the stunned officer and shouted in a strained, guttural voice.

"Stop him!"

Tom pushed his way through the elevator doors and flung himself inside as the officer turned and ran toward him. "C'mon! *C'mon!*" he shouted as he repeatedly punched the "Down" button. A moment later the officer's hand appeared in the gap and began pulling one of the doors open. Tom picked up the IV stand and crashed it into the officer's fingers. A piercing howl punctuated the air as the officer released his grip. Tom then lunged forward and began frantically pressing the doors closed. He'd nearly succeeded when the enraged face of the officer appeared in the thin gap between them. A quick flash of steel caught Tom's attention. He looked down to see the barrel of the officer's sidearm wedged between the doors. Before he could act, a fireball of light erupted from the barrel as a searing bolt of pain ripped through his chest. A second flash quickly followed, this one strangely silent, as another bullet tore through his body.

Keep it together. Keep it to—

Tom slowly slid to his knees, his strength drained. He vaguely noticed the elevator doors opening, the terrified face of the police officer shouting words he couldn't hear. He looked down at his chest. A dark, sticky stain of blood covered his hospital gown and was pooling on the ground beneath him.

They'll need bleach to clean up this mess, he thought calmly as he dropped backward onto the elevator floor.

The officer reached for his radio and disappeared into the hallway. Tom stared vacantly at the ceiling. The coldness of the floor was seeping rapidly into his body. His vision began to blur and darken as a familiar face now hovered over him. He gazed up at the solemn face of Alex and smiled until the darkness met the cold.

Lots and lots of bleach.

Chapter 63

Jeri loosened her grip on the knife.

"Me? You were after me?" she asked, glaring at Chip. The older man nodded. "But that doesn't make any sense. Why would you go to all this effort for me?"

Chip narrowed his eyes on her irritably. "You know, you've been suffering from this lack of confidence ever since your father died. I thought it was finally starting to wear off, but perhaps I was wrong."

Jeri eyed him coldly. "You didn't know me before my father died."

"Of course I did," Chip replied. "I've known you your whole life. You just weren't allowed to know *me*."

"And why was that?"

"That was our agreement," Chip said with a shrug. "Your father and I had made some seriously powerful enemies in Washington. Regardless of how well we'd hidden our tracks, there was still a risk of being found. So we decided long before you came along that we wouldn't let anything—or any*one*—from our past lives become a part of our new lives. It was just too dangerous. Of course, that didn't keep the two of us from grabbing the occasional drink together and exchanging stories. Your father could never wait to show me pictures of his little girl and tell me everything you were up to." He paused for a moment, his stern expression softening. "That's how I got to know you, Jeri. I watched you grow up through those pictures and those stories. Your father and I used to joke that I was your secret godfather. But to tell you the truth, that's how I really felt."

Chip turned and stared pensively at the view.

"The last time your father and I talked was just a few weeks before he died. I think he knew something was wrong, but he certainly didn't want to talk about it. We talked about the usual stuff . . . how proud he was of you and how he was convinced you were even more brilliant than he ever was. I remember he was especially proud at that moment because you were finishing up your master's degree in economics. He said he could only imagine what incredible things you'd be doing in a few years."

Jeri looked away from Chip for a moment, her eyes wet with tears.

"The only reason I suspected something might be wrong was because he asked me for a favor. It was only the second time your father had ever asked me for a favor, so I knew it had to be serious."

"What was the favor?"

"He asked me to keep an eye on you."

"And this is how you repay him?" Jeri asked angrily, wiping at her face. "By kidnapping me into your agency?"

"That's right," Chip said firmly as he turned and met her stare. "And I have no regrets about it. Do you think it's been easy watching you waste your life away in a forgotten old saloon for the last year while you quietly mourned the loss of your father? Is that what you think he wanted for you? Is that even remotely close to what you've wanted for yourself?" He stepped forward and narrowed his blue eyes on her intensely. "I brought you here—I brought you *into this*—for two reasons. The first was because I owed it to your father. The second was because I owed it to you. He was right—you *are* brilliant—and I need you. *We* need you."

Jeri looked at him skeptically for a moment before shaking her head. "And you expect me to believe that becoming a terrorist is the best use of my skills?"

The older man smiled. "You still don't understand what we do."

"Then tell me, Chip!" Jeri demanded. "Tell me what you do!"

Chip nodded his head toward the open doors of the van. "I'd prefer if he did that."

Jeri glanced outside. A short distance away, a tall figure stood at the edge of the bluff, staring out at the sea. Even with his back toward her, Jeri immediately recognized his thin frame and short, curly dark hair.

"Why should I ask him?" she asked quietly.

"Because as of this moment I'm officially retired," Chip replied. "I've been doing this shit for far too long. It's time for me to sit down at a bar and drink a beer without having to worry about you or them or some goddamn assignment. Not that I won't still worry . . . but I'm hoping that'll fade with time." He looked out at the lone figure of Chilly standing on the bluff. "He's a lot younger than I am, and a helluva lot better at this than I ever was. I'm sure you two will get along just fine."

Jeri looked at him skeptically. "You promise he won't try to kill me?"

Chip laughed and gave her a sympathetic smile. "I promise. Just go out there and talk to him."

Jeri looked at the knife in her hand for a moment before tucking it carefully into her pocket. "Fine," she said firmly as she walked past Chip and stepped out of the van. She took a few steps before pausing and looking back. "But if he so much as looks at me funny, I'll carve him like a pumpkin."

═══

An arid wind blew steadily against Jeri's back as she marched across the rocky, sun-scorched ground. Her eyes flickered nervously from the spindly, thorn-covered branches of ocotillo growing around her to the dark-haired figure standing at the edge of the bluff. A short distance ahead, Chilly stared out at the sea, ignoring the incessant wind as it ruffled his jeans and white T-shirt. Jeri moved toward him cautiously, avoiding anything on the ground that might crack underfoot and announce her presence. Every few steps a sunbathing lizard darted nervously from her shadow. When she was finally within speaking distance, she stopped and stood silently, her eyes fixed on his broad shoulders.

"It's nice, isn't it?" Chilly asked without turning around.

Jeri stepped back in surprise. A loud snap immediately punctured the silence as her foot landed on a dry branch. *Goddammit!* she inwardly screamed at herself, chastising her own stupidity. She then took a deep breath and forced herself to look around at the view.

"Yes," she said quietly. "It's beautiful."

"Warmer than usual for this time of year," Chilly mumbled. "Feels almost like summer."

"You've been here before?" Jeri asked.

"Many times," he replied, waving her forward. "Come up here. I want to show you something."

Jeri glanced around warily before stepping forward. The ground rose gently toward the edge of the plateau before terminating in a nearly vertical drop to the deserted beach below. She approached the edge, careful to stay well out of arm's reach, and looked down.

It was clear that a fall from the bluff would be fatal.

"See that?" Chilly said, pointing toward a small, dome-shaped island that stood stark white in the center of the bay. "That's Isla Raza. Believe it or not, that little lifeless-looking piece of rock is home to more than three hundred thousand nesting birds. That's why it's so white . . . all those countless birds shitting on it for god knows how many years." He shrugged. "Ironic, isn't it?"

Jeri shook her head. "In what way?"

"That something so pure from a distance is really just covered in shit." He turned and looked at her. "Anyway, welcome to Mexico, Jeri."

Jeri didn't respond as she studied his face in the full light of day. For the first time she was able to clearly see her Mysterious Joe's Last Stand Guy from the letters and photos. He stared back at her calmly, his thin, chiseled face and large, intelligent brown eyes smiling with humor. Looking at him now, Jeri realized he was even more handsome than she had remembered from the bar.

She broke her stare and pointed at his chest. "You're not wearing your usual outfit."

Chilly glanced down and nodded. "I know . . . I apologize. I thought my Joe's T-shirt could use a little time off. To be honest, it was in desperate need of a wash." He turned and again looked out at the view. "Did you like my letters?"

"Of course I did," Jeri replied. "How could I not? Your descriptions of the places, your stories about the people around you, your completely warped sense of humor . . . I loved all of it." She reached into her pocket and wrapped her fingers around the handle of the utility knife. "But what I loved most of all were your cleverly hidden messages to Chip regarding the status of your latest victims."

Chilly smiled as he stared down at the turquoise-colored water beneath them. "Me too," he said quietly.

Jeri watched him expectantly. "So?" she finally asked, taking a step closer.

Chilly glanced over at her. "So *what?*"

"Chip said you were going to explain everything to me."

"He did? Wait, let me guess—did he tell you he was retiring?"

Jeri glanced behind her. In the distance the older man was leaning against the van watching them. He raised his arm and waved.

"Well, yeah . . . he did," she replied as she turned and gave Chilly a quizzical look. "What difference does it make?"

"I should have known," Chilly said, shaking his head. "Do you have any idea how many times Chip has pulled this stunt? He's retired more times than Sugar Ray Leonard." He turned and once again focused his attention on the view.

Jeri glared at him as a sudden wave of anger erased her timidity. Without thinking she walked over and grabbed him roughly by the arm. "Listen," she said, twisting him toward her, "I don't give a damn about Chip's retirement status. I just spent twelve hours stuffed inside an oversized toolbox wondering if someone was going to put a bullet in my head. And now I'm stuck in the middle of Mexico with a murdering pen pal and an old man who wants me to be a part of his *agency*—whatever the hell that means. My entire world has been turned upside down because of you two, and I'm *done*. I want some fucking answers. So tell me," she said, quickly pulling the utility knife from her pocket and pressing the blade to his throat. "What am I doing here, and why should I believe you're anything more than a terrorist?"

Chilly glanced down at the knife before looking admiringly into Jeri's eyes. "Nicely done."

"Thank you. Now start talking."

He stared at her intently with a tight, serious expression. "Do you know how many people under the same circumstances have attempted what you just did?"

"No, and I don't care."

"Less than one percent," Chilly replied matter-of-factly. "I'm serious. We've run this scenario countless times before, but no one's ever tried this. Regardless of how scared or angry they've been, no one's ever used that knife to confront me. That's impressive."

Jeri pressed the knife harder against his neck. "I swear to god, if you don't start explaining what this is about, I'm going to—"

Chilly suddenly leaned his body back away from the sharp blade. At the same time he deftly grabbed her wrist and snapped her arm violently upward. In an instant Jeri was lifted off the ground and propelled toward him. She collided against his broad chest as he wrenched her arm overhead, forcing her to lose her grip on the knife. Jeri then watched in stunned silence as her only weapon flew high into the air above them before sailing over the edge of the bluff. Her eyes followed its tumbling descent to the beach far below, then glanced anxiously at Chilly. His handsome face hovered just inches from hers. He stared back at Jeri with a placid, friendly expression as he slowly lowered her arm, his muscular body pressed firmly against hers.

He then gently released her wrist and took a step back.

"Recruitment, Jeri," he said calmly, reaching into his back pocket. "That's the answer to your question. To *all* of your questions."

Jeri watched as he pulled a cigarette from a mangled pack and quickly lit it. His dark, intelligent eyes narrowed on her as he inhaled. "What are you talking about?" she asked.

"I'm telling you what we do," he said. "We're not terrorists. We're corporate recruiters."

Jeri eyed him skeptically. "You don't really expect me to believe that, do you?"

"Yes, I do."

"Okay, then convince me."

Chilly gave her a thin smile as a gust of hot, sandy wind swept over the bluff, whipping the smoke from his cigarette into oblivion. "Did you read the book?" he asked flatly.

"Yes, I did," Jeri replied. "What else was I supposed to do on the drive down?"

"Care to give me a quick summary?"

Jeri cocked her head in irritation. "Is this a test?"

Chilly smiled. "Everything's a test, Jeri."

"Fine, here's your summary," Jeri replied curtly. "My father believed that the world's economic power was going to shift from major governments to large multinational corporations. He based this belief on a fundamental rule of evolutionary biology—that an organism's size and strength are dictated by the limitations of its environment. Of course, 'environment' is better defined as 'economy' in this sense, but the principle still applies. My father understood that while a government's growth and power are limited by the boundaries of its own economy, those same limitations are far broader for global corporations. Of course, if you believe my father's premise, then you know it's only a question of time before the world's largest corporations grow into the 'corporate states' he described. Once they do, they will become the new economic and financial world powers: the 'global apex predators' that control everything around them. From the governments that set the laws, to the media that cover the news, to the consumers who purchase the products—the corporate states' collective political and economic influence will be inescapable. From that point forward, nothing will be as it appears. Corporate-driven wars designed for pure economic gain will be sanctioned by governments and fought under the guise of humanitarian or ideological differences. Corporate-controlled media will subvert the true facts to coincide with their own agendas. And the rest of us—the consuming masses—well, most of us won't have a clue that anything ever changed in the first place."

She crossed her arms and glared at him harshly. "How was that?"

"That was perfect," Chilly replied. "Which means I don't need to explain just how much power your father entrusted to Chip when he handed him that book. You're a smart woman, Jeri. You know that everything your father predicted in those pages is coming true. Imagine being handed something that predicted the evolution of the global economy twenty-five years before it happened. Imagine the doors that information would open for you. Christ, the money you could make on Wall Street alone would be in the billions." He took a deep drag of his cigarette and shook his head. "It would be so easy to abuse that knowledge, to use it for your own selfish ends."

Chilly paused and tossed his cigarette onto the ground before crushing it under his foot. He then turned and looked at her. "But what if you didn't?"

"Excuse me?" Jeri asked, taken aback by his stare.

"What if you decided to take that knowledge and use it for good? You know . . . to protect those things that needed protection. Or to help regulate those things that were beginning to grow beyond anyone's control."

"That sounds great," Jeri answered sarcastically. "And just how would you do that?"

"By manipulating things from the *inside*," Chilly replied, his mouth creasing into a grin. "After all, even the world's largest corporations have their weaknesses. For all their power, they still have one serious vulnerability—and that one vulnerability just happens to be their single greatest asset."

"Which is?"

"Their *human capital*—the people at the top. Of course, I'm not talking about the executives. The guys in suits will come and go. No, I'm talking about the geniuses with a vision of tomorrow and the scientists sitting in laboratories, discovering the next big idea. They're the ones who really matter. They're the ones the corporations can't afford to lose. More importantly, they're the ones that competing corporations will do anything to get their hands on."

He paused and gave her a conspiratorial smile.

"And that's where we come in. Our little agency was created by Chip for one primary purpose—to recruit the world's top talent. More specifically, we *acquire* some of the more critical personnel within giant multinational companies—or 'corporate states,' as your father liked to call them—and *redistribute* them to their smaller rivals. You might say our agency is the business equivalent of Robin Hood. When it comes to human resources, we steal from the rich and give to the poor."

"And how often does 'recruit' really mean 'kill'?" Jeri demanded.

"Never."

"Oh, really?" she said, shaking her head. "Then what's your excuse for killing Petronus Energy employees?"

"I don't need one," Chilly shrugged. "No Petronus employees have been killed. We just made it look like they were." He raised a finger to his lips and smiled. "But keep that to yourself. That's one of our little trade secrets."

Jeri glared at him in surprise. "You *faked* their deaths?"

"Yes, we did."

"But why?"

"I said these corporations are vulnerable, not stupid. They know the value of their people better than anyone—which is why most of their best talent is usually hidden away in hard-to-find facilities or some far corner of the world. That's why the people we recruit can't just disappear. It would raise too many eyebrows. Their departures have to be more *definitive*—hence the reason for making everyone believe they're dead."

"And exactly how do you do that?"

"The process is always the same," Chilly replied. "After we've identified the recruit, we find a suitable *package*. The package is just a fresh corpse . . . someone unfortunate enough to have died in the local area who matches the recruit's sex, height, and basic body type. Once we've got a suitable package, we figure out a scenario for falsifying our recruit's death that looks and feels plausible, like a car accident or some random act of terrorism. Then we put the final touches on the package, put the scenario in play, and, when nobody's looking"— Chilly looked at her sternly and snapped his fingers—"we take them."

"And these smaller corporations . . . they pay you to do this?" Jeri asked.

"Yes," Chilly answered, nodding. "Quite a lot, in fact."

"Right, of course they do," Jeri replied. "Unfortunately, that doesn't sound very much like recruitment to me. It sounds more like slavery."

"On the contrary," Chilly replied, giving her an odd grin. "Imagine a company wanting you so badly they're willing to blow up half a city block to get you. Do you really think they'd go to that much trouble without making it worth your while?"

Jeri stared at him suspiciously. "Wait . . . please don't tell me that you—"

"We're not bad people, Jeri," Chilly interrupted. "Despite everything that might lead you to believe otherwise, we're not murderers or terrorists. Hell, we're not even home-wreckers. We won't take a job if the recruit in question has kids or a spouse. And we don't just take any assignment."

"What do you mean?" Jeri asked.

"Well, take Petronus, for example," Chilly said as he lit another cigarette from his crumpled pack and gazed out at the sea. "The five people we recruited aren't just ordinary researchers. All of them are leading experts in the field of alternative energy development.

"Unfortunately, what nobody bothered to tell them while they were happily working away in their laboratories is that Petronus has actually been systematically stockpiling their alternative energy discoveries for the sole purpose of keeping the demand—and of course price—for oil at a premium. After all, the company owns roughly forty-three percent of the world's current untapped oil reserves—and a new alternative energy source could pose a significant threat to the value of all that beautiful crude. So what do they do? They collect all those brilliant ideas from their brightest people and quietly lock them away. Luckily, our five new recruits are going to be heading up research for a corporation that will actually turn their ideas into real-life technologies."

He turned and looked at Jeri.

"That's why we took this assignment. Some things are simply too important to be left in the hands of their corporate keepers. Some ideas are too vital to be kept from the world." He paused and took a drag of his cigarette. "Are you starting to understand the true nature of what we're doing here?"

Jeri nodded. "And then there's me," she said somberly. "I was recruited the same way as the others, wasn't I?"

"Correct."

"Which means Joe's Last Stand Saloon is now a smoking pile of rubble, and the rest of the world thinks I'm dead."

"Correct again."

"And you're telling me no one else was killed in all this?"

Chilly looked at her in silence for a moment. "Not by us," he said quietly.

Jeri spun on her heel and began walking along the edge of the bluff. She walked slowly, deep in thought, before eventually turning and pacing purposefully back to Chilly.

"Why didn't you just tell me the truth from the beginning? Why didn't you just ask me to be a part of this?"

"Because that isn't how this works," Chilly replied, shaking his head. "Look, Jeri, I know exactly how you feel right now. You're coming into this the same way as the rest of us. None of us were *asked* to do this . . . none of us. You don't bring people into an agency like this by asking. There's too much at stake if someone says no. We're brought into this brave new world the same way as our clients—without a choice." He laid his hand gently on her shoulder. "But I promise that once you see what you've been brought into, you'll come to the same conclusion as the rest of us. That there's nothing else in this world you'd rather be doing."

Jeri gave him a sharp look. "And what if I still said no?"

"You won't."

"But what if I did?"

Chilly took another drag of his cigarette and shrugged. "Well, since no one's ever left before, I'm not entirely sure. Most likely you'd just get a nice severance check and a one-way ticket to any-where in the world. Excluding Arizona, of course. Oh, and a shot of diaverol to erase your memory. But that's about it."

Jeri watched as a grin creased his face.

"I'm just kidding, Jeri."

"Sure," Jeri replied. "About everything but the diaverol."

Chilly's expression grew serious. "Your father only asked two favors of Chip in his lifetime. The first was to take his book and to do something good with it. The second was to look after his daughter when he knew he was dying. That first favor brought this agency into being, and the second brought you into this agency. If that isn't a textbook definition of 'destiny,' I don't know what is."

He stepped forward and stared intently into Jeri's amber-colored eyes. "So what do you say? Are you ready to get started?"

Jeri turned and looked out at the shimmering blue water beneath her. The wind had lightened to a gentle, sea-scented breeze, and the full warmth of the afternoon sun now engulfed her. A memory of her father filled her mind, his handsome young face smiling at her as he lay stretched out on a rock along a mountainside trail. She closed her eyes and let the memory slowly fade into darkness. The pleading cry of a seagull drifted through the air as the wind teased the locks of her hair. She took a deep breath and opened her eyes, then turned and faced Chilly.

"I'm ready," Jeri said assertively. "So when do we begin?"

"Tomorrow," Chilly answered, glancing wryly at the van in the distance. "We've got a retirement party already scheduled for today."

"Fine. Tomorrow it is," Jeri replied. She then stepped forward and gave him a calm smile. "By the way," she said, extending her hand, "I don't think we've been properly introduced. I'm Jeri . . . Jeri Stone."

Chilly looked at her curiously for a moment before taking her hand. "It's nice to meet you, Jeri," he said, squeezing her hand gently. "I'm Chilly." He quietly leaned toward her, his handsome face easing into a grin. Jeri felt her face blush with heat as he pressed his mouth against her ear and whispered softly.

"But you can call me Sam."

about the author

Photo © C. T. Wente

C. T. Wente lives in San Diego, California, with his wife, Linda. *Ice Man Cometh* represents his first full-length fiction novel.

For more information on the author, including upcoming novels, please visit www.toddwente.com.